DESTINY

DESTINY

PREQUEL TO THE NAVY JUSTICE SERIES

DON BROWN

Mountainview Books, LLC

ACKNOWLEDGMENT AND BACKGROUND

To the more than one hundred thousand readers from around the world who have become fans of the Navy Justice series, I would like to thank you for reading and also for your kind comments which often have come to me by email at just the right time.

Many of my readers have called for more of Zack Brewer, the swashbuckling, young Navy JAG officer we first meet in my novel *Treason*. For those of you expressing this sentiment, let me assure you that your message has been heard. In the not-too-distant future, Lord willing, Zack will be back!

But years before Zack ever received his commission in the U.S. Navy, his grandfather, Walter Brewer, faced a unique military challenge of his own that would require personal bravery to survive. That challenge was called World War II, and the battle that would threaten Walter's life took place on June 6, 1944, in Normandy, France. And, as will be seen, Walter will face even greater battles that follow.

This novel, *Destiny*, was actually penned two years before *Treason*. But *Treason* quickly found its way to publication in 2005, in large part because of the enormous popularity of the television show, JAG.

Now, nine years later, I am pleased to finally present the first novel that started it all, *Destiny*, a novel that is one of my sentimental favorites and that serves as the prequel to the Navy Justice series.

I hope you will enjoy getting to know Walter Brewer and, through him, I hope that we can come to a better understanding of the genetic, DNA makeup of his grandson, Zack.

Thank you for reading and God bless America!

Don Brown
Charlotte, NC
July 20, 2014

DEDICATION

Seventy summers now have passed since 1.3 million Allied soldiers, sailors, marines, and airmen assaulted the beaches at Normandy, France in what would prove to be the largest, greatest, and deadliest amphibious assault in the history of the world.

They called it "Operation Overlord," and the renowned broadcaster, Tom Brokaw, has aptly referred to the Americans who carried it out as, "the Greatest Generation."

It is hard to argue with Mr. Brokaw's assessment.

When we see the iconic black-and-white images from Normandy, of American landing craft opening into a spewing spray of German machine-gun fire, or of soldiers' bodies washing in the surf as their buddies, crouched and low, stepped over them, advancing through smoke toward craggy cliffs beyond the beaches, the full story of Normandy is often overlooked.

Hours before the first bombardment from naval gunfire, before the first brave soldiers advanced in virtual suicide-waves onto the beaches, another story was unfolding. In the minutes just before midnight, at 2230 GMT, or 11:30 local time on June 5, 1944, C-47 transport planes jam-packed with U.S. paratroopers from the 82nd and 101st Airborne Division began taking off from airfields in southern England.

Their mission: to parachute in behind enemy lines, to cut communications, to establish communications checkpoints, and to kill Germans.

At forty-eight minutes after midnight, paratroopers from the newly-minted 101st Airborne Division, also known as the "Screaming Eagles," began leaping from the C-47s over the French countryside. Fighting through thick cloud cover, navigational difficulties, and German antiaircraft and machine-gun fire, the men of the 101st would continue their parachute drops under dark skies for most of the hour, from 00:48 a.m., until approximately 01:40 a.m.

In the great epoch battle that would follow on the beaches

with the rising of the sun, the "Screaming Eagles" of the 101st would mark history as the first Allied soldiers to land on enemy soil to begin the battle, and the first to spill blood in the liberation of Europe.

This novel is dedicated to their memory.

Don Brown
Charlotte, NC
July, 2014

"The 101st Airborne Division has no history; but it has a rendezvous with destiny."

—Major General William C. Lee, U.S. Army
At the Activation Ceremony of the 101st Airborne Division
Camp Claiborne, Louisiana. August 16, 1942

PROLOGUE
NUREMBERG, GERMANY
NOVEMBER 9, 1938

They bowed their heads over the simple wooden table. There were three of them, and they joined hands over the steaming meal in an unbreakable circle of love.

The rabbi's prayer, uttered in lilting Hebrew, had been passed down through the generations from Abraham.

"Oh, for the reasons to give thanks!

"For a warm home and loving family.

"For a faithful God.

"For a congregation committed to the good works of the Lord.

"For a wife, beautiful and loyal, who has stood by me from the beginning and cared for all my needs—in the kitchen, in the bedroom, in the synagogue, in our home."

Solomon had spoken of a wife like his Rachel in the last passage of the Proverbs. God had seen fit, in His infinite wisdom, not to give them children of natural childbirth, but He had blessed them through adoption.

Young Anna, a Gentile by birth with adorable locks of red, curly hair, would be raised Jewish. And she never would have been raised in the faith had Rachel not been obedient to God's call.

"Bless the LORD, O my soul, and all that is within me, bless His holy name!"

They released their hands and raised their heads.

Grateful and satisfied for the bounty of the Lord's beneficence, the rabbi reached across the table for a piece of freshly-baked bread. His mouth watered as his fingers caressed the soft loaf. The fresh aroma seeped into his nostrils, and he thanked the Lord again.

"What was that?" Rachel said.

The sudden, bright flash from outside turned the rabbi's head from the table.

Outside the window, a ravaging fireball lit the dark sky. Across the alley, a ferocious flame engulfed the wooden frame of the temple.

"God, please help us!"

What was happening?

As he stood, the front window exploded. Shards of glass flew in every direction. The wave of heat swooshed in through the shattered bay window.

The Gates of Hell had opened in their front yard.

A second loud crash! Another stone had shattered the rest of the windowpane, sending Rachel into a blood-curdling scream.

The rabbi looked down. His daughter, Anna, slumped to the floor. Blood gushed in a pool from the gash in her scalp. The stone had struck her skull.

"Anna! Anna! Please wake up," Rachel screamed through a stream of tears.

"Anna! Wake up for Papa! Anna!" The rabbi fell to his knees, pleading and praying.

"She is not breathing." Rachel pulled Anna's head against her chest, rocking her like a little girl cradling a rag doll.

The rabbi rose to his feet, backing away several steps.

His eyes scanned from left to right, first to Anna and Rachel, then out the front window to the burning synagogue, then to the kitchen counter.

The blade glistened against the images of the leaping flame, now towering into the starry sky.

He grabbed the knife and charged out the front door into the cold night.

There! Standing behind the bushes! He locked eyes with the assailant.

An eye for an eye.

A tooth for a tooth.

1

Had he done the right thing by dumping her? After all, she *had* cheated on him. And with his own brother at that.

But then again, it happened before they were engaged.

And all they were doing—she and his brother—was making out in *his* car out by the tobacco barn. At least that's what he thought they were doing.

He never actually saw them necking or kissing or whatever. His brother wasn't even in the car when he caught her sitting there, stuck in the mud in a rainstorm, by the tobacco barn.

Still, the circumstantial evidence condemned her. The disheveled, blonde hair. The red lipstick smeared onto her chin and neck. Her white blouse pulled slightly down, exposing part of her tanned shoulder.

In his mind, he still saw the look of shock on her face when he showed up, before Billy returned on his tractor to rescue his damsel in distress.

It took months, but she humbled herself to the point of asking his forgiveness. Perhaps this marked the first time Ellie

Williams had asked for forgiveness of anyone. What pride she must have swallowed when she wrote him that letter two months after the fact.

Of course, her apology in one sense marked an admission of guilt, like a murderer confessing to the crime. Before the confession, rather before the "apology," he tried imagining that the smeared makeup, wrinkled clothing, and disheveled hair might have been caused by something other than his younger brother, his very own flesh and blood, acting like a dog in heat with his girlfriend. Although he welcomed her apology and was shocked by her showing a modicum of humility, it did nothing to stem his vivid imagination.

"I see you found your tickets, Mr. Brewer," the conductor said in a whispered voice.

Walter opened his eyes and saw the conductor again towering over him. "Lucky thing. Last thing I need to do is lose our tickets on the way home from our honeymoon," Walter joked. "I'm sure sleeping on a cold, hard bench at Union Station would go over real well in the first week of marriage."

"She looks like she's sleeping well right now," the conductor said.

"She's bushed. We've had a whirlwind week. We got married at four in the morning on Monday the thirtieth so we could hop a six-o'clock train for our wedding trip to D.C." Walter handed the tickets to the conductor, who stashed them in the inside pocket of his jacket.

"Early-morning wedding, sir?"

"You can say that again. Not too many guests. Just us and the preacher."

"I'm happy for you and the misses," the conductor said.

"Thank you." Walter again closed his eyes as the train began inching forward and took his sleeping bride's hand. It felt warm and soft.

Sure, he loved Ellie. At least he *thought* he did. He had tried forgiving her for the afternoon necking session last October.

After that, he even asked her to marry him last Christmas Eve. She cried with joy when he slipped the ring on her finger in her living room under the Christmas tree. It was the same ring his late father had given his mother.

She had waved her diamond-studded finger around the house that night, hugging her mother and father. Then they celebrated with some of Jimmy Williams's famous Christmas eggnog. All four of them had piled into the car for the short trip to Grace Episcopal Church in downtown Plymouth for midnight services.

And then, trouble.

Walter opened his eyes. An hour must have passed, he guessed. He looked out the window and saw the sun rising over the frosty Virginia countryside as the Norfolk Southern Engine #387 barreled south through the chilly morning air.

The stillness of the rolling hills flashing by the cabin window reminded him of his grandfather, who fought for the Confederacy in these very fields.

Granddaddy Brewer would approve of what he had done this week, wouldn't he? After all, the old man had preached the importance of perpetuating the family name, which ultimately required the cooperation of a good woman.

Walter dozed off, again, falling asleep to the rhythmic clickety-clack of steel wheels rolling over riveted iron tracks.

Ellie got what she deserved when Jessie Manning came along. No, Jessie wasn't Ellie Williams, not in the looks department anyway. Still, Jessie possessed an intangible attractiveness. Shy. Demure. Pretty. The brunette, nineteen-year-old granddaughter of Christian missionaries to China, Jessie turned heads in her own way, and he found that pleasing.

Besides, he and Ellie were the economic mismatch made in heaven. Or perhaps hell, depending on one's perspective.

The filthy-rich product of Saint Mary's Boarding School in Raleigh, marking the best private education money could buy, Ellie strutted about with a self-absorbed air as the only child of Plymouth's wealthiest man. By contrast, Walter, the grandson of a Martin County tobacco farmer, a cash-strapped, impecunious tobacco farmer, had learned the virtues of hard work by the sweat of his brow, by steamy hot hours in the summer tobacco fields, and by shooting deer and squirrels for food in the winter.

If Ellie ever saw a drop of sweat, who knew how she would react? The mental illusion of combining the concepts of Ellie and sweat together—or of Ellie and work together, for that matter—seemed as far removed as heaven was from hell.

That was another thing that bothered him. She had tried using her daddy's money to lure him. "You'll never have to work menial jobs," she'd often said.

And then she dangled the most enticing carrot of all.

The offer had come from "Daddy" Williams himself on Christmas Eve of 1930, the night they got engaged. With a glass of heavily-spiked eggnog in his hand and a beaming smile on his face, Jimmy Williams promised to pay for Walter's books, tuition, room, and board for him to attend Carolina. "Right after the wedding, of course," Jimmy had added, with a jolly "Merry Christmas" followed by an affectionate slap of Walter's back.

Jimmy and Ellie knew that attending the South's greatest university in Chapel Hill was his life-long dream. They knew what would make him salivate.

Ellie urged him—in fact, almost pleaded with him—to consider the offer to attend the University of North Carolina courtesy of Jimmy Williams's big, fat checkbook.

"We can go to law school after that," she said. Besides, she wouldn't mind living in married student housing for a while. Or so she said. It would even be an adventure while in school, before they came back to Plymouth to set up his law practice on Water Street.

Walter almost took the bait, and would have, had he not hated handouts. He would go to Carolina someday, Lord willing, but not on someone else's dime. He would save his money and pay his own way.

When he got a job as a rural mail carrier in his hometown

of Jamesville—a decent paying job at that—Ellie turned up her nose at the news. "A mailman? Walter, you could go to law school!"

Her attitude had infuriated him. At a time of widespread unemployment, with folks lining up at soup kitchens in Williamston, Plymouth, and Little Washington, he had been blessed with a chance to earn a steady income. Her snide comments about him not having to be a mailman made him want to dump her.

But somehow, in a strange way that he could not understand, Walter had a tough time letting go of Ellie Williams. The images of her blue eyes, blonde wavy hair, magnetic smile, shapely legs, and pencil-slim waistline often held court in his dreams. Then there was her personality—a quick-witted, friendly snobbishness he found stimulating.

In many ways, she was the perfect package. Maybe too perfect.

Why had she chosen him? This he never understood.

She moved among the good-looking upper class, the debonair likes of young attorneys, doctors, and bankers. Her romantic dalliances and conquests had included handsome athletic types, including the starting quarterback of the State College football team from her days at St. Mary's boarding school in Raleigh.

Walter could look in the mirror. He was of average build, maybe slightly better-than-average looks.

All things work together for the best, and it was a good thing he had caught her cheating with Billy. It was just another sign, he finally decided, that they were too different. That it would never have worked.

So he'd dumped her, again. She cried and threw the ring at him.

It had now been six months since he had seen her or talked to her. He had never told her about his engagement to Jessie. Fact is, he had never even told her about Jessie. He should have told her, he knew. He just couldn't bring himself to do it.

Walter Brewer turned to his dozing bride, massaging her on the back of her neck.

"Wake up, sleepy head. We're almost there."

Jessie smiled at him as she returned to consciousness. "Where are we?"

"We're in Nash County, ten minutes from the station."

"What time is it?"

Walter pulled out the gold pocket watch Ellie had given him last Christmas. "A little after five o'clock in the afternoon."

"Thirteen hours on a train. I'll be glad to get off." Jessie rubbed her eyes. "So, do you think your brother will be on time to pick us up?"

"Billy had better be there, if he knows what's good for him," Walter joked.

"And what if he's not? You're gonna make him sit in the corner with his nose against the wall?"

"Either that or ban him from using my car on weekends."

"You *are* a harsh one!" She laughed.

❖

The train slowed as a large black-and-white sign with the words *Rocky Mount, N.C.* came into view. Jessie, who sat next to the window, strained for a look outside.

"I can see the station, Walter." Her voice rang with excitement. "I can start decorating our new home for Christmas."

"Great," Walter replied. "I'll start getting our baggage out of the overhead compartment."

As the locomotive ground to a halt releasing a long sigh of hissing steam, Walter stood in the aisle and popped open the compartment over their heads.

"Walter, I don't see Billy anywhere."

"I guess he'll be sitting with his nose in the corner tonight." Walter chuckled. "Don't worry. He'll be here."

While Walter retrieved their suitcases, Jessie again surveyed the waving crowd just outside the train.

"Walter, I see Billy! He has somebody with him!"

"Who is it?"

"I can't quite see. But she *is* beautiful," Jessie said.

"A girl? Billy's got a girl with him?"

Walter stooped down to try and get a glimpse.

"I don't see anything."

"Walter, it looks like that girl you were engaged to—Ellie Williams."

Walter laughed as he tickled his new bride under the chin. "You are so amusing."

"Stop it, Walter. I'm not kidding. Look!"

2

Her deep, blue eyes shot through the windows of the passenger cars, darting back and forth in search of their target.

Walter felt the sweat beading into cold drops on his forehead just below his hairline. With his right hand, he wiped away the clammy moisture. He could not, however, alleviate the severe abdominal knotting caused by the sudden, unexpected sight of his beautiful, sassy, and sure-to-be-hellacious ex-fiancée.

Hell hath no fury . . .

He took two deep breaths.

I should have told her about Jessie.

"I wonder why she's here with Billy," Jessie said.

I should have told her about the engagement.

"Walter?"

Get hold of yourself, Walter.

"Walter!"

Keep your cool. Be friendly. Don't ruin the end of your honeymoon, no matter what.

He motioned for Jessie to step off the train first. Then he stepped down onto the curb—right into the faces of his younger brother and ex-fiancée. "Brother Billy! Ellie! It's great to see you both!"

"Welcome home, you lovebirds," Billy shot back.

"Walter, I'm so happy for you." Ellie threw her arms around him and gave him a big bear hug. Dressed to kill and looking as fine as ever, Ellie sported a well-fitting, red-and-black silk dress.

"And Jessie, congratulations. You have a great one." Ellie released Walter and gave Jessie a much briefer congratulatory hug.

"Thank you," Jesse said. "How sweet of you to come."

What in the world is going on?

"Here, let me help you with your bags."

"Thank you, little brother," Walter said. "Don't mind if I do."

An uncharacteristic chattiness had beset Billy. Two sentences within thirty seconds. At least his rambling broke the awkwardness of this bizarre situation.

"We're parked right over here." Billy pointed to the far corner of the gravel parking lot as he led the foursome toward the Model A Ford.

"So. Did ya'll have a good drive up here?" Walter asked.

"Let's say it was exciting," Ellie answered. "Your brother drives a bit faster than you." She smiled at Billy, who smiled back. Then she winked at Walter.

"He's always been kind of a reckless driver," Walter fumbled for words to keep the conversation going.

"I hope you'll let your reckless brother drive us at least one more place before we drop you off at your new home," Ellie responded.

"And where is it that my reckless brother wishes to drive us?" he asked.

"Billy?" Ellie batted those irresistible blues at Billy as if she expected him to answer Walter's question.

Poor Billy did not stand a chance if she had been blinking her eyes like that at him on the way up here.

"Billy?" Ellie again summoned his name.

"Oh, yeah. Uh, we're going to the Carton House."

Ellie whispered into Billy's ear, "The Carleton House, Billy. Not Carton, but Carleton with an *L*."

"Excuse me," Billy said. "We're going to the Carleton House to celebrate."

"You sure you want to go there, little brother? I know it's just around the corner, but the ticket's pretty pricey."

"Nonsense, Walter," Ellie answered for Billy. "We want to celebrate and treat you and Jessie to a first class dinner in honor of your wedding."

What's with this we stuff? At least I know who's picking up the tab—the Williams trust fund.

"That's sweet," added Jessie.

The foursome walked into the marble-floored parlor of the lavish old restaurant. A brilliant crystal chandelier hung overhead in the entrance of the dining establishment, the restaurant of choice for doctors, lawyers, and politicians in Nash, Edgecombe, and Wilson Counties. The Restaurant's proprietor, Chet Borders, had been a fraternity brother of Ellie's father, Jimmy Williams, years ago and remained friends with the Williams family.

As a result of the never-ending Williams family connections, the quartet got a personal escort to their secluded table by Mr. Borders himself, where a bottle of expensive champagne awaited them, chilled in a bucket of ice. As the brothers held chairs for the ladies to be seated, Borders wasted no time pouring the sparkling alcohol into the four glasses that had been preset.

"Ladies and gentlemen, I understand congratulations are in order," Borders said.

"Congratulations indeed!" Ellie added. "Mr. Borders, I'd like to present the lovely newlyweds and good friends of mine, Mr. and Mrs. Walter Brewer."

"Welcome to the Carleton House, Mr. and Mrs. Brewer. Over the years, we've had a number of newlyweds and honeymooners dine with us. And any friends of the Williams family in Plymouth are friends of ours."

"Thank you for the hospitality," Walter said. "We've heard great things about the restaurant."

As the distinguished-looking restauranteur walked away, Ellie reached over and whispered something into Billy's ear, who then spoke up.

"I'd like to propose a toast to my brother and my new sister-in-law." With Billy's toast, the clanking of four glasses converged over the center of the table, as Billy and Ellie followed with sizable swigs of the light bubbly stuff.

Both Walter and Jessie left their flutes untouched on the table.

"Oh, I hope we didn't make you feel uncomfortable." Ellie sneer-smiled. "I'd forgotten. Walter's not much of a drinker."

"That's okay," Billy interrupted with a chuckle. "Neither is Jessie, for that matter. If they don't want it, I'll be glad to help 'em polish it off."

"To that, I propose another toast," Ellie said with a tinge of sarcastic enthusiasm. "To the newlyweds! May they forever be happy!" Billy and Ellie downed the rest of their champagne, while Walter and Jessie switched to their glasses of water.

Five minutes later, Ellie polished off glass number two and ordered a second bottle. Billy kept up with her, glass-for-glass.

Jessie glanced at Walter as Ellie half-slurred another announcement. "We've toasted the newlyweds. And now, I believe Billy has an announcement to make. Billy?"

"What's the hurry? How 'bout another drink first?" Billy smiled and gulped more champagne.

"At least we know who's *not* driving home." Walter's half-joke fell flat before Billy and Ellie's spirited drinkfest.

"Okay Billy, you should have had enough champagne to calm your nerves by now," Ellie teased. "Let's hear that announcement."

"Uh, well." Billy hesitated, looking sweaty across the forehead as he guzzled the remaining half a glass of champagne in one swoop. "Well, let me put it this way. Walter ain't gonna be the only married Brewer brother."

Walter saw Ellie cringe when Billy used the slang term *ain't*.

"What do you mean by that?" Walter demanded, leaning forward and staring into the eyes of his baby brother.

"Well," Billy muttered, pouring more champagne in his glass.

"Tell him, Billy." Ellie smiled as she placed her hand on his and shot a glance of satisfaction at Walter.

"Well, okay. Me and Ellie."

Ellie interrupted him midstream and whispered in his ear, "Ellie and I, Billy. It's *Ellie and I*."

"Oh, yeah, Ellie and I. Well, we're gettin' married!"

Walter felt every drop of blood drain from his face. He looked at the smirk on Ellie's face, her big blues batting with obvious satisfaction as she looked at one brother, then the other.

"Congratulations," Jessie broke the silence.

"Thank you Jessie," Ellie shot back. "I'm *so* much looking forward to being part of the family."

"When's the big day?" Jessie continued.

"Saturday the nineteenth."

"The nineteenth of what month?" Jessie asked.

"The nineteenth of December," Ellie said.

"That's right around the corner," Jessie said.

"We know, Jessie. But when you know something's right, there's no point in wasting time. And for some reason, I always wanted to get married on the nineteenth. Just a silly thing, I guess," Ellie said. "You know, my birthday's on the nineteenth of August. But that fell on a Wednesday. And I hear that Wednesday's not a good day to get married. So the next available Saturday the nineteenth is December, just two weeks away."

"I guess it doesn't matter what day you get married if you love each other," Jessie observed.

"Ah yes . . . love." Ellie took another drink of champagne. "Love *is* in the air, isn't it? And speaking of love, we want you both in the wedding. We were going to get married at my church. I'm a member of Grace Episcopal in Plymouth. But unfortunately, Janie Morgan Outen is getting married that day. So we're getting married at *your* church in Jamesville!"

"You're getting married at First Christian in Jamesville?" Jessie asked.

"Yes, and won't that just be sooooo convenient," Ellie said with a smirk.

"If you'll excuse me, I think I'll step into the ladies' room." Jessie got up and walked away from the table, disappearing in the general vicinity of the ladies' restroom.

"That's a good idea," Billy blurted. "I'm headed that direction too."

Now, alone at the table with Ellie, Walter looked in her eyes and began a whispered interrogation. "I didn't know you and Billy were dating."

"We weren't," she snapped, "until you left on your honeymoon. Besides, I didn't know *you* were getting married."

"I'm sorry. I probably should have mentioned it to you."

"*Probably* should have mentioned it to me? How nice of you to come to such an obtuse realization."

"I . . ."

"We were engaged, Walter," Ellie snapped.

"I . . . Well . . . We broke that off months ago."

"We? Did you say *we* broke off the engagement?"

"Well . . ."

"Well, I'm just glad that *we*, after careful and mutual discussion and deliberation, came to this joint and rather well thought out decision. And I especially appreciate the input I was allowed on the matter." She grabbed her full glass of champagne without looking at him. "Bottoms up." Another gulp. "So in conclusion, it's good to know that *we*—as you say—broke that off months ago."

"Okay. Okay. So it could have been handled better." Walter looked around. He lowered his voice to just above a whisper. "I'll take responsibility for that, and I apologize. But what's this engagement thing with Billy? You can't be serious. You say you've only been seeing him a week?"

"Billy and I did make out by the tobacco barn once," Ellie quipped. "Remember the time you caught us? That one time in the tobacco field, combined with a week of dating while you and sweetie were on your honeymoon, should be more than enough time on which to make a decision for a permanent relationship."

"Ellie, stop being sarcastic. This is your future you're talking about. And Billy's too."

"What's the matter, the big brother newlywed getting jealous as soon as he gets back from his honeymoon?" Another swallow of alcohol.

"Of course, I'm not jealous." Walter's blood boiled hotter by the second. "But a week? Come on, Ellie. That's not enough time to decide to get married."

"You would know about short engagements, huh?"

"Ellie, that is uncalled for!" When several heads from adjacent tables turned in his direction, he resumed his refrained-but-strained whisper mode. "You and I both know Billy's not your type. What are you going to do at the end of the day? Discuss Elizabethan literature? Or maybe you could take a cozy stroll around downtown Plymouth and chat about the Federalist Papers while you watch the lazy Roanoke roll by." Walter felt like grabbing her flute and downing the rest himself. "You'd be bored with him in two weeks." A gulp of water. "Who proposed to whom, anyway?" Another swig.

"Walter, of course Billy *thinks* he proposed."

"He *thinks* he proposed? Like I don't know you put the idea in his head. What are you trying to do, Ellie? Are you trying to marry Billy to punish me?"

"Now Walter, you know me better than that."

"I know you all too well. And I know your favorite Shakespearean quote, Ellie."

"About hell hath no wrath . . ."

"Like a woman's fury," he said. "Yeah, that's the one."

"Tisk, tisk, Walter. What's it to you, anyway?" Ellie said. "You don't care about me."

"That's not true, and you know it."

"It's not? Look at you now!"

"Just because I married Jessie doesn't mean I don't care about you."

"Walter, do you remember the last thing you said to me that day in June at your house?"

Walter paused for a moment. "About the rain check, right?"

"That's right. You promised me a rain check, and then you disappeared without a word," she muttered under her breath.

"I just apologized for that."

"Let me put it this way. Let's just say poor Billy is the rain check you promised me."

"I don't understand, Ellie. It sounds like you're using Billy as some kind of pawn or something."

"*Moi? C'est ne pas possible, Monsieur.*"

"Cut the French, Ellie. You're half inebriated."

"Inebriation seems the appropriate course of action under the circumstances, don't you think?"

"Seriously, can you look me in the eyes and tell me you even love Billy?"

"Walter. We both know the answer to that question, don't we?"

"Yes, we do. Which is why you should not marry him. It's not fair to marry someone you don't love."

"Now Walter, I never actually admitted that I don't love Billy, did I?"

"You admitted it without admitting it."

"What's the matter? Don't you want me in the family? Having me as your sister-in-law a little too close for comfort, big boy?"

"That's not it. I just want . . ."

"Hello. I'm back." Jessie had returned from the ladies' room.

"Jessie!" Ellie's tone changed from sarcasm to syrupy sweet, causing Walter's stomach to turn. "Walter was expressing his congratulations," she slurred. "You two need to mark your calendars for the nineteenth."

Just then, Billy returned to the table. "Billy and I want you and Walter to serve as our best man and matron of honor. Isn't that right, honey?"

3

Ingrid Schultz never felt comfortable with her husband's nocturnal activities. Politics kept him away from home too much, especially in the evenings. Lately, every night he seemed to trot out the door to some secret meeting, conspiring with his black-shirted friends in clandestine support of their new hero, Adolph Hitler.

Things were somewhat better since Hitler became chancellor. Heinrick got his factory job back, and they had at least some money and some food on the table. But Heinrick's fixation with politics had strained their marriage. It started two years ago on the night he had heard Hitler speak in Nuremberg, and from there it had exploded into an obsession.

On this evening, she prepared bratwurst, his favorite meal. She hoped the aroma of seasoned cabbage and freshly-baked cornbread would encourage him to enjoy a relaxing dinner and spend time with the family. But once again, he inhaled his meal and barely spoke to her or their girls except to announce that he would be gone again tonight.

As she scraped dishes from the dinner table, she heard him

rummaging in their small upstairs bedroom. Within minutes, he hustled down the steps and into the kitchen, his slender six-foot frame dressed in black pants and a black turtleneck. He had pulled a black ski cap over his head, covering all but a shock of his sandy-blond hair.

"What's with all the black tonight, Heinrick?"

"No special reason. Sorry, but I shall be late coming home. I must go now."

As he rushed for the front door, she stepped in front of him and held her hand straight out to block his rapid exit.

"What occasion could be so special that you could not stay and enjoy your favorite meal with your family? Can you not even stay for *Apfelstrudel*? Can't you see how disappointed your daughters are? They made the dessert for you."

Ingrid hoped that mentioning apple strudel would make his mouth water. He rarely turned it down. She watched him as he stopped in the doorway. His head turned and she saw his eyes fall on their daughters, Leisel and Stephi, who were both sitting at the table waiting for him. Did he not know that his girls, at ages seven and five, were the most beautiful children in Germany? With their papa's blonde hair and their mother's green eyes and curls, each gave him a stare that should have made his heart melt. Surely the sight of his precious girls sitting at the table with his favorite dessert, waiting for him, would make him pause and stay just a few more minutes.

"Save the strudel till I return," he said. "We are working on a special project for the Party tonight."

"What do you mean 'a special project for the Party?' And who is 'we?'"

"That information is classified."

"Classified? I'm your wife, Heinrick! What could be so classified that you can't or won't tell your wife what you are doing in the wee hours of the night?"

"I'm sorry, Ingrid. I wish I could tell you. But my activities are classified for reasons of national security."

"National security, you say?" Ingrid snarled. "Heinrick, you're a factory worker. How are the nighttime activities of a twenty-eight-year-old factory worker essential to national security? That's an imaginative ruse. I'm beginning to think there is another woman."

"How dare you degrade me! You would demean my occupation as a factory worker? And you would accuse me of infidelity? You shall not speak to me in such a matter, woman. My activities this night *are* a matter of national security. And I declare to you that the time is coming when I shall no longer be subjected to the bowels of a hot factory, but I shall bring glory to the Fatherland in service to our Führer. The last laugh will be upon those who make fun of me and my occupation. That goes for you too, Ingrid." His blue eyes pierced the air in a blazing fury, and one of the veins in his left temple bulged, as often happened when he lost his temper. "And I tell you," he shook his finger at her, "that my daughters shall see glory and greatness because of the example I shall set for them and because I shall point them in the right direction. They shall be eternally grateful."

Ingrid hesitated before responding, hoping that he would cool down. "Speaking of your daughters, Heinrick, aren't you going to say goodnight to the girls before you leave?"

"*Ja. Ja,*" he mumbled as he walked over to the table and kissed each girl on the forehead. Then he shot out the front door without even acknowledging Ingrid.

"*Auf Wiedersehen*, Heinrick," Ingrid sighed, as if saying good-bye to a closed door which had just been slammed in her face would cure her desperate need for companionship. "*Auf Wiedersehen.*"

Ingrid gazed into the full-length mirror in the couple's living room. Her girlish figure had not left her, even after two babies. Her wavy, shoulder-length red hair complemented her smooth face and green eyes. She still looked pretty, she thought, but apparently not pretty enough to distract Heinrick from politics. Turning from the mirror, she reached for a handkerchief and dabbed her eyes.

Heinrick tried slipping into the back of the dimly-lit beer hall. Nine other men, all dressed in similar black garb and head gear, were seated in two rows. They were taking instructions from a military officer, an SS captain, dressed in a black uniform with a swastika armband. He was short, cleanly shaven, fit, and with a Napoleonic complex like his supreme commander. Heinrick knew that Captain Helmut Klinger would not let even the slightest tardiness go unnoticed.

"Good to see you could make it tonight, Schultz," Klinger growled as the other nine wheeled around and stared at Heinrick.

"My apologies, Commandant. Domestic obligations."

"Ah, yes. Domestic obligations. I am sure the Führer and the Party will understand. After all, I suppose these so-called 'domestic obligations' at least help provide the population base to support the rank and file, if not the leadership, of our great army. Right, Schultz?"

Heinrick wanted to crawl in a hole. The commandant, the title Klinger insisted on being called, was a stickler for punctuality. Even a thirty-second delay would send him into a frenzy. If Ingrid had gotten dinner ready earlier and had not delayed him with the silly interrogation about his activities, he would have been on time. It was her fault, stupid woman.

Hopefully, the commandant would not retaliate by blocking his participation in tonight's classified mission, the details of which remained secret. Rumor had it that those selected to participate would enjoy a bright future with the Party and possibly the military.

"My profound apologies to you and my colleagues, Commandant. You have my word that it shall not happen again."

Klinger paused for a moment. "Now that Schultz has attended to his domestic obligations, perhaps we can proceed, eh?"

Thankfully, the commandant seemed uninclined to press the matter. Heinrick sat down on the back row as the commandant extracted a white envelope from his jacket.

"Gentleman, I hold in my hand classified orders for tonight's operation. Prepare to stand at attention for the reading of the orders." Klinger paused, his eyes sweeping his ten volunteer subordinates in Hitleresque fashion.

"*Achtung!*"

With the sharp bark of that single order, twenty leather jackboots stomped in unison against the varnished hardwood floor of the empty beer hall as the ten-member platoon mounted to attention.

"From Reinhard Heydrich, Director of Security Service, to all operatives, friends, and supporters of the Third Reich.

"Two days ago, November 7, 1938, Ambassador Ernst vom Rath, the third secretary of our German embassy in Paris, was shot by an infidel Jew named Hershl Grynszpan. French authorities took Grynszpan into custody. I regret to inform you that earlier today, November 9, 1938, Secretary vom Rath died from gunshot wounds."

Klinger paused, allowing the announcement of vom Rath's death to sink in.

"Secretary vom Rath, a family man, served as a loyal servant of the Führer and the Third Reich. Both Reich Minister Josef Goebbels and the Führer have expressed their condolences to the family. However, in our grief we must never lose track of our resolve to punish those members of the evil Zionist movement whose hands drip with the blood of this murder.

"Your retribution shall be swift, devastating, and effective. May those who would shed innocent German blood get a foretaste of their bloodthirstiness. In the name of our Führer and of the Third Reich, good luck and Godspeed."

A master of melodrama, Klinger let his voice hang for a moment.

"At ease, gentlemen! You may take your seats."

Klinger resumed. "Tonight for the first time, our squadron is called into action in service to the Party. This action is highly classified and may be discussed with *no one* outside the confines of this room. Anyone breaching security will be shot."

The idea of that woman questioning the classified nature of our operations! If she could only hear this now, Heinrick thought as Klinger continued his briefing.

"You shall be divided into two elite commando units of five men. Team A shall consist of Von Reuben, Becker, Graff, Rödl, and Struben. Von Reuben is commando leader. Team B shall consist of Brandt, Shroeder, Kleinschmit, Heidelmann, and Schultz. Brandt is Team B commando leader."

Heinrick got chills to hear the name *Schultz* included as part of Commando Team B.

"All over Germany tonight, a handful of elite commando teams just like yours, comprising the brightest and most talented Germany has to offer, shall retaliate for the murder of Secretary vom Rath.

"But unlike the murdering Jews, we shall show our compassion and respect for human life by attacking only property, which of course the Jews prefer over life anyway. Our message shall be resolute. Attack our people and we shall retaliate with fury and abandon!"

The group burst into applause at the inspiring words of revenge.

"Commando Team A shall strike business properties controlled by the Jewish conspirators. By disrupting Jewish business interests, we will slow the flow of money used to finance assassinations and other organized criminal activity. Specific targets will be revealed by your team leader as you are being transported to the sites."

"Commando Team B will strike at the heart and soul of these filthy murderers. You gentlemen shall attack the personal residences of the conspirators who seek our annihilation. Then you shall also carry out incendiary operations against the Temple Beth-El. This so-called synagogue spreads anti-government propaganda to the population. Your team leader shall provide details in transit. Your actions will serve as a stark reminder that vigilante murders such as the cold-blooded killing of our ambassador shall rain down consequences! You will be armed with Mausers if fired upon. However, you are not to fire except in self defense. I repeat, do not fire unless fired upon. You will be comforted to know that German police forces will stand by to arrest many wealthy Jewish conspirators."

"*Achtung*!"

The two teams of five jumped to their feet.

"As you carry out your mission this night, remember the

family of Secretary vom Rath. Attack in the name of the Führer. Attack for the Glory of Germany! Any questions?"

Not a soul spoke up.

"Very well, then. Heil Hitler!"

"Heil Hitler!" came the unified response.

"Go now. We will reassemble here in three hours to discuss damage assessment."

4

NUREMBERG, GERMANY
NIGHT OF THE BROKEN GLASS
NOVEMBER 9, 1938

Team B! Follow me! Let's go! Move it! Move it!"

Apparently relishing his appointment as commando leader, twenty-five-year-old Wilhelm Brandt assumed the role of drill sergeant, motioning his four subordinates into the back of a small troop transport truck just outside the beer hall.

Heinrick hopped into the back and sat on one of two wooden benches which had been bolted to the bed of the truck. Several dozen bricks and stones were stashed on the floor along with six military rifles. Heinrick also noticed about twenty aluminum containers, each filled with two gallons of gasoline.

"Men, smear shoe polish on your faces," Brandt barked orders as the truck rolled off. "I want no one seen. It is now 7 p.m. We are rolling on schedule. Estimated time to first target, fifteen minutes."

Almost immediately, Heinrick and his buddies were black from head to toe. Only the whites of their eyes gleamed in the dark.

"I have orders from the commandant. We will hit three banks, a house, and a synagogue. You will divide into teams of two. Schultz and Schroeder are together. Kleinschmit and Heidelmann are also together. I will remain with the driver to defend the truck if attacked."

"Kleinschmit and Heidelmann will hit three Jewish banks. These banks have been involved in financing subversive activities. They are the Schwartz Brothers Bank, Silverstein Bank, and Bank of Rothschild. They are all located in the Jewish financial district on Heidelberg. As you attack, one of you hurls stones at the property while your partner covers with his weapon in case there is a need for deadly force. Decide amongst yourselves who does what. Just get the job done. Questions?"

"*Nein*," they all said in unison.

"Very well. Halt the truck."

"Kleinschmit, Heidelmann, we will drop you here and rendezvous in one hour. Be swift, and Godspeed."

As Kleinschmidt and Heidelmann rolled out the back, Brandt turned to Lars and Heinrick.

"Schroeder and Schultz, your job is most crucial. You will first attack the residence of a Jewish diamond merchant. Then we move to the most important part of tonight's operations."

"What is that?" Heinrick asked.

"See the gasoline?"

"*Ja.*"

"We will burn the temple the commandant referred to. I will provide more details after the first attack."

The truck pulled to a halt. Heinrick felt a rush of adrenaline.

"We are here. Schultz and Schroeder, your target is 114 Regenbogen Straße. Cut straight through this wooded field to the right of the truck. You will find a small path between the trees. It is about one hundred meters to the other side. Be swift."

Heinrick and Schroeder hopped out the back and moved through the dark wooded lot to stake out a position just outside the house. Each man carried a rifle and a black satchel with bricks and stones.

Crouching down behind a tree on the perimeter of the

front yard, Heinrick and Schroeder scoped the outline of the large house against the stars. No lights were on. No one appeared to be home.

"You go, and I'll cover you," Heinrick said.

"Okay, we'll switch next time."

Heinrick cocked the Mauser as Schroeder sprinted across the yard, his black silhouette blending into the night and out of sight. Heinrick strained to see his accomplice to no avail.

A minute passed. Each additional second dragged into a seeming eternity as he waited, his rifle pointed in the direction of the house.

The loud sound of shattering glass broke the eerie silence. The smashing sound reverberated through the woods. Heinrick cringed. His heart raced. Then came another crashing sound, followed by a third. Quick footsteps approached through the darkness. He aimed the rifle toward the sound.

"Run, Schultz!" Schroeder shouted. "Run! Keep us covered!"

As Schroeder bolted past him running back through the woods, Heinrick fell in behind, his rifle strapped over his shoulder.

"Schroeder, Schultz," Brandt's voice came from the darkness as they neared the vehicle. "This way. *Mach schnell.* Hurry up."

Breaking through the woods, they turned right and followed Brandt's orders.

"Let's go! In the truck."

Panting and out of breath, the duo tumbled into the back of the truck as it sped off.

"Did you accomplish your mission, gentlemen?"

"*Ja.*" Schroeder responded.

"Were you spotted or followed?"

"Nein," Heinrick answered. "No one home."

"Very well. Then listen carefully. Our next mission is most dangerous. We will attack the house and the Temple Beth El across the street. We expect the house to be occupied. It is the home of Rabbi Judah Goldstein and his swine family. Goldstein has been spreading Zionist propaganda subversive to the

Reich. The flames may bring out active Jewish resistance. Be prepared to shoot if necessary."

Brandt took a swig from his canteen.

"Schultz. Your job is the house. Schroeder, you gas the temple. I will cover you both, and the driver will also provide armed backup. We shoot to kill if the Jewish pigs interfere. But our timing must be synchronized for maximum effectiveness. Neither of you acts until my order. Understand?"

"*Ja*," Schroeder responded.

"What about you, Schultz? Are my orders clear?"

Heinrick hesitated. He had privately hoped for passive rifle duty again. Stoning someone's house did not sit well with him, not even the house of a Jew. But if this would deter more assassinations and if the Führer had ordered it, so be it.

"Of course. I am ready to act."

"Very well. We arrive in five minutes."

The truck stopped on the street between the rabbi's house and the temple. Lights inside the house revealed people stirring behind the large front window. They appeared to be having a late dinner. Across the street, the dark temple was barely visible.

"Schultz, stay here. Wait for my order. Cover us with your rifle. I will be back."

Heinrick waited while Brandt, Schroeder, and the driver each lugged several gallons of gasoline from the truck to the synagogue.

As he waited alone, every sound seemed amplified. In the eerie silence of the night, he heard a rustling sound coming from the ditch about twenty feet behind the truck. He cocked and pointed his Mauser toward the sound, uncertain of its source. His hands shook, and with his finger on the trigger he aimed at the noise.

The rustling from the ditch continued. Someone was moving in the leaves. Heinrick thought about signaling for help, but doing so might give away his position. He considered abandoning his post, but that would be treason. The dark night was his ally. He held his position.

The noise grew closer. He *had* to try something. But firing his Mauser without an identifiable target would be foolish. If he were wrong, the gunshots would foil the operation.

He let go of the trigger and reached for a brick. He would smoke these Jews out so he could get a clean shot. As the rustling sound got closer, he hurled the brick in the direction of the noise. A screeching sound came from the ditch. Heinrick prepared to fire.

Two black cats scampered out of the ditch and ran across the street just behind the truck. He took a deep breath. Heinrick hated cats, but never had he been so relieved to see one.

How sounds in the dark play tricks on the mind.

"What was that?" Brandt whispered as the trio returned for more gasoline.

"Nothing. Just some cats playing in the ditch," Heinrick whispered back.

Heinrick watched as Brandt, Schroeder, and the driver grabbed more gallons of gasoline and headed back across the street toward the temple. Though it was hard to see well, his eyes had by this time grown accustomed to the dark. The silhouettes of the three Nazi commandos drenched the base of the white wooden building with petrol.

A moment later, Brandt returned with instructions.

"Listen, Schultz. We soaked the target around the foundation. The temple will explode once Schroeder lights the match. But for maximum psychological impact, our timing is crucial. The Zionist rabbi must witness his kingdom engulfed in flames just as soon as the bricks fly through his front window. No delay. Understand me? No delay."

"*Ja.*"

"Schroeder will torch the place, and the second you see the flames you throw the bricks. Is that clear?"

"Very clear."

"On my command, you will charge toward that large front window and send three bricks into the dining room. Understood?"

"I understand, Brandt."

"Oh, and Schultz. There's one other thing."

"What is that?"

"We will be right behind you with our rifles aimed and ready to fire. Don't fail to act."

Heinrick did not respond. He wasn't sure if the last comment was a threat to shoot *him* if he failed to carry out the mission or a promise of protection if the Jews retaliated.

Brandt looked down at his watch. "Be ready, Schultz. Ten seconds. On my count."

Heinrick's heart raced. His breathing grew heavy. This was his first military operation on behalf of the Reich.

The sudden burst of heat from the fire warmed the back of his neck. In a perverse way, in a perverse instant, the heat felt comforting against the cold night air.

The crackling, popping sounds behind him were the sounds of a raging fire, a fire consuming wood at a blistering pace. The reflection of the angry flames off the window of the house showed the fire dancing off the white wooden synagogue like a thousand little demons, then lapping into the night sky like a burning tower.

Heinrick did not turn around. He kept his eyes fixed on his target, on the window. Then the sound of Brandt's voice bellowed from behind. "Five, four, three, two, one. Now, Schultz. Go! Go! Go!"

He sprinted in a crouched position toward the large pane-glass window, ducking under some shrubbery about ten feet to the right. He reached into his sack and grabbed the first brick. Closing his eyes, he hurled it toward the center of the large pane window. The earsplitting sound of shattering glass broke the calm night. He unloaded his second brick and then his third.

A blood-curdling scream arose from the house. A woman's voice! As the explosion of heat and flames warmed his back, his curiosity drew him toward the shrubs outside the broken window.

"Schultz. Let's go!"

He heard Brandt's call, but he had to see what the screaming was about. He peeked over the bushes and looked inside the window.

A young man and a woman sat on the floor sobbing. They

were looking down at something, but he could not tell what. Maybe he had broken some valuable china or crystal with the brick. Jews would be upset over the destruction of such valuable property. After all, they loved money more than life.

He raised his head a little higher over the bushes, straining to see what the fuss was about. From this angle, he saw some locks of curly, red hair on the woman's knee. He moved closer, angling for a better look.

A little girl rested in the woman's lap. Her head gushed with blood. She must have been struck by one of the bricks. She looked about seven years old, the same age of his eldest daughter, Leisel. Her face appeared ghostly white. She looked unconscious—perhaps dead.

Heinrick wanted to vomit. He felt himself heaving but could not throw up. How could he have committed such an act? He only intended to smash glass—not hurt anyone—especially not a little girl.

He stood just a few feet outside the window, peering in at what he had done.

The flames from the synagogue lapped the sky behind him. The heat intensified. He felt like the Gates of Hell were closing in on his back.

"Move, Schultz. Let's get out of here!"

Heinrick froze. As the heat and flames intensified, the man in the window looked up. His eyes locked with Heinrick's, the fury of his gaze boring into Heinrick's soul. The man bolted out the front door with a knife in his hand.

"Move it, Schultz! Now!" Brandt commanded.

But Heinrick stood frozen. The rabbi charged him with the knife raised over his head. In a fleeting millisecond, Heinrick decided this was his deserved fate for killing the girl with the curly, red locks.

The sharp sound of a rifle cracked the night air and broke Heinrick from his trance. The rabbi bent over. Brandt yelled again.

"Move now, Schultz, or we shoot you too!"

Blam!

The rabbi flinched again. A second shot had been fired for

good measure. He tumbled to the ground, lifeless, as the shot echoed off the burning building. His instinct taking over, Heinrick turned and sprinted to the truck silhouetted by the blinding flames of the synagogue burning in the night. He glanced back over his shoulder before he jumped in.

The woman, her white dress soaked in front with her daughter's blood, had rushed into the front yard and crouched over her husband. As the truck engine revved, the woman looked up at Heinrick and his cohorts. With the flames illuminating her, she stood and started running toward them.

The truck screeched off, and as the distance and darkness separated them from the woman, her screams faded.

The truck disappeared around a bend in the road, leaving the woman out of sight.

"Shake it off, Schultz."

Showing no remorse for firing two rounds into the rabbi's stomach, Wilhelm Brandt tried giving Heinrick a pep talk as the transport truck sped back to the beer hall.

"Look. There will be civilian casualties in war. That's going to happen. That Jew girl was in the way. Remember who started this. The Jews started this fight by murdering our ambassador. The girl's blood is on their hands, not yours. You did your duty."

"I know, Brandt. But we technically aren't at war yet."

"What do you mean, not at war? The Jews murdered our ambassador in cold blood! They started this. Not us!"

"But our duty wasn't to attack a girl. We were ordered to attack only property. You heard the commandant. We could be shot for this."

"Shot? Are you crazy, Schultz? We will be commended for this. Besides, we were authorized to use deadly force to defend ourselves."

"*Ja.* But the girl was not a target for deadly force under our rules of engagement."

"You weren't using deadly force, Schultz. You didn't fire your gun into the house. You did what you were ordered to do. You just threw some stones. That's not using deadly force.

Besides, you don't know that the girl is dead, and you don't even know that your brick struck her, for that matter."

Heinrick paused for a moment. Brandt had a point. Perhaps the girl was only shaken up.

"No, but I know that the rabbi is probably dead."

"So what? I fired my weapon to prevent you from getting stabbed in the heart. And if you'd moved out when I ordered you too, we would have evacuated before I had to shoot the guy. But you froze, he came out with the knife, and I had no choice."

Heinrick paused for a moment. Brandt took another swig from his canteen and continued his lecture.

"Besides, Schultz. The last thing you want is for the commandant or higher Party officials to think you are soft on the 'Jewish Question,' right? With this line of talk, they'll think just that."

This time, Brandt paused and reached for something under the bench. Heinrick cringed, thinking the Nazi team leader may be grabbing for a handgun to put a final end to the discussion. He breathed a sigh of relief when the "handgun" turned out to be a bottle of beer which had been stored for celebratory toasting of the mission's success.

Brandt tossed the bottle over to Heinrick. Then he grabbed another bottle and popped the top off.

"Look, Schultz. It's time to celebrate. We've carried out our duty. Now, you and I go back a long way in the factory. We are about to move into an elite class as dependable Party operatives. It would do no one any good and it would change nothing for you to continue this type of indecisive talk. Tell you what I will do. If you drop the matter, my lips are sealed. *Ja?*"

Brandt's points resonated with Heinrick. Had he not frozen, had he just run back to the truck when ordered, maybe the rabbi would be alive. Maybe he was responsible, not just for one death, but two. Heinrick felt sick. These were unarmed citizens, not invading Allied soldiers. But what was done was done. No point belaboring it.

Plus, an official inquiry could reveal that Heinrick had not followed orders or that Brandt had fired unnecessarily. Perhaps the former explanation would prevail, that his own failure to evacuate in a timely manner led to the shooting. But Brandt could be disciplined for not controlling his subordinates. Thus, either of them could be punished. Better to keep quiet.

Heinrick's sense of self preservation kicked in. "Okay, Brandt. You're right. We just followed orders. If anybody asks, the guy rushed out with a knife trying to attack us while we were fleeing the scene. No more discussion from me."

"Good. I thought you would see it my way. Then let's toast our victory and toast the beginning of our glorious new career. *Feiern, wir Schultz! Prost!*"

Heinrick raised his beer for the celebratory toast Brandt had suggested. Their bottles clanked in triumph of a successful mission. Plastering a fake smile on his face, he guzzled the beer, trying to drown the image of the little girl with the red, curly locks.

5

BREWER HOME
JAMESVILLE, NORTH CAROLINA
NOVEMBER 13, 1938

Jessie was having problems sleeping. She didn't know what time it was, but she knew it was sometime between midnight and dawn. That made today November thirteenth.

Seven years ago today, Walter had proposed. From that day forward, she and Walter always joked that the thirteenth day of any month would be a lucky day for them. Walter loved anniversaries, and later today they planned to drive over to Little Washington after church for dinner by the Pamlico River to celebrate. The way she felt as she squirmed in the bed, Jessie doubted that the dinner by the Pamlico would take place.

Sitting up, she squinted at the miniature grandfather clock above the mantle. It looked like five o'clock. Then five slow gongs confirmed that her eyes were not playing tricks.

She rolled off the bed and onto the cold, hardwood floor. Walter slept like a dead man, and she wasn't about to wake him. Sundays were the only days he could sleep past five o'clock.

Walter was half awake when Jessie got up at five-thirty to light the wood stove and knock the chill out of the air. By six o'clock, the aroma of fresh coffee brewing wafted from the kitchen into the bedroom, arousing him like a pack of smelling salts. Slipping into a robe and slippers, he tiptoed into the kitchen to pour a fresh cup of the black brew to jumpstart his day.

In her yellow bathrobe, Jessie sat at the kitchen table weeping, her head buried in the Sunday morning newspaper. Walter came up behind her and rubbed her shoulders.

"Should I call Dr. Papineau?"

"No, not yet," she said through heavy sobbing. "It won't be long. Just not yet."

"What is it, then? Is it something I did or said?"

"No, it's got nothing to do with you, Walter."

"Then what?"

Jessie raised her head from the table, dabbing her eyes with a napkin.

"Here, read this." She handed him the front page of his favorite newspaper, the Sunday edition of the Raleigh *News & Observer*.

"Unemployment Figures Down? That's good news. Why would you be upset about that?"

"No, look at the bottom right."

"Nazis Launch Widespread Attacks Against Jews. Is that the article you want me to read?"

"Just read it."

"Okay. Give me a minute."

Berlin (AP) - A massive, coordinated attack on Jews throughout the German Reich occurred on Wednesday night, November 9, 1938. President Roosevelt and the U.S. State Department have condemned the attacks as rumors circulated around Washington that the United States may break diplomatic relations with Germany over the incident.

The attacks came after Herschel Grynszpan, a 17-year-old Jew living in Paris, shot and killed a member of the German Embassy staff there in retaliation for the poor treatment his father and his family suffered at the hands of the Nazis in Germany.

On October 27, Grynszpan's family and over 15,000 other Jews, originally from Poland, had been expelled from

Germany without warning. They were forcibly transported by train in boxcars then dumped at the Polish border.

For Adolph Hitler and Propaganda Minister Joseph Goebbels, the shooting in Paris provided an opportunity to incite Germans to "rise in bloody vengeance against the Jews."

On November 9, mob violence broke out as the regular German police stood by and crowds of spectators watched. Nazi stormtroopers along with members of the SS and Hitler Youth beat and murdered Jews, broke into and wrecked Jewish homes, and brutalized Jewish women and children.

All over Germany, Austria, and other Nazi-controlled areas, Jewish shops and department stores had their windows smashed and contents destroyed. Synagogues were targeted for vandalism, including desecration of sacred Torah scrolls. Hundreds of synagogues were systematically burned while local fire departments stood by and watched the buildings burn. The attacks lasted into the next day and are being referred to as "Kristallnacht," which translated into English means "The Night of Broken Glass."

Officials estimate that 7500 businesses and 267 synagogues were destroyed. Ninety-one Jews are confirmed killed as a result of the violence.

Walter finished the article and looked up. Jessie was still crying.

"Honey, this is horrible news. But we've known that this Hitler is crazy. This is no surprise."

"You just don't understand, Walter."

Jessie was right. He did not understand. Maybe this crying was a hormonal thing. Over the past seven years, he had learned that a woman's hormones were as unpredictable as predicting an Atlantic hurricane off the Outer Banks. Predict landfall, and it would turn east toward Bermuda. Predict clear skies, and it would strike with fury. Walter would pretend he understood it even if he didn't.

"I understand that you're upset. You're sensitive to the needs of innocent people who've been persecuted for their religious beliefs. You're from a family of missionaries. I'd expect you to be upset. That's one of the reasons I fell in love with you."

Jessie stared at him like he had no clue. "You still don't understand, do you?"

"I'm sorry, Sweetie," he said. "I can't read your mind this morning."

She hesitated and dabbed her eyes again.

"This article—it just brought back a flood of memories."

"A flood of memories about what?" he asked.

"These poor Jews."

"I know. It's a real shame," he said.

"I know how they feel to have their homes attacked. It happened to me, remember?

Then it hit him.

The article had triggered a flashback to June of 1931, when her home was ransacked by laid-off workers from the pulp mill in Plymouth and her dogs were shot. The workers were retaliating against her father, blaming him for the layoffs.

That's why she's so upset.

"I'm sorry. I was insensitive. Of course I remember. I was in the middle of it."

"It's just that this article—there's such a wave of emotion when I read it. I thought about Jeb and Bear and the horror on my little brother's face. People are so cruel.

"I can still see it like yesterday. Our house shattered and ransacked when we got home from church that Sunday. Our dogs shot and piled on top of each other in the back yard." Tears came to her eyes. "I'll never forget what they wrote, in the dogs' blood, on the back of the house—'More layoffs means death to the milk snatcher and his family.' They called Daddy a milk snatcher, Walter. And my poor little brother, N.R., saw all of it."

"I know. I know. But that was a long time ago." He rubbed her shoulders some more. "N.R. is twelve years old. He'll be a teenager next year. Your folks are back in the house. The economy has picked up. Most of the laid-off workers are back at work."

"I know Walter, but they were cruel."

"But there's no more danger." He held her in his arms. "Not anymore. And look on the bright side. You moved in with us, and we got married."

She smiled. This was a welcome sign. "I know. All things work for the best for those . . ."

"Jessie?"

Jessie's face winced. Then she bent over and pressed both hands against her stomach.

"My stomach. Walter, I think it's time. Please call Dr. Pap."

Dr. Ernest Papineau rolled up to the Brewer house at 6:45 a.m. By seven o'clock, one of his three nurses, Joyce Roebuck, had also arrived. Joyce, a stout woman of fifty-some years, had never been married, largely because she wasn't overly appealing to the eye. But her homely appearance and her nurse's training turned out to be a good thing for Dr. Papineau, assuring that she remained available to assist him with deliveries on weeknights, weekends, and holidays. The deal worked out well for Joyce, as she got paid time and a half for her off hours availability.

Dr. Papineau and Joyce took Jessie to the back bedroom and banished Walter to the den. By eight o'clock, he had gulped down five cups of coffee. The knock on the back door came as he was pouring cup number six.

"Ellie?"

"Walter, your mother called. She said Jessie was having some problems."

Ellie Williams Brewer, even after seven years and two children, could still turn heads in a room, at church, at the beach, or any other place she chose to grace with her presence. Unlike most women in Martin County who managed to retain a fifteen-pound permanent layer of fat with each baby, Ellie had given birth to "Little" Billy and Margaret but barely gained any weight and returned to her pre-pregnancy figure within weeks. Now twenty-six, Ellie was aging like the finest of wines.

Billy remained loyal and treated her like royalty. What red-blooded American male wouldn't? She had the looks and the money. The Williams trust fund had provided for a comfortable lifestyle. The fund had purchased a large, two-story, Civil War-era house at the corner of Washington and Third Streets in Plymouth where they resided. At Ellie's insistence, the couple attended Grace Episcopal at least three Sundays a month, where she retained her membership. Billy remained a member of the Jamesville Christian Church and attended about once a month, sometimes accompanied by Ellie and sometimes alone.

Despite moving to Plymouth and becoming a "quasi Episcopalian," Billy seemed to be, in the words of their late grandfather Baldy Brewer, "as happy as a dead pig in the sunshine." Though living in Plymouth, he remained a good ol' Jamesville boy through and through.

The domestic bliss Billy enjoyed had not found its way to Ellie. She had not found it by marrying the country boy brother of her ex-fiancé.

Her relationship with Billy, at least in front of Walter, demonstrated aloofness. She seemed bored with him. The two rarely talked—at least in public—and when they did speak, the substance of their conversation was often no deeper than "Margaret needs a diaper change."

Billy wasn't sharp enough to figure out he'd been used as a platform to get back at Walter for breaking the engagement. Observing his sister-in-law over the years, Walter became more convinced that the Ellie-Billy marriage was a colossal mismatch.

Walter suspected that her eyes were still on him. She had dropped many hints to that effect over the years. She always gravitated toward him at family gatherings. She married Billy— he was convinced—to become the permanent forbidden fruit in his life. She would be there always to provide a salacious temptation for him. She knew the effect she had on him. This would be his punishment for breaking the engagement and dumping her.

"Sorry." Walter caught himself. "Of course. Please come in."

"What does the doctor say?" Ellie asked as Walter hung her overcoat on the coat rack.

"Dr. Pap's back there with Joyce Roebuck now. Jessie read an article in the paper this morning. It got her upset. He thinks the emotional reaction induced premature labor."

"But she's not due for another month, is she?"

"No, she's not," he said. "Doc and Joyce looked worried."

"Will she be all right?"

"They haven't said. Joyce always looks cheerful. She didn't seem so happy this morning."

"What did Jessie read that got her so upset?"

"Would you like some coffee?"

"Sure."

"Come with me into the kitchen." Ellie followed him and took a seat at the kitchen table. "Still two teaspoons of sugar and a tablespoon of milk?"

"You remember?" she asked.

"Of course I do." He handed her the morning newspaper. "Here. Read this. The article's at the bottom right."

Ellie had finished the article when Walter returned with her coffee. "I hope that's not too strong," he said.

"I've never known you to botch coffee."

"I botch a lot of things."

"Maybe a few major items, but never coffee," she said.

"So what did you think of the article?" he asked.

"I can see why it upset her, Walter. It reminded her of the time those hoodlums killed her poor dogs."

"How'd you know that?" he asked.

"I was with you when it happened. Remember?"

"That's right; you were," he said.

"You know, a Sunday afternoon?" She persisted. "You had gone in the kitchen to make me some iced tea and we got a knock on the door?"

"I remember."

"I remember it like yesterday. It was the first time I'd ever seen Jessie. She came to the door with her father. You told me they were some people from church. She looked like she was crying then. No doubt this news might bring back those memories and upset her. It would upset me."

"Your memory never ceases to amaze me, Ellie."

She took a sip of coffee. "We remember the things that are important to us."

"I remember that when I got back that day you were gone."

"You could have found me if you'd wanted. But no point in talking about that now."

"You're right," he said.

"Right now I want you to let me help you and Jessie if I can. Why don't you let me take the kids home with me? I know they'd love to play with Uncle Billy and their cousins."

"They're all three upstairs asleep. I may take you up on that when they get up. How long can you stay?"

"As long as you need me."

"I appreciate that."

"Jessie's a sweet person and a wonderful sister-in-law. That's why you married her. I wish I had her character."

Ellie's comments were interrupted by a knock on the kitchen door. It was Dr. Papineau.

"Walter, could I talk to you?" Pap's face looked ashen. It was the look of a doctor who had lost a patient.

"Maybe I better leave," Ellie said.

"No, please stay," Walter responded. "What's the matter, Doctor?"

"Walter, Jessie went into premature labor. We've had some problems. I wish I had good news."

Walter felt sweat breaking out on his face. "Jessie? Is she okay, Doctor?"

Pap hesitated, looked down at the floor, and then looked at Walter. "I'll be honest with you, Walter. It's too early to tell. She's lost a lot of blood. She may be all right. But I've seen it go both ways at this point."

Walter sat in shock. Ellie fidgeted with her coffee cup, her eyes glued to the doctor.

"What about the baby?"

Pap hung his head. "Walter, there were two babies. Jessie had twins."

"Twins?"

"The babies were small, Walter. That's why we didn't know ahead of time."

"How are they?"

Pap hesitated again.

"Jessie had a boy and a girl. The boy seems okay from what we can see, although he's very light. He weighs five-and-a-half pounds. But your daughter . . ." Dr. Papineau's voice vacillated. "There was a problem with the umbilical cord. She's hanging in there right now, but . . ."

"But what, Doctor? Go ahead and shoot it straight."

"I'm sorry Walter, but it just doesn't look good for her. We'll try and stabilize them here. Then I want to get all three to the hospital in Plymouth if we can. But I wouldn't hold out too much hope."

"I don't understand, Doctor. Why don't we just get them to the hospital now? Wouldn't that be the best thing?"

"They're not strong enough. I think your son can go in a while, maybe. But with Jessie and your daughter, it's wait and see. I'm going to call in two other nurses to help. They should be here in a little while."

"Can I see them now?"

"I don't think that's a good idea. Not while they're critical. When the other nurses arrive and we get things calmed down—maybe then. I'll let you know."

Dr. Papineau left the room. Walter stared out the kitchen window at the large pecan tree just in front of the smokehouse in the back yard.

"Walter?" Ellie could not get him to answer. His eyes began filling with water, still focused on the old pecan tree.

She stood behind him and began massaging the back of his neck and his shoulders.

"It's going to be okay, Walter. I promise."

6

They desired privacy, under the circumstances, so they planned an informal, intimate farewell to their baby daughter. Yes, that seemed to be the thing to do. They weren't sure why if felt right. It just did.

Invitations would be limited to close family members, the pastor, and of course the funeral director from nearby Williamston, the county seat. It would be a short service, simple but elegant, something befitting the short life they were celebrating.

The church was small, perhaps ten rows of pews on each side, separated by a red carpet running down the middle from back to front. Three stained-glass windows adorned the walls on each side, tinted yellowish, allowing enough light from the outside sun to filter into the sanctuary. But the thick tint of the windows did not allow anyone from the outside to see in or anyone from the inside to see out.

They gathered in the chancel of the church and stood near the simple, marble pedestal. On it sat a white coffin, so small that it looked almost like a shoe box. At the base of the pedestal against the red carpet, two arrangements of flowers—one from Grace Episcopal in Plymouth and the other from James-ville Christian Church—commemorated the baby girl's brief stay on earth.

All were standing except for Jessie, the surviving baby, and the three other Brewer children, who were seated like stair steps according to their age and height on the first-row pew of the church. A handful of people milled around the chancel area, but the rest of the small church sanctuary was empty.

Jessie had been released from the hospital the day before. She looked frail, having survived the past six days from nutri-ents and antibiotics pumped into her veins from a clear glass bottle dangling above her hospital bed. Yesterday, Dr. Papineau removed from her inner forearm the long, painful, stainless steel needle that had been connected to the bottle by a rubber feeding tube.

A big, purple bruise covered half her arm, perhaps because the nurses at times had been overly aggressive with her dosages. Or perhaps the nurses had missed the vein and had to re-stick her arm. Walter wasn't sure what caused the bruising and decided not to mention it to Jesse because he didn't want to call attention to it.

Looking weak and dazed from her near bout with death, Jessie sat in the wheelchair just in front of her three older chil-dren, Virginia, Hardison, and Caroline, stroking their baby brother's head as he sucked on a warm bottle of milk. She refused to let anyone pry the prematurely-born infant from her clutch.

Nine days old, oblivious to everything around him except the white fluid now filling his miniature belly, Zachary Mitchell Brewer, the fourth living child of Walter and Jessie, would never remember this day. He would be told of his twin sister Mona, of her arrival fifteen minutes before him, of their one week on earth together, and of her death at the end of that week. Beyond that, Mona Shephard Brewer would be a name only to the boy, a twin sister he never knew.

This being the case, Walter worried about the wisdom of exposing his infant son to the cold. He had thought maybe it would be best to leave him home with Cousin Eva Gray or perhaps Ellie, that maybe Jessie should just skip the funeral. She was so weak.

When Walter had suggested these ideas, Jessie would have none of it. She was determined to attend the funeral and equally determined not to release the baby. She'd lost one baby and she wasn't going to let the other out of her sight, not even for a minute.

Walter capitulated when Dr. Papineau said that baby Zack "will be fine if he's kept warm with blankets."

"Besides," the doctor reasoned, "Jessie has drawn her will to live from the baby. Maybe holding him in her arms will help her get through the funeral."

Pastor Bobby Holliday looked at Walter. It was time.

Walter leaned over and whispered in Jessie's ear. She nodded but kept her eyes on Zack as Walter rolled her wheelchair to within a couple feet of the pedestal holding the little casket.

He turned to Virginia, Hardison, and Caroline. "It's time to say good-bye to baby sister."

Virginia took Hardison by the hand, leading him to within inches of the right wheel of Jessie's wheelchair. Caroline made a beeline for Walter, who stood to Jessie's left with his hand resting on her shoulder.

"Let us all hold hands and form a circle around the casket," Pastor Bobby Holliday said. He gave the small group time to comply.

"Let us pray. Lord, your servants have come here on this day to say good-bye to Mona Shephard Brewer, the precious baby daughter of Walter and Jessie. Little Mona never got to grow up with her family in Jamesville, Lord. Instead, You brought her home to Yourself. We do not always understand Your ways or Your purposes, but nevertheless, in You we commit our trust.

"O Lord, we stand today holding hands in a small circle around her small body. Soon that circle will be broken, as we return this precious child to whence she came. For as You have said, 'From dust that we were formed, and to dust we shall return.'

"We pray that though the circle will be broken this day, that one day it shall be mended together again. That by Your merciful hand, one day Walter and Jessie will have a relationship with their baby daughter, that little Zack—and we pray Your blessings on him—will know his twin sister, and that Virginia, Hardison, and Caroline will be mended to this one they have lost so young in life.

"And we are reminded of the preciousness of life, oh Lord, that all life, no matter how old, no matter how young, is precious in your sight. May we all gather again one day under Your eternal light, basking in the glory of thy only begotten Son.

"For it is in His name and for His sake that we pray, Amen."

The undertaker, in a gray suit and wearing white gloves, cradled the baby's casket in his arms then walked down the center aisle and out the front door.

7

Heinrick opened his eyes. He pushed himself up in the dark and wiped sweat from his forehead. He had seen her again. Or had he? Was this a bad dream? Was his mind playing tricks on him in the dark? This was the fourth night he had awakened with her face in front of him. He wasn't sure if he was having a nightmare or being haunted by a ghost.

On the night of November ninth, he had seen her unconscious with her head bleeding in her mother's lap. But in his dreams, she appeared standing by his bed. Her face was beautiful and unmarred by the scar of a brick. Her complexion was lily-white and her cheeks rosy-red, almost matching the locks of her hair. He wasn't sure why she had red hair. He had never seen a red-headed Jewish girl. Maybe she was adopted.

Jewish or not, adopted or not, dead or alive, she was very real, at least in his imagination. Sometimes she smiled. Sometimes she cried. Sometimes she spoke. When she spoke, her voice sounded like an angel's voice. At least it sounded like what Heinrick imagined to be an angel's voice. Her message was always the same:

"Read the book. Before it's too late."

Her voice always woke him from his sleep. He was never sure if he heard the voice in his dreams or if she was in the room. The uncertainty was unnerving. Each time, he woke up in a cold sweat, frightened and confused. Perhaps he was going mad.

"I don't understand! What book do you want me to read?" He spoke aloud.

"Heinrick, who are you talking to? Are you talking in your sleep again?"

Ingrid was a light sleeper. In the nights following the ninth, she lost plenty of sleep from Heinrick's squirming in bed. She knew something was wrong, but Heinrick would not reveal the details of his operation, let alone tell about the girl. Revealing the details of confidential military operations could lead to execution.

"It's nothing. Maybe something I ate."

"I don't believe you, Heinrick. You haven't been eating much of anything. And you've been twisting and turning in your sleep for a month now."

"Sorry, Ingrid. I will try and be still. Go back to sleep."

But Ingrid could not sleep. Neither could Heinrick. She got up and headed downstairs.

"Where are you going?"

"To bake some gingerbread men."

"It's three in the morning!"

"*Ja*, and in two days it will be Christmas. We don't have any sweets for the children."

"Can't it wait till tomorrow?"

"It *is* tomorrow. Besides, if you could've waited till tomorrow to start talking, I could have waited to start baking. Now I can't sleep."

Heinrick gave up as Ingrid headed down the steps. He slipped back under his blanket and closed his eyes.

"Papa?"

Heinrick rolled over and saw his seven-year-old daughter Leisel standing in the doorway.

"Yes, sweet girl?"

"Stephi and I cannot sleep, Papa."

"Why can't you sleep, Leisel?"

"Because Mommy woke us up."

"I know. Mommy has gone downstairs to bake some gingerbread men, and when you wake up, I'm sure she will give you some. Now go back to bed."

"But Papa?"

"What now, sweet girl?"

"Will Mommy make some gingerbread women and some gingerbread boys and girls, too?" Leisel asked.

"I'm sure she will, and we can eat the whole gingerbread family, just like we do every Christmas. Now go back to bed."

"But there's just one more thing I must tell you, Papa."

"Just one more thing. Then to bed."

"Me and Stephi are cold, Papa."

To provide moral support to her big sister, five-year-old Stephi Schultz peeped around the door, her big rag doll wrapped in her arms. The doll, which she found under the Christmas tree last year and named Eva, was her constant companion.

Heinrick gazed for a moment at his girls standing at his bedroom door. In their flannel blue pajamas with curly blonde locks and big blue eyes, together they formed the most persuasive and the cutest diplomatic team the world had ever known.

"Hallo, Stephi."

"Hallo, Papa."

"Are you cold too?"

"*Ja*, Papa."

"Eva isn't keeping you warm?"

"No, sir. My feet are cold. Eva won't keep my feet warm," she said.

Heinrick knew what they were hinting at, and by now his resistance to their scheming had long since melted.

"So do my girls want to cuddle with Papa?"

"*Ja, Ja!*" said Stephi, bounding with joy that Heinrick had read her mind.

"Please? Please can we cuddle?" pleaded Leisel.

"Okay. Come on. But first you must give Papa a big kiss!"

Filled with excitement, the girls jumped on the bed, gave

Heinrick a slurpy kiss on each cheek, and crawled under the covers. Within minutes, both were asleep on each side of Heinrick.

By four in the morning, the sweet aroma from gingerbread cookies in the oven mixed with the evergreen scent from the Christmas tree at least gave the small house a holiday smell. Ingrid considered going back to bed for an hour but decided that she just wasn't sleepy enough. Maybe she could rest even if she couldn't sleep.

She sat down alone in the den and closed her eyes. Just as she felt herself starting to doze, she was interrupted by an unexpected ring of the front doorbell. Who could be visiting at 4:30 a.m. on Christmas Eve?

She got up, tiptoed over to the door, and looked through the peephole. A man stood outside in the cold, dressed in a black uniform. She could see his breath in the freezing air. He looked like a military officer of some sort. She pulled her robe closed and opened the door.

"Frau Schultz, I presume?"

"*Ja?*"

"Pardon the interruption, madam. I am Commandant Klinger of the German Verfügungstruppen."

"You're from the SS?"

"That is correct."

"What can I do for you, Commandant?"

"I need to speak to your husband."

"He's upstairs sleeping. Is there anything I can do for you?"

"I have an urgent telegram for your husband. It's from Berlin."

"But it's Christmas Eve. Can't it wait?"

"Madam, the telegram is from Der Führer."

Ingrid wasn't sure if her throat had fallen into her stomach or if her stomach had leapt into her throat.

"Heinrick's not in trouble, is he?"

"Madam, the telegram is confidential." The man's eyes glared, and he spoke in a businesslike, intimidating voice. "And while I am a patient man," he rested his hand on his pistol, "our time is running short. Please understand that compliance with our request is not optional."

Ingrid got the message. Either she got Heinrick out of bed or the commandant would invite himself and his friends in for Christmas cookies.

"I am pleased to be of service to you, Commandant. Please wait here. I will tell Heinrick that you wish to see him."

"Very well, madam."

Ingrid climbed the narrow staircase to their small bedroom, where she found Heinrick sleeping on his back with Leisel under one arm and Stephi under the other.

"Heinrick!" Ingrid whispered, not wanting to awaken the girls.

"The cookies smell good," Heinrick mumbled, sounding half asleep.

"It's not about the cookies. You have a visitor!"

"A visitor? Who?"

"He's in a black uniform. He calls himself the Commandant. He says he is with the SS."

"The Commandant?" Heinrick snapped up.

"Do you know him, Heinrick?"

"*Ja.*" He sat up with his eyes wide open.

"Who is he?"

"That information is classified," he said.

"There you go again. What do you mean by classified?"

Heinrick ignored the question. "Go back downstairs and tell the commandant I will be right with him."

"Very well, Heinrick." Ingrid felt her hands shaking. She descended the staircase to deliver the message. She walked to the front door. "Heinrick will be with you soon, *Herr* Commandant."

"Aah, something smells wonderful, Frau Schultz. Would you happen to have a cup of coffee you could spare for an officer of the Reich?"

Ingrid hesitated. "Yes, of course, Commandant. Please come in." She directed him into the kitchen. "Please be seated, sir. How do you like your coffee?"

"An SS officer drinks his coffee black and powerful, which are the colors and characteristics of the great war machine that our Führer is assembling for the glory of the Reich."

She ignored the comment, for his words and eyes gave her all the comfort of having a viper in her house, slithering up at her table for breakfast. She extracted a cup from the cupboard and poured some coffee into it. "I hope you will find this suitable, Commandant."

"*Danke*, Frau Schultz."

"My pleasure."

She looked up and saw Heinrick bounding down the steps. He had donned himself in the same black turtleneck and trousers he had worn the night of November ninth, the last time he had left the home for some cryptic Nazi party function.

"Commandant!"

"Schultz!" Klinger jumped to attention, extending his right hand, palm down, toward Heinrick. "Heil Hitler!"

Heinrick shot back the Nazi salute. "Heil Hitler, *Herr* Commandant."

Ingrid cringed at her husband's rigid military bearing. She knew he was a follower of Hitler, but that salute felt creepy.

"Schultz, I have a telegram for you. Please read it."

Heinrick took the telegram from the commandant and opened it.

> From: Adolph Hitler, Chancellor
> To: Heinrick Schultz
> Re: Induction into German Special Forces
> Date: 24 DEC 1938
>
> Thank you for your valor and heroism in service to the Reich. Your loyalty and courage displayed on the evening of November 9, 1938 have proven your value to your country.
> Because of your service, you have been selected as an officer candidate in the German Special Forces to serve in the SS-Verfügungstruppen. You will report to Induction Processing Headquarters, Berlin, no later than midnight December 25, 1938.

Congratulations.

Respectfully,
Adolph Hitler
Chancellor

"I take it I am not the only recipient of this telegram."

"No, but you are part of an elite handful selected. Your work at Temple Beth-El was, shall we say, impressive to the Party."

Heinrick thought about the red-headed girl. He felt queasy.

"But the telegram says I am to report by midnight?"

"That's right, Schultz. I need you to gather your things and come with me now."

"What are you talking about?" Ingrid demanded. "It's Christmas Eve! I knew nothing of this. You can't just march off and leave us like this without warning, Heinrick!"

"Schultz, I suggest that you speak with your wife about the privilege and honor it will be for her to be the bride of a German Special Forces officer. Obviously, she doesn't understand the prestige and stature that has just been bestowed on her. If she keeps her nose clean and keeps her mouth shut, she will move in social circles with the elite of Germany."

"I will speak with her, Commandant. But it is short notice. And it's Christmas Eve. What about my job at the factory?"

"You've resigned and your position has been filled."

"But . . ."

"Everything is taken care of. I realize it is Christmas Eve. But der Führer is seeking Special Forces officers who can drop what they are doing at any time and report for service to the Reich. What is more important, Christmas or service to der Führer? Now if you are coming with me, I need you to gather some toiletries and a change of clothes now."

"Very well, *Herr* Commandant. But could I have just a few moments alone with my wife?"

"Take twenty minutes; then we must go."

Ingrid followed Heinrick upstairs.

"Heinrick, what's going on?"

"The Führer has selected me to serve in the German Special Forces."

"What are special forces?"

"That's classified."

"If you say 'classified' again, I'm going to scream!"

"Okay."

"Heinrick, it's 4:45 a.m. on Christmas Eve. I've had no notice. What am I to tell the girls? How long have you known?"

"Ingrid, you know I've been doing some classif—" Heinrick caught himself about to utter the forbidden word. "I mean, some secret work for the Party. But I swear to you, I had no clue about this."

"So what will you do, Heinrick?" A desperate look set into her eyes. "Are you just going to leave us on Christmas Eve?"

"Of course I do not wish to leave," he said as he threw some slacks and sweaters into a small suitcase.

"Then why are you packing your suitcase? I thought the commandant said 'If you're coming with me, I need you to gather your things.' That sounded like it wasn't definite that you have to leave."

"I know he said that, but this is not optional."

"Not optional? Then why would he say 'if you're coming?' That sounded optional to me."

"I don't think it's optional because of the Führer's telegram."

"Come on, Heinrick. The commandant made it sound like the Führer sent you a personal telegram. Now we discover that the same telegram went to others as well."

"It doesn't matter, Ingrid. It was issued in the name of and by direction of the Führer. And is says clearly"—he opened the telegram again—"'You will report to Induction Processing Headquarters, Berlin,' not 'You have the option of reporting' or 'You may choose not to accompany the commandant if you wish,' but 'You *will report*.' Here. Read it for yourself."

He tossed her the notice. She read it and shook her head, and he saw the look of worry on her face. "I see your point."

"Besides Ingrid, even if it *were* optional, they've already eliminated my job at the factory. I would have no place for work. For your sake and for the sake of the girls, these are not the kind of people we want to cross."

"What do you mean by that?" she asked.

"Just trust me, Ingrid. You didn't believe me when I told you I was involved in activities affecting national security. Now you see my importance to the Reich. So trust me when I say we don't want to cross these people."

"Okay, Heinrick. I'll trust you this time. But when will you be back? Will you be gone all the holidays?"

"I can't say. The telegram provides no information. Maybe this is some sort of one-day indoctrination thing. Maybe they'll let us come home on leave." Heinrick didn't believe a word of it. Deep down, he knew he would be gone for a long time.

"I can't bear to see you out the door, Heinrick."

"Then stay up here with the girls." He grabbed her and gave her a long, passionate kiss. Then he kissed each of his sleeping daughters on the cheek.

"I love you. I will contact you with more information as soon as I am permitted."

He hugged her once more, then headed downstairs, suitcase in hand.

Ingrid heard the front door close. The Nazi visitor had taken her husband, and her gingerbread family was burning in the oven.

8

Darwin McCloud sat in the corner of the fortified basement and sipped a glass of Pinôt noire. To him, the redeeming thing about this New Year's Eve was that the year 1940 was about to come to an end. Darwin wished 1940 had skipped the calendar altogether. He hoped that the bottle of expensive wine would numb some of the pain and drown out the sounds of the air raid sirens as he slipped into the new year.

The pale-looking, twenty-year-old only child of a Royal Navy captain lived with his mother, a baroness with distant blood ties to the Royal Family, in a posh flat in London's Kensington District. Even before the Nazis bombed London, the year had been an emotional bomb for him. His parents' final divorce in the first week of January had gotten things off to a bloody miserable start.

A devout Anglican, Darwin interpreted the Holy Scriptures literally and thought divorce was sinful. He had pleaded with his parents not to separate. When they did, he begged them to reconcile.

They ignored him and signed the divorce papers. One week after finalizing their divorce, Edward and Juliana

McCloud were off gallivanting with eligible members of the opposite sex.

Though the winds of war were blowing across the European continent by the beginning of 1940, Darwin hardly noticed. His preoccupation with his parents' divorce blinded him from international events or anything else for that matter.

Looking for a diversion, Darwin turned to the theatre. He landed the lead role in Plutarch's *The Life of Marcus Antonius*.

On September ninth, the Luftwaffe began blitzing London. Air raid sirens, the whistling of bombs dropping, and thunderous explosions rocked the city night after night. One bomb struck the theatre. Darwin got lucky, but his stint as Marcus had gone up in smoke.

A dozen of Darwin's friends were not so fortunate. Many were killed within two weeks of the bombing. Londoners, terrified by air raid sirens, scrambled each night into bomb shelters, the underground, or any other place of refuge they could find.

Hell rained from the skies. Nothing remained sacrosanct. Even Buckingham Palace was bombed. For years, Captain Edward McCloud of the Royal Navy had pushed Darwin to pursue a career in the military. Either the Royal Naval College or Sandhurst would've suited the father's ideal wish list for his son.

But the father's suggestions did not resonate with the son. A military career did not stir Darwin's fancy. All those rules and regulations would stifle his creativity. Darwin wanted to sing and act.

Now the Prime Minister, Mr. Churchill himself, had called the nation to arms. Darwin may have been an actor, but he was first and foremost British. That meant having a profound sense of duty to the crown and to country. The Nazi air force shook Darwin from his personal malaise. *Marcus Antonius* was over. He wanted to find a way to help. But how?

Because its large dome was so visible, St. Paul's Cathedral became a convenient bull's-eye for the Germans. On October 10 at 5:55 a.m., a large bomb fell on the east end of St. Paul's. It exploded between the roof and the high tower, destroying the chancel area. The bomb provided Darwin's answer—or so he thought.

On Friday morning, the eleventh, he took a cab over to the church to talk with some of the firefighters about volunteering. "The duty is dangerous," they said. "You would need to be on call around the clock. Jerry loves dropping incendiary bombs, the type of bomb that spreads fire," they told him. "You will have to fight fires, handle live fallen bombs, and dodge falling chunks of glass and concrete."

These fellows, most who were serving because of their love for the church, were exhausted and shorthanded. Several chaps had gotten no sleep and still had smut on their faces from the night before. They needed all the help they could get. Moved by their sacrifice, Darwin volunteered on the spot. He knew the danger, but even if he were killed, his death would be part of a noble cause. Maybe this type of death would make his father proud of him. He reported for duty the next day.

Sunday, December 29, 1940 seemed to be one of the heaviest days of bombing yet. Because of the ferocity of the attacks that day, St. Paul's postponed its morning services. Only the firefighters were in the cathedral, and they had been on watch all night.

Darwin reported for duty that morning and gathered in the watch captain's spaces in the basement with other members of his shift. He poured a cup of black coffee as his new pal, Edwin Reece, lit a cigarette. Reece, a bachelor machinist who lived alone in London's less-affluent South Side, was not a member of St. Paul's. He served here as watch commander because the cathedral was a national landmark, and he wasn't about to let Jerry have the satisfaction of destroying any symbol of British nationalism.

Reece, at age thirty-nine, was rough, gruff, and blue collar. From Darwin's perspective, the relationship with Reece had been a godsend. Getting to know someone from a different social stratification helped get his mind off his parents' divorce.

Darwin grew comfortable enough with Reece that he revealed his mother's nobility. He discussed his father's military career and his feelings about the divorce. He would never mention these personal matters to the other members of the crew, lest they have yet another reason to rib him. But Reece, in a gruff yet gentle way, seemed to understand him and always lent an understanding ear without being judgmental.

In Reece, Darwin found someone he could trust with anything. Not many other people in his world fit that category.

The chitchat in the watch captain's quarters began picking up as Reece took a draft from his cigarette. Darwin had taken one swig from his hot cup of coffee when the air raid sirens started blaring outside.

"Be on guard, gentlemen! Jerry's on the way!" Reece said.

"At least they could let a chap finish his coffee," Darwin joked.

"Look on the bright side, McCloud. Jerry will provide enough heat to keep your coffee warm." This was Roger Olsen, the deputy watch commander.

"Very funny, Olsen, ol' boy," Darwin shot back as the sound of roaring airplanes and antiaircraft fire from outside grew louder by the minute.

As Darwin took a second drink from his coffee mug, the building shook from a rocking thud and he heard the shattering of glass. Hot coffee sloshed over the front of his shirt.

"Tally ho, gentlemen! Secure your equipment! To your stations! Immediately!" Reece barked.

The entire crew charged upstairs to assess the damage. An incendiary bomb had flown through a stained-glass window and into the main worship area of the cathedral. The bomb had spread fire across the back benches and up the wall.

"Williams, Heath! Hose down the walls. McCloud, Anderson, start getting water on those benches!" Reece yelled. The flames on the walls were brought under control, but the flames on the old wooden pews were tougher to contain. Yellow fire jumped along the pews, spreading from row to row. Black-and-white smoke billowed into the high rafters and into the dome of the giant, ancient cathedral.

"Gentlemen, we need a firewall around these benches, or the whole interior of the cathedral will be in smoke and flames.

Grab your axes! We're going to rip out row four and row twen-ty-one!"

Reece's strategy was to tear out at least four rows of the benches and contain the fire between rows five and twenty. The men responded to his orders, but the flames leapt toward the chancel area in the front of the cathedral faster than the men could work. Reece needed more workers ripping out the pews. The problem was that his volunteers were working with light-weight pick axes. They needed the heavier sledge axes which were stored in the watch captain's spaces below.

"I need three volunteers to come with me! On the dou-ble!" Reece ordered.

Reece and three volunteers rushed back downstairs past the crypt to the watch captain's space. Reece went in first and started passing axes to each man.

"Men, take your axes to rows four and twenty. I'll be right there."

Darwin looked up and saw the three volunteers emerge from the basement stairwell with axes. Reece was not with them.

The axes were dispatched to the appropriate rows as the firemen ripped the benches out of the flame's path. As Darwin continued hosing down the flame, a huge explosion rocked the building from below. Darwin looked up again. Still no sign of Reece.

"Somebody go check the situation down below!" Darwin yelled, still pouring water on the middle section of the pews.

"I'll go have a look!" Olsen volunteered.

Five minutes passed. Flames from the burning benches gave way to the stream of water from the fire hoses. Darwin worried that neither Olsen nor Reece had appeared.

He kept his eyes glued on the smoke-filled stairwell leading down to the basement. Straining to see through the smoke, he saw the image of a firefighter at the top of the stairwell.

"Help! We need some men down here with pick axes, now!" This was Olsen's voice. Darwin's stomach knotted.

"What's the situation below?" one of the firefighters yelled.

"A concussion bomb hit the watch captain's spaces. The whole area is destroyed."

"What about Reece?" Darwin shouted.

"He's buried under some rubble. I tried to reach him but couldn't."

"Did he say anything?" someone asked.

"No. Nothing."

"Is he alive?" someone else asked.

"Can't tell," Olsen replied.

Darwin threw down his water hose, grabbed an axe, and ran through the smoke down to the basement. Fallen rafters, chunks of mortar and steel were blocking the entrance to the watch captain's space. Pitch darkness made visibility difficult. Darwin shined his torch through the rubble but could see nothing.

"Reece!"

No answer.

"Reece!" Darwin's voice echoed through the crypt. Still no answer. "You better answer me, ya bloody drunk, or I'll pull you out of there and personally feed you to Jerry!"

Olsen arrived with three axe-toting firemen, their torches illuminating the full wreckage caused by the bomb.

"Where is he, Olsen?" Darwin demanded.

"There, look down low." Olsen crouched to knee level and shined his torch through some bent steel beams. Shaking, Darwin reached down and pointed his torch in the same direction. About fifteen feet away, pressed under a concrete slab, he could see a boot and part of Reece's pants leg.

"Reece! Reece!" Darwin screamed as he pulled against the concrete but could not move it.

"You've got to calm down, man!" Olsen pulled Darwin back. "We can't help if we panic."

The sight of Reece's legs, motionless, lifeless, made Darwin feel as if someone had dumped a bag of ice on his head and shoulders. "We must get him out, Olsen!" A helpless panic set in his body. "He's my best friend! We must get him out!"

"Okay. We're going to get him," Olsen said. "You men get your axes. Start breaking through that rubbish. The five of us will remain here and work on getting Reece out. I'll go upstairs and tell the others to join us when the fire is under control."

It took three hours before the men had cleared enough debris to reach Reece. Darwin wanted to crawl under the space to be the first to reach him, but Olsen ordered two of the men to restrain him. Instead, Olsen himself lay flat on his belly and inched toward the fallen watch commander.

"Okay, men. I've got a rope around him. Let's pull him out," Olsen ordered.

Olsen crawled back out and shook his head at the crew. Darwin refused to accept Olsen's obvious body language as being indicative of anything. He watched as the rope tugged Reece's stiff body from under the rubble and into full view.

"Don't leave me, Reece! Ya can't leave me, man! Ya can't go now! I've got no one else." Darwin repeated through his sobs.

Olsen's men pulled Reece, his face ghastly white and his eyes frozen open, onto a fire blanket. Darwin leaned over the body, then buried his head in Reece's chest. Reece had been his only friend—and the only person on earth, besides his mother and possibly his father, that he loved.

A couple of the firefighters started to reach down to restrain Darwin again, but Olsen waved them back.

"Just give the chap a few minutes, boys," he said.

Olsen waited then finally spoke up. "McCloud, ya gotta let him go now."

But Darwin would have none of it. He couldn't bear to leave Reece there on the floor.

"McCloud, Reece was strong and brave. He'd want you back at your station. Let him go. This is a war. We've got work to do," Olsen said.

Darwin ignored Olsen's instructions.

"Okay, boys." Olsen motioned to the firefighters to pull Darwin back. He followed them up the steps into the cathedral as the rest of the crew stayed behind to take care of Reece's body.

The escorts led Darwin to the front door of the great cathedral, where Olsen met them.

"Let him go, boys," Olsen instructed, as he gave Darwin a handkerchief.

"Darwin." Olsen usually called him McCloud. "There's a lull right now in the bombing. I don't expect another raid for at least thirty minutes. I'm sending ya home for the day. Take some time and come back when you're ready."

"But I'm okay now," Darwin protested.

"No you're not, son. We can't have you here in this state. I have no idea how you'll react when Jerry starts bombing again. You could get yourself killed or get one of us killed. We want you back and we need you back. Just not today."

"Okay, Olsen. I'm leaving. I'll be back."

"Good."

Darwin lumbered through the smoke, sloshed through standing water and walked by the smoldering pews in the sanctuary, then down the front steps of the great cathedral and hailed a cab for Kensington. The cabbie dropped him off at his Kensington flat just before the next wave of bombing started. He joined his mother in the fortified basement they used as a bomb shelter.

She said she knew something was amiss, but he refused to talk about it. Instead, he contemplated the brevity of life. Had he completed his cup of coffee that morning, he would be dead. Instead, he lost the best friend he ever had. He would trade places with Reece if only he could.

On New Year's Eve, 1940, as he finished the last drops of the bottle of Pinôt noire he had been nursing, Darwin McCloud concluded that life was too short to deny who he was. Yet he had to be discreet. Revealing his true identity to the wrong person could destroy him, especially under the circumstances.

His mother might understand, only because they were so much alike. His father never would understand or approve. The information in the wrong hands could destroy his father's military career. People like Darwin were not allowed in the military. But he needed to confess his feelings to someone or he would explode. He had to find someone to talk to.

9

THE OUTER BANKS OF NORTH CAROLINA
EASTER MONDAY
APRIL 14, 1941

Ellie pulled a towel over her legs to avoid the beating rays of the Carolina sunshine. She never liked the beach at Nags Head. Way too much wind. Plus the inebriated sailors on liberty from Norfolk could not seem to resist the urge to whistle at a hundred decibels whenever they happened to stumble within a stone's throw of wherever she sunbathed in a skimpy swimsuit. While she appreciated the flattery from these tattooed drunken studs, their shrill catcalls made it impossible to concentrate on her book. Sometimes other factors made concentration difficult too.

She adjusted her shades and glimpsed at Billy splashing around in the surf with Little Billy and Margaret. For all his faults and shortcomings and despite the fact that he was a bore, Billy Brewer was a good father to her children. For that, he deserved credit.

She sat on the beach trying to concentrate on her new novel, *Gone with the Wind* by Margaret Mitchell. She'd just gotten into the book, an exciting, romantic page-turner set in the Civil War.

But the wind kept flapping the pages around so much that

she closed the book, closed her eyes, and just listened to the wind and waves washing across the sandy shore. With the warm Easter sunshine basking on her face, Ellie felt as relaxed as she had in months. Burying her feet in the warm sand, she drifted into a light sleep. She awoke and saw Billy standing over her.

"Ellie."

"Oh Billy, how long have you been standing there?"

"Not long. I just got out of the water," he said.

"How long was I asleep?"

"I don't know. Fifteen, maybe twenty minutes."

"Billy, where are the kids?" she asked.

"Oh they're down playing in the surf."

"In the *surf?*" Her motherly instinct kicking in, Ellie rose up and locked eyes on her children, scrawling in the wet sand a few feet from the water's edge. "Billy, Margaret's only three years old. You've got to keep your eyes on her every second."

"She's just having some fun in the sand, Ellie," he said.

"But I'm just not comfortable with her being that close to the ocean."

"Ellie, there's something I wanna talk about."

"That's fine. But first, please go get Margaret and bring her closer up here so I can keep an eye on her."

"She's fine, but whatever you say, Ellie." Billy cuffed his hands around his mouth, forming a manual megaphone. "Billy! Margaret! You young'uns come on up this way!"

"That's not doing any good, Billy," she sniped. "You can see that didn't faze them one bit. I *asked* you to go get them."

"Oh, all right," he grumbled as he headed down to the surf.

In a few seconds, Billy returned with Little Billy under one arm and Margaret under the other.

"Mommy, I'm hungry. Can we have something to eat now?" Little Billy asked.

"You'll have to ask your daddy to go get the picnic basket out of the car, son," she said.

"Wait just a minute," Billy protested. "Don't you remember, Ellie? I said there's something I want to talk about. And I wanna talk about it before we eat."

"I'm sorry. You *did* say that," Ellie said. "Kids, why don't you go over there and build Mommy a sand castle?"

"Oh, boy!" Little Billy shouted. "Come on, Margaret." Little Billy found a spot in the sand a few feet from where Ellie was sunbathing, and Margaret waddled over to help him.

"So, what did you want to talk about?"

"Well . . . You know how Roosevelt signed that new draft law last year?" he asked.

"Of course. It's all you and Walter talked about for a solid week," she said.

"I've decided I don't want to get drafted."

"I don't blame you for that. Who would?"

"What I mean is . . . I want to have some control over the situation."

"You and every other man. Control is a man's greatest aspiration," she said.

Billy hesitated for a moment. His face displayed the typical befuddled confusion he so often displayed in reaction to any comment deeper than *supper's ready.*

"Never mind," Ellie said. "How do you propose to control this draft thing? Do you want Daddy to make a call to the draft board for you? You know he'll be glad to."

"No, I wouldn't feel right about that."

"Billy, Daddy's got a lot of IOUs on the Washington County Draft Board. And you *are* his son-in-law. That's the safest way I can see you getting out of the draft."

"That ain't what I had in mind."

Ellie cringed every time he said *ain't.* She tried breaking him of slang years ago with limited success and had long since given up.

"Okay, what *did* you have in mind?" she asked.

"I've been thinking about enlisting."

"Enlisting? In the Army?"

"Don't ya see? That's how I could have some control over the situation," he said.

"By signing up for the Army?"

Billy smirked. She'd seen it on his face a thousand times—a cross-grin look that displayed half his teeth and made his left nostril twitch. The smirk came whenever he had deluded himself into believing he had outwitted her. She hated the smirk and could predict that the I-might-not-have-any-book-sense comment would soon follow.

"Ellie, for somebody with so much book sense, you've still not figured it out yet?"

"Okay. You've got me, Billy. My 'book sense' has eluded me."

"Not the Army, Ellie. The Navy. I'm thinking about signing up for the Navy."

"The Navy?"

"That's right, the Navy," he said.

"And this will solve your draft dilemma because?"

"My draft *what?*"

"How will enlisting in the Navy solve your draft problem?"

"Because if I enlist in the Navy, I won't get drafted by the Army."

"Oh I see," she said. *Here it comes.*

"See, I might not have any book sense, but at least I've got some common sense!"

Ellie snickered under her breath. *Just like clockwork.*

"And your common sense tells you that the Navy would be preferable over the Army?"

"It's not just common sense that tells me that, Ellie."

"What else tells you, pray tell?"

"Ellie, it's a historical fact that the Navy's more prestigious than the Army. In fact, the President was the Secretary of the Navy and so was Teddy Roosevelt. In fact, Teddy Roosevelt did serve in the Army. But when T.R. was the President, he liked the Navy so much he started the Great White Fleet."

She didn't have the heart to tell him that F.D.R. served as *Under*secretary of the Navy, not the secretary. But Billy's observation about T.R. was impressive.

"I'm impressed. Have you been reading about Teddy Roosevelt?"

He hesitated. "Not really."

"Then how did you know all that about the Great White Fleet?"

"Walter told me."

"Walter's not thinking about going in the Navy too, is he?"

"Walter ain't got . . . I mean Walter don't have . . . I mean Walter's got no reason to want to go. He's already got a good government job."

"But Billy, you've got a job too."

"Come on, Ellie. My job doesn't amount to much. All I do is work shift work in the mill and help with the tobacco crop in the summer when I'm off from the mill. I mean, the Navy'd be a chance for me to make somethin' of myself."

"Billy, you know you don't have to work at Kekeauver, and you don't have to pursue your agricultural endeavors either. I've told you a thousand times there's seed capital to start your own business if you want."

"And I've told *you* a thousand times that I don't feel right taking so much from your daddy. I mean he's bought our house for us. I appreciate what your daddy does. But a man's gotta be a man."

"Billy, you are your own man." She touched him on the shoulder. "Yes, we lived in Jamesville for a while before we moved to Plymouth. That was your idea. Little Billy was born there. You agreed to move to Plymouth because it would be ten miles closer to your work at Kekeauver. Remember?"

"You've always got an answer, don't you, Ellie? But that's not the point. Look, I'll probably get drafted anyway, and if I get out ahead of the pack, the Navy's a chance for me to prove something. I could get promoted before everybody else gets drafted."

"You're serious about this, aren't you?"

"Yes, I am," he said.

"Mommy! Daddy! Look at our sand castle!" Little Billy shouted, running to Ellie and Billy with Margaret waddling close behind.

"That looks great!" Ellie said.

"Now can we eat, Mommy? I'm still hungry. You said we could eat when we build you a sand castle," Little Billy protested.

"Tell you what."

"What, Mommy?" Little Billy asked.

"Mommy just needs to talk to Daddy a few more minutes. If you and Margaret can find Mommy a few sea shells in your bucket, we'll have cookies with lunch. Okay?"

"Really?" Little Billy said.

"I want cookies!" Margaret shouted.

"Then go find Mommy some shells, and we'll have lunch and cookies!"

Ellie watched as the kids walked out of earshot, looking for shells just about twenty feet away.

"So what about *them*, Billy? You are a father, and they need their daddy. Aren't you worried about leaving them? And isn't this a very dangerous situation you'd be getting into?"

"Of course I'd miss 'em. I'd miss everybody, and I'd miss you. But Ellie, if I'm getting drafted anyway, there's nothing I can do about it. President Roosevelt has signed the draft law. As far as the danger goes, I've done a lot of thinking, and the Navy's not as dangerous as the Army."

"Why do you say the Navy's not as dangerous?"

"Think about what's been happening. The Germans have a huge army. They've attacked Europe and bombed England, but they've not got much of a navy. When the draft starts picking up, way I figure it, Uncle Sam'll need a big whopping army to go over there and fight the Germans. And that's where the real danger is, Ellie. In the Army, not the Navy. So one of the reasons I want to sign up *is* for them. And for you too. I've got a much better shot at coming home alive in the Navy than the Army."

"You *have* thought through this, haven't you?"

"Of course I have. It's just common sense, that's all."

"Just don't make any rash decisions. But whatever you want to do, I'll support you."

Billy smiled.

Ellie reciprocated, with great effort, silently convinced that her husband had lost his mind.

10

LONDON
EASTER, 1941

Nazi bombs rocked the British capital city through the first few months of 1941. But after Reece's death, Darwin had developed a numbness to it all. The fires, the blasts, the destruction, the air raid sirens, and the smoke—none of it bothered him after Edwin Reece died.

The death caused Darwin to examine himself and his relationship with Reece. He felt alone and didn't care if they killed him too. Somehow, some way, on the other side of eternity perhaps he would see Reece again. Saturated by his new sense of indifference, he returned to his post at St. Paul's with a fearless attitude toward the Luftwaffe.

On Easter Sunday, Darwin attended church services with his mother. As choruses of "Up From the Grave He Arose" cascaded around him, Darwin bowed his head—in shame. Four months had passed since his New Year's resolution.

He had repeated it over Reece's grave and resolved that he would fulfill it. He would deal with the demons within him. He would talk to someone.

He would admit—to someone he could trust—who he really was.

On Easter Monday, April 14, 1941, Darwin stopped by the watch captain's spaces and asked for the day off. Olsen was short-handed but must have sensed that Darwin needed the break.

A distracted firefighter was a dangerous firefighter—at least dangerous to his fellow crew members.

Olsen consented, and Darwin went home. Pacing about, he hesitated and tried to talk himself out of it.

No one really has to know this dark secret, do they? After all, I've lived with this all these years. Maybe I can keep living with it. But then again, I promised over Reece's grave that I would deal with it. Show the courage Reece showed. Do it for him.

Darwin hailed a cab to the home of the Reverend Charles P. Brooks, one of the staff members at St. Paul's. He arrived at the modest stone flat in Sutton about two in the afternoon and knocked on the door.

Brooks, a tall bachelor in his late twenties, came to the door wearing a clerical collar.

"Yes? May I help you?"

"Reverend Brooks, I'm Darwin McCloud. I'm from St. Paul's. I serve on the Fire Brigade. We've met a couple of times."

"Ah, yes. What can I do for you, Darwin?"

"Reverend, I believe I may need counseling of some sort."

"Counseling? You don't say. What sort of counseling might you be in need of?"

"It's rather personal. I wanted to know if I should set an appointment."

"Regretfully, we cannot maintain ordinary office hours at St. Paul's these days, not with the bombing. I suppose now would be a jolly-good time for me if it's okay for you."

"Splendid. That is, if you don't mind." *I suppose there's no getting out of this now.*

"Of course. Please come in and have a seat. Would you care for some tea?"

"Tea would be wonderful, Reverend. Thank you."

Brooks returned with a silver pitcher and two cups of tea.

"Now then, Darwin, have you ever had counseling of any sort before?"

"No, I can't say that I have. I suppose I haven't needed it. This would be the first time."

"I suppose there are several basic axioms we should go over before we start. First is the clergy-parishioner privilege. This means that anything you say here will remain confidential—not to be repeated outside the confines of these walls. Do you understand?"

"Yes. That's good to know."

"Secondly, we want you to relax and understand that the only bad question is no question at all. Can we agree on that?"

"Yes, of course, Reverend. I will try and relax and ask questions."

"You can dispense with calling me Reverend. You can call me that in public if you'd like, but for purposes of our session, we've found that we've been more successful by striving for a level of informal intimacy. So if you'd like, feel free to address me as Charles."

"Very well then, Charles."

"Good. So then, Darwin, tell me about yourself. Why do you feel you need counseling?"

"It's a matter that's very hard to talk about."

"Of course it is. We all have deep, dark matters that are hard to discuss. Don't feel badly about that. You aren't alone."

"Oh, I feel very much alone in this struggle. Rev—I mean, Charles. I've struggled with this issue for years. And I'm reluctant to discuss it, because if the information ever got out it could destroy me."

"Whatever the issue is, Darwin, God knows about your struggles. He loves you and accepts you just like you are."

"I believe that God accepts me. But if this information were made public, I'm afraid there are so many others who would reject me, especially my own father." Darwin's eyes met Brooks's then wandered to the far wall where various diplomas were framed and hanging.

"No father should reject a son, Darwin, no matter what," Brooks said. An awkward moment passed. "Tell me about your father. What about him makes you think he would reject you?"

"Perhaps a better word would be *disown*. Not only would he reject me; he would disown me."

"All right. I'll let you choose your own words. Why would your father disown you?"

"My father is an officer in the Royal Navy. He's the captain of the destroyer HMS *Defender*. He's a rough-and-tough type. For years, he's pushed me to join the military. On my seventeenth birthday, he got me applications for Sandhurst and the Royal Naval College. The applications never got filled out."

"I take it you weren't interested in following in your father's footsteps in a military career?"

"Part of me would very much like to serve in the military, not only to serve the crown, but to make Father proud of me. He divorced Mother last year. I pleaded that they stay together, but they ignored me. Sometimes I think that if I served in the military, I could establish some credibility with father and maybe he would listen to my arguments for reconciling with Mother."

"There's nothing wrong with desiring to please you father. And promoting the reconciliation of your parents is both admirable and biblical. But I do have a question for you, Darwin."

"Ask away." Darwin sipped a cup of tea.

"If part of you would like to serve in the military, why don't you just volunteer? The Army's going to need all the help it can get."

"Charles, that goes back to my dark secret. Let me put it to you this way. They don't accept my type in the military. And if they were to find out about me, they'd ridicule me and then kick me out in disgrace."

"I see." Charles cleared his throat. "Let me ask it this way. What sorts of things are you interested in?"

"I love song, dance, and drama. I'd like to be a professional actor."

"Sounds like you're very talented. Nothing wrong with the arts."

DON BROWN

"I'm also interested in the affairs of the Anglican Church, which is one of the reasons I volunteered for the fire brigade at St. Paul's."

"Then you and I share a common interest."

"I suppose we do."

"Tell me about your mother. Would she be accepting of you if your secret were out?"

"Mother would be more accepting than Father, no doubt. We have a special bond."

"What is your mother's name?"

"Juliana. Juliana Windsor McCloud."

"Her maiden name is Windsor, as in the House of Windsor?"

"There's a semblance of truth to that. My grandfather is distantly related to the Royal Family. Mother was born as Baroness Juliana."

"So your mother is nobility, eh?"

"As was grandfather. But you'd never know unless you had a reason to know. She's treated accordingly in the circles she runs in, but to the chap on the street, she would simply introduce herself as 'Juliana McCloud.' Of course, I think Father married her because he believed being married to nobility would advance his naval career."

"You mentioned that you and your mother have a special bond. Tell me about that."

"Soon after mother and father were married, my father began focusing on advancement within the Royal Navy. He volunteered for arduous sea duty. Mother remained at home, alone, to raise me. Of course, we had a number of nannies, but I was with Mother more than the nannies. She took me everywhere.

"With Father at sea, Mother became interested in the church, in music, and in the theatre. As a boy and as a teen, I went with her to dozens of plays in the theatre district. Through her, I learned to love and appreciate drama."

"So I take it that you're more like your mother than your father."

"Yes, you hit the nail on the head."

"Lots of people are more like one parent than the other. Nothing is wrong with that."

"But Charles, in my case it's different. I'm not just more like my mother than my father. I'm not like father at all. In fact, I'm not like most other men. And that's the problem I need to confess."

Charles paused for a moment and sipped some tea. "You know, Darwin, I think I know what you're going to say. If it's what I think it is, we've had others with the same issue. And I want you to know that I don't think any less of you no matter what you say, and neither does God."

"Thank you. I needed to hear that," Darwin said.

"And it's been my experience that those who have this problem feel much better once they confess the inward struggle and get it off their chest. The best thing to do is just take a deep breath and come out with it."

Darwin slowly inhaled, then exhaled, then slowly inhaled again. Then another exhale. "Very well, Charles. Here goes. Charles, I'm a . . ."

"It's all right, Darwin. Let it flow."

11

Billy, Ellie, and the kids got home from the beach around six o'clock that evening. The large white house at the corner of Third and Washington Streets near downtown Plymouth was still strewn with chocolate Easter eggs and baskets from the previous afternoon. Little Billy and Margaret each grabbed a handful of chocolates and scooted upstairs, hoping to stuff their faces before Ellie could intervene.

Billy still had the Navy on his mind.

He had not mentioned his idea to the kids yet but made a number of cryptic comments to Ellie on the drive back from Nags Head. With the kids upstairs feasting on chocolate bunnies, Billy again broached the subject. This time, he wanted to float the idea by Little Billy and Margaret, and he wanted to do it now.

"Margaret, Billy, ya'll come back downstairs. Mamma and I want to talk to you about something."

"You mean you want to tell them something," Ellie told him.

"This needs to be a joint thing, Ellie."

"I don't think so, Billy. I told you I'd support your

decision and I will. But if you get killed and they think I encouraged you to go, they'd never forgive me."

"I already told you, Ellie. The Germans can't compete with our Navy."

"Look. I said I'd *support* you. But that's different from *encouraging* you to go," she said.

"And I need to prove I can make something of myself without the support of the Williams trust fund."

"Oh Billy, stop being so sensitive. You knew what you were getting into when you asked me to marry you."

"Did I ask you or did you ask me?"

Getting insightful, are we? Better not give him a direct answer to that question. "Billy, you know you wanted to marry me from the very first time you seduced me behind your granddaddy's barn."

"Oh, yeah? Is that why you were engaged to Walter after that?"

"But you know I dumped Walter for you, my big sailor man." She playfully rubbed the back of his shoulders. "Of course, there's no point in rubbing it in to Walter."

"You don't think I'm dumb, do you?" he asked.

"I refuse to answer the question on the grounds that it may incriminate me."

"You think I'd tell my own brother I stole his fiancée from him? You know that's *our* secret, Ellie."

Little Billy and Margaret came down the stairs, a blond-headed, blue-eyed tandem sporting a copious supply of chocolate smeared on their faces.

"Are you sure you want to do this?" Ellie asked. "You can think about it some more. Remember what I said. Daddy can make one call to the board and this whole thing goes away."

"I know. The great Jimmy Williams waves his magic money bags, and the whole world's problems are solved."

"Billy, don't talk about my daddy that way. You make it sound like he's a criminal who tries to bribe his way out of trouble."

"Just let me handle this, Ellie."

"What is it, Daddy?" Little Billy asked.

"You remember last summer when we went to Albemarle Beach at the sound?" he asked.

"Yeah, Daddy!" Little Billy responded. "Can we go back to the sound?"

"Maybe we can. But first you have to answer a question."

"What's that?" Little Billy asked.

"Remember the game we played?"

"We played Navy war!" Little Billy shouted. "I was the submarine and you were the battleship! And I bombed you with clam shells and pecan shells. Pow! Pow!" Little Billy started making explosion noises and gesticulating with his hands, trying to engage his daddy in playing the war game right there in the living room. "Let's play that again, Daddy!"

"Hang on a second, Little Billy. First, there's something I want to tell you."

"What's that, Daddy?" Little Billy asked.

"Do you know what the draft is?"

"Yes. I heard Uncle Walter talk about it. That's when you have to go in the Army."

"That's right, Billy. Now guess what?"

"You've been drafted in the Army?" Little Billy asked.

"No. But Daddy *might* be in the Navy," he said.

"The *Navy*?" Little Billy's eyes widened with excitement.

"That's right. The Navy."

"Wow." Billy looked at Ellie as Little Billy seemed to think for a moment. Margaret appeared more concerned about licking chocolate off her fingers than the announcement her father had just made.

"Does that mean you'd be on a ship?"

"Yep. Daddy's going on a ship."

"Wow!"

"So what do you think about that?"

"Can I be in the Navy, too?"

"When you get to be big enough you can."

"But Daddy, I *am* a big boy. I'm seven *and a half*!"

"Okay, Billy. You're right. You *are* big enough. You're just not quite old enough. But I tell you what. Maybe you can come see Daddy's ship when it's in port. How would that be?"

"Really?"

"Really."

"Daddy, does that mean you get to bomb some Germans?"

"I don't know, son. We'll just have to see."

"That's not fair. *I* want to get to bomb some Germans."

"No you don't, Little Billy," Ellie protested. "Nobody needs to bomb anyone." *We're raising a warmonger.*

"When can I see your ship, Daddy?"

"I'm not in the Navy yet. So it might be a little while before we can see Daddy's ship. But if you'd like to, we can drive up to the Navy base in Norfolk on Saturday and look at some *real* Navy ships."

"Billy, what have I told you about making plans without checking our schedule?" Ellie demanded.

"But I want to go see some real Navy ships, Mommy."

"Okay, that's fine," Ellie said, resigned that hers was a hopeless cause. "Go back upstairs now children."

Little Billy scurried upstairs to his chocolate stash, his little sister in tow, mumbling gleeful utterances about the Navy all the way up the stairs.

Billy looked at Ellie, sporting an arrogant grin on his face and reeking with satisfaction at the boy's response. "I'd say that went pretty well, don't you think?"

"Like father, like son."

"What do you mean by that?"

"Testosterone. It must be a male thing."

12

I feel so tongue-tied," Darwin said. "Being the son of a career naval officer, I don't know. This is so hard to admit. Although Father and I have been estranged, I don't want to hurt him. If this gets out, it will damage Father's career."

"It's okay, Darwin. Just say it. Remember, your secret goes no farther than these walls," Charles said.

Darwin breathed deeply again, trying to muster the courage to confess the thing that would destroy him, especially during this time of war. "I'm a . . ."

"Go ahead," Charles said.

"I'm a . . . How do I say this?"

"Yes?"

"I'm . . . a pacifist! There! I admit it. I'm a pacifist!"

"You're a *pacifist*?" Charles looked incredulous. "*That's* what you wanted to admit?"

Darwin paused for a few seconds then smiled. "Yes, and I already feel somewhat liberated. If there were some way to make this philosophy of mine go away, I could feel good about serving in the military and make Father proud."

"Is there anything *else* you wanted to confess to?"

"Like what?" Darwin asked.

"Oh, never mind." Charles hesitated then continued. "But I have another question for you, Darwin."

"What's that?"

"Why did you feel you needed to make that particular confession to an Anglican priest?"

"Because I need guidance on whether a true Christian can serve in the military."

Charles cleared his throat. "First, there's ample evidence that there were Christians in the military during the time of Christ and that Christ acknowledged these military personnel as Christians."

"Really?"

"Yes. An example comes to mind from the Gospel of St. Matthew. The Roman centurion came to Christ and asked for healing of his servant. Christ offered to come to the centurion's home, but the centurion responded that he wasn't worthy of having Christ in his home and that all Christ needed to do was to say the word and the servant would be healed. Do you remember that story, Darwin?"

"Yes I do, but I don't understand why that makes it acceptable for a Christian to serve in the military."

"Think for a moment about Christ's response to the centurion. He said that He had found no one in Israel with such great faith. What do you think Christ meant by that?"

Darwin hesitated. "I suppose He meant that the fellow had faith that Christ would heal his servant."

"True. But the meaning is deeper than that. The faith isn't just in what Christ would do, but in *who* Christ is. The centurion had faith in Christ. That means he was a Christian. In other words, here is a soldier, one whose military duty may require killing, yet Christ recognizes him as a man of faith."

Darwin paused for a moment to think. "I suppose I see your point."

"And the story of Cornelius is found in the Book of Acts Cornelius and his family are described as devout and God-fearing. So Cornelius served as an officer in the very army that put Christ to death, yet he is described as a Christian too."

"But doesn't Christ suggest that we should turn the other cheek? And if a fellow asks for our shirt, we should give him our coats. How can we act this way if we aim to kill the poor fellow, even if he *is* a jerry?"

"That's true, Darwin. But we do have to view all scripture in proper context. In neither of those cases is Christ referring to national conflicts in which a state of war exists. He is referring to interpersonal situations which occur outside a state of war. This means we should not exact personal revenge out of vengeance. If someone insults us or cheats us, we should not respond with an eye for an eye as some of the Jews were suggesting with their questions."

"So Christ was responding to a question about an eye for an eye?"

"Precisely. More tea for you?"

"Yes, please," Darwin said. "So Christ was not a pacifist?"

Charles sipped a spot of tea. "Heavens, no. Christ combated evil. He resisted the devil in the wilderness. He rebuked the Pharisees. He drove the moneychangers out of the temple. But when spat upon and beaten, He refused to retaliate."

"But doesn't that prove he was a pacifist, the fact that he let them beat on him and spit on him and crucify him without retaliating?"

"Absolutely not. In God's plan to redeem mankind, Christ had to die. He had to be crucified as part of the plan. He died for our sins, then conquered death three days later. Revelation predicts that Christ will return as a warrior, in splendor and glory to battle his enemies. Hardly the actions of a pacifist, eh?"

"So I could go to war and preserve my status as a Christian?"

"Of course. Christ predicted there would always be war. War is a part of the fallen condition of our world."

"I understand. Yet one thing remains beyond my comprehension."

"And what would that be?" Charles asked.

"How can I fulfill my duty as a Christian to spread the gospel to the Germans if I have to kill them?"

"Because the Nazi government represents evil, you can, as a Christian, fulfill your duty to kill the military agents of that government. Yet you should pray for the salvation of those you are duty-bound to kill."

"I have a duty to kill them, yet I must pray for them at the same time?"

"If England is at war with Germany and you are ordered into battle on behalf of the Crown, then yes, your duty is both to pray for your enemies *and* to accomplish your mission."

Darwin swallowed more tea. "Sort of paradoxical, isn't it?"

"Yes, paradoxical indeed. But that is the Christian's duty in wartime," Charles said.

"How thought provoking." Darwin stood. "Perhaps I should go."

"Darwin, before you leave, there's something I have for you. Wait a moment please." Charles left the room, and a moment later returned with a book in his hand. "A gift from me. It's the King James Version Bible, translated into German. Perhaps it will remind you to pray for your enemies."

"Thank you, Charles. I'll remember that."

Darwin shook Charles's hand and walked out the front door, down the cobblestone steps to the street, and hailed a waiting cab. "Kensington, please." He got into the back seat of the car, and as the cabbie rolled forward, he studied the German Bible.

As the taxi passed by St. Paul's where Reece had died from German bombs, Darwin wiped a tear from his eye, then glanced again at the Bible.

I shall pray for my enemies, and then I shall kill them.

13

On the first Saturday in October, Ellie decided to take a late afternoon walk. Downtown Plymouth basked in unseasonable warmth for this time of year, the effects of the final days of a lingering Indian summer.

She followed the same route every day, turning right out her front door then following the sidewalk down Washington Street to Water Street, which paralleled the Roanoke River. As usual, she walked down the banks of the Roanoke just behind the businesses on Water Street and stopped to spend a few minutes alone watching the river flow slowly from left to right. She stood on the banks of the river alone, with no one else in sight, as the handful of merchants along the street always closed their shops at noon on Saturdays.

Yet despite being alone on the riverbank, she did not feel lonely. The kinship she felt with the river gave her comfort. The lazy, old river seemed to be a living thing, a silent comforting friend on which she could cast her thoughts. It was the heart and soul of her heritage—a reservoir of history—an eternal artery linking Jamesville with Plymouth. She, like the river, would always be linked with Jamesville.

She sauntered along the bank for about a block before cutting back up to Water Street, where she strolled past the antebellum bricks of Grace Episcopal.

Often she stopped in front of the church to gaze at the cross atop the old steeple. Standing on the sidewalk at the same spot along Water Street where she had stood on December 6, 1930—the night of the club Christmas party—her walks never failed to stir memories of that evening.

Sometimes she felt guilty. Billy had been gone since July, and here she stood on a sidewalk in front of Grace Episcopal, reliving a romantic memory with his brother from eleven years ago. Many times she had wondered what if. Sometimes she dwelled on it. Sometimes her thoughts were fleeting.

On this warm Saturday afternoon, she walked past the church and headed back home, her mind turning to Little Billy's show-and-tell project due on Monday. The boy brought a note home from his teacher last Wednesday announcing the assignment, and both she and he were stumped coming up with ideas.

Before going home, she needed to stop by the Plymouth Post Office to check her box. Often she got letters from Billy, sometimes to her, more often to the kids. While she wasn't good about writing back, she insisted that Little Billy write his daddy on a weekly basis. Margaret wasn't old enough to write but insisted on "signing" her name on the bottom of Little Billy's letters. Margaret got a kick out of writing her daddy, and Ellie imagined that Billy got an even bigger kick out of "reading" her portion of the letter. Today, she found a solitary letter in the post office box from Seaman Billy Brewer at the Naval Training Center in Great Lakes, Illinois, addressed to Billy Brewer, Jr. at 302 Washington Street, Plymouth, North Carolina.

Good. This will make Little Billy's weekend.

"Read it to everybody." Ellie handed the letter across the kitchen table to her son. She figured he would need her help reading it, but he loved opening letters addressed to *him*. He ripped open the envelope.

"Look, Mommy! There's a picture of a ship in the envelope." Excited, Little Billy handed the picture to his mother.

"Hmm. USS *Arizona*, BB-39. I wonder what BB-39 means."

"Can I have the picture back, Mommy?"

"Here." Ellie handed him the photo. "Do you want to read the letter, or do you want me to?"

"You can read it while I look at the picture."

"Okay. Give it here." Ellie took the letter while Little Billy gazed at the photo. "It's dated August 29, 1941. That would have been one week ago today. Here goes."

Dear Billy,

I hope you and Mommy and Margaret are doing fine. Daddy misses you all very much.

Guess what? I've got some exciting news! Daddy's going to be on a battleship! Isn't that great? And the news is even better. It's the biggest and most powerful battleship in the whole Navy! It's called the USS *Arizona*! It's over 600 feet long and has big powerful guns that can shoot shells for miles. It's also the most famous ship in the Navy.

Daddy is going to be a gunner's mate on the Arizona. That means I get to fire big 50-caliber machine guns at enemy airplanes. The ship is going to be stationed in Hawaii and will be in the Pacific Ocean. I will be going to Hawaii to meet the ship in November. But first I have to get some more training in firing the weapons.

Here's a picture of the Arizona. It was taken from a Navy airplane.

I get some leave next spring and will be able to come see you.

Take care and tell everybody I love them and I miss them.

Love,
Daddy

"Wow! Daddy's going to be on a battleship! I can't wait to tell everybody at school."

"Is this the first you've heard about Hawaii, Ellie?" said Becky Estep, the college-student-turned-nanny Ellie had recently hired from Sweet Briar College in Virginia.

"I guess it says something that he would make the announcement in a letter to his son," Ellie said.

Becky gave Ellie a curious look. "I just thought of something."

"What's that?" Ellie asked.

Maybe Little Billy could incorporate the battleship in his show-and-tell for science."

"Yeah, Mommy! Can I? That's a great idea!"

"I'm sorry. I didn't mean to speak prematurely," Becky said.

"That's all right," Ellie said. "But how would he go about relating a battleship to science?"

"He could talk about displacement."

"Displacement?" Ellie looked puzzled.

"Yes. I mean water displacement. It has to do with how a ship floats," Becky said.

"Yeah, Mommy. Please?"

"I suppose it sounds as good as any other idea we've come up with. But I don't know that much about how the physics works," Ellie said.

"We covered it last year in a physical science lab at Sweet Briar. I'd be happy to help him if you'd like."

"Thanks, Becky. You just solved my problem."

Billy Brewer, Jr. had never been so excited to set foot on the campus of Washington Street School. Before the eight-thirty bell rang, he was waving his picture in front of all his friends.

"Guess what? *My* daddy's gonna be on a *battleship*! It's called the USS *Arizona*, and it's the most famous ship in the Navy! See?"

The boy held up an eight-by-ten-inch glossy black-and-white official U.S. Navy photograph of the dreadnought. "Here's a picture he sent me!"

"I want to see!" said one little boy.

"No, give it to me!" demanded another.

"Is your daddy really on that ship?" A wide-eyed, pigtailed little girl asked.

By nine in the morning, the picture had caused sufficient commotion that not a single student in Mrs. Neil Asby's second-grade class was unaware of Billy Brewer's assignment to USS *Arizona.*

When Mrs. Asby called on young Billy for show-and-tell, he again announced that his daddy was "gonna be on a battleship, the most famous and powerful in the Navy." He passed the picture around for everyone to see again and took a stab at explaining the theory of water displacement in second-grade language. "A ship floats because the water around it holds it up. If a ship gets a hole in it, it would sink. But if a ship doesn't have a leak, it will float. A ship is heavy. But the water around it is heavier than the ship. That's why the ship floats, because the water is heavier than the ship."

Little Billy's performance earned him an A-plus for show-and-tell that day. On this Monday, October 7, 1941, Billy Brewer, Jr.'s daddy became the most popular daddy at Washington Street Elementary School.

14

TRIPOLI, LIBYA
NOVEMBER 1941

Heinrick had seen more than his share of sandstorms. North Africa, it seemed, was nothing but sand.

Since arriving as an intelligence officer attached to General Rommel's staff in February, he had spent most of the year in Libya.

His only respite from the blistering Sahara came in June when Rommel dispatched him on temporary assignment to Crete, where German forces had routed the British and taken control of the strategic Mediterranean island. By August, he returned to Africa, briefing Rommel's senior staff on his findings. There would be no more temporary assignments off the continent.

The assignment to Erwin Rommel's staff was a political plum for Heinrick, reward for loyalty to the Party and "bravery and heroism" in the attack on the Jewish synagogue.

Rommel, the Desert Fox, was the brightest mind in the German military. He would become Heinrick's ticket to the highest places of power in Berlin. With his assignment to Rommel, Heinrick had aligned with a rising star. As an intelligence officer, Heinrick got plenty of face-time with the general himself, usually in the form of briefings on the activity and strength of the enemy.

But the job wasn't always so glamorous, especially the repulsive battlefield examinations when his intelligence team dug through dead bodies and equipment looking for any clues left by the enemy. Heinrick soon discovered the horrific stench of the battlefield.

So many of the dead, both British and German, died with their eyes and mouths wide open. The buzzards enjoyed plucking a corpse's eyeball as a pre-meal delicacy, leaving a gaping bloody socket to boil in the searing afternoon sunshine. Perhaps out of respect, the birds seemed to leave the other eyeball in place, preferring to instead pick at the meat around the neck and face.

Heinrick grew callous to the shocking sight of such blood and gore. He was not as thick-skinned, however, when thinking of his family back in Nuremberg.

Since that Christmas Eve in 1938 when the commandant plucked him from his home in the middle of the night, Heinrick had seen precious little of Ingrid and the girls. He did not return for Christmas that year as he had hoped, and though he was allowed to write letters to assure them he was well, he was not allowed to reveal his whereabouts. He would not see home for another four months. His sudden return in April of 1939, resplendent in the immaculate, black uniform of an SS officer candidate, was an answer to prayer for Ingrid, Leisel, and Stepphi. Screams and tears of joy were the order of the day, followed by tears of sadness when he informed his girls—the collective term he used for his wife and two daughters—that he had only three days of leave. His departure in April was harder on them than his disappearance in December had been.

When Germany invaded Poland in September, leave became a rare commodity for young military officers. He did manage a couple of days the week before Christmas 1939, which the girls loved. But he was gone again until September of 1940. That was the last time he had been home.

He took solace in knowing that Ingrid and his daughters were better off, at least economically, than they had been in years. The Party was taking care of its own. Yet he missed them greatly, especially in the lulls. He wrote as often as possible. Sometimes the letters got through. Sometimes they got lost. Always there was a delay of weeks or months.

By the middle of November, 1941, his heart ached for his girls. Late at night on November 20, he flipped on the small lamp beside his bunk and began penning a letter to Ingrid.

20 November 1941

Dearest Ingrid,

Someday, when there is peace under German rule of the world, I will bring you to the places where I was honored to serve the Führer and the Third Reich. I will bring you to the Sahara, but not for long, for the blistering heat would be too much for your fair skin. I will bring you here so that you may have a brief glimpse of the oppressive environment in which so many brave sons of the Fatherland sacrificed so much for the swastika-laden banner.

As the Christmas season again approaches, my mind turns to our family. I think of you, of the girls, of our humble home in Nuremberg, of our Christmas tree, and of logs crackling in the fireplace. When you and the girls huddle around the fire to stay warm and when you look into the hot flame and see the wave-like mirage the hot gases make at the tip of the flame, think of me.

For as I look in every direction over the barren landscape of a wasteland they call Sahara, where the summertime temperature climbs to 120 degrees, I too see the wave-like mirage that you see in our fireplace. Through binoculars, the waving atmosphere is more pronounced on the horizon.

There is always suspense, an uncertainty, sometimes an ominous fear of what looms on the other side of the waving wall of air. Sometimes, we see dark objects appear in the midst of the wave. Our hearts beat fast as we try focusing our binoculars and our telescopes on the objects, which as they grow closer seem larger, darker, but no less intelligible to the eye than they were fifteen minutes earlier.

We sometimes feel a collective sense of relief when the

objects break through the wall and appear in our binoculars as a herd of camels or a nomadic tribe scouring the desert for shade or water. But sometimes there is no relief—not when the objects materialize into a British scout party or troop transport trucks or tanks with their barrels aimed squarely at us.

Many times during this past year, the murky mirage has materialized into a military machine. But each time, our forces have beaten them back and brought glorious victory to the Fatherland. In May, they launched several offensives against us, trying to dislodge us from our positions here in Libya.

The sight of an army emerging through a desert mirage from a distance is frightening. But the face of war up close and in the wake of battle is dreadful beyond description. As part of the general's intelligence team, I have become an expert, for better or worse, at staring into the face of war.

After the enemy's failed attacks on us in May, my team waded through what seemed like thousands of British bodies and tons of wrecked equipment in conducting our intelligence evaluation of the scene after the battles.

In June, the general dispatched me, along with three other intelligence officers, to Crete to assess conditions following our victory there. Fortunately, the battlefield carnage was not as significant as in Libya. We spent three weeks on the island, which is a very mountainous and desolate place off the coast of Greece. We hit the Brits hard with a great parachute attack, with many of our forces literally floating from the skies and onto the island. We overran the Brits there and sank a cruiser, HMS *Calcutta*. The ship was trying to evacuate fleeing British troops. When the ship went down, we captured many British prisoners, and our team spent time interrogating them through the use of translators. If you had been there, you could have helped us translate. I think your English is better than some of the translators assigned to us.

While in Crete, we received word of Operation Barbarossa, which as you have heard was launched June 22. The Führer has long warned of the dangers of communism. He spoke of the dangers and inefficiency of Communist Russia on the night I heard him speak at the labor hall in Nuremberg in 1936.

Now Operation Barbarossa will stamp out the most powerful communist nation so near to our eastern border. I must confess that part of me wanted to go to the Russian front when I heard the news. Yet I am very grateful and honored to serve in Africa on the staff of the most brilliant military tactician in the army, General Rommel. The general and many members of his staff believe it's only a matter of time before the Americans join the fight. Therefore, we must be diligent in defeating the British, and we must be ready if the Americans get involved.

As I write this letter, I am back in Libya and have been here since returning from Crete in July. As of today (November 20) the Brits are trying yet another offensive against us. This one has been going on for a couple of days. I expect the result will be the same, that Afrika Korps will defeat them yet again. The Brits have no leader who can match the military genius of the Desert Fox.

I hope that my letter to you has not been redundant. I realize that I covered several topics I wrote to you about in earlier letters, but I do not know if those letters reached you. I hope this does in time for Christmas.

Tell the girls I love them, and know that I love and cherish you.

All my love,
Heinrick

15

Bridge, sonar," came the voice over the loudspeaker near the helm of the British warship, HMS *Defender*.

"Go ahead, sonar." Captain Edward McCloud surveyed the gray, choppy waters of the North Atlantic from the bridge of his ship.

"Captain, we've received an urgent message from the USS *Greer*."

"Bring it up," Edward said.

"Aye, sir."

"Convoy duty. Heck of a way to earn a living, Steve," Edward said to his personal friend and the chaplain of the destroyer squadron, Lieutenant Commander Stephen McKibben. The chaplain, an Anglican priest who had known Edward for years, was on the ship's bridge at the captain's invitation, along with the executive officer, the helmsman, and the conning officer.

"Playing a deadly game of chicken with German submarines? You know you couldn't stand life any other way, Captain," McKibben said. "Anything less mundane and you'd wither like a dried-up raisin, sir."

"You know me well, Steve," Edward said.

"I should. We've known each other for a long time," McKibben said with a sly grin. "Besides, it isn't like you're playing Russian roulette only for the rush of adrenaline. I'm a chaplain and not a line officer. But still, I would say there's a slight bit of importance to the national interests attached to our duties here. Hmm?"

"So true," Edward said. "These convoys from America now represent Britain's only lifeline to the free world. Not even our friends in the Royal Air Force, who fought so brilliantly in repelling the Germans during the blitz of London, can work their magic without supplies. Sever the lifeline and starve the victim.

"Hitler knows it, Churchill knows it, and Franklin Roosevelt knows it too." He paused. "Forgive me for stating the obvious. Sometimes a commander needs to reassure himself of the obvious, even if everyone else knows it."

"Not a problem, Captain," McKibben said. "That's one of the reasons you're an excellent sea captain, your ability to focus on the mission. And God bless FDR. Standing up to the isolationists in America like Charles Lindberg, who would let us rot on the grapevine."

"Yes, well, we should have a drink to FDR when this is all said and done."

"Excuse me, Captain," the executive officer said. "Petty Officer Crowley is here from sonar with that urgent message."

"Send him in," Edward said. The young petty officer made a beeline for the captain and handed him the teletype message. Edward unfolded it.

FLASH

From: Commanding Officer, USS *Greer*
To: Commanding Officer, HMS *Defender*
Subj: Enemy U-boat Coordinates

1. Sender has been escorting Convoy #27143 [New York-Liverpool.] Be advised of successful U-boat infiltration of convoy. Damage includes three merchantmen sunk, two

oilers disabled and on fire. One, possibly two, U-boats suspected.

2. Be advised sender last lost sonar contact of target bearing course of 93 degrees at 25 degrees west, 61 degree north at 11:03:35 GMT. Headed your direction. Good hunting.

Edward looked at his watch, then the clock on the bridge.

"Last contact was fifteen minutes ago. At that course, he's headed just south of us."

"Awaiting your instructions, Captain," the executive officer said.

"Very well," Edward said. "Mark course at one-eight-two degrees, ahead three quarters."

"One-eight-two-degrees, ahead three quarters," the executive officer said back.

"Have sonar mark these coordinates. Go active sonar immediately," the captain ordered the petty officer from the sonar room.

"Aye sir," the petty officer said, as *Defender* turned left in the choppy waters, beginning a southerly course to hunt the German U-boat.

"Alert me of the first possible contact," Edward said.

"Aye sir," the executive officer said.

From his chair on the bridge, Captain Edward McCloud watched with pride as his crew carried out his orders with immediate precision. The hunt was on. *Defender* was ready to kill. Or be killed.

"Perhaps I should go below," Lieutenant Commander McKibben said. "Not much a chaplain can do from the bridge just before battle."

"Why don't you stay up top for this one, Steve? And look on the bright side. If we get torpedoed, you'll be the last to go down—with me. Besides, we could use the blessings of the Almighty right about now."

"Very well," McKibben said. "I serve the Lord wherever I am ordered to go."

"Like the good sailor that you are," Edward said. "Besides,

there's nothing we can do right now except wait . . . and listen. Tell you what. I'll have the steward bring up some tea while we wait." Edward caught McKibben's eye. "And watch." The captain summoned his personal steward and ordered a pot of tea from the galley.

"A high stakes game of life or death over a pot of tea," McKibben said. "If I survive this, I should write a book some day."

"Be sure to put in your book that if we had been under aerial assault, your captain would've sent you below to take cover. But since we are facing a potential submarine attack, he was simply trying to keep you as far away as possible from the point of impact."

"You never cease to amaze me, Captain."

"All in the name of self interest, Commander. I want the Lord's man close to me if I am going to die."

"I think it is the *Lord* you want close to you if you are going to die, not necessarily His man."

"Reverend Stephen McKibben, the ever-insightful theologian," Edward said as the steward from the galley brought in a silver tray containing a pot of hot tea. The steward unfolded a small portable table and left the pot and cups beside the captain's chair.

Chaplain McKibben poured two cups and handed one to the captain, then said, "At the captain's suggestion, I propose a toast to FDR."

Edward chuckled. "Hot tea wasn't the beverage I had in mind for the occasion, but why not? To FDR, for providing a lifeline to England."

"Don't forget Scotland and Wales," McKibben said, as the two old friends clanked their cups of hot tea.

"So, do you miss them?" McKibben took his first sip.

"Miss who?" Edward said.

"Juliana and Darwin, of course."

"Playing the role of the marriage counselor moments before battle, are we?" Edward said. "I'm afraid you're too late, Reverend. Baroness Juliana and I are now divorced. And my son and I are, well, shall we say . . ."—Edward sipped his tea as his eyes looked out the bridge at the gray North Atlantic horizon—"different?"

"Which of course explains the presence of the large, glossy photographs of them both in your stateroom," McKibben said.

Edward again sipped his tea, unsure about whether he would let this subject matter continue.

"Of course I miss them. What kind of a question is that?"

"Care to discuss it?" McKibben asked.

"Not now," Edward said.

"Not a problem, sir."

"It's just that," Edward said, "you know as well as I that I'm married to the Navy, Steve. Ours was a marriage of convenience and design. Sort of window dressing, service to the Crown. The lovely lady of nobility and her handsome young naval officer. Over the years, having to live for the sake of maintaining that picture grew unfair, especially to her."

"Think we're handsome, do we?" McKibben asked with a grin. Steve McKibben was the only officer in the entire destroyer squadron who could get away with such banter with the captain.

"Of course not. Neither handsome nor young. But that's the picture every young lady of nobility in England wants to imagine, and they all seem to be looking for naval officers."

"But do you still love her?"

Edward took a long sip of tea before answering. "Of course I do. But now we have three complicating factors. First, we're now officially divorced. Secondly, the Royal Navy is a jealous mistress. Thirdly, we are at war."

"But we won't always be at war," the chaplain said.

"No," Edward said. "And an hour from now, I might be a frozen corpse on the bottom of the Atlantic, depending upon whether I find the Nazi U-Boat commander first or he finds me."

"Life does present some complications, eh Captain?"

"Complications indeed, Reverend."

McKibben sipped his tea. "And what of your son?"

Edward looked around, unsure whether to continue this personal line of questioning on the bridge of a warship.

McKibben had just been assigned as chaplain to the destroyer squadron one week ago, and although he and McKibben had been boyhood friends, this was the first personal conversation they had had. The hum of the engines and the activity going on around them, with the crew monitoring charts and fidgeting with gadgets, gave them some privacy. At least nobody seemed to be listening.

"I dreamed he would follow in my footsteps and become an officer in the Royal Navy. Tried to steer him to the Academy. I even introduced him to Churchill once. Winnie put in a plug for the Navy at my request. But Darwin is far more like his mother than me. Looks like her. Acts like her. While I've been at sea, she's raised him to love the church and the theatre. At one time, I thought he was going to seminary."

McKibben cleared his throat. "And something would have been wrong with that?"

"No, not at all. It wasn't my first preference, but I pointed out to him that he could've become a Royal Navy chaplain."

"And that didn't go over well?"

"Darwin sings and dances and acts. I wanted him to become a naval officer. But my son is a *toe dancer*. I tell you, I wonder about him, Reverend."

"A toe dancer whose pictures you have all over your state-room."

"If you're asking if I love him, of course I do. But I cannot... I have never been able to communicate at all with him. There is a great gulf between us, regrettably."

"Bridge, sonar." The blaring sound of the loudspeaker cut off Edward's comments.

"Go ahead sonar," Edward said.

"Sir, we have contact with target. Possible German submarine."

"Bearings."

"Course bearing three-one-zero degrees. Range three thousand yards, Captain."

"That means he's circled to the southeast and is heading right toward us," Edward said. "XO, sound general quarters. All hands to battle stations!"

"Aye, Captain." The ship's executive officer, its second in command, pushed a button on the bridge, under which was a small label with the words *General Quarters*. Alarm bells went off all over *Defender,* creating a sound that resembled a fire drill.

With the alarm bells still ringing, the XO pressed another button activating the ships loudspeaker system, and in a tense voice announced, "General Quarters, General Quarters. All hands to battle stations." The exec let about thirty seconds pass, and then with bells still ringing, repeated over the loud-speaker what he had just said.

"General quarters! General quarters! General quarters. All hands to battle stations!"

Steve McKibben looked out from the bridge to the deck below and saw sailors, now clad in gray helmets and orange life pre-servers, scrambling about the deck like mice running from a cat. His heart surging, McKibben strapped on his helmet, which looked like all the others except for the small white cross painted on the front.

"Bridge, sonar!" came the voice over the loudspeaker.

"Go ahead, sonar!" Edward said.

"Sir, we have contact with a second target. I repeat, a *second* target. Range one thousand, five hundred yards and closing. He's off our starboard, sir."

"Where did that come from?" Edward said.

"No explanation, sir. He just appeared on the screen," the sonar operator said.

"Helmsman, hard about right. Now!" Edward ordered.

"Hard right. Aye, sir."

The helmsman turned the wheel to the right, causing the ship's starboard to dip close to the waterline as it came about. Edward and Steve grabbed the railing by the captain's chair. As the ship turned, Edward said to his chaplain, "I need you to start earning your pay, ol' boy."

"What can I do, sir?"

"We're outnumbered two to one. One of these U-boats has somehow slipped into firing range, undetected by our sonar. We're pulling to the starboard to make ourselves less of a sitting duck. If he hasn't gotten his torpedoes off, our defensive maneuver will guarantee he gets off a first shot. I need a prayer to the Almighty, and I need it now. That's an order, mister."

"Aye, sir," the chaplain said.

"Bridge, sonar."

"Go, sonar."

"Captain, we've got two fish in the water, sir. Torpedoes closing in, sir."

"Acknowledge, sonar. Fire control, bridge."

"Fire control."

"Lock coordinates on closest enemy submarine, range one thousand, five hundred yards. Fire depth charges on my command."

"Coordinates locked. Ready to fire on your command, Captain."

"Stand by, fire control."

I hope that's a command I live to issue.

"Captain, forward lookout has a visual on two inbound torpedoes, sir," the executive officer announced.

Edward looked through his binoculars straight off the bow. The white streaks in the water were on parallel courses about a thousand feet out and closing toward his ship. One was about a hundred yards in front of the other.

He pressed the microphone button activating the ship's loudspeaker. "All hands, this is the captain. Brace for possible torpedo impact. Prepare to launch lifeboats."

The two white streaks in the water raced closer to the ship. Binoculars were no longer necessary to see them. All eyes on the bridge were fixed on the explosive devices racing towards the bow.

The hard-right maneuver was now complete. By bringing the ship to a position facing the enemy U-boat, Edward had reduced the target area from seven hundred feet—the length of the ship—to less than sixty feet—its width. It was easier to hit the ship from the side than head on.

On the other hand, a strike to the bow would mean definite death to the *Defender*. Edward had reduced the chances for a strike but exposed the most vulnerable area, the ship's bow. McKibben saw sweat dripping off the captain's forehead as he continued elevating silent prayers to the Almighty that the "fish" would miss.

The first one zipped just past the ship's port, about fifty feet off the railing. The second whizzed no more than ten feet off the starboard.

"Close, but no cigar!" Edward blurted. "Fire control, bridge. Launch depth charges, now."

"Aye, Captain."

Defender rocked as exploding powder sent the depth charges hurling forward. First there were splashes in the water about a thousand feet in front of them. Then the explosions sent great plumes of water against the cold, cloudy sky.

Edward looked forward with his binoculars. Nothing yet.

"Bridge, sonar."

"Report."

"Captain, U-boat has lost his engines. Looks like a strike, sir."

Edward again looked through his binoculars and saw black oil floating to the surface in the midst of bubbles.

"All engines idle," Edward ordered.

"Engines idle," the helmsman repeated Edward's command then pulled back on the gears to slow the ship's progress.

"Fire control, bridge. Prepare to launch depth charges on my order. Same coordinates. I also want five-inch guns ready in case she surfaces with hostile intent."

"Acknowledged, Captain. Awaiting your order," the fire control officer said.

"Bridge, sonar."

"Go ahead, sonar."

"Captain, it sounds like he's blowing his tanks. He's trying to bring her to the surface."

"Roger that, sonar." Edward watched the bubbles blowing with greater frequency on the surface. He watched as the bow of the submarine pushed through the surface, then the conning tower, and the stern.

"Bridge, fire control. Awaiting your instructions, Captain."

"Hold fire, gentlemen. There's not much she can do to us on the surface. "

Steve McKibben looked down and saw the entire crew with their collective eyes fixed on the crippled German sub, now bobbing in the rough waters of the North Atlantic. The hatch popped open on top of the sub's conning tower, and men with life preservers on began scrambling along the deck of the submarine.

A few fell overboard as the crippled boat rocked in heavy seas. Inflatable rubber lifeboats were launched, and men started crawling into them and paddling away from the doomed warship.

Edward watched through his binoculars as the sub's bow began to list upwards, pointing at a forty five-degree angle to the cloudy sky. Then as it rose almost vertically, the sub slipped under the surface to its watery grave.

"Captain, should we commence rescue operations?" the executive officer asked.

"Not yet, XO," Edward said.

"Bridge, sonar."

"Report, sonar," Edward said.

"Captain, second U-boat has disengaged and is making a run out to sea."

"Skipper, should we mark course and pursue?" the executive officer asked as four lifeboats with German sailors bobbed in the rough waves several hundred yards off the bow.

Should I give pursuit and let these men perish? Edward wondered. There's no doubt about what a Nazi destroyer commander would do in my shoes. These submarines just sank thousands of tons of supplies headed for England and killed sailors and crewmen in the American convoy. I should leave them to the sharks, he thought to himself. Then again, some of them are just boys, conscripted into service against their will. Some of them have fathers back home. Some of them have sons.

Make a decision, Edward. If you don't pursue now, the other U-boat will be out of your reach. Free to destroy other shipping. You're the captain. This is your call.

"Commence rescue operations, XO. You've got the con," Edward said.

"Aye, Captain."

Edward turned to his old friend, Steve McKibben. "Meet me in my stateroom, Chaplain. I think it's time to finish that toast to Mr. Roosevelt—with something other than tea."

16

From the quarterdeck of the USS *Arizona*, Seaman Billy Brewer rubbed his eyes as the sun crested Diamond Head, just a few miles to the east of the large American Naval Base at Pearl Harbor. For the last few weeks, with the *Arizona* moored with the U.S. Pacific battleship fleet at Ford Island, Billy had found himself looking forward to sunrises.

Especially on Sunday mornings.

That was because the sun rose in the east—from the direction of his family. It was like God sending him a big, orange, warm ball which he imagined had been launched by Little Billy in Plymouth floating west across America and then across the Pacific to remind him that the kids and Ellie were alive and well and doing fine.

He missed them more than he imagined he ever would when he came up with the idea of enlisting in the Navy. The separation had made him wonder how he wound up with such a pretty, sophisticated wife. He was just a plain, simple tobacco farmer's grandson from Jamesville. Yet somehow, he was married to the envy of eastern North Carolina, the beautiful Ellie Williams.

He looked toward the rising sun and remembered the last time he saw her. It was at the bus station in Plymouth the morning he shipped out for boot camp at Great Lakes. She had looked into his eyes and spoken one of those quotations she liked to speak. "Absence makes the heart grow fonder," she said. "You'll see what I mean."

And she was right. He wasn't much of a reader and he wasn't an educated man like his brother, but he had heard that saying before. He'd never given much thought to it, but now he knew. His heart ached by the great divide of time and distance from her.

Billy looked out at the beautiful aqua sparkling waters of Pearl Harbor, at the light, choppy ripples reflecting the rising sun. If he had to be separated from his family, at least the unrivaled, scenic beauty of Hawaii provided some consolation. If only Ellie could see this place. The beaches back home, Nags Head and Albermarle Sound, were pretty in their own right.

But nothing like this.

One day, when he got out of the Navy, he would bring Ellie here. Maybe even the kids too, if he could afford it.

And if he couldn't afford it, maybe he'd swallow his pride and dip into the Williams trust fund to finance the trip.

Billy snapped a salute as a Navy commander in summer whites, whose black-and-gold shoulder boards showed him to be a Christian chaplain, walked onto the quarterdeck from the catwalk.

Probably headed to morning chapel.

When the officer of the deck waved the chaplain aboard, Billy dropped the salute and looked around at the still-sleeping gray warships.

A few white-clad sailors were moving about on the deck of *Arizona*. On the deck of USS *West Virginia*, the same scene was unfolding. The same was true for the deck of USS *Nevada*, at least from what Billy could see. Just a few sailors scurrying about, unfolding the American flag with buglers in place, getting ready for morning colors. Most of *Arizona*'s crew and the rest of the Pacific battleship fleet was asleep down below decks. Even Admiral Kidd was down below somewhere.

At least the war was in another part of the world and America wasn't involved. It was a good thing. Many of his ship-mates were sleeping off hangovers. Too much whiskey.

It was just his luck. On this clear, beautiful Sunday morning, he was stuck with quarterdeck duty. Not that Billy would be sleeping off a hangover. For the last few weeks, he had discovered that Sunday mornings were the most peaceful time of the week. A time for a couple of hours when it seemed he had paradise all to himself.

Were it not for quarterdeck duty, he would have already caught a boat ashore for an early-morning church service followed by a late-morning breakfast of scrambled eggs, bacon, and pineapple juice at his favorite Honolulu café, the Pacific Breeze. Then he would catch a cab down to Waikiki Beach, spread a towel on the warm Hawaiian sand, and pen a letter to Ellie and the kids and return to the ship when liberty expired at eighteen-hundred hours.

Billy checked his watch.

7:55 a.m.

"What's that idiot doing?" Someone shouted as the buzzing roar of an airplane engine grew louder.

Billy looked to his right out over the bay and saw a fighter bomber flying into the entrance of the harbor, hugging close to the surface and flying inbound at maybe twenty feet off the water.

Rat-a-tat-a-tat-a-tat-a-tat-a-tat-a-tat-a-tat-a-tat!

"What the . . ." someone shouted as bullets from the fighter cut down the center of the harbor, spraying a wave of water high into the air.

"Here comes another fool!" someone else shouted.

Boom!

"They ain't ours!" Billy heard someone yell.

"They're Japs!" the officer of the day screamed. "Sound general quarters!"

Black smoke suddenly billowed from one of the other battleships. Billy felt his heart sink as air raid sirens cranked up around the harbor. Now dozens of planes were swooping in from the harbor entrance.

Alarm bells were now ringing on the *Arizona* and other ships.

"Battle stations! Battle stations! This is no drill! All hands to battle stations!"

Billy sprinted to his battle station, a 50-caliber antiaircraft gun, as wave after wave of torpedo bombers bore down upon the aqua-blue waters of the gorgeous harbor.

For twenty-eight-year-old Billy Brewer, the screeching sound of the approaching aircraft was surreal. How could this be happening?

The sun was shining. His shipmates were sleeping. The carriers were at sea, and the American planes at Hickam Field were still grounded. This was not supposed to be happening. Not in this, the most beautiful of all places Billy had ever known.

No one at Pearl was on guard. Billy's shipmates were sleeping like sitting ducks before a double-barrel shotgun. Neither the Navy nor the Army had prepared Billy or anyone else for a surprise attack.

There would be plenty of blame to smear around later. But he might not be around to witness the blame game. Now was the moment of truth. In a few moments, it would be Billy Brewer against the entire Japanese Navy.

In a flash, his mind began racing from the palm and coconut trees of Pearl to the tobacco and peanut fields of Carolina; from his shipmates to his family; from his wife Ellie to his kids Little Billy and Margaret; from his brother Walter's last hug before shipping out to his first deer, shot on their grandfather's farm outside Jamesville.

Billy had fired a gun many times. But never in anger. Never in war. Now in this picturesque paradise, Billy's adrenaline kicked in. He knew the attack was coming. The planes were now in his gun sight and bearing down on the *Arizona*. It was time to lock and load.

Billy engaged his firing mechanism as thunderous explosions occurred all around the *Arizona*. Water and fire sprayed everywhere. Billy wheeled around and squeezed the trigger. The 50 millimeter shook like a loud jackhammer, spraying a wave of lead into the deep-blue sky. More explosions as smoke, fire, and water sprayed everywhere.

Billy winced at the sparks and the sound of ricocheting bullets from a Japanese Zero bouncing on the steel around his head. The near-miss only made him more determined.

Billy fired again, hanging on to the powerful, vibrating, antiaircraft machine gun as it sprayed another round at the enemy. This time, a green dive bomber with the Rising Sun emblazoned on its fuselage burst into flames. Bull's-eye! He kept firing. A Japanese Zero started smoking. But more smoke was billowing from the crippled American battleships moored in the harbor. The planes kept coming. Too many planes, not enough bullets.

His mind ran in slow motion, the sight carrying him back to Grandaddy Brewer's Martin County farm, to a field called the John Grey Field. Named for a beloved slave who died a hundred years ago, the field had an old tobacco barn in the middle of it and a large beehive in the far corner. Now in the midst of battle, Billy remembered his granddaddy reaching into the beehive for the honeycomb. How Billy loved sucking on fresh honeycomb. But Granddaddy never got stung because he was always wearing long, thick gloves.

Here at Pearl Harbor, Billy had no gloves.

Now in a surrealistic two-dimensional mind frame, Billy was at the same time fighting the Japanese and walking across the field toward the beehive. As black, billowing clouds of smoke blocked the sun's rays, Billy squeezed the trigger again with one hand. With his other, he reached back to Martin County, to his granddaddy's beehive. With each step across the field, the roar of the bombers and the buzzing of the bees grew louder. As he reached his gloveless hand into the swarm of bumblebees, a deafening explosion rocked the ammunition magazine of the *Arizona*. The blinding fireball blasted Billy into the air, the fire burning his arms and legs before splashing him into the oily, flaming waters below.

The splash doused the flames off his back and pants legs. He bobbed under then back up. His leg throbbed as he tried treading water, his eyes focused on his ship. Bobbing up and down, struggling to stay afloat and dodge the patches of fire on the water, he saw USS *Arizona* spewing an inferno of flames and a torrent of black smoke from her magazine rack.

He felt the salt water burning the gash in his back. Blood bubbled up under his arms, and he felt dizzy. He gasped for air then inhaled water. His natural instincts forced him to cough violently, which sent his head under again.

Help me, Jesus.

When Billy kicked his feet to resurface, it felt like a blunt axe swung against his shin. His mind wandered to Ellie's last smile, then Margaret's curls. He kicked once more, enduring enough pain to stay afloat for a last thought of Little Billy asking him "Can I be in the Navy too?"

With the stabbing in his knees growing more violent and with his own blood floating around his neck, he tried floating on his back, praying that a rescue boat would pick him up. Overhead, the sky was black with buzzing hornets—not Grandaddy's bees. Airplanes with red meatballs painted under their wings.

The meatballs began to blur. The booming explosions sounded more distant now. Muted, they yielded to a ringing in his ears. In the distance, he heard the Jamesville Christian Church choir. At homecoming. When he was a boy.

Amazing grace, how sweet the sound.

Grandaddy!

A wave of salt water sloshed over his head and into his mouth. Billy choked, heaved, coughed, and slipped under the water.

On December 9, 1941, Ingrid received Heinrick's letter via the local postal carrier, postmarked from German Military Command in Tripoli. The envelope had been opened and the letter had been cleared by military censors. Ingrid read the letter and wept. Heinrick was still alive.

Despite Heinrick's desire to go to the Eastern Front, Ingrid had a bad premonition about Germany's war with Russia. She had hoped since the invasion in June that Heinrick would be spared being sent there.

She and the girls would celebrate at dinner tonight, knowing that her husband and their father was safe—for the time being—in North Africa. Next day, she penned a response.

December 10, 1941

Dear Heinrick,

Your letter speaks of the desert, but to us your letter was like water to dehydrated nomads.

None of the other letters you spoke of had reached us, and we had heard nothing from you in more than a year. We are so grateful to learn that you are alive and that you are safe with General Rommel in North Africa.

It sounds as if this General Rommel is a wise and prophetic man—especially about the Americans. I'm sure you have heard what has been reported here on German radio and also on the BBC, that the Americans were attacked in Hawaii by the Japanese and that our government is now in a state of war with the Americans. Since it was the Japanese who attacked them and not our nation, perhaps their armies will head to the Pacific and leave Europe to Germany.

Since you have been gone, Stephi has taken up the violin. She is taking lessons from Frau Brauberger of the Nuremberg Symphony. She is progressing quite nicely. Frau Brauberger is having her learn a few pieces by Wagner. She says that Stephi may be ready to audition for the Nuremberg Junior Youth Symphony by next spring. She is practicing an hour every day, working toward that goal. She has her papa's drive and determination. You would be so proud of her.

Leisel has been busy at school and is doing well in her ballet classes on Tuesday and Thursday afternoons. We were required to purchase her a pair of new pointe shoes because we have some great news. Your oldest daughter was selected to dance in "The Nutcracker" over the holidays! She was among a handful out of over 200 who auditioned. She will be in "The Sugar Plum Fairy." I have never seen her so excited as when she got the news. She did not sleep for three nights. Her performance will be Sunday night, December 21. I wish you could see her in her costume. She is so beautiful. Her only disappointment is that her papa won't be able to make it. Think of her that night, Heinrick.

As for me, I too have embarked upon a new venture. In July, I was approached by three members of the local Party about teaching English at the academy where the girls attend school. The committee knew of my background and said that English would be valuable in the future, as Germany would someday occupy Britain and possibly America. Because of the opportunity for extra income and also because things are so lonely here with you gone, I accepted the position. I was a little rusty at first, but now I have gotten more comfortable and am enjoying working with the youngsters.

The job helps the daylight hours pass more quickly. At night, once the girls have gone to bed, I prepare my lesson for the next day or grade examinations.

We are proud of you, Heinrick. You are a credit to our nation and this family. But the girls and I hope for peace soon so that you can return to us. We love you. Write us again soon.

With Love,
Ingrid

17

The last seven days were the toughest Ellie had ever endured. The uncertainty of Billy's fate had destroyed her appetite. She lost weight, and for the first time in her adult life, the daughter of Plymouth's most prominent businessman was looking a bit less than glamorous—and people were starting to notice.

To her dismay, the local press in Washington and Martin Counties had taken an interest in Billy's whereabouts.

The Martin County bi-weekly, the *Enterprise,* featured a front-page headline on Tuesday, the ninth of December. The story was short and poignant, almost like an obituary before the fact.

Not to be outdone, Plymouth's weekly newspaper, the *Roanoke Beacon,* countered with its own front-page story on Wednesday, the tenth.

Fate of Plymouth Man Stationed on Battleship Still Unknown. Congressman Bonner Visits Family.

Billy Brewer, son-in-law of prominent Plymouth businessman Jimmy Williams, was stationed on board the USS

Arizona when Pearl Harbor, Hawaii was attacked by Japanese torpedo bombers on Sunday, December 7. Brewer, a former Kekauver employee and a native of Jamesville, joined the Navy in July and trained in Great Lakes, Illinois before being assigned to the *Arizona* in Hawaii in October. As of the date of this publication, Brewer's whereabouts remain unaccounted for. However, the Navy has released figures showing that most crew members of the *Arizona* died in the attack.

Brewer married Ellie Williams of Plymouth at Grace Episcopal Church in December of 1930. The couple has two children and the family resides at 302 Washington Street, in the historic Windley-Ausbon house. Ellie Williams declined to comment, but Jimmy Williams spoke to the Beacon about his son-in-law. According to Mr. Williams, Billy is a very brave man who had been working at the mill and joined the Navy because he wanted to serve his country. "Billy wanted to prove himself," Williams said. "He didn't wait to be drafted. He volunteered for the Navy. He is a true hero."

Since Sunday's attack, a stream of visitors and even some dignitaries have dropped by the Williams home on Washington Street to offer support. Congressman Herbert C. Bonner, a close friend of Jimmy Williams, visited with Ellie Williams yesterday and then had dinner with Jimmy and Nancy Williams at their home on Woodlawn Road before returning to Washington. Yesterday, Ellie Williams also received a telegram from Governor Melville Broughton, according to her father. "We're thankful for all the encouragement Ellie has received during these difficult days and especially appreciate the telegram from the governor and the visit from Congressman Bonner. I think the congressman's visit lifted Ellie's spirits."

Plymouth Mayor Archie Riddle, who also had dinner with the Williamses and Congressman Bonner, released a statement to the Beacon about the fate of Mr. Brewer. "The attack on Pearl Harbor strikes not only the heart of our nation, but it strikes at the heart of our community, as one of our own families has been affected. I've known Ellie Williams Brewer from the time she was a little girl. We've seen her grow up into a lovely young lady, go off to St. Mary's, and return to Plymouth to start a family of her own. Leone and I call upon all citizens of Plymouth and Washington

County to join us in prayer as we remember Ellie, Billy, and their family in this time of uncertainty for them and in this dark hour in our nation's history."

The *Beacon* article stirred up a commotion in both Jamesville and Plymouth. To the few who had not already heard, the article served notice on everyone that Billy's fate was twisting in the wind.

Ellie detested the circus of visitors constantly knocking at her front door. Many had come because of the article. The lineup of curiosity seekers, many whom she did not know or hadn't seen in years, seemed like a week-long Halloween in December. She had no news and no candy for these Yuletide goblins and wished most of them would go away and leave her alone.

Becky Estep had been a godsend, especially in the last week. More than proficient in the kitchen, Becky kept hot meals on the table for the kids and urged Ellie to eat, to no avail. She cared for the children and provided companionship during the lonely night hours. She also shielded Ellie from what seemed like a deluge of humanity waiting outside for news from Billy. When the doorbell rang, which occurred often during the day, Becky would greet the curiosity seekers, answer their questions, and turn them away by saying that Ellie was resting.

One person not turned away was Congressman Herbert C. Bonner, who arrived unannounced with Jimmy. Ellie knew Bonner and his predecessor, former Congressman Lindsey Warren, for years.

Of course, it's not all that hard to get to know a congressman when your daddy is one of his biggest contributors in a relatively poor district. Both men had visited the Williams estate on Woodlawn Road many times and had bounced Ellie on their knees when she was a little girl.

Bonner arrived in the middle of the afternoon on Tuesday the ninth, just long enough to offer his best wishes to Ellie and to vow that the Federal Government would do all in its power to locate Billy. The consummate politician, he brought candy for Little Billy and Margaret and then left for a meeting with Mayor Riddle and Jimmy Williams. Altogether, he had been in her home no more than fifteen minutes.

Despite Jimmy's comments in the *Beacon,* Bonner's visit did nothing to lift her spirits. To her, a visit from a congressman was no big deal. Her stomach had been in knots since news of the attack, and it wouldn't have mattered if her father had brought down FDR himself to encourage his daughter. She didn't feel like seeing anyone at all, with two exceptions—her brother-in-law and her pastor.

On Sunday the fourteenth, Ellie did not attend services at Grace Episcopal. The last thing she needed at the moment was to get out in public and get pummeled with a barrage of questions. Becky prepared an early lunch for the family, cleaned the kitchen, and asked Ellie to step into the parlor.

"You still didn't eat your lunch, Ellie. I'm starting to think I'm losing my culinary touch."

"I'm sorry, Becky. You're a great cook. Just look at how the kids cleaned their plates. I'm sure my appetite will return soon enough."

"Ellie, I'm worried about you. You've *got* to eat something. You're going to lose your strength. Do I need to call your brother-in-law down here at every meal to keep you from starving yourself?"

The comment grabbed Ellie's attention. Becky had never made a reference to Walter before. "What do you mean by that?"

"I'm sorry. I didn't mean anything at all. I . . . well, I'm sure Billy would want you to eat something."

"But what did you mean by that comment about my brother-in-law?" Ellie persisted.

"I was out of line, Ellie. I shouldn't have mentioned it. What I really—"

"Becky," Ellie interrupted. "It's okay. You can tell me anything. You're not gonna get fired, and I won't hold it against you. Go ahead, what did you mean about my brother-in-law?"

"It's just that Walter seems to be the only one able to get you to eat anything. And also it's . . . I think I've said enough."

"Go ahead, Becky. You can't start a comment like that and leave it hanging."

"Are you sure you want to hear this?" Becky wished she hadn't opened her mouth.

"It's okay, Beck. I need to know what other people are thinking."

"I haven't talked to other people."

"All right then. What are *you* thinking?"

"It's just the way you and Walter look at each other."

"You detect something in the way we look at each other?"

Is it that obvious, or is this girl that sharp? Ellie wondered.

"Maybe it's nothing. I shouldn't have said anything."

"No, I'm glad you did. You know I want you to tell me what's on your mind. And I appreciate all you've done for the kids and me these past few months. We'll miss you, but I hope you have a great time over the holidays with your family."

"Ellie, I've been thinking. I don't feel right about leaving you and the kids, especially under the circumstances."

"Don't be silly, Becky. The kids are out of school. I'll be able to manage. Besides, I can take them to Mother's if I need a break. You deserve some time with your family."

"Ellie, I never had a big sister. I've grown so fond of the children over these months. I feel like *you* are my family too. I feel like I need to be with you. I *want* to be with you when the news comes."

"You want to be here to support me when I get word that my husband has been killed, don't you?"

"I want to be here either way. Besides, Mayor Riddle made the comment the other day that no news may be good news. There's still reason for hope," Becky said.

"I appreciate your kind words, but my instinct tells me otherwise. Some people are hoping against hope that Billy's still alive. All the signs are ominous. Billy was on the ship that took the biggest hit. There was a huge explosion before it sunk. Over a thousand men went down. Even the captain of the ship and an admiral died. Anybody with half a brain knows the statistical odds are not good. I'm not about to delude myself into thinking otherwise."

"I know it doesn't look good, Ellie. All the more reason you still need someone if the news does come. I mean, there will be a lot of decisions that would need to be made, and the last thing you would need to do is have to make those decisions and worry about the kids too."

"As far as I'm concerned, there's only one real decision still outstanding," Ellie said.

Becky was silent—probably unsure whether to pursue this discussion. But it was obvious Ellie wanted to talk about it. "What decision would that be, Ellie?"

"Where to bury him. That is, if we ever find him. Daddy thinks we should bury him at Grace Episcopal here in Plymouth. But Billy was no Episcopalian. Not even close. He was a Jamesville boy. I think Jamesville Community Cemetery would be more appropriate."

"Why does your father favor Grace Episcopal Cemetery?"

"Because if Billy's buried there, Daddy thinks I would be buried beside him. Daddy and Mother already have their plots there. Burying Billy there is Daddy's way of ensuring that the whole family would be in the same cemetery. He won't say this, but I know him. He's afraid that if Billy is buried in Jamesville, I would be buried there beside him. The thought of having his little girl buried anywhere other than . . ." Ellie caught herself.

"Ellie, you're too young to think about where you're going to be buried," Becky said.

"I'm old enough to know that Jamesville Cemetery is not much of an option, at least not for me."

"You don't want to be buried with your husband?"

"Becky, you've been with us going on five months now. You're a sharp girl. You can read between the lines. That's very obvious from this conversation. But Billy was a fabulous father, and Little Billy worshipped the ground he walked on. Helping him deal with this is going to be the hardest thing I have to do."

"All the more reason I would like to stay over the holidays. Ellie, I'd stay free of charge. Please consider it."

As Ellie smiled and took Becky's hand, the sound of a slamming car door from the street in front of the house grabbed her attention. Ellie looked out and saw a black Model A with U.S. Government tags. Two tall and slim naval officers in service dress-blue uniforms emerged and headed up her front walkway.

"Becky, a couple of naval officers are out front. We're about to get our answer. Could you please take the children upstairs and keep them there until I call you down?"

Becky's face flushed white. She looked like she felt more nervous than Ellie. "Of course. I'll get them right now."

Becky rushed the children upstairs as the officers rapped on the front door.

"Good afternoon, gentlemen."

"I'm Lieutenant Commander Jeffrey Lettow from the Naval Station in Norfolk. This is Lieutenant Dennis Ornsby of the Navy Chaplain Corps. We're looking for Mrs. Ellie Brewer."

"Commander, Lieutenant. I'm Ellie Brewer. I've been expecting you. Please come in."

The officers removed their covers as Ellie motioned them to sit on an antique davenport by the front window in the living room. Ellie sat in a pink wingback chair across the room. A sunbeam streamed through the window behind the officers, illuminating the middle of the living room floor.

Ellie had replayed this moment over and over in her mind for the past week and had resolved to remain calm. Her efforts were failing. Now she felt her heart pounding like a jackhammer against her chest. She looked down and saw her hands trembling.

"Commander, in my mind, I thought I was ready to hear this news. I've been preparing myself for this all week. But right now, I'm not sure I can take it alone. Could I call my pastor and my husband's brother to see if they could be here with me if you're planning to announce my husband's death?"

Ornsby looked at Lettow, who nodded. Receiving the approval of his superior officer, Lieutenant Ornsby spoke up. "Mrs. Brewer, take all the time you need. Call whomever you'd like. We can stay all afternoon or even into the evening if we need to. If you prefer, we can leave and come back later."

"No, that won't be necessary. Just wait here please." Ellie went into the kitchen and dialed Swan 3-3295, the number for Grace Episcopal Rectory. Within seconds, the warm voice of Reverend Francis Fordham was on the line.

"Father Francis?"

"Yes?"

"This is Ellie."

"I'm glad you called, Ellie. I was hoping to stop by and see you later this afternoon."

"Father, a couple of naval officers have just come to the door. Could you come sooner?"

"I'll be there in two minutes."

Ellie hung up the phone and with her hands shaking dialed Swift 2-3875, Walter's number in Jamesville.

"Hello?"

At the sound of Walter's voice, Ellie broke into sobs.

"Ellie, is that you?"

Ellie tried to catch hold of herself. "I'm sorry, Walter. Two naval officers are here. It's about Billy. I thought I was ready for this. I guess I'm not."

"I'll be there in fifteen minutes."

As Ellie hung up with Walter, she could hear Francis Fordham come through the front door and speak with the officers.

"I'm Francis Fordham from Grace Episcopal here in Plymouth. I'm Ellie's pastor."

Ellie could hear Commander Lettow speak up. "Good to meet you, Reverend Fordham. I'm Lieutenant Commander Lettow and this is Lieutenant Ornsby. I'm sad to say we're here on bereavement detail. Mrs. Williams wanted to call you and her brother-in-law, I believe."

"Have you told her anything yet?"

"No sir, not formally," Lettow responded. "I think she knows, but she requested we delay the formal announcement until you and her brother-in-law arrived. Of course, we honored her request."

"Where is she now?"

"I think she's in the galley. Excuse me, the kitchen."

"It's all right, Commander. I was enlisted Navy, serving in the Atlantic in the Great War."

When Fordham opened the kitchen door, Ellie was silently weeping. Still outfitted in his black shirt and white collar from the morning's homily, the friendly bear of a man in his late fifties walked over to her and gave her a gentle hug. Then he offered her a handkerchief.

Dabbing her eyes, Ellie spoke up. "I feel so guilty, Father Francis. I was never a good wife to Billy. If I *had* been a good wife or if I had been better than I was, maybe he wouldn't have left."

"It's all right, honey. Billy would have been drafted anyway. Nobody thought that Hawaii, of all places, would be attacked. You can't second-guess yourself. You *have* been a good wife, and you *are* a great mother."

"Father, would you offer the officers something to drink please? I'm being a terrible hostess."

"Absolutely."

Fordham prepared glasses of iced tea for Ornsby and Lettow. Then he went back into the living room, where Ellie heard him engage the officers in small talk for a few minutes. Ellie was still alone in the kitchen when she heard Walter arrive and introduce himself to the naval officers.

"Hi. I'm Walter Brewer. I'm Billy's brother."

"I'm Lieutenant Commander Lettow. This is Lieutenant Ornsby. We're from the Navy in Norfolk."

"Where's Ellie?"

"She's in the kitchen, Walter," Ellie heard Fordham say.

His appearance at the door brought her to her feet, her heart leaping for the first time. She wrapped her arms around him and sobbed.

"This is it, Walter. They're going to tell us Billy is dead."

"I know, Ellie. Billy was brave, and he'd want us to be brave."

Walter rubbed her head for a few minutes until she gained her composure. "Okay Ellie, let's be brave like Billy.

Let's go out there and deal with this news. We'll all get through this."

Ellie wiped her eyes as Walter put his hand on her back and led her into the living room. She sat in the same pink chair with Walter standing behind her.

"Commander," Walter spoke up. "We are ready to receive your news."

"Very well," Lettow began. "Mrs. Brewer, on behalf of the President of the United States, it is with deep sorrow and regret that I must inform you that your husband was killed in service to his country in the Hawaiian Islands on December 7, 1941. As you know, your husband was stationed on board the USS *Arizona*, which took very heavy damages and was sunk in the Japanese surprise attack on Oahu. While I realize this news is of very little consolation in your time of bereavement, it is also my duty to inform you that your husband will receive the Navy Cross posthumously for valor displayed before he was killed. Seaman Brewer was spotted manning a 50-caliber antiaircraft gun and single-handedly shot down several Japanese aircraft in the early minutes of the attack. He was brave and heroic against heavy odds."

With Walter's hand on her shoulder, Ellie took a deep breath and spoke up. "Thank you for helping us bring closure to this, gentlemen. I am proud of Billy, and I'm sure his son will be proud that his father died a hero."

"You have every right to be proud, ma'am," Lettow said.

"Commander, I take it Billy's body was recovered?" Walter asked, his voice quaking.

"As you may have read in the press, most crew members of the *Arizona* went down with the ship. Seaman Brewer's body was recovered floating in the harbor. We made a positive identification by dental records and his military dog tag."

"What are our burial options, Commander?" Ellie asked.

"Ma'am, your husband is entitled to burial with full military honors, if you so choose. A number of those whose bodies are being recovered are being buried in Hawaii. There's a new cemetery on Oahu called the Punchbowl, which is high on a hill overlooking Diamond Head. It is a gorgeous place.

Or, if you prefer, we can ship him back home to North Carolina for burial."

Ellie looked at Walter then spoke resolutely. "Gentlemen, bring my husband home. We will set the funeral at the First Christian Church in Jamesville, burial to be in Jamesville Community Cemetery with full military honors. I want my son to see his daddy buried as a hero."

18

Red Underton, the postmaster of the rural Jamesville post office and Walter's on-the-job supervisor, was doing 35 miles an hour in his Model A and was already halfway along the ten-mile route to Williamston. The fifty-five-year-old Underton, who long ago was saddled with the nickname "Red" not only because of the color of his hair but to a lesser extent his face and neck, was once a rural carrier like Walter and Skillet. He became postmaster when the former postmaster, Poss Adams, died fifteen years ago.

As postmaster, Red was one of the few Jamesville residents with a telephone in his home. Last night, Red got a call from Billy Bob Peele, a prominent Williamston lawyer just appointed chairman of the local draft board. Billy Bob had requested a meeting with the postmaster at 9 a.m. but did not give a reason. Red speculated that he would be asked to serve on the board as a representative from Jamesville. Given the chance, Red decided in advance that he would accept.

When Red arrived at the law offices of Peele and Martin, he was escorted into a large office with burgundy carpet and judges paneling overlooking the Roanoke River.

Billy Bob, an old-time southern lawyer who could reportedly "charm a bullfrog into a fryin' pan," slapped Red on the back with one hand and grabbed his arm with the other as if the two had been best friends for years.

"Come on in, Red. It's good to see you, ol' boy. Have a seat."

"Good to see you, Billy Bob. We're always happy to come to the big city," joked Red. People from Jamesville always referred to both Williamston and Plymouth as "the big city," though each sported a population of only about two thousand.

"How'd y'all get along with the fruitcake run this year?"

Billy Bob was asking about a Jamesville tradition whereby the post office delivered more than five hundred fruitcakes to all the local citizens during the week before Christmas. The fruitcakes were baked by an elderly widow who started the tradition twenty-five years ago as a way to spread good cheer when her husband died. Billy Bob Peele oozed so much charm, Red thought for a moment that the silver-haired lawyer actually cared about the fruitcake run.

"We did all right," replied Red. "Had 'em finished by about two o'clock Wednesday afternoon."

"Heard Walter wasn't involved this year, but I reckon that's understandable under the circumstances."

"Walter's had it tough, Billy Bob. Billy Brewer was a good man. Now Walter feels responsible for his own family and Billy's too. That's six young'uns he's gotta be a daddy to."

"I'm afraid the war will affect lots of good men, Red. I guess you heard about the Japs bombing our air base in the Philippines last week?"

"I just read about it in the *News and Observer*," Red said.

"And that Hitler and his Italian lackeys declared war on us just as soon as we declared war on the Japs!"

"I think it's gonna be a long, drawn affair. Listen, if there's any way I can be of assistance to the draft board, please let me know."

"I'm glad you said that, Red. You know, we've been getting a lot of pressure from the Office of War Mobilization about excessive deferments."

"I'm sure," replied Red.

"With all these attacks and declarations of war, President Roosevelt wants full mobilization, but it seems like everybody and his brother are looking for some sort of deferment. This puts the board in a tough spot."

"I don't envy you, Billy Bob, but we sure appreciate what you're doing."

"Red, I hope you'll still appreciate me when we get done this morning."

"How's that?" The Office of War Mobilization's been getting on us about excessive occupational deferments in the public service areas."

"The public service areas?"

"You know, the highway crews, hospital workers, school teachers, police department, even the post office."

"The post office? Billy Bob, I've got two rural carriers. Walter covers the area south and east of Jamesville down to the Washington County line. Skillet covers west of town to Gardner's Creek, halfway up here to Williamston. And me and Eva Gray—We're too old to get drafted."

"I know how you feel, Red, and it's not just the Jamesville Post Office that we're talking about here. Shucks, we're looking at Robersonville, Oak City, and Williamston too. All those post offices are more overbloated than Jamesville."

"Overbloated?" Red interrupted. "Billy Bob, like I said, we ain't got but two carriers. That sure ain't overbloated."

"No offense meant, Red. It's not just you," the lawyer said. "We'll be talkin' to the postmasters in all those towns. We'll also talk to the police chiefs, the sheriff, the hospital administrator, and the head of the highway department. But Red, the military needs more bodies, and we can't justify one-hundred-percent deferments."

"Billy Bob." Red wasn't comfortable with the direction of the conversation. "If you take away one of my carriers, whether it's Walter or Skillet, the one who's left will have to cover the entire area from the Washington County line just outside Plymouth to Gardner's Creek, pert' near all the way to Williamston. I know Jamesville's only got five hundred folks, but that's about three thousand people out in the country. And there ain't no way one carrier can cover it all in a day."

"Red, the board met yesterday afternoon, and word had already made it back here about how well you and Skillet worked together on the fruitcake run."

"First of all, the fruitcake run is just in Jamesville proper and a few farms outside town," the postmaster said. "It ain't the whole area 'tween Williamston and Plymouth. And second . . . wait a minute. You tellin' me the board expects *me* at my age to go back on a rural delivery route *and* serve as postmaster?"

"With your experience, you do know the job better than anybody in the whole county. Look Red, here's the point," Billy Bob Peele leaned forward and looked Red straight in the eye. "The board won't tell you how to run your post office or get the mail out. You're the senior postmaster in this county, and I know you've forgotten more about mail delivery than the draft board will ever know."

Billy Bob's flattery softened Red's resistance somewhat as the lawyer came to his point.

"What the board needs from you, Red, is a recommendation."

"What kind of a recommendation, Billy Bob?"

"Assuming—and I mean just *assuming*—we had to lift the deferment status of Walter or Skillet, what would you recommend? And Red, before you say anything, I want you to know that the board has authorized me to tell you that your recommendation—based upon your recognized expertise in the area—will be the final word."

"When you say *assuming*, Billy Bob, do you mean the board *definitely will* lift the deferment status of one of my carriers, or do you mean it *might* lift the deferment status?"

"Nothin's decided yet, Red. I'm just interviewing all the postmasters to bring a report back to the board. That's why we need your recommendation."

"That's a tough call, Billy Bob. Both are good men. On the one hand, Skillet has two years' seniority over Walter. And you know in government service, seniority is usually the ultimate factor. On the other hand, Walter's situation is unique, just losing his brother and all at Pearl Harbor. Like I say, he's got two families to tend to who need him here. 'Course Skillet's got a wife and two young'uns too, and they need him at home. And the United States Mail needs 'em both.

"You want my recommendation? Here it is. Based on my expertise, I think you should go first to the larger post offices at Williamston and Robersonville. They've got carriers to spare. We ain't got none. So, there. There's my recommendation, Billy Bob."

"Thank you, Red. I'll take your recommendation back to the board. We sure appreciate your time."

Red had driven to Williamston expecting to be appointed to the draft board. Driving back to Jamesville, he was unsure what had happened. Was Billy Bob simply seeking information, or was the board planning to draft one of his carriers?

Should he say anything to Walter and Skillet? Wouldn't they want to be prepared if their deferment status was about to be lifted? Yet the prospect of going to war was the last thing they needed to hear right now, especially Walter and his family. Besides, Red had recommended that both were essential personnel, and in the end, Billy Bob seemed to accept the recommendation. Silence was the best policy, Red decided. No point in raising worries over nothing.

⚜

NEW YEAR'S EVE, 1941
WALTER BREWER HOME
JAMESVILLE, NORTH CAROLINA

Walter Brewer awoke to the sound of sizzling bacon and the smell of fresh coffee brewing from the kitchen. He rolled over and looked at the alarm clock. Five o'clock. Time to get up.

He couldn't remember a time when he was more ready to see a New Year's Eve, which meant that in just a few short hours he could say good-bye to 1941, a horrible year he'd just as soon forget.

After finishing his bacon, eggs, and cheese grits, Walter kissed Jessie and headed for the post office. He arrived at six-thirty. As usual, he was the first at work. Walter liked it that way. In the quiet hour alone, he had more time to think.

He started sorting mail for the morning run. In the first bunch was a familiar envelope from Williamston—the same type of envelope he had delivered to Sammy Chesson, to his brother Billy, and to many other Martin County farm boys. The addressee in this case, however, was Walter Lawrence Brewer of Jamesville.

This isn't happening.

Standing alone and half-stunned on the cold concrete floor in the back of the Jamesville Post Office, he ripped open the package.

Local Board No. 1
December 30, 1941
Martin County
001
County Court House
Williamston, North Carolina

ORDER TO REPORT FOR INDUCTION

The President of the United States
To Walter Lawrence Brewer

Order No 1004

GREETING

You are hereby notified that you have now been selected for training and service in the ARMY. You will, therefore, report to the local board named above at the Courthouse, Williamston, North Carolina at 10:30 a.m. on the 14th day of January 1942.

Signed: Billy Bob Peele, member or clerk of local board.

D.S.S. Form 150
U.S. GOVERNMENT PRINTING OFFICE.

"Three weeks!" He banged his fist on the mail sorting table.

"Three weeks after the Navy buries my brother, the Army pulls me from my family!"

"How much do they expect from one family? This is a bunch of bull!"

His angry voice reverberated in every corner of the empty building.

"Here's what I think of your draft notice, Billy Bob!"

He kicked the mailbag, sending hundreds of letters in every direction across the concrete floor.

"I did all I could, Walter. I recommended against this. I'm sorry."

Red Underton was standing in the doorway, apparently having walked in at the end of the tantrum. "This ain't over, Walter," Red said. "The post office will try and get you deferred. The war can wait. Right now, you need to be here with your family."

19

Walter declined Red's offer to take the rest of the day off. Though Red meant well in offering, Walter needed some thinking time alone in the country. Dropping letter after letter in sparsely-scattered mailboxes, Walter found his soul embroiled in an emotional tug of war. Rage, revenge, and sorrow would give way to compassion, patriotism, and love.

Livid about the timing of the notice, he also fumed at the Japanese, and despite his Christian upbringing, he felt great satisfaction by imagining machine-gun fire sprayed into a squadron of Japanese pilots.

Then the thought of vengeance would give way to the human face of war—a face he knew all too well—to the cold reality that war means the loss of husbands, fathers, and brothers.

Around three-thirty, Walter delivered his last package, a large envelope to the Hershel Daniels farm in the Dardens community, about seven miles east of Jamesville. The fifteen-minute drive back to town gave him time to finish crafting his words to Jessie. But the closer he got to home, the deeper his thoughts got sucked into a mental whirlpool. As the Model A closed to within a couple miles of town, Walter decided on a last-minute detour.

"Happy New Year, Walter! Please come in." Pastor Bobby Holliday opened the back screen door of the small wood-framed Jamesville Christian Church parsonage as Walter made his way up the steps.

Though never much on gut spilling, the day's events had left Walter tongue-tied, and he needed some advice from the pastor on how to break the news.

"Afternoon, preacher. Got a minute?"

"Absolutely, brother Walter. Come in and sit a spell. Fannie Mae, bring Walter some sweetened iced tea, please."

As Fannie Mae Holliday poured sugar-sweet iced tea from a big tin pitcher into a Mason-jar glass, Walter cut to the chase.

"Preacher, I've got something I want you to read." Sipping the glass of tea with one hand, Walter handed the draft notice to the pastor with the other.

Holliday opened the envelope, read the notice, and paused with his head bowed for about a minute before saying a word.

"The Lord works in mysterious ways. Have you told Jessie about this yet?"

"No, preacher. That's why I stopped by here. I need to know what to say, how to say it, and when to say it. Any ideas?"

"Won't be easy, Walter. Jessie is a strong woman; you know that. She was a pillar of courage during Billy's whole ordeal, but this . . . I don't know. There's only so much anyone can weather in such a short time. She has great composure, but I'd be surprised if she could accept this right now. I'd be happy to ride over to the house with you to break the news."

"That's mighty kind, preacher, but that doesn't help me figure out what to say."

"Then let's take a few minutes and see if we can sort through this. When did you first get the notice?"

"First thing this morning. About six-thirty."

"And you haven't told anybody yet?"

"That's right."

"Tell me what you've been thinking."

"Tell you the truth, preacher, I've been feeling guilty."

"Guilty? The draft notice isn't your fault, Walter."

"It's not the draft notice I'm feeling guilty about. It's my reaction to the notice."

"How's that?" Holliday asked.

"Our family's got a long tradition of military service."

"I'm aware of that," Holliday replied.

"Grandaddy Baldy served under Stonewall. Daddy was in France in 1918, and then Billy went into the Navy."

"You feel guilty for not wanting to carry on that tradition?"

"No preacher, just the opposite. As I've been riding around thinking all day, I've halfway changed my mind. I do want to carry on that tradition. And I'm feeling guilty because if I pursue this, the war will take me away from the family."

"Walter, based on that paper in your hand, you may not have much of a choice. So don't feel guilty about what you can't control."

"That's not all that's eating me, preacher. The more I think about it, I want to kill some Japs. I want to kill 'em because of what they did to Billy."

"First off, the way things are going overseas, you might be killing Germans instead of Japs. What you're feeling is natural. But the Lord commands us to love our enemies and forgive our transgressors. The fact that you feel guilty shows that your conscience is working, that you have a good heart."

"More like a selfish heart, preacher."

"Why do you say that?"

"As much as I want to go to war, I also want to stay here with Jessie and the children. I feel selfish for wanting to stay home while other fathers have to go fight."

"Walter, that's not selfish. That's just making your family a priority. Besides, I'd say you have a right to be selfish considering what happened to your brother." The preacher paused. "Walter, let me be honest with you. Red Underton called me this morning."

"What'd he say?" Walter asked, worried that Red had reported his tantrum to the pastor.

"He was concerned about you. He did say you were very upset this morning."

"I need to go by and apologize to him for losing my temper."

"No, Walter. You don't need to apologize to anyone. What you need to do is come with me to see Dr. Papineau."

"Dr. Pap?" Walter looked confused. "What? Do you think I need some nerve pills?"

"No, it's not that at all. Come on. I'll drive."

20

Ernest, that was ten years ago. You've got to let go of the guilt," Mary Grayson Papineau, Dr. Ernest Papineau's elegant-looking wife of forty years said to her husband. "You did everything you could. We've been over this a thousand times."

"I know, Mary Grayson." He cast an affectionate glance at her. "But Billy's funeral just brought up all the memories again." Ernest Papineau slumped in the leather wingback chair in his study and sipped a glass of brandy.

"Ernest, you didn't kill Billy. And you didn't kill his father. And you didn't kill that baby, either. You did everything you could just to save Jessie and the little boy."

"I've thought of both situations repeatedly. Lord knows I've lost enough sleep over it. True, I'm at peace believing I could do nothing more for that baby. It was a miracle that Jessie survived. Doesn't make me feel better though. But Richard Brewer . . . I just don't know. If I'd said no, if I'd gone with my instincts, I'm convinced Richard Brewer would be alive today."

"Richard was a workaholic, Ernest, like most of the

tobacco farmers around here. He was the one who insisted on going to work the next morning."

"Yes, but he had a fever of 104 when I got to his house the night before. When the fever broke at midnight, he asked me if it would be all right to go back in the fields the next day. At first I said no, but he kept pleading. Said the family needed the money. I should have stuck to my instincts, Mary Grayson. But I didn't. I told him against my better judgment that it might be okay to go back in, provided the fever was still down the next morning and only if he would take it easy."

"I know, honey. I've only heard the story a thousand times over the last ten years. But you know what? Richard Brewer was going back in the tobacco fields the next morning come hell or high water. He knew you didn't think it was a good idea."

"Who knows what he knew?" Dr. Ernest Papineau rose from the chair in his study and turned his back on Mary Grayson. He gazed out the back bay window of his study and onto the rolling Roanoke River behind him. He'd replayed the events of that day in his mind a thousand times before.

Now, he would replay them once more in his mind, to spare Mary Grayson from having to hear the story again: Richard Brewer was up by four the next morning, following Ernest's house call. By four-fifteen, Richard was along the dark gravel roads collecting the help for the day's work. That day was hot, about 102 degrees with stifling humidity. When an afternoon thunderstorm followed by a dose of heavy rain cut short the workday about three o'clock in the afternoon, Richard, in pouring rain, ordered the helpers into the wagon and delivered them all to their muddy destinations.

Dr. Pap, who waxed eloquently when he was drinking and rambled even more so in his thoughts, took another sip of brandy.

"I still think I could have stopped him." Pap took yet another sip.

"Honey, you went to his house the night before. You gave him pills. You gave him compresses. You said that he broke into a profuse sweat by midnight and that the fever was gone by one in the morning. Now, is that what happened? Because if that's what happened, you can't keep second-guessing your-self. You did your job. You broke the fever. He had no symptoms when you left, and then you came home."

"Yes, Mary Grayson. I know we've been over this a thousand times, but—and I'm sorry you're having to hear it again—you know how the brandy makes me talk, and that's what happened."

She walked over and put her hand on his shoulder. "It's okay Ernest, if you need to repeat it ten thousand times, I'm here for you."

"You're a good woman, baby." He hugged her, and with brandy in hand, paced across the floor. He took a substantial nip of the liquor. "I should have known when I got back to his house at nine o'clock the next night, he was pale as a ghost and had a fever of 106 degrees. None of the pills in my magic medicine bag, none of the compresses on his hot forehead, none of my specialized training could do a thing to bring him back. What happened, Mary Grayson, is that he was dead within twenty-four hours, and those boys, Walter and Billy, were without a father all because I didn't follow my instincts."

"Ernest, let's go over this again. Richard Brewer told you the family needed the money. He would have gone to work no matter what you did," she said.

"I know. I know. I've heard you say that before, my dear. But maybe if I'd just given him the money he would have stayed home. You know how easily I could have done that? A day's wages for him would have been nothing to me. Now, Billy's gone." Pap felt tears welling in his gray eyes. "Jessie nearly died in labor. She and Walter lost a child, and Billy's children—just like Billy and Walter—are without a daddy."

"Ernest, you've got to snap out of this," Mary Grayson said with forcefulness in her voice. "You know as well as I do that Richard Brewer would never have accepted a dime from you. He was too proud."

She walked over to him and put her hands on his shoulders, gently massaging his tight muscles.

"That feels so good." He kissed her hand.

She kissed the top of his head. "I know how much you love that family, Ernest. But you didn't kill Richard, you didn't kill Walter's baby, and you didn't kill Billy." She leaned over and kissed him on the forehead. "There was nothing you could do about any of it. It's all water under the bridge."

Dr. Papineau sat there sipping his brandy and enjoying the light shoulder massage. "Maybe not, honey. But there's something I can do."

"And what is that?" she asked, still massaging his shoulders.

"I can make sure no one kills Walter."

Walter and Pastor Holliday pulled into the long driveway leading to the Papineau home. A large, five-bedroom brick house situated on five private acres overlooking the Roanoke River six miles east of Jamesville, Dr. Papineau lived in what the locals referred to as the "mansion on the Roanoke." He'd built the house as a retirement home and moved there six years ago. Before that, he lived in a more modest white frame house on East Main Street in Plymouth.

Though considered opulent by Jamesville standards, no one in town seemed to mind that Pap in his latter years lived a relatively-luxurious lifestyle. Doctors were expected to have money, and this physician in particular had been good to so many of the locals.

Walter and the pastor were greeted at the front door by Mary Grayson Papineau.

"Please come in, gentlemen," she said in a slow, aristocratic southern drawl.

"Ernest asked that I show you to his study. He's tied up for a couple of minutes and will be right with you."

Within five minutes, the sixty-five-year-old doctor appeared in the study, still draped in a white overcoat with a stethoscope hanging around his neck.

"Preacher, Walter. Thank you for coming."

"Walter, I know you've been drafted," Papineau began as Walter looked puzzled.

"It doesn't matter how I know; I just know."

"Your intelligence sources are correct," Walter replied.

"I know a number of patients who have been through this, and I wanted to talk to you about what to expect." Papineau continued. "When you report to the courthouse, they are going to load you on a bus and haul you down to Fort Bragg in Fayetteville. You will be subjected to a haircut and a few tests. Then you will be taken over to base medical for an induction physical. You have to pass that physical to be called into service."

"You should know that the base doctor in charge of induction physicals is a good friend of mine, Doctor Alban Ferguson. Fergie and I were in medical school together and were lab partners. We also interned together. We still correspond and have even vacationed together a few times over the years.

"The point, Walter, is this. No one from Fort Bragg gets a medical clearance to go into the Army without Dr. Ferguson's approval. I've just finished dictating a letter for Dr. Ferguson which I would like you to deliver to him when you arrive for your physical. This letter is my recommendation that you receive a medical deferment from active duty service in the United States Army. I have written seven of these letters, and every one of my patients has gotten medically deferred."

"Doctor, why do you recommend a medical deferment?" Walter inquired.

"It goes back to the incident when you were about fourteen years old. We almost lost you to tobacco poisoning. That incident, I am convinced, had a severe debilitating effect on your heart. Any kind of exposure to chemicals or high-stress situations could be fatal."

Walter flashed another look of bewilderment at Papineau. "Doctor, why haven't I ever heard anything about this before now?"

"I've been monitoring the situation all these years. But there's never been a need to tell you before now. Just trust me, Walter. I'm doing what's right for you and your family. Do you trust me?"

"You know I trust you, Dr. Pap."

Walter had gone to the preacher seeking advice on how

best to tell Jessie about the draft. Now he was even more confused. He had better think of something quickly.

He was almost home.

21
WALTER BREWER HOME
JAMESVILLE, NORTH CAROLINA
JANUARY 2, 1942

New Year's Day, 1942 passed without Walter and Jessie mentioning the draft or the heart problem to the children or anyone else. Both thought breaking the news would be pointless, as there was insufficient information on the heart condition. And since Walter may not have to serve in the Army because of the doctor's letter, there was no sense jolting the kids with the draft notice.

But first thing in the morning on Friday, January second, Jessie called on her first cousin, Ollie Ruth Askew, whose husband A.C. had had a massive heart attack several years back. Without sharing details of Pap's letter or the draft notice for fear of flaming the Jamesville rumor mill, Jessie extracted the information she sought from Ollie Ruth.

A.C. had been treated by a well-known heart specialist at Duke University Hospital in Durham named Antonio Bowser. Jessie even got a telephone number for Dr. Bowser.

By ten o'clock that morning, she had the doctor's uncooperative receptionist on the line.

"This is Jessie Brewer in Jamesville. My husband needs an appointment with Dr. Bowser as soon as possible."

"What seems to be his problem, Mrs. Brewer?"

"He's been diagnosed as having a heart condition, and we need to get a second opinion."

"What is the condition?"

"Let me get the letter so I get this right. The doctor calls it severe brachycardia, and the letter says it came from massive toxic poisoning."

"Really?"

"Yes, ma'am, that's what it says."

"I've never heard of that before."

"I'm just reading what the letter says."

"Is he having any symptoms such as dizziness, shortness of breath, or chest pain?"

"No, I don't think so. But we have a local doctor who has made this diagnosis and felt like we needed a specialist."

"All right, excuse me for a moment and let me check the doctor's schedule." After about thirty seconds, the receptionist returned. "Yes, Mrs. Brewer. Our first available appointment will be Thursday, February fifth, at two o'clock."

"I'm sorry, I didn't catch your name, ma'am," Jessie replied, thinking that if the Army didn't buy Dr. Papineau's letter, Walter would be long gone by February fifth.

"My name is Mrs. Ward. I'm the appointments secretary for Dr. Bowser."

"Mrs. Ward, we can't wait that long. My husband has been drafted and has to report to the Army in ten days. We need to know about this condition before he leaves. I just don't trust the Army medics to be able to make a diagnosis."

"Mrs. Brewer, I sympathize with you. But the doctor's schedule is packed between now and then. We can't do anything before that unless he's having symptoms or unless this is an emergency."

"Mrs. Ward, is there any way the doctor could work us in on the weekend or in the evening? We'd be willing to meet him anytime and pay extra, but we just need to see him soon."

"I'm sorry ma'am, but that just won't be possible," Mrs. Ward sniped back. "It's going to be February fifth at the earliest."

Jessie paused, trying to think of something to say.

"Are there any other heart specialists in your clinic who could see my husband sooner?"

"We have two other doctors, Dr. Berman and Dr. Honeycutt. I'll be happy to check their schedules if you'd like."

"Please do."

As Jessie mumbled a silent prayer, she could hear the receptionist leafing through some papers, presumably the doctors' appointment books.

"Let's see . . . it looks like Dr. Berman's first appointment is . . . Well, no, that won't work . . ."

Jessie bit her lip as the receptionist fumbled about.

"Dr. Berman could see your husband on . . . Monday . . . February the ninth."

"What about Dr. Honeycutt?"

"I was just checking on that. Let me see . . . Dr. Honeycutt... Dr. Honeycutt . . . We could work you in with Dr. Honeycutt on the ninth of . . .

"Please say January," interrupted Jessie.

"February."

"Did you say January?" Jessie hoped against hope.

"No ma'am, Mrs. Brewer. Dr. Bowser's first available date is February fifth, and both Dr. Honeycutt and Dr. Berman would be available February ninth."

"Could you give me just a second?"

"Sure."

Jessie's mind was racing for a solution. She knew February would be too late but felt she had no choice.

"We'll be there the fifth."

"All right, Mrs. Brewer, we'll see you Thursday, February fifth, at two o'clock."

Jessie hung up the phone and walked into the kitchen, where Walter was sipping a cup of coffee and reading the *News and Observer*.

"Walter, I just got off the phone with the doctor at Duke."

"What'd they say?"

"Pack your bags, honey. We're going up there January the fifth."

"The fifth is in two days—this coming Monday."

"That's right."

"I'm very surprised they could work me in that early. How'd you pull that off?"

"Trust me, Walter, it wasn't easy."

22

On Sunday night, January 4, 1942, Jessie and Walter dropped the kids off in Plymouth with Ellie, who had agreed to watch them for a few days while the couple was out of town. Ellie had accepted Becky's offer to remain through the holidays and felt that having Walter's kids for a few days would be manageable. Plus, it might be good for Little Billy and Margaret to have their Jamesville cousins visit.

Walter dared not mention to Ellie that he had been drafted. No point in adding more stress on the heels of Billy's death. She was still not over the funeral and had not mustered enough curiosity to probe further into the circumstances surrounding the trip.

He roused Jessie at four-thirty Monday morning, January fifth. After a quick breakfast, he fired up the Model A and they were westbound on Highway 64, following a route that would take them through Williamston, Rocky Mount, and Raleigh before reaching Durham, about 120 miles west of Jamesville.

Though accustomed to driving in the cold, dark hours before sunrise, this morning he felt somewhat awkward, his natural instinct telling him to brake each time the Model A's headlights illuminated a rural mailbox belonging to one of his customers. This urge subsided when they crossed west over Gardner's Creek and beyond the Jamesville mail route.

By now, the heater in the old car had the cabin toasty warm. Rumbling down the highway at 45 miles per hour, they were all alone on the road, passing fields and barns but not a single car between Jamesville and Williamston. Walter looked over at Jessie, who had dozed off, her head resting on a pillow propped against the passenger door with her long, brown hair pulled over her left shoulder away from the window. Walter had always relished the early morning as a time of peace and solitude when he could do some of this best thinking. As the car passed through Williamston and on toward Robersonville, he glanced again at his sleeping bride and reflected on the events of the past few days—first the funeral, then the draft notice, then the letter from Dr. Papineau, and now this trip.

"Where are we, Walter?" Jessie had been dozing for two hours.

"We've just passed Raleigh," he said. "We should be at Duke in about twenty minutes."

"You look deep in thought. What've you been thinking about?"

"Oh, just about Billy and Ellie. You know, same thing."

In this case, the "same thing" meant he was thinking about catching Ellie with Billy behind the barn twelve years before. Believing that some things are better left unsaid, Walter had never shared the details with Jessie. He didn't want Ellie to look like a hussy.

But truthfully, he had never gotten over it. He once loved Ellie, even enough to marry her. But the image of the smeared makeup and ghostlike look on her face when he caught her with Billy proved emotionally insurmountable for him. And he had never reconciled the question of whether he would have married Ellie for love or for money or for the prospect of having his education paid for by Jimmy Williams.

"Did you have a good nap?" he asked.

"About as good a nap as possible with my head jammed against a cold car door for two hours."

"Well, you know we've got to protect that pretty head of yours. Anybody who can convince a high-powered heart doctor to see a patient like me on two days' notice has got to have some brainpower in her head."

Walter's comment reminded Jessie of the predicament she was in. "You give me too much credit, honey." In less than half an hour, she would face Mrs. Ward, the crotchety-sounding lady whom she must somehow circumvent to get her husband to Dr. Bowser.

Would Mrs. Ward fall for the we-got-our-months-mixed-up-and-drove-three-hours-please-see-us routine? Somehow, the idea of this lady capitulating at such a sob story seemed unlikely. But Jessie knew she had to try something. She *had* to know whether Walter was sick, whether this mysterious heart condition was a product of Dr. Papineau's imagination. Besides, a scheduling mixup, even a fabricated one, would not get them arrested, and if Walter found out what she was up to—well, that was the least of her worries.

The couple pulled into the Duke University visitors' parking lot about forty-five minutes ahead of Walter's "appointment." With a little time to kill, Walter suggested they stroll about the campus, which neither he nor Jessie had ever visited.

The tobacco magnate, James B. Duke, had dropped millions on the old Trinity College in Durham to form a great Methodist University honoring his father in the Piedmont area of North Carolina. On a cloudy day such as this one, the strong stench of flue-cured tobacco saturated the air in and around Durham, descending like a blanket on the Duke campus and seeping into the classrooms, dormitories, and hallways of the university.

Walking across the campus with Jessie, Walter was reminded of the old adage *beauty is in the eye of the beholder.* That old saying applied to the architecture and atmosphere of Duke. Some said the gothic architecture was stately. But to Walter, it seemed out of place, nestled in the tobacco stench of Durham

County. On this cloudy day, the buildings looked gray and dismal. The campus felt cold, the academic equivalent of a funeral parlor.

Nor were the students friendly. Known as the University of South New Jersey at Durham by students at Chapel Hill because the largest segment of the Duke student population hailed from the Garden State, Walter and Jessie discovered that the students would look the other way when within speaking distance and remained largely unresponsive to a simple *hello*. This was the antithesis of the hospitable atmosphere found in Martin County or any other place in North Carolina, for that matter.

Walter wondered what Jessie thought about the place. But no matter. He wasn't here to critique the campus or the personality of its students. Walter had come to Duke because it had a reputation of having one of the best medical programs in the country and because his wife had insisted upon it. Meandering their way to the main entrance of Duke Medical Center, they were given directions by a security guard to the cardiology wing. At the entrance of the wing, they were given more directions by the duty nurse to the offices of Drs. Bowser, Berman, and Honeycutt.

"Go down the hallway and turn left then take the first hallway on the right, Suite 100."

At this point, Jessie's instincts took over. "Excuse me, nurse, but do you have a waiting area for my husband while I go down there and get us checked in?"

Walter interjected before the nurse could respond. "Jessie, I'll just walk down there with you. I mean it's almost time for my appointment, and we might get separated in this big hospital."

Jessie shot back. "Walter, you know how doctors are. They're always running late. We'll probably be here all day before they work us in."

"Either way, ma'am. We have a waiting area around the corner which you're welcome to, sir, or there is a waiting area in the doctor's office."

"Thank you, nurse, but I'll just walk with my wife on down to the doctor's office." Walter wondered about the bizarre exchange. Jessie's forehead broke into a cold sweat as they opened the door to the doctors' offices.

"Wait right here, Walter." Jessie pointed to some chairs in a waiting room outside the receptionist area. "I'll check us in and be right back."

"Okay, but don't be long." At Walter's reply, Jessie breathed at least a temporary sigh of relief at Walter's cooperation. Now for the real challenge—dealing with Mrs. Ward and getting to the doctor. Participating in this type of charade was against everything Jessie stood for. But she felt like she had no choice. The doctor's office *had* been uncooperative, even a bit belligerent. On top of that, her husband's life was at stake. If the specialist would just verify Dr. Papineau's diagnosis, she could keep Walter home and make sure he got the medical treatment he needed.

Besides, didn't Rahab from the Bible tell a little white lie when it meant saving the lives of the Israelite spies?

Mustering an air of confidence, Jessie marched from the waiting room to the receptionist's desk in the adjoining room. Sitting alone behind the desk was a cute, petite young lady in her early twenties.

Here's a case where looks sure don't match the crabby old voice, Jessie thought to herself.

"Mrs. Ward?" Jessie asked.

"No, I'm Miss Bunker. Mrs. Ward's in the back assisting Dr. Berman. Would you like me to get her for you?"

"Oh, no, no." Jessie was relieved Mrs. Ward was absent. "Please don't bother her if she's busy."

"Is there anything I can help you with?"

"Yes, we had an appointment with Dr. Bowser for the fifth."

"Your name please?"

"Brewer. It's for my husband, Walter Brewer."

"Let me see." Miss Bunker paused as she studied the appointments calendar. "I don't have you on here for today. Are you sure of the date?"

"Yes, ma'am, we were told that Dr. Bowser would see my husband on the fifth."

"We must have some kind of mixup. Wait right here."

"Wait a minute." Jessie tried to stop her, but Miss Bunker disappeared into a back hallway. About a minute later, she returned, accompanied by a gray-haired older lady wearing granny glasses secured by a chain around her neck.

Miss Bunker was speaking to her older colleague as the twosome returned. "Mrs. Ward, this lady says her husband has an appointment for today, but I can't find her anywhere on our calendar." Jessie did not like the sudden change of expressions on their faces.

"I'm Mrs. Ward." The lady's voice was cold. "May I help you, ma'am?" Her question was punctuated in a drum-like cadence. For Jessie Brewer, now was the moment of truth.

"My husband had an appointment with Dr. Bowser."

"And your husband's name?"

"Walter Brewer." Jessie tried to remain resolute.

"Brewer? Didn't I talk to you on the phone last week?"

"I talked to somebody," Jessie answered. "I was told my husband had an appointment for the fifth, so we drove three hours to be here this morning."

"Didn't I tell you that we're booked solid this week and we could see your husband only if it was an emergency?"

"I remember you saying the fifth." Jessie stammered and uttered a silent prayer requesting forgiveness for the lie she was about to tell.

Lord, forgive me. "He, uh, is having chest pains."

"I don't remember you saying anything about that, Mrs. Brewer." Mrs. Ward sounded incredulous.

"Uh, the chest pains started after we spoke, Mrs. Ward."

"Wait here, please." Mrs. Ward, agitated, disappeared in the back, while Miss Bunker waited without saying a word to Jessie. About a minute later, she returned with a scowl on her face, slamming a clipboard on the receptionist's desk.

"You know, Mrs. Brewer, I have a mind like a steel trap. I don't forget telephone calls, and I can smell a rat whenever someone is trying to manipulate the medical system to avoid military service to our country. My uncle lost his leg in France in 1917 when he stepped on a mine. But—"

Jessie interrupted. "Mrs. Ward, I can—"

"Let me finish please." Mrs. Ward cut Jessie off mid-sentence. "But you're lucky Dr. Bowser is a lot more lax in his attitude about these things. Just to be on the safe side, he's going to work your husband in this morning, overriding my recommendation against it, I might add. But this better be legitimate."

"Thank you, Mrs. Ward. And I *am* sorry about your uncle." Mrs. Ward did not respond. But at least Jessie understood in part why she had made such an issue of the matter. Jessie walked back into the waiting room and sat down beside Walter.

"Everything alright?" Walter asked. "You look a little pale."

"They will see us in a little while," Jessie answered.

About thirty minutes later, young Miss Bunker appeared at the waiting room door. "Mr. Brewer, Dr. Bowser will see you now."

Miss Bunker led the couple by the receptionist area— where Jessie got the evil eye from Mrs. Ward—and on into the back examination room.

"The doctor will be right with you."

Jessie deliberated on whether to tell Walter that he was having chest pains. But she knew Walter wouldn't lie about the matter and would disapprove of her having done so.

Within minutes, a tall, slender, dark-looking man with a white coat walked into the examination room.

"Hi, I'm Charles Bowser." For the first time that day, Walter and Jessie detected warmth from someone's voice associated with Duke. This was a welcome change.

"Nice to meet you, Dr. Bowser," Walter responded.

"You too. I understand you're having some chest pains, Mr. Brewer?"

"Chest pains?" Puzzled, Walter looked at Jessie. She didn't return the glance. "Not exactly, Dr. Bowser."

"No?" The doctor sounded confused. "Let me recheck your chart. Shows chest pains. Odd. What can we do for you?"

Walter showed him the letter from Dr. Papineau. Bowser took a few minutes to read over the letter.

"I'll bet this got Mrs. Ward excited," Bowser said with a chuckle.

"Mrs. Ward?" Walter looked confused.

"Doctor," Jessie spoke up for the first time. "Walter doesn't know anything about Mrs. Ward. I have been dealing with her."

"It's just as well," Bowser snickered. "Mrs. Ward seems to think her patriotic duty is to single-handedly eliminate every medical excuse that might keep someone out of the military. If the patient's on his death bed with an incurable disease, it doesn't matter. Mrs. Ward still thinks they need to be on the front lines."

"At least she's patriotic," Walter remarked.

"Whatever floats her boat," Bowser said. "She's been around here since Robert E. Lee was in the saddle, so we just kind of roll with the punches." Bowser paused, reading Papineau's letter in detail. Then he looked up at Walter and adjusted his glasses. "Bradycardia, eh?"

"That's what Dr. Papineau says," Walter said. "I'm not sure what that means. But he's been my family doctor for years and seems to think I should get a military deferment. Frankly, this doesn't sit right with me, and I wanted a heart specialist to check it out. If I get a deferment, I want it to be for a legitimate reason."

"Dr. Papineau's a good doctor," Jessie interjected. "He's treated Walter all his life. I'm sure he's right about the military deferment. We just wanted to check it out and see how serious this is. Walter's brother was killed at Pearl Harbor."

"I'm sorry to hear about your brother." Bowser seemed to sense the potential difference in agenda between husband and wife. "But I think you did the right thing to at least have it checked out. Walter, could you unbutton your shirt? I'd like to listen to your heart."

Bowser put a cold stethoscope on the upper left area of Walter's bare chest. "Hmm. A bit slower than normal. Breathe in for me, Walter."

23

LONDON
JANUARY 5, 1942

By early 1942, the ravaging airborne bombardments that killed Edwin Reece and thousands of Londoners had subsided, at least for the time being. Churchill's Spitfires, though greatly outnumbered, had outdueled Goering's Messerschmitts. Hitler's failure to bomb the British into submission redirected his ambition elsewhere. Frustrated by British resistance, the Nazi jackboot turned its fury to the east—to Russia.

All this Nazi attention on Russia and Africa created a false sense of security in the British Isles. Most Brits knew that the silent, wind-swept skies above their wispy island-nation were a deceptively peaceful tapestry, a placid and eerie contrast to the greatest tempest in the history of mankind now brewing across the English Channel.

Mr. Churchill had said the Battle of Britain was over, but the battle for Europe was about to begin. Even still, the British enjoyed this temporary respite for their homeland during the holiday season of 1941.

Seaman Darwin McCloud of the Royal Naval Reserves was pouring a glass of wine at his mother's dining room table in Kensington. He had duty over the New Year's weekend, and Monday, the fifth, was his first real chance to celebrate with her.

A candlelight dinner of wild rice, duck, and champagne set a relaxing stage for mother and son to ring in the New Year five days late.

"I'd like to propose a toast, Mother, but I have so much on my mind I don't know where to start."

"Are you asking *me* to assume the honors?" Juliana asked.

"Not necessarily, Mother. Just exploring our possibilities."

"Your father would have some witty saying from naval lore. What was it he used to say about Lloyd George?"

"Ah, yes," Darwin chuckled. "It was that monotonous dialogue they would sing in the officers' wardroom to the tune of 'Onward Christian Soldiers.' Something like 'Lloyd George knew my father, Father knew Lloyd George?'" Darwin burst into laughter. "And then it repeats itself, over and over again to the same words?"

"That's it! Now you're catching on. Sip your champagne, darling, and maybe it will come back to you!" Juliana smiled. "I want to hear you sing the silly thing!"

"Shame on you, Mother. Trying to turn your only son into a sot and it's not even New Year's!" Darwin took a sip and smiled. "Okay. Here goes. To the tune of 'Onward Christian Soldiers' . . ." Darwin burst into laughter again. "Are you sure you want me to sing this, Mother?"

"Yes, of course! In honor of your father."

"And my superior officer, I might add," Darwin interjected.

"To Captain Edward McCloud!" Juliana said.

"Here, here!" Darwin raised his glass as Juliana joined him. "There, Mother, you *did* propose the first toast of the new year!"

"Yes, I suppose I did."

"And to your ex-husband at that!"

"And to *your* father. To his health and safety as he commands his ship somewhere in the cold, treacherous waters of the North Atlantic."

"I'll drink to that, Mother."

"I suppose I sound rather silly. I mean, I *did* divorce the man."

"Don't feel silly. I miss him too. Besides, I've been praying for reconciliation."

"My son, the matchmaker. Trying to put his parents back together when he doesn't even have a girl of his own."

"I had a close friend, though."

Juliana paused, as if not knowing how to react or what to say. "Yes. I know you still grieve the loss of your friend. Let's raise our glasses in his honor, shall we?"

"To Reece. May he rest in peace."

Darwin raised his glass as Juliana sipped her champagne and paused for a moment.

"Darwin, do you mind if I ask you a personal question about Reece?"

"Mother, you know you can ask me anything."

"I feel a little silly asking this. But what is it that made Reece so special?"

"The truth?"

"Yes, the truth. If you feel comfortable telling me."

"Mother, here is the truth. The thing I loved so much about Reece was that he reminded me so much of Father."

"Of your father?" Juliana looked puzzled. "I don't understand. Your relationship with your father has been distant, sometimes tumultuous."

"Precisely. But don't you see? Like Father, Reece was big, strong, and brave. He was a man's man."

"A *man's man*? I didn't think you cared too much for muscular men, Darwin," she said. "I mean, you've never taken an interest in . . ."

"What, Mother? I haven't taken an interest in what?"

Juliana paused again. She looked as if she wasn't sure if there was a question Darwin wanted her to ask or if she had already said too much. "It's just that I fail to comprehend your attraction to Reece if he reminded you of your father."

"Mother, all my life I yearned to have a relationship with Father. I've wanted him to love me and to accept me. As close as you and I have been, Mother, and as much as I love you, I've needed a man in my life. I've needed father's love too, but he was never home. And when he was, he never accepted me for who I am. Perhaps I am who I am because he was gone. Reece was the first man to take an interest in me. He made me feel special. It was as if I was having a loving relationship with my father—the loving relationship I missed with my real father—through Reece. That's the best I can describe it."

"You mean your relationship with Reece was like a father-son relationship?"

"Not totally. Our relationship was more complex than that. But yes, I suppose there is a bit of truth to that. He was big and masculine; I was frail and scrawny. Sort of the way I would be compared to father. Yet Reece accepted me, yes, he *loved* me for who I was. Even to this day, Father has barely even acknowledged my enlisting in the Reserves."

Juliana looked across the table at him, her eyes and face illuminated by the flickering candlelight. She sipped her champagne, her eyes fixed on him.

"Oh Mother, I know that look on your face. You're wondering if I've been involved with, shall we say, inappropriate activities with members of the same sex."

"Is that a statement or a question?" she asked.

"Which would you prefer?" he asked.

"Answering my question with a question, are you?"

"You don't want me to address the issue, do you, Mother?"

"The issue has nothing to do with my love for you, Darwin."

"Again, you make my point for me."

Juliana paused, taking yet another sip. "I dare not ask how. But I've a feeling you're about to tell me."

"You said the issue has nothing to do with your love for me, right?"

"Yes, son. That's right. This issue that you're struggling with, whatever it is, does not affect my love for you."

"So you *do* love me, right, Mother?"

"That's a ridiculous question."

"So *you* love me, and *we've* never done anything inappropriate with one another, right?"

"This isn't Oedipus Rex," Juliana snapped, then smiled and sipped her wine. "Who do you think I am, Queen Jocasta?"

"Very funny, my queen. But my point is that just because two men love one another doesn't mean the love is immoral or in any way impure."

"You're trying to convince me of something, Darwin."

"Jesus loved Peter. There was nothing immoral about that. And all I ever wanted was Father's love and attention. But I've never done enough to make him proud of me."

"You are who you are, son. You are the way God made you. And I'm sure that your father *is* proud of you. Don't read too much into the fact that he hasn't made much out of your service in the Reserves. We are in a war."

"Yes, we are. And it's not right that Father should have to be away at sea getting shot at with torpedoes from U-boats in the North Atlantic while my part is to ride in a patrol boat just off the coast of Dover."

"Darwin, I'm sure that watching our coastline is of the highest importance to our defenses. Please don't sell yourself short."

"I don't mean to downplay the significance of coastal defenses. But my work was more dangerous at St. Paul's during the Blitz." Darwin paused to sip some champagne. "I feel I need to do more, Mother. That's all."

"You've volunteered for the Reserves, Darwin. You're pulling weekend military duty. What more can you do right now? It isn't your fault the Germans stopped bombing us and attacked Russia."

"I can help take the attack to the Germans, like Father is doing."

"Darwin, I'm your mother. I know when you have something on your mind. What is it?"

"A Special Forces unit is being formed this spring. They've opened the opportunity to reservists." He paused for a sip of champagne. "I've decided to volunteer."

Juliana did not respond, but instead, speared at her duck and rice. She looked at him. "Darwin, I know you better than anyone. Why do you keep me guessing with all this double talk about Reece and now this reference to Special Forces." She looked almost afraid to ask any more questions. "So what is— what do you call it—a Special Forces unit?"

"Special Forces are highly-trained, forward-deployed combat units—units on the vanguard of the fighting. These units are ready to move at a moment's notice for service to His Majesty anywhere in the world."

"Sounds like you've got all the jargon down. What is this Special Forces going to be called?"

"The unit is to be called the Royal Naval Commandos. If accepted, I would go to Ardentinny for training. If I make it through the initial training sessions, we would be training at Achnacarry where we would be required to master rock climbing, amphibious assaults, and battlefield survival under ardent circumstances."

"Is it dangerous?"

He picked up his glass, sloshed the wine in a swirling motion, and studied it for a moment against the burning chandelier. "I cannot lie to you, Mother. Yes, both the training and the operations we would engage in could be perilous."

"Perilous, you say? Why are you doing this to me, son?"

"Mother, I'm not trying to do anything to you. I am only trying to serve God. Someone must go. It may as well be me."

"You're trying to serve God? By putting yourself in one of the most dangerous military situations you could be in? This wouldn't have anything to do with proving something to your father, would it?"

"I'm not sure which question you want me to answer first, Mother. Am I hoping to prove something to Father? Yes. Honestly, I am. I want him to be proud of his son, and part of me hopes that becoming a Special Forces member will make him proud. But I *do* look at this as an opportunity to serve God. After all, the whole continent is oppressed. Someone will have to be on the front lines when our forces go back in, and someone must also minister to the Germans. If I die, perhaps Father will remember me as a hero much in the same way I remember Reece."

"But what about me?" Juliana took him by the hand and looked him in the eyes. "I want you alive, son. Look at you. You're talking about rock climbing and amphibious assaults and battlefield survival. All that sounds so demanding. I know we're at war, but Darwin, you're an actor. You're not a soldier or a sailor."

"Yes, Mother, I'm an actor. But you know what Shakespeare said—'The whole world is a stage and we are all but actors upon it.' I would still be an actor, just playing the role of a Special Forces commando for a while. Besides, as you've pointed out, I am rather, shall we say, physically pusillanimous."

"I never said such a thing."

"Then, perhaps weak or scrawny would better describe your view of me."

"Be realistic, son. I'm just concerned for your physical safety."

"Look on the bright side, Mother. They say that most of the candidates will wash out in training. Perhaps I will flunk and be assigned back to my boat at Dover. Then all of this would be academic, wouldn't it?"

"Somehow I have a feeling you won't wash out. You are awfully determined once you set you head on something."

"But you do hope I don't succeed in the training, don't you, Mother?"

Juliana looked at him, almost coyishly, as if she wasn't about to reveal her true feelings. "I love you, son."

"Happy New Year, Mother."

24
DUKE UNIVERSITY HOSPITAL
DURHAM, NORTH CAROLINA
JANUARY 5, 1942

Mr. Brewer, your test results are in." Charles Bowser strolled into his office where Walter and Jessie had been waiting about twenty minutes.

"Am I gonna live, Doc?" Walter asked.

Bowser sat, adjusted his glasses, and glanced at his charts. "I think you're going to live, Mr. Brewer. But I *do* think that Dr. Papineau is at least partially correct in his diagnosis."

"You think Walter needs a military deferment?" Jessie asked.

"Possibly, but not necessarily."

"But you *are* saying that he *possibly* needs one?" Jessie persisted.

Bowser cleared his throat and adjusted his glasses again, perhaps hoping to send the message to Jessie that it was not necessary to cross-examine him after every sentence.

"Shoot it straight, Doc," Walter said.

"Dr. Papineau diagnosed you with a condition known as bradycardia. In simple terms, that means a slower than normal heartbeat, anything slower than sixty beats per minute. In your case, Mr. Brewer, your normal heart rate is fifty-five beats per minute.

"So he *does* have bradycardia, just like Dr. Pap said?" Jessie asked.

Walter had seen this side of her before—that rare but dogged role which sometimes came out, in which she could mimic a relentless prosecutor.

"Jessie, let the man talk."

Bowser glanced at his notes, trying to suppress a grin. Then he again adjusted his glasses and looked at Jessie. "Yes, ma'am. Your husband does *technically* have bradycardia."

Bowser looked over at Walter. "Now, does that mean you're in any kind of danger? Maybe and maybe not. The issue is *why* your heart is slow. Some athletes, for example, have slow heartbeats because their hearts are strong and relaxed from exercise. In your case, Dr. Papineau thinks your condition is from tobacco poisoning when you were a kid. His concern is that your heart could be compromised by additional stress."

Jessie looked puzzled. "I don't understand, Doctor Bowser. Dr. Papineau recommended a military deferment. Don't you agree with him?"

"Jessie, the man is *trying* to tell us what he thinks."

"It's all right, Mr. Brewer."

Bowser paused, apparently to collect his thoughts. "That's a complicated question, Mrs. Brewer. We put your husband's heart through some rather rigorous stress testing. The purpose was to look for danger signs under prolonged exercise. The good news is that he passed those tests. After reviewing the charts, I think he could serve in most military positions. However, he *does* have bradycardia, and his doctor feels that stressors or chemicals may compromise him. Therefore, he is technically eligible for a medical deferment."

"What are you saying, Doc?" Walter asked.

"He's saying you should take the deferment, Walter."

"Mr. Brewer, I'm saying that this could go either way. I think you'll be fine, but you could also take the medical deferment. At least there's a legitimate diagnosis."

"See? He said take the deferment."

Walter looked at Jessie. His subtle hints for her to talk less and listen more were not resonating. "Jessie, the doctor's not a potted plant. And he said that I *could* take it, not that I *should* take it."

He looked apologetically at Bowser. "What do you think I should do?"

"There's a doctor in Chapel Hill who's an expert in tobacco poisoning. I've arranged for him to see you later this afternoon."

"You want me to see another doctor?"

"When we're talking about your heart, we want to be safe. And I think two heads are better than one. I want to see if we can establish or rule out tobacco poisoning as a cause for your condition. The doctor in Chapel Hill is better equipped to do that than we are here at Duke."

"What's his name?" Walter asked.

"Guthridge. Dr. Dean Guthridge. He's a cardiac toxicologist. He specializes in poisons and their effect on the heart. I just want to run Dr. Papineau's tobacco theory by him."

Walter looked at Jessie. "I've always wanted to go to Chapel Hill anyway. If Doc Bowser thinks it's a good idea, we may as well go while we're up here."

"It's only about eight miles over there," Bowser interjected. "He's at North Carolina Memorial Hospital on the southern part of the UNC Campus. My staff will give you directions. I'll have a courier take your file right over."

Jessie was irritated with Dr. Bowser. Why not just tell Walter that the military was a bad idea and leave it at that? On the other hand, Bowser said that Walter was *technically* eligible. This would give her plenty of ammunition. Unless Guthridge messed things up. Deep down, she worried that this new Dr. Guthridge, this cardiac whatever he was, might override Dr. Papineau and convince Walter that the Army would be safe.

Walter was excited to visit Chapel Hill, a place he had heard so much about but had never actually seen. Following Highway 15-501 from Durham, he crossed the town limits and parked the Model A just in front of "Silent Sam," the rifle-toting statue of a Confederate soldier overlooking Franklin Street where the UNC campus converged with downtown Chapel Hill.

Stepping on the Carolina campus for the first time brought back a rush of memories and a flood of what-ifs. He remembered the night when Jimmy Williams, half full of liquor, offered to pay his full tuition to this very place, conditioned of course upon marrying Ellie.

As they walked past the Old Well, past the South Building, and through the Quad toward the hospital, it was obvious why the old campus was the pride of North Carolina and the gem of the great Southern universities.

With lovely Georgian architecture blending subtly into the oak and pine orchards of Piedmont, North Carolina, Carolina carried the proud mantle of being the oldest of the state universities, first founded in 1789. This was where Walter and the brightest sons of the South had dreamed of coming to college. Even in the dead of winter, the campus was beautiful beyond description.

Maybe it's a good thing Jimmy didn't show me the campus before he made his offer. I can only imagine what this place would look like in the springtime, with all these dogwoods and azaleas in full bloom.

They walked past the Bell Tower and Kenan Stadium and finally reached Memorial Hospital, where they were led back to the cardiac wing by an orderly. At the end of a dark corridor on the right, an opaque glass pane on a wooden door proclaimed "Dean Guthridge, MD," and under that, "Cardiology."

"Welcome to Chapel Hill, Mr. and Mrs. Brewer. I'm Dr. Guthridge. Most of my patients call me Dr. Gut. We've been waiting for you." A short, humble man with thinning white hair and granny glasses, Guthridge spoke through his nose, producing a classic Kansas twang.

"I've never had a doctor take me in without a thirty-minute wait. I hope that's not a bad sign," Walter said.

"Not at all. Dr. Bowser phoned and sent your charts over. He asked me to review your chart and give a second opinion. I know you've got a long drive, so we wanted to work you in."

Jessie spoke quickly. "Dr. Papineau recommended a

medical deferment, and Dr. Bowser said that a deferment could be granted under the circumstances."

Guthridge chuckled. "I guess if I recommend otherwise that means I'm outvoted, huh?"

"Doctor, I'm not trying to avoid the draft," Walter said.

"But he certainly doesn't need to go if he has a medical condition. Especially since his brother was killed at Pearl Harbor," Jessie interjected.

"Dr. Bowser made a note about your brother in the records. I'm very sorry."

"Thanks, Doc. But please don't let that influence you. I'm just trying to find out if I have a heart condition."

Jessie again spoke up. "Technically, you *do* have a heart condition. Dr. Bowser said so."

"Yes, Jessie, but it doesn't sound that serious, and he also thought I would be okay if I were in the military."

"Walter, he said the deferment could be supported from a medical standpoint."

"We'll see what Dr. Guthridge has to say. That's why we're here."

"For goodness sake, Walter! How many opinions do we need? You saw what the Navy did for Billy." Jessie turned her plea to Guthridge. "Are you a father, Dr. Gut?"

"Yes, ma'am. Three kids and two grandkids."

"Good. Then you'll understand where I'm coming from. We have four children at home. Walter's dead brother has two young children. Walter's now got six children to take care of. That's why we think it's important for him to take care of himself and maybe get some treatment for his condition here in Chapel Hill over the next few months. Walter's got a good job with the Federal Government, and we can pay for the treatment."

"Mrs. Brewer, you can relax. I'm not going to send your husband to the Army."

"You're not?"

"No, I'm not. I don't plan to override the medical deferment recommended by Dr. Papineau."

"Really?" Jessie felt a sudden sense of relief.

"Yes, ma'am. I'll give your husband my opinion on whether he would be at risk from a medical standpoint if he goes in the Army. He can still take the deferment if he wants. That will be up to him. I'm just going to draw some blood to try and determine if the tobacco poisoning is related to the bradycardia."

"I'm sorry, Doctor Gut. I didn't mean . . ."

"Think nothing of it, Mrs. Brewer. Now, if I could just ask your husband to step back with me. We'll draw some blood, and we should have some results in a half an hour."

An hour later, Dr. Gut was back in the waiting area with test results in hand. "Mr. Brewer, we've tested for trace elements of nicotine and all other known carcinogens used to poison tobacco for bugs. Your blood work looks exemplary."

"I guess that means I don't have tobacco poisoning."

"It means that I can't find anything linking the bradycardia to tobacco poisoning. It's possible there's a link, given your medical history, but I can't find any medical evidence to support it."

"But Dr. Papineau has been his doctor all his life. He knows Walter best!" Jessie protested.

"Jessie, the doc just said my blood work looked good. You want him to say I'm on my death bed?"

"That's not it, Walter. It's just that Dr. Pap—"

"Mrs. Brewer," Guthridge interrupted. "I'm not impugning Dr. Papineau. It's possible that an unknown carcinogen may have caused the reaction and thus the condition. There *was* apparently a symptomatic correlation. I'm just saying your husband's blood work is clean. That's good news."

"What about military service?" Walter asked. "What should I do?"

"Again, Mr. Brewer, it's up to you. I agree with Dr. Bowser. You *do* have a condition which makes you technically eligible for deferment. If you wish to take the deferment, you could get away with it. However, based on your stress tests and now your blood work, I doubt you would be at risk beyond the normal hazards of the military."

"So you're saying that he *is* eligible for deferment?"

"Yes, ma'am, I'm saying that *technically* he is eligible. Dr. Papineau's letter makes him eligible."

"But you're also saying I'll be okay physically if I go?" Walter asked.

"I'm saying I don't think you'll have a heart attack or any type of heart failure from natural causes."

By the time Walter and Jessie got back to Jamesville that evening, they had bickered for three hours over their respective interpretations of the two specialists' opinions. During the drive home, Jessie had repeated the phrase *technically eligible for deferment*—a phrase she thought she heard from both Dr. Bowser and Dr Gut—more than a hundred times.

Walter, on the other hand, was not so jaded in his interpretation of the doctors' reports. He was torn between his duty to the children, his wife, his sister-in-law, and doing what was right. He didn't know what was right. He didn't want to shirk his duty based on a technicality.

He took Jessie home and then headed to Ellie's house in Plymouth to pick up the kids.

25
JAMESVILLE COMMUNITY CEMETERY
11:15 P.M.
JANUARY 5, 1942

Walter had never visited a cemetery at night before. As he turned left on Highway 171 in Jamesville and drove slowly past his house, he looked to see if any lights were on. All was dark. Jessie had gone to bed.

He pressed the accelerator. The Model A clanked over the railroad tracks a quarter of a mile past his house. He slowed down again. The Jamesville Community Cemetery was just another hundred yards past the tracks on his left.

He wheeled left off the road, killed his headlights, and cut the engine.

This was a place he'd visited many times before. Most of his visits were in the context of graveside services after funerals. Sometimes he'd walked the short distance here from his home on Sunday afternoons to visit his grandfather's grave. But never at night.

The full moon blazing overhead illuminated every tombstone in the ten-acre graveyard. At the back center of the field was a large white cross, maybe ten feet tall, that had long ago been planted in the ground, a symbol that nearly every corpse was at one time at least a professing Christian. Glancing across the field of grave markers from his car, Walter wondered how many professions of faith had been real. He wondered about the souls of the dead, where they might be now. He thought about heaven and hell, about the verse in the Bible that says "Narrow is the road that leads to eternal life, but broad is the road that leads to destruction."

Could most of the people buried here be in hell now?

He reached into the glove box, pulled out a flashlight, then got out of the car.

Around the backside and perimeter of the cemetery, the tree line stood clearly against the night sky, visible under the stars to the East. Walter pulled out his pocket watch. In forty-five minutes, it would be midnight. Jessie was probably asleep, so he would take his time.

Ellie predicted he would seek a place of solace to find an answer to his dilemma about the draft. She was right. This was the place. He flipped on the flashlight but decided it wasn't doing much good with the bright moon out.

Strolling a few paces down the gravel cart path toward the back of the field, Walter looked to the left for Billy's grave. It should be easy to find, with fresh dirt and flowers still present. But at this time of night and from this distance, all the head-stones looked the same. If he could only find some sort of landmark. He took another ten paces or so, still squinting toward the left side of the cemetery.

The two taps on his left shoulder shocked his heart into overdrive. He pivoted to his rear.

Billy?

No one was there. At least no one he could see. Just the Model A parked by the road at the edge of the grave markers, its chrome bumper glistening in the moonlight. He took a deep breath, exhaling a frosty fog into the crisp, night air. His heart pounded inside his black leather jacket like a jackhammer crushing concrete.

"I just made a cup of hot chocolate for her, brother. That's all."

Am I going mad, or is my imagination playing tricks on me? Get a hold of yourself, Walter. You've been under a lot of stress. Nobody's there.

He turned around and took another step towards the back of the cemetery, still looking for Billy's tombstone. With his heart still thumping from the imaginary tap on his shoulder, a rustling sound near his feet stopped him dead in his tracks. This time, he flipped on the flashlight and pointed it in the direction of the sound. The bright eyes of a big calico cat reflected in the beam of light.

"Hey, kitty, kitty."

At least I've got a little warm-blooded companionship out here.

He reached down to pet the furry feline. The big cat accepted a few seconds of affection with a roaring purr before scampering off, where it curled up at the base of a grave marker. Walter's eyes followed the cat. The moonlight revealed the name on the tombstone where the cat had stopped.

Mattie Satterthwaite
1845-1931
John 3:16

"Thank you, kitty cat," he whispered, as if speaking might awaken someone. "Miss Mattie" Satterthwaite, a legendary Sunday school teacher around Jamesville, was buried in the same row as Billy. He turned left and walked straight across Miss Mattie's grave.

Billy should be about seven or eight plots over.

As he squinted across the fluorescent-like glow of headstones, the silhouette of dozens of flowers on one of the graves came into view. He had found Billy.

With his eyes locked onto Billy's resting place, he tip-toed over several other graves, stopping at Billy's feet. He paused, gazing at his brother's freshly-erected headstone.

It was amazing how so little could say so much about Billy. This showed the fragility of life, that a person's entire existence on Earth could be boiled down to a few lines within the limited space of a granite marker. With Ellie's help, Walter had authored the words on Billy's epithet. But the grave marker hadn't been ready in time for the funeral. This was the first time he read the words chiseled in granite.

Billy Mitchell Brewer
Seaman, U.S. Navy
July 12, 1913-December 7, 1941
Father, Husband
Navy Cross Recipient
In God We Trust

Maybe his answer was somewhere on the headstone. He began to reflect on the words he had written about his brother.

Father, husband. *Maybe that's my answer. I've got to take care of my kids and be daddy to yours too. Maybe you've given enough for both of us. Maybe I need to stay here and be a husband and a father. Maybe that's why Dr. Pap wrote the letter.*

Navy Cross recipient. *You've raised the bar with this one, brother. You're now the highest decorated combat veteran in the history of Martin County. I wish there was some way I could tell you they decorated you for heroism. You were awarded the highest medal in the Navy for your courage. Only the Medal of Honor is higher. You've left us with a legacy and a legend. I know we were different in so many ways, but I'm so proud of you. How can I hide behind a letter and refuse to serve, when you gave your life for this country?*

In God we trust. *I'm trusting You, God, for an answer. But I don't have one yet. Please give me clear direction before this night is over.*

Walter stood there for a few minutes, gazing up at the stars. He found the Big Dipper, then the North Star off to his right.

If I follow that star about a thousand paces, it would take me straight home, where Jessie and the kids are asleep. Maybe that's where I should go—home. Maybe I should forget this whole thing and follow the doctor's orders.

As he watched the North Star, a meteor streaked across the sky from Southwest to Northeast.

If I follow that star about a thousand miles, I'd be in the middle of the North Atlantic, on my way to Europe, where the Army will soon be engaged. Maybe I should do my duty and follow that star.

He stood there a bit longer. There were no more streaking stars. In the stillness of the night, he still had no answer. There was another grave he needed to visit.

He turned right and followed the North Star about twenty paces. There were no fresh flowers on this grave, but its occupant had influenced Walter's life as much as anyone. He stood at the foot and looked at the marker.

Zachary Lawrence Brewer
"Baldy"
April 8, 1840-October 4, 1930
17th NC, Co F, CSA
"Deo Vindice"
Psalm 46: 1-2

Walter remembered Grandaddy Baldy bouncing him on his knee so many times as a boy and regaling him with stories of Company F of the seventeenth North Carolina. The seventeenth had seen bloody action in two last-gasp Confederate victories around Petersburg, both at Bermuda Hundred in May of 1864 and again at Cold Harbor on June third. In both bloody charges, the seventeenth North Carolina anchored the right flank of the Confederate Army, and Baldy, on the edge of the Confederate charge, had his arm shot off.

His brother had given his life. His grandfather had given his arm. Both had sacrificed for causes in which they believed.

Ellie was right. The family heritage of sacrifice was too compelling. Walter had made up his mind. He would tear up Pap's letter and join the Army.

He was not ready, however, to leave the cemetery. There was one other grave he needed to visit before he left. This would be the toughest visit yet. Seeing this grave one last time before he left would be painful. But it was something he had to do.

Off in the distant West towards Williamston, the rumbling of the railroad tracks was stirring the peace on the crisp winter's night. The sound of the midnight train barreling in the dark, clacking across the tracks just a stone's throw from his house, had over the years become an audible security blanket as he lay in bed with his eyes fixed on the ceiling.

Instead of disturbing the sleeping people of Jamesville, the three horn blasts from the powerful locomotive were like midnight music to their ears, muffled by the walls and closed windows of their homes.

Walter closed his eyes as the rumbling and roar of the engine came to a deafening crescendo. The powerful high beam on the front of the locomotive swept its blinding light across the edge of the cemetery. Even with his eyes closed, Walter could see the powerful beam through his eyelids.

Standing here in the cemetery, only a few yards from the tracks, the noise level was almost ear-splitting. He opened his eyes as the engineer blasted the horn, its high squelch echoing and reverberating off the tombstones all around him. If ever there was a noise to wake the dead, this was it.

The powerful engine sped past him, heading east toward Plymouth. With the sound of the locomotive now fading in the distance and only the clacking of box cars lingering, Walter waited a bit longer for the caboose to barrel by. He wanted silence and solace for this last graveside visit.

With the train now out of earshot, a blanket of peaceful tranquility seemed to descend over the place like never before.

He took a deep breath and walked across three graves to the left of his grandfather's. The moonlight lit the baby's head-stone with what seemed to him an angelic glow.

Mona Shepard Brewer
Infant Daughter of Walter and Jessie
November 13, 1938-November 20, 1938
With Us For A Short Time
But Loved For All Eternity
Until We Meet Again
Commended Into The Hands
Of Almighty God

Walter dropped to his knees, his hands embracing the top of the stone. "I love you, sweetie. Daddy loves you. Daddy will always love you."

He was choked with emotion. The three-year gulf since his baby's death had done nothing to ease the pain. Nothing was harder for him than visiting her grave. He had never been able to visit it without crying.

"Daddy has to go to war. I have to say good-bye for now."

Tears streamed down his face.

"But look on the bright side." He took his right hand off the tombstone and wiped the water from his face. "Daddy may be with you soon."

He stood and started walking away from the grave. Then he stopped in his tracks and looked back one last time. The cat had curled up on the grave in front of the headstone.

"Night-night, sweetie. Sleep well till I see you again."

26
HMS *ARMADILLO*
ARDENTINNY, SCOTLAND
MARCH 1, 1942
2 A.M.

The jackbooted Royal Marine drill instructor kicked the empty metal trash can across the tile floor. It sounded like a cymbal crashing two inches from their sleeping heads. Then he flipped on the light switch in the barracks.

"Up! Up! Up! You pusillanimous wretches. You call yourselves men? I've never witnessed such a group of feminine-looking fairies! Just settled down for a long winter's nap, had you? On your feet, ladies. Move! Move! Move!"

Darwin rubbed his eyes and pulled the covers off his body. He'd never been screamed at at two o'clock in the morning before. Twelve hours ago, he had checked into the Royal Naval Commando Training Facility in Ardentinny, near the beautiful West Coast of Scotland. He'd filled out his paperwork and was directed to the barracks, where he was told to get a good night's sleep and be ready to start military orientation at seven o'clock in the morning. But the fellow hovering over him, wearing the black beret, the camouflage fatigues, and holding the long billy club had other plans.

"Up! Up! Stand at attention!" The drill instructor shouted, now banging his billy club on the heads of the metal-framed cots. A couple of whacks missed Darwin's head by a few inches as the sergeant stomped down the aisle tormenting his sleepy-headed targets. "Stand at attention and do not move!"

Within seconds, thirty-five underwear-clad male subjects of the British Crown were standing at barefooted attention on the cold floor.

"Did you sweet pussycats think you'd get up at seven, have a leisurely breakfast on your first day, and then commence with learning how to be Royal Naval commandos? Hmm?"

There was no answer.

"Oh, I see. Having trouble hearing, are we?" The Royal Marine drill instructor took eight paces down the center aisle between the two rows of men standing at attention and did an about-face. "I said, did you sweet pussycats think you'd get up at seven, have a leisurely breakfast on your first day, and then commence with learning how to be Royal Naval comman-dos?"

Still no answer.

"You! What's your name?"

"Richardson, sir," came the response from the big man with bulging muscles who was looking straight ahead. "Ian Richardson."

The drill instructor got in Richardson's face and screamed, "Mr. *Ian* Richardson, do you have a hearing problem?"

"No, sir. Not that I'm aware of."

"Well, then, Mr. *Ian* Richardson. Can you explain to me why you, as the physically largest member of this class, did not answer your drill instructor when I asked you and your ship-mates a simple question, not once, but *twice?*"

The big man hesitated.

"I'm waiting, Mr. *Ian* Richardson, for your answer!"

"With respect, I thought the question was rhetorical, sir."

"*Rhetorical?*" Now the drill instructor had the ammunition he needed. "Do you hear that, pussycats? Mr. Ian Richardson thought my question was *rhetorical*. All right, Mr. *Ian* Richardson. I want you to repeat after me. I."

"I," Richardson said.

"Am," said the instructor.

"Am," said Richardson.

"A dumb," said the instructor.

"A dumb," repeated Richardson.

"Hippopotamus!" said the instructor.

"Hippopotamus!" repeated Richardson.

"Sir!" barked the instructor.

"Sir!" said Richardson.

"Now let's put that together, Mr. Richardson. Say 'I am a dumb hippopotamus, sir!'"

Richardson complied.

"Now that you've admitted that you are, in fact, a dumb hippopotamus, I want you to hit the deck and give me fifty *rhetorical* push-ups, Mr. *Ian* Richardson."

"Yes, sir!" Richardson barked then hit the floor on all fours and started doing push-ups.

"That's a pansy push-up, Mr. Richardson," the instructor yelled, rapping his billy club on the floor beside Richardson's head. "You will kiss the floor each time you go down then fully extend your arms when you push up. I want to see your lips kiss the deck on each extension."

Richardson pushed up, then kissed the floor, then pushed up again.

"That's better," said the instructor.

"You!" the drill instructor now turned his attention to another member of the group. "You think something is humorous, do you?"

"No, sir," the recruit said.

"Then perhaps you would like to explain the presence of the Cheshire smirk that is emblazoned across that rodent-looking face of yours?"

The Cheshire smirk that had been emblazoned across the recruit's rodent-looking face vanished.

"What is your name, mister?"

"Ashton, sir."

"Mr. Ashton, since you seem to think something is humorous and have the audacity to deny that you think something is humorous after I was a personal witness to that rat-faced grin of yours, you will repeat after me."

The drill instructor brought his nose so close to Ashton's nose that the two were touching. He screamed, "I am a rat-faced weasel."

"I am a rat-faced weasel," Ashton said.

"Louder, you vermin!"

"I am a rat-faced weasel!" Ashton said.

"Now, Mr. Weasel, I want you to hit the deck right beside our dumb hippopotamus, Mr. *Ian* Richardson, and give me one *hundred* push-ups. And kiss the floor with your stinking rat-faced lips, mister. Now!"

"Aye, sir!" Ashton got on all fours as the drill instructor walked up and down the line of recruits, searching for another potential target.

"What's your name, mister?"

"McCloud, sir. Darwin McCloud."

"Is this yours, Mr. McCloud?" the instructor asked as he held up a shirt on the end of his billy club. "What's the matter? Your mummy never teach you anything about hanging your clothes in a closet?"

Here it comes. Just don't say anything cute.

"Yes, sir."

"Then perhaps you could explain to your shipmates here why I found it on the floor when I came in?"

Darwin hesitated.

"Got a hearing problem, little fellow?" It was a clear reference to Darwin's physical stature. At five feet, four inches tall, Darwin was the smallest of the commando candidates.

Lord, give me wisdom.

"No, sir."

"I'm waiting, and your shipmates are waiting to hear why you have chosen to be such a slob on this our first day together, *Miss* McCloud."

"I have no excuses, sir." Darwin held his breath.

"Then I suggest you hang this in your closet and fall back in at attention, immediately."

The drill instructor turned away, stamped to the front of the barracks, then looked down the aisle of recruits.

"Now, then. By your very presence here this morning, you

pathetic-looking misers seem to think you have the gravitas to become part of one of the most elite fighting units in service to the Crown, Royal Navy Commandos. That, gentlemen, remains to be seen. If what I've seen so far this morning is any indication, I have my grave doubts.

"My name is Sergeant George Loomis. And for the next few weeks, for the few of you who might make it through this program, I shall be your mother, your father, your aunt, your uncle, and most importantly . . ." Loomis hesitated then whacked his billy club against one of the metal lockers. "Most importantly, I shall be your worst nightmare.

"You shall refer to me as Sergeant Loomis or sir. I, on the other hand, provided you haven't screwed up too badly for the day, shall refer to you as Commando Candidate McCloud. Or Commando Candidate Winstead.

"You are about to undergo the most rigorous training in the British military. You will climb rocks, swim for miles, jump off cliffs, handle with precision advanced weaponry, and learn to kill with your bare hands. This training is not for the meek." Loomis stepped in front of Darwin and stared at him for a couple of seconds, then turned away. "Look around you, gentlemen. There's a good chance half of you won't make it out of this training. For the half of you who do, there is an even better chance half of you will be dead within the next twelve months.

"There are plenty of places in the Navy for you to serve, places which would substantially lower the statistical chances of your imminent death. Only a special breed of killer should bear the title of Royal Naval Commando. If you wish to be reassigned to other duties, you may step forward now. There will be no record that you were ever here. In other words, the Royal Navy is giving you the opportunity to gracefully exit at this point, and it will never be held against you should you request reassignment elsewhere.

"Very well, then. I am holding my pocket watch in my hand, and I will give you sixty seconds to step forward. On my mark. Go."

I'm not afraid to die, Darwin thought. My eternal destination is secure. But what becomes of Mother if I die? With

Father gone, who will care for her? She would love nothing more than for me to step forward.

"Forty-five seconds.

"Fifteen seconds.

But what would Father think if I stepped aside? Nothing, if he never knows I was here. But even if the military doesn't tell him, Mother would. He would know I resigned or washed out. I volunteered for this because of him. I shall stay because of him.

"Time! All right. No resignations, I see. Very well. My job, to put it bluntly, is to wash you out. But look on the bright side. Better have me amputate your testicles than have the Germans do it." He whacked the billy club three times on the closest locker. "Any questions?"

There were none.

"Very well. Get into your utilities and fall in in front of the barracks in ten minutes. We will begin our *bonding time* with a six-mile run. Upon our return, we will commence a regimen of calisthenics and then start special military orientation. Move! Move! Move!"

27
NEAR TOBRUK, LIBYA
MARCH 15, 1942

From the front passenger's side of General Rommel's staff car parked high on a ridge, Heinrick looked through his powerful binoculars at the desert floor, about five hundred yards down range. His initial view was nothing but a sea of sand—by far the most plentiful commodity in this God-forsaken wasteland. He flicked his wrists upward and saw the far horizon, where the desert met the sky. The thick waves of heat lapping to the heavens blurred the view. If the British approached from the horizon, they would not be visible until their forward infantry stepped through the mirage-like wall dead ahead.

He swept his binoculars to the left. The black iron crosses painted on the sides of the panzers brought goose bumps to the back of his neck. There were hundreds of them lined side by side, their barrels pointed from left to right. Their motors roared like a light, continuous thunder in the distance. The awesome firepower of the Third Reich made him proud to be German.

He allowed his binoculars to linger for a moment at the sight of the Nazi war machine. He knew already from experience that within a few hours many of the men he could see working around the tanks would be dead, that many of the tanks poised now for the attack would serve as crumpled, charred mausoleums for their crew.

The same would hold true for the enemy. But he tried not to think about that for the moment. The glory of battle was at the precipice of battle. And for the moment, the sight before him was glorious.

Heinrick moved his binoculars in a slow, sweeping motion back to the right. Something black shot across his field of view. He stopped, slowly inching the glasses back to find what he had seen.

They were nomads, and they were running across the desert floor as the sound of thunder grew louder. There were six of them—a man, a woman, and four children. The woman was out front, carrying an infant.

The man brought up the rear. With one hand, the man guided his camel. With the other, he held the hand of his daughter. Two little boys were running single-file between their mother and their father.

The sound of thunder was augmented by lightning. The blasts from the tank barrels were like bursts of fire. Hundreds of plumes of black smoke rose from their barrels as the panzers charged onto the battleground. Heinrick looked to his right. British tanks, hundreds of them also, were pouring over the ridge charging at the German position, their barrels hurling heavy doses of fire and lead.

He looked back to the center of the battlefield, trying to find the nomad family. Shells, both British and German, pummeled the desert near where he had seen them. The dust and cloudy smoke made visibility impossible. As both the Germans and the British charged into the smoke cloud, Heinrick could do nothing but watch.

Six hours later, it was over. On this day, the British had turned and retreated, leaving the Wermacht in control of the territory. Tomorrow, he knew, the outcome might be different.

The perimeter having been secured, Heinrick and his staff drove their cars down into the sun-baked valley of sand. As their vehicles approached the battlefield, the stench of death surrounded them like a cloud of putrid ammonia. For all the glamour of serving on General Rommel's staff, for the prestige of briefing him on intelligence matters, and for the excitement of being seen at his side in front of some of the most important people in Germany including the Fürher, there was a price to pay.

That price was scavenging through dismembered, blood-ied, decaying human bodies. This was the part of his job Hein-rick hated.

He pulled the cloth mask over his face to block the brunt of the stench. "Stop here!" He raised his hand over his head to signal the two following open-topped troop trucks.

The British tanks—what was left of them—resembled burned, salvage metal at a junkyard. Smoke and steam still rose from hundreds of sources across the battlefield, as buzzards picked the faces and eyeballs of dead soldiers strewn one on top of another.

"Out of the trucks! This is where we begin," Heinrick ordered. "You know the routine. Check the bodies of the offi-cers first. Then the tank drivers. This will serve as our collec-tion point. I am to be immediately notified of anything unusual."

"*Jawohl, Herr Kapitan,*" came the collective response as the fifteen soldiers and officers assigned to the collection detail poured out the back of their trucks.

Heinrick stepped out of the command truck with a clip-board and began scribbling notes. As his men prodded the bodies, he would begin a damage assessment report, first counting the number of British tanks destroyed within their immediate area of about a thousand square yards. His assistant, Lieutenant Hans Kohlman, would begin with a body count.

The sound of a single shot echoed throughout the smol-dering tank graveyard "Hit the deck!" Heinrick shouted as the men in his squad lunged for the ground. "What was that?"

"Over here, *Kapitan*!" came the voice in German. Heinrick recognized it as that of Sergeant Rupert Sternam, one of his squad members.

Heinrick took a breath, rose to his feet, and followed the

direction of the voice around the back of a bullet-riddled British troop carrier. Lieutenant Kohlman followed behind.

Sergeant Rupert Sternam was standing behind the truck with his sidearm drawn, pointing at something on the ground.

"It was still alive," Sternam said.

Heinrick's eyes followed the direction of Sternam's gun and saw the camel. Its right back leg had been blown off and its head was bleeding, courtesy of the sergeant's sidearm. Five feet in front of the camel lay the bodies of a man and a little girl.

His mind raced back to November 1938, to the brick crushing the little Jewish girl's head, then back to Libya again.

"The camel, *Kapitan*. I put it out of its misery," Sternam said. "It was still breathing."

Read the book.

"Did you say something, Lieutenant?" Heinrick asked.

That sounded like a girl's voice.

"*Nein, Herr Kapitan*," Lieutenant Kohlman said.

"Sergeant. Get a shovel and bury that little girl," Heinrick said.

"*Jawohl, Kapitan*," Sergeant Sternam said.

"May I remind you that you have an appointment with General Rommel in two hours, *Herr Kapitan*?" Lieutenant Kohlman said as Sergeant Sternam double-stepped to the nearby command truck for a shovel.

"*Ja*. I am aware of my schedule with the general, Lieutenant. So what is your point?"

"Permission to speak freely, *Kapitan*?"

"Speak."

"*Kapitan*, as your second in command, my role is not only to help ensure the success of our mission, but also to ensure that my commanding officer, who in this case is you, *Herr Kapitan*, emerges in the best possible light."

"Get to your point, Lieutenant," Heinrick snapped as Sternam returned with the shovel.

"Respectfully, *Kapitan*, with so little time before your briefing and with so much intelligence that needs to be gathered in so short a time, would it be wise to divert the sergeant's time with so trivial a task as burying a nomadic girl, when he could be spending that time lifting potentially-important documents from the bodies of the enemy?"

Heinrick bit his tongue. "Have we no humanity, Lieutenant? The shells of our tanks killed the girl and her father."

"With respect, sir, it might have been the shells of the British. We've seen civilian casualties before. This girl was but a nomad whose path accidentally crossed the advance of the Third Reich. She is destiny's victim. Not ours."

"Give me the shovel, sergeant!" Heinrick ordered in an angry voice. "And resume your examination of the bodies in that tank. Report back to me if you find anything." Then he turned to his lieutenant. "You're right, Lieutenant. This nomadic girl is but a victim of destiny, unworthy of the time of a professionally-trained sergeant of the Third Reich. I shall dispose of this trivial matter myself."

28

Darwin kicked off his Boondocks, hung his military blouse in the small, aluminum closet beside the flimsy steel-framed cot he had been assigned, and flung himself face-up on the lumpy mattress. He crammed the small, feather-stuffed pillow under his head and stared up at the ceiling. He was dressed in his socks, military trousers, and a tee shirt.

Most of his classmates, the ones who had not dropped out of training, were milling past his cot in a single line waiting for what might be a lukewarm shower before dinner, if they were lucky. Most would have their shower served ice cold.

Sergeant Loomis had given them thirty minutes to shower and report to the galley—as it was called on a naval facility—where dinner would be served, followed by additional instruction on the art of special warfare. By 2100 hours, the "plan of the day" called for special warfare training to conclude for the evening.

Time was tight tonight, as always. In order to shower, get out, get dressed, and report to the galley, the commando candidates would need to spend no more than twenty-five seconds in the shower. Fatigued, they filed silently by Darwin without paying much attention to him or the couple of other trainees who were electing cot time over standing in line for a shower.

After special warfare training, they would return to this very aluminum Quonset hut, collapse on these flimsy, steel-framed cots, and try to get some sleep until four o'clock in the morning when their day would start with a ten-mile run followed by a five-mile swim followed by breakfast. Of course, their day *could* begin prior to 4 a.m., if Sergeant Loomis felt up to a midnight trash-can-kicking episode.

Darwin closed his eyes. Today he had nearly washed out of the program. It was an exercise, Loomis said, that was designed to teach the commando candidates effective hand-to-hand combat against larger opponents.

"If you can break this board, you can pulverize your opponent by a swift and unexpected whip-kick to his Adam's apple," Loomis had said. "This technique is ideal for situations where the fighting is down to bayonets and bare fists. You have to strike the throat. Kick high, quickly, accurately, and with power."

Most of the commando candidates handled the exercise with ease. Ian Richardson, for example, smashed the board to splinters on the second try. But Darwin, at five feet, four inches, had trouble kicking high enough to reach the board.

"Come on, McCloud," Loomis had said to Darwin the second time he landed on his rump. "These Germans aren't midgets. That might be high enough if your enemy is one of the seven dwarfs."

"You may not be physically tall enough to handle this exercise, laddie." Loomis stared down at Darwin, sprawled on the grass. "You missed the board by more than a foot on the third kick. You've got to get through this or I can't let you go on, son."

Loomis bent over and whispered in Darwin's ear. "You don't have to do this, McCloud," he spoke low enough that the other commando candidates could not hear him. "There's no disgrace in resigning from this training. Most people, even most members of the military, aren't cut out to be commandos. You're here as a volunteer. You had the courage to try. I commend you for that."

In other words, you're too small and not physically strong enough to cut this, McCloud. Don't make me be so blunt about it.

"One more shot, please sir," Darwin had responded. This time, his foot reached the small board, smashing it like a twig.

A mild round of applause followed from his shocked classmates who were gathered around him in the circle.

"Not bad," Loomis grudgingly said. "Now fall out and go to the barracks."

"Aye, sir!" Darwin saluted and walked back to the barracks. His foot was killing him and he grimaced as he walked back, but he dared not show a limp.

When the line for the shower shortened a bit, he decided he would get up off his cot. Perhaps a short shower would make him feel better.

Thank you, Lord, for Your intervention today. I would have washed out if it weren't for You.

Darwin opened his Bible to the Psalm he read every night just before dinner. He soaked in every word, worshiping his Creator as he read. It was a Psalm of David, number one hundred twenty-one. Darwin knew every word by heart but delighted in reading it every day anyway.

> I will lift up mine eyes to the hills
> From whence cometh my help?
> My help cometh from the LORD,
> Which made heaven and earth.
> He will not suffer thy foot to be moved;
> He who keepeth thee will not slumber.
> Behold, He who keeps Israel
> Shall neither slumber nor sleep.
> The LORD is thy keeper;
> The LORD is thy shade upon thy right hand.

The ruckus from the back of the barracks broke his concentration. It was Ian Richardson, and his tone was not pleasant. Richardson had been on a warpath recently, especially when Loomis wasn't around.

At six feet, three inches tall and weighing two hundred

twenty pounds, Richardson had succeeded in using his size, strength, and bravado to bully the smaller commando candidates when he wanted his way.

"You've got thirty seconds to get out of the bloody shower, Winstead," Richardson screamed.

Richardson's displeasure was directed at Commando Recruit William Winstead, normally a quiet fellow who kept to himself.

"Bug off, Richardson," Winstead said from the bowels of the shower.

Winstead's response sent a shock wave throughout the barracks.

Darwin looked back toward the shower area and saw Richardson deliver a hard punch to Winstead's midsection that landed with a crunching thud. Winstead howled, and with his face writhing in contortions, he heaved a few times, struggling to catch his breath. The white towel that had been covering him dropped to the floor. Winstead heaved again, then collapsed naked.

Darwin hopped off his bed, ran to the back of the barracks, and covered Winstead with the towel. Then he took Winstead's arm, pulled it around his shoulder and struggled to help him to his feet. Winstead felt like a limp, heavy load.

"A little help, please," Darwin said, struggling to balance his shipmate. Commando Candidate Peter Ashton, himself a previous target of Richardson's wrath, rushed to assist.

"If it isn't the rector come to rescue the flock," Richardson sneered. "The rector" was the term Richardson had given Darwin because of Darwin's nightly ritual of reading Psalms.

"Richardson," Darwin said in an even voice, "Why don't you take Winstead's advice and bug off?" The remark sent another shock wave through the Quonset-hut barracks.

Darwin and Ashton helped Winstead to his cot.

When Winstead lay down, Richardson mouthed off again. "If you weren't such a big guy, McCloud, I'd clean your clock."

"All right, Richardson," Darwin said, "if it makes you feel better to clean my clock, then have at it." He walked over to where Richardson was standing, right in front of the shower, and stopped so close to Richardson that his nose was nearly touching Richardson' chest.

The contrast could not be starker—a face-off between one man, a short, former actor, and a tall, well-chiseled former dock worker.

"Go ahead, take your shot, Richardson." Darwin spoke in a calm voice. "Do what you have to do."

I'm about to get my jaw broken. Perhaps worse.

Richardson cocked his balled fist and reared back, staring down into Darwin's eyes. Darwin looked back but kept his arms down and did not flinch or assume a defensive posture. Richardson pulled his fist back farther, then sent his fist barreling toward Darwin's nose.

He stopped his punch in the air an inch from the smaller man's face. Still, Darwin did not flinch.

I will lift up my eyes . . . From whence comes my help?

Richardson stood there for a moment with his balled fist frozen in front of Darwin. Then he dropped his fist and said, "You're not worth me breaking your face, Rector McCloud."

My help cometh from the LORD, Maker of heaven and earth.

Ian Richardson turned away and stepped into the shower. *Thank God.*

Darwin returned to attend to Winstead, now lying face-up on the cot.

"How are you feeling, mate?" Darwin asked as he put his palm on William Winstead's forehead.

"He's still out of breath," Ashton said. "McCloud, you're either bloody brave or a bloody fool."

"More like the bloody fool." Darwin covered Winstead with a blanket.

"Hip, hip!"

Darwin turned around and looked at his shipmates still standing in the shower queue. Their collective eyes were glued on Darwin, Ashton, and Winstead.

"Hurray!" came the response from a handful of the commando candidates.

"Hip, Hip." More voices joining in.

"Hurray!"

"Hip, Hip!"

"Hurray!"

The final *hurray* included a bombastic chorus of thirty enthusiastic voices.

Darwin felt himself blushing as his colleagues slapped him on the back.

"Atta boy, McCloud," said one.

"Richardson needed someone to stand up to him," said another.

I'm sure Richardson is hearing all this. I can't wait to see his reaction when he gets out of the shower.

Thirty seconds later, Ian Richardson stepped from behind the plastic curtain wrapped in a towel. All cheering ceased.

Barefoot, Richardson walked down the narrow aisle separating the steel cots. He stopped beside Darwin's cot, glowering at him. Darwin's eyes did not meet his.

Richardson then walked to his locker and got dressed. It was over—for the time being.

My help cometh from the LORD, Who made heaven and earth.

29

In the eight weeks since Commando Training Class 003 had reported to HMS *Armadillo*, no one had been granted liberty, a chance for a brief break off base. That unexpectedly changed on Saturday, May 2, 1942 at noon when Sergeant Loomis entered the barracks and announced that liberty would commence immediately and end at midnight on Monday, May 4, 1942. Thirty-six hours were being granted for the worn-out candidates to do anything they liked, but they could not travel more than ten miles off base. It was a welcome announcement.

As others ventured into Ardentinny and the surrounding countryside in search of excitement, Darwin remained alone in the barracks on Saturday night, the second of May. His shipmates were on a self-anointed reconnaissance mission, hoping to find the local pubs overflowing with Scottish beer and wine, and most importantly, local Scottish lasses in need of companionship.

When he awoke at dawn on Sunday morning the third, he rose up on his elbows, squinted his eyes, and noticed about half of the pub seekers had found their way back to the barracks where they had crashed on their flimsy cots and were sleeping off their self-inflicted hangovers.

Not enough lasses to go around, I suppose.

Flinging off the sheets, he sat there for a moment then stood up. The floor was colder to his feet than the first night when Loomis had chased them all out of bed.

Still wearing the white boxers and white tee shirt he had been sleeping in, Darwin made his way to the back of the barracks to freshen up. The strong stench of vomit infiltrated his nostrils.

The drunken fools could have at least tried to clean up their mess. Remind yourself never to go drinking with the lads, Darwin.

He had the shower all to himself this morning, and after taking advantage of a couple of extra minutes to lather up and let the warm water flow over his back, he shaved and threw on his dress uniform.

Tiptoeing in full dress uniform down the center aisle of cots between his snoring, hungover classmates, he closed the front door behind him and walked across the base, out the front gate, and across the street. His destination— the small Presbyterian church he had noticed the day he reported for training.

The church, small and brown, sat on a corner just across the street from the main gate. A few people were seated in the sanctuary when he arrived just before eleven o'clock. He sat alone on the very back pew, and with the organ playing a prelude, he watched people trickle in.

The man and woman who sat on the pew just in front of him looked late fortyish, maybe fifty. They turned around and glanced at him. He noticed they did not sit next to the aisle, but left space for at least one other person to sit.

Soon the reason for the space on the pew arrived. Her hair was red and wavy. Her eyes were green, and her teeth were as white as the full moon. She wore a kelly-green dress, the hemline cropped to just below her knees. Around her neck was a strand of modest white pearls. The backs of her calves were well-contoured in her seamed stockings. She too turned and smiled at Darwin before she sat. Her glance lingered a bit longer than the man's or the woman's, as if she was reluctant to break eye contact.

"Hello Mother," she whispered to the woman in a distinguished Scottish accent, loud enough for Darwin to hear.

"Hello, Sally," came the whispered reply of the woman followed by a hug and a brief kiss to her daughter's cheek.

Darwin looked up as the minister motioned for the congregation to rise.

"Let us open our hymnals to page . . ."

His eyes rested on the rearview contour of the redhead. The dress accentuated her narrow waist, draping her graceful curves below.

His gaze fell on her black pumps, then like an elevator, rose slowly back upward.

Nice hair. Lots of body for a redhead. More like an auburn color. Nice figure too. Especially from this angle.

He snapped his eyes closed.

What am I thinking? Forgive me, Lord.

She looked at her mother standing beside her then shot a glance over her right shoulder, her eyes catching his. She smiled and faced forward so as not to linger.

They felt like sparkles in his body. Thousands of them. Warm, tingling sparkles, flowing from the top of his stomach, rising through his sternum and tickling the bottom of his throat. Triggered by her look. Or maybe it was her smile that set them off. This was a feeling that twenty-year-old Darwin McCloud had never associated with a woman before.

So this is what it is like. How can I even focus?

Darwin closed the Presbyterian hymnal and put it in the rack on the back of the pew where the redhead and her parents were sitting. The service was over. He wasn't sure what the sermon had been about. He hesitated as the congregation began to spill into the aisle—perhaps out of curiosity—before heading into the aisle and out the front door.

The sun had burned off the morning cloud cover, causing Darwin to squint as he strolled across the luscious, green grass, across the church grounds, and toward the street. *The grass is the color of her eyes.*

When traffic cleared, he would go back to the base, grab some lunch, and return to the barracks for a Sunday afternoon nap.

"Excuse me, lad." Darwin felt a hand on his right shoulder. He turned and saw the man who was seated on the row just in front of him in church. He was not a tall man, maybe five feet, eight inches with a slightly-rounded waistline, salt-and-pepper hair, and a ruddy face.

"I'm William Cameron. I didn't catch your name." The man spoke in a thick Scottish accent. Darwin looked at the man. Then his eyes swept the front lawn in search of his daughter. Nowhere. His eyes caught William Cameron's again.

"I'm Darwin McCloud, Mr. Cameron. It's a pleasure."

"You're a commando recruit, are ya, lad?"

"Yes, sir. This is our first weekend of liberty. I wanted to visit your church."

"Where ya from?"

"London, sir."

"Well, Mr. McCloud of London," the man said, his hand still on Darwin's shoulder. "I was wonderin' if ya might be able to join me and my family for lunch today."

Darwin's heart quickened. "Sir, I would be honored, but I would hate to impose."

"Nonsense. It's just me and my wife and my daughter. There's a-plenty to eat. We'd consider it an honor to have your fellowship."

"I would consider it a privilege, Mr. Cameron. I don't have to report back to the base until tonight."

"Good. Then it's settled," William Cameron said with a twinkle in his eye. "Our house is about three blocks that a-way. You can walk with me. My wife and my daughter left a few minutes ago to get a-started on things. They were kinda hopin' you'd say yes."

A broken brick walkway in the small front yard crossed through a meticulously-manicured garden of blooming daffodils, petunias, and roses leading to the porch of the modest stone home. Spring was in the air on a gorgeous, sun-baked Scottish afternoon, as William Cameron put his hand on Darwin's back and ushered him through the front door and into the small living room.

"Elizabeth, Sally, we're here!" he called with a tinge of excitement in his voice that matched the twinkle in his eyes.

The woman he had first seen in church stepped in from the kitchen. She was a pretty lady in her forties, slim, with her graying blonde hair in a bun.

"This is my wife, Elizabeth," William Cameron said with pride.

"I'm Darwin McCloud. It is a pleasure, ma'am," Darwin said.

"Please call me Elizabeth," she said. "Welcome to our home, Darwin. We are honored to welcome British servicemen who visit our church."

What a lovely lady. Sort of reminds me of Mother. I don't feel extremely comfortable calling her Elizabeth. I feel like I'm calling one of Mother's friends by her first name. But if she insists.

"Your hospitality is appreciated, Elizabeth."

Darwin's gaze left Elizabeth Cameron as the third family member appeared in the small den. Her eyes were on his, his on hers. The smiles were unabashed.

"And this is our daughter—"

Darwin wasn't sure who said that. The girl's name faded from earshot. The sparkles reignited as the sight of her face enraptured him.

I feel like a bloody fool. I didn't even catch her name.

"Hello Miss, I'm Darwin McCloud from London. I have to apologize. I didn't catch your name."

"Hello, Darwin. I'm Sally," she said in a slight Scottish accent not as thick as her father's. Her voice sounded like velvet, conveying deep warmth. "Welcome to our home."

"The pleasure is mine, Sally."

"Well then," William said. "Shall we proceed to the dining room?"

It was a square mahogany table with a bouquet of flowers in the midst of perfectly-set silverware. Elizabeth Cameron directed seating arrangements. Darwin sat beside Sally and across from Elizabeth. William sat across from his daughter.

"Tell me, Darwin," William said, "I assume ye are a Christian, being as ye were in church and all."

"Yes, I am," Darwin said.

"Good. Then you won't mind us sayin' a little blessing, would you?"

"I would be honored to join you in saying grace."

"We also have a little family tradition when we say grace," Elizabeth said. "We all join hands around the table." Then, without waiting for a response, she reached out and took his hand and bowed her head. Darwin looked to his right and saw Sally's hand extending in his direction.

The electric current was immediate when their palms touched and even more so when their hands clasped in a tight grip. William Cameron launched into a long blessing. Darwin was glad the old man was longwinded, especially when Sally seemed to give him an extra little squeeze a couple of times.

Was that my imagination?

". . . . in the precious name of our risen Lord and living Savior, the Lord Jesus Christ. Amen."

Elizabeth Cameron released Darwin's hand, but Sally lingered, giving him a little squeeze before letting go. Their eyes met again, and they exchanged fleeting smiles.

I never believed in love at first sight.

Until now.

30

Land of my high endeavour,
Land of the shining river,
Land of my heart for ever,
Scotland the brave.

Perhaps one would assume that the only son of a baroness and a Royal naval captain would be well-traveled. Not so with Darwin. He had been confined within the borders of England for most of his life with only brief exceptions.

Once Juliana took him to Nice, France on the French Riviera for a summer holiday. Twice had he ventured across the northern border of England into Scotland. Once as a boy, he and Juliana had accompanied Father to Holy Loch on naval business. Several years ago, he traveled with Juliana for a weekend to Edinburgh on a castle tour.

His earlier forays were so brief that he had little memory of them. In the last four months he had made up for lost time and lost plenty of sleep doing so. In June, he penned his first letter to Juliana from his quarters at the Royal Naval Commando Training Centre in Ardentinny, in Northwest Scotland.

June 3, 1942

Dear Mother,

I am writing you from my quarters on board HMS Armadillo. I know what you're thinking. You're worried that I'm writing you from a ship out in the middle of the ocean surrounded by German U-boats. But don't worry, Mother. HMS *Armadillo* isn't a ship like HMS *Defender*. Armadillo is the name of the Royal naval training facility here in Ardentinny.

When I announced that I was volunteering for the commandos, I knew the training would be rigorous, but I had no way of grasping the full effect of what would be demanded—not only physically, but also psychological. Twenty hours of sunlight coupled with constant running, swimming, forced marches, karate training and storming chilly beaches with rifles, grenades, rocket launchers, and live explosives can have an adverse effect on a fellow's ability to catch some sleep.

Before one can catch a nap, some marine gunnery sergeant will bark additional orders to scale a rocky cliff and then pile us in a landing craft so they can dump us in the middle of Long Loch wearing full gear, giving us an equal opportunity to either freeze, swim, or drown.

While the training is indeed arduous, I'm having a jolly ol' time. It's quite amusing to watch some of these big-muscled chaps who seem to be afraid of heights and who are skittish about jumping into freezing water.

In one exercise early in the training, we were standing atop a rocky cliff when they instructed us to dive into the cold deep waters of the loch about thirty feet below. When the sergeant gave the instructions, I looked around and could see the visible apprehension which had suddenly descended on the faces of these big guys.

The sergeant asked for volunteers, and seeing none, I stepped forward. I think I shocked everyone. The reaction was something like "McCloud—you?" You see, Mother, they believed I would wash out of the programme early on. My reaction was, "Of course, why not?" Then I proceeded to dive across the cliff head first, streaming toward the deep blue water below. I must confess I did a bit of praying during the descent. The fall was actually kind of fun, but the water was bloody cold.

I popped to the surface, where the frogmen yanked me into the rubber raft and threw a blanket over me. Up top, I could hear some of my colleagues cheering—at least those who had not yet soiled their swim trunks. I heard the drill sergeant yelling, "See, if McCloud can do it, you can do it! He's the smallest chap out here, for heaven sakes."

I just looked up and enjoyed the moment, all the while receiving "attaboys" from the frogmen manning the raft. My colleagues on the cliff nervously formed a line, and one by one, began to sheepishly leap off. At least the first three jumped.

Then the fourth guy was a fellow named Richardson. This chap stands about six feet, three inches tall and weighs every bit of two hundred twenty pounds. Richardson is a strong fellow who seems to get his thrills picking on little guys. He certainly has gotten some mileage at my expense, as I suppose I was the most visibly available target.

Richardson had, up to this point, outscored everyone on the speed and strength drills. He'd been a bit cocky about his performances, and though it appeared he would easily graduate, he certainly was not in line for the award of Mr. Popularity. A number of the fellows were clearly intimidated by him, as he tended to make use of his brute strength and boorish personality to get his way when the drill instructors were not around.

Yesterday, Richardson's target was a candidate named Ashton. Ashton likes to rise half an hour early to polish his boots. In front of everyone, except the drill instructors, Richardson accused Ashton of being too ambitious and too noisy. When Ashton contended that he had not been noisy and asked for a show of hands if anyone thought he had been so, Richardson shoved him to the deck and threatened to break his neck if he ever again got up before the other members of the class. Suffice it to say that Ashton has been enjoying an extra half hour of sleep for the last week.

Therefore, we all expected the mighty Richardson to leap off the cliff immediately, beat his chest, and utter some primal scream like Tarzan, lord of the jungle as he descended to the waters below. The scenario did not play out as we expected. It seems that our big he-man friend had a slight case of acrophobia. He started towards the edge of the cliff then he stopped. Even from our vantage point below, we could see his face was white as a ghost. "Come on, Richardson, jump!" the trainers shouted.

Ol' Richardson backed up about fifteen feet and then ran toward the cliff again. As he reached the edge, it was like a brick wall stopped him in his tracks. This time, we could see terror on his face. Some of the fellows in our rafts who had already taken the plunge were laughing. None of the guys at the top thought it was funny. It was as if the big fellow's fear was spreading a sense of panic. I thought the whole incident was sort of amusing but couldn't bring myself to laugh.

Finally one of the Royal Frogmen yelled, "Richardson, if you want to be a Royal Naval commando, you can jump now or pack your bags and go back to Manchester!" That brought a round of jolly laughter from the audience in the raft section. I suppose the humiliation got the best of the big fellow.

He backed up, appeared to take several deep breaths, and started walking toward the edge. Just about five feet before the edge, he closed his eyes and took off running, leaping into space with his eyes welded shut. At first it appeared he would go in feet first, but his wailing arms altered his angle of entry, and for an instant we were concerned he might actually land in the raft. He missed us, barely, but all the arm waving during the descent resulted in the biggest belly flop you have ever seen! The splash was like a tidal wave, spraying cold water all over our raft.

Yet another round of laughter erupted at the funny sight, but I couldn't bring myself to snicker. I felt sorry for him, despite the fact that he had gotten plenty of laughter at my expense. As my colleagues were having their jollies, I rolled into the cold water and swam to the area where he had gone under, about twenty feet from the raft.

He popped to the surface with a look of total embarrassment on his face. I helped him swim toward one of the empty rafts and got in the raft with him. I told him not to worry about the snickering, that he had made it and done a good job. I told him that we were a team and that we were behind him. Afterwards, even Ashton and Winstead encouraged him.

As of today, Richardson is still in the programme, but is, to say the least, seemingly a bit more humble—for now anyway.

I miss you, Mother, and will write again when I can.

With all the love a son can muster for his mother,
Darwin

Juliana received the letter on Friday the tenth. By Sunday night, her reply was finished.

July 12, 1942

Dearest Darwin,

I've just gotten back from church, where many people asked about you today. Chief among the inquirers was Rev. Charles Brooks, who conveys that you have been in his prayers. I related to him some of your adventures as set forth in your letter of June third. Like me, he found the story of poor Mr. Richardson very amusing. He insisted that I remind you that "the bigger they come, the harder they fall!"

Yet, he was also very proud of the compassion you showed for Richardson, the way you swam to him and showed him encouragement when he had perhaps deservedly become the laughingstock for others. That's the thing that makes you so special, Darwin. You are different from the crowd and always have been. I am so blessed to have you as a son.

I've read in the papers that the war, at least for the moment, seems to be concentrated in North Africa and Russia. The BBC also reported that the Americans have scored some major naval victories against the Japanese in the Pacific at Midway and Coral Sea. Apparently, they sunk several aircraft carriers.

The papers are saying the Coral Sea victory may have stopped or at least delayed a Japanese invasion of Australia. If so, that's a good thing because I'm not sure how Britain can defend France against the Germans and Australia against the Japanese at the same time. Oh well, I'll leave such strategic thinking to Mr. Churchill and the war council. Frankly, I wish the Yanks would dispense with the Japanese and send their ships this way to help protect Britain. I would feel better about the Royal Navy and your father if the Americans were here in full force.

While it is a welcome change to be able to attend worship services and not worry so much about an air raid siren, I continue to worry about your father. Not a word has been heard from him since before you left. My largest fear is that his ship will sail into a nest of U-boats and . . . well, no point in spelling out details. At this point, I must assume that no news is good news.

I also fear for you, my son. But I am proud of you more than you will ever know. You are very brave to have voluntarily undertaken such difficult training on behalf of the Crown. I know your father will also be proud.

Take care, and know that you remain in my prayers.

All my love,
Mother

31

ROYAL NAVAL COMMANDO GRADUATION CEREMONIES
HMS *ARMADILLO*
ARDENTINNY, SCOTLAND
AUGUST 1, 1942

Darwin opened his eyes at the sound of the clanging alarm clock. It was five o'clock in the morning on Saturday, the first day of August, 1942. He squinted, then sat up on his rack while his shipmates slept. He opened his Bible. This morning he read through the thirteenth chapter of First Corinthians on charity and love. What a coincidence that his morning study would fall on this beloved chapter at a time when he felt he was beginning to better understand what true Christian love was all about.

He closed the Bible, closed his eyes, and silently prayed.

Lord, thank you for your blessings upon my life. May my time here in the Commandos and my time in Ardentinny be used for Your glory alone. Thank you for bringing Sally into my life, and I pray that you would lead me by your Holy Spirit, this day and every day for the rest of my life.

Darwin opened his eyes, and when he did he felt a great love for his mother tugging his heart. He stood, reached in his locker, and took out a pen and paper and began to write a letter.

August 1, 1942

Dearest Mother,

I arise this Saturday morning facing, not the rigorous demands which have characterized my training these past three months, but rather as the sun crests the eastern sky, I find myself preparing for the pomp and pageantry associated with the celebration of a crowning achievement.

Today is graduation day. And this morning at 10:00 a.m. I am to report to the parade grounds here at HMS *Armadillo,* where along with my surviving classmates, I shall receive the designation of Royal Naval Commando. I wish you could be here today. I also wish Father knew. Please tell him, if you see him, what I am doing for the Crown. Also tell him that I love him.

You were right, Mother. I made it as you predicted. I give credit to God Who helped me complete the training when most here thought at first that I would never make it. I am now the smallest RNC in the Navy. Perhaps that entitles me to some distinction. If so, perhaps I will find out in a couple of hours.

I had hoped to return to England to visit you after graduation, but I am afraid circumstances will not permit that now. Instead, I will remain here in Scotland a while to receive my orders. Pray that I will fulfill God's will in my life.

Whatever His will may be, I would not argue if He would have me return to Scotland after the war to settle here. I had forgotten how lovely and charming this place is. Over the past three months, I have fallen in love with this proud land of clans and lakes and green highlands.

You should know, however, that my affinity for England's northern neighbor is not totally generated by the beauty of the terrain. I speak, rather, of beauty of another sort.

You see, Mother, I have met someone.

I met this person on weekend liberty while attending First Presbyterian Church of Ardentinny. This person is wonderful and fulfills me in ways no one ever could.

I know you, Mother. You're probably worried that my new friend is like Reece.

Hardly.

What is this person's name?

Oh, how I love teasing you, Mother. You will definitely approve.

Her name is Sally Cameron. She's twenty years old, an inch taller than me, and has the prettiest auburn hair I've ever seen. We've been spending a lot of time together, at least all my free time—what little of it there has been. She's wonderful, and I've told her all about you. She can't wait to meet you.

I suppose I should stop here and leave the rest to your imagination.

Take care of yourself until we meet again.

All my love,
Your son

At 9:50 a.m., having dropped the letter at the post office, Darwin reported to the parade grounds at HMS *Armadillo* and fell into the end of the growing line of newly-minted commandos. He arrived a few minutes early, hoping to soak up every vestige of this moment. Already, the blustery summer breeze was whipping off the loch, scattering some paper programs across the parade grounds. The grass was a deep, lush green—the color of the Scotland he now loved.

A few yards in front of the single line of commandos, a small wooden platform and podium had been erected for the occasion. To the left of the platform, a military band and bag-piping unit were warming up. Within a few seconds, the big chap from Manchester fell into the line just to Darwin's left. Richardson greeted Darwin with a friendly and affectionate pat on the back.

"Morning, McCloud," Richardson whispered.

"Morning to you too, Richardson," Darwin replied. He half expected Richardson to say something else, but the big guy fell silent.

Darwin's eyes rolled to the right of the podium toward the grandstand section reserved for members of Parliament, VIPs, and guests. With his head pointed to the podium but his eyes looking so far to the right that he felt like his eyeballs were about to pop out of their sockets, he strained to see who was in the stands. He couldn't care less about the MPs. They had been commonplace during his childhood. Rather, he hoped to see the one special guest in possession of the only ticket he was allotted for the ceremony. Three months ago, only one person in the world who would have gotten his ticket. But today Juliana's slot had been reserved for Sally Cameron.

Darwin hoped Sally would come. But he wasn't sure that she would. She had grown emotional as graduation day approached, facing the reality that Darwin's military obligations would separate them at least for a time.

From this vantage point, everyone in the full grandstand looked the same. Darwin was tempted to turn his head to look for Sally, but he knew better than to break his military bearing.

"McCloud," Richardson whispered again.

"Awfully talkative today, are we?" Darwin replied.

"Thank you."

"Thank you for what, Richardson?"

Richardson paused, as if trying to get up the nerve to say something. "I never would have made it if it weren't for you."

Darwin was stunned. Richardson had changed for the better since the embarrassing incident on the cliff. He seemed mellowed and wasn't trying to bully others. But Darwin never imagined ninety days ago that the bullish giant would ever bring himself to utter the words he had just spoken.

"Shut up, you big brute, before you make us both start crying."

Commander Graham Reynolds, executive officer of HMS *Armadillo*, led a small group of dignitaries onto the platform. Clad in full dress blue uniform, Reynolds approached the podium and surveyed his smart-looking line of commando candidates standing at parade rest before him. Satisfied that everyone was in place and ready to proceed, Reynolds barked into the microphone. "Company. Attention on deck!"

Darwin and his classmates snapped to tight attention.

"Ladies and gentlemen, distinguished guests, and members of Parliament, I am Commander Graham Reynolds, Executive Officer of HMS *Armadillo*. On behalf of His Majesty King George the Sixth, our Prime Minister Mr. Churchill, and our

Commanding Officer, Captain Al Rudy, I welcome you to HMS *Armadillo* for the graduation of RNC Class Number Three. Please rise and come to attention for the playing of our national anthem."

A long drum roll commenced as the guests and dignitaries rose to their feet. Just behind the podium, Darwin watched the Union Jack and the Royal Naval Ensign flapping in the wind. The cold, deep waters of Long Loch, glistening one moment and gray the next as the wispy clouds played a game of peek-a-boo with the sun, served as a panoramic backdrop to the ceremonies.

The color guard commander broke the momentary silence, his sharp command echoing across the parade grounds.

"Pree-zent Arms!"

The color guard snapped their rifles into position as the drum roll ceased. A reverent and patriotic silence pervaded, except for the gusty breeze and the waves washing up on the shore of the loch about a hundred yards from the parade ground. The clouds parted as the water turned again from gray to blue. The band broke into a slow, melodic introduction to the most beloved tune in all of Britain.

Darwin could hear singing from the grandstands. The voices were untrained, yet no cathedral choir had ever sounded more majestic to his ear.

> God save our gracious King,
> Long live our noble King,
> God save the King!
> Send him victorious,
> Happy and glorious,
> Long to reign over us,
> God save the King.

"Order, Arms!"

As the color guard pivoted and marched out of view, Commander Reynolds again approached the podium.

"Ladies and gentlemen, it is my privilege to present the commanding officer of HMS *Armadillo*, Captain Al Rudy."

Reynolds sat as Al Rudy, a short, ruddy-faced man,

approached the podium. Darwin knew Rudy by reputation. The salty naval veteran was Edward McCloud's contemporary, and the two had been shipmates early in their careers. Despite the connection, Darwin never made his presence known to Rudy. The last thing he needed was an accusation that he had passed the training only because of his father's connections with the commanding officer.

The weather-worn seadog stepped up to the microphone. "Ladies and gentlemen, distinguished graduates Royal Naval Commando Class Number Three, my words today will be short, for our duty is long. We are at war. You, our new shipmates, have been trained in the most sophisticated battle techniques the world has known. You conquered your rigorous training with distinction. You have earned the right to be called Royal Naval Commandos."

A burst of applause.

Rudy continued. "As you know, the motto of the Royal Naval Commandos is 'Imprimo Exulto'—first in, last out. And in many cases, you will be the first ones in and the last ones out. Britain shall depend upon you. For some of you, your call shall come sooner rather than later. Some shall pay the ultimate sacrifice. There's a bloody good chance the man to your left or the man to your right will not make it. But you were aware of the risk before you volunteered.

"We are at war against the most evil enemy in the world's history, an enemy that tried bombing us into submission. He bombed our streets. He attacked not military targets, but residential neighborhoods, killing not soldiers and sailors, but innocent women and children. Like a coward, he hid high in the sky, seeking safety within the confines of his airplanes. But how wrong he was. This enemy got a taste of the Royal Air Force, and he could not break the backs of the British people. And it was a taste he did not like!"

Another round of applause broke the speech.

"This enemy has also gotten a taste of the Royal Navy! As we stand here this day, the two most powerful German battleships ever commissioned, the *Graf Spree* and now the *Bismark*, rest on the bottom of the Atlantic thanks to your Royal Navy.

Let that be a lesson to Mr. Hitler, that when he tangles with Britain's finest, he will have a price to pay!"

Rudy stopped for another round of applause.

"Ours is a grave duty. And in contemplating that duty, I leave you with the words of the Apostle Paul to his adopted son Timothy. Let us fight the good fight! Let us finish the race! Let us keep the faith!"

Rudy stopped, looking up and down the line of his newly-minted commandos.

"Go now, gentlemen, and do your duty."

Rudy sat down as Reynolds concluded the ceremonies.

"Ladies and gentlemen, at the conclusion of the ceremonies there will be an opportunity for you to meet with and congratulate our commandos in the reception area of the old hangar just about one hundred yards north of the parade grounds. Thank you for your attendance."

Reynolds signaled the class company commander to take charge of the troops. The company commander saluted the executive officer, then pivoted and faced the line of newly-graduated commandos.

"Company. Ah-ten-chun on deck!

"Left face!

"Forward, march!"

The company pivoted left and began marching in step to the sharp cadence of the snare drum as Reynolds and Rudy whipped open-handed salutes. The bagpipers joined in, filling the air with shrill tones of "Scotland the Brave."

At this moment, nothing seemed so soothing to Darwin's soul as the sound of the bagpipes. If the world were really a stage, and if we are but actors upon it as Shakespeare said, this was a role Darwin was relishing more than any other he had played. Never was he so proud to be British.

Marching toward the reception area with chills running down his spine, Darwin thought of Captain Edward McCloud.

If only Father could witness this moment, to see his son transformed from a fledgling actor with no real ambition to a Royal Naval commando with a beautiful female companion.

They marched into the reception area, where champagne

flowed everywhere and thousands of strawberry crepes sat on a hundred silver trays. Breaking ranks, Darwin and his new comrades mingled among the well wishers. Juliana had invited friends in Parliament to say hello to Darwin, and they happily obliged, calling him aside while the other commandos chatted amongst themselves.

Darwin smiled, nodded, and looked for a gracious exit as William Fox and Trent Archer, the two MPs from the districts adjoining Kensington, regaled one another with jolly ol' stories about Edward and Juliana.

"Gentlemen, if you'll excuse us for a moment."

The familiar voice from behind him shocked Darwin.

"By all means, Captain," Archer replied.

Darwin pivoted and saw the uniform of a Royal Navy captain. Surprised at the sight before him, the loud cackling and hobnobbing of the MPs faded into the background.

"It appeared, at least from my vantage point, that you needed some relief, son."

Darwin stood speechless.

"It's all right. You can speak. I know firsthand that you are familiar with the uniform of a Royal Navy captain."

"My apologies, Captain. Perhaps I should introduce myself. I'm Darwin McCloud."

"Yes, I know," Captain Rudy responded. "You're Edward and Juliana's son. Your father and I go back a long way. I've had my eye on you since you reported for training."

"You have, sir?"

"Certainly. Your mother called three months ago. It was good to hear from her, although I was sorry to hear about the divorce."

"Mother called you, Captain?"

"Yes. But don't get the wrong idea. She wasn't asking for any special favors to advance your military career."

"I don't understand."

"Darwin, your mother was convinced that you would be physically unable to pass the training. She was afraid you would irreparably injure yourself. And I must say that as we initially reviewed your charts, I had doubts myself. She made me promise that, for your own good, I would expel you from the program at the first sign of weakness."

"Sir, I know Mother meant well. But I must apologize for her actions. I also want to apologize for not having introduced myself earlier. I didn't want to create the perception that I was receiving a special favor by virtue of Father's connections."

"So I speculated. And I admire you for that. And I just wanted to let you know that your actions on the cliff that day, the way you were the first over the side and the way you showed compassion for Richardson when he probably didn't deserve it, constituted a remarkable display of courage and leadership."

"Thank you, sir."

"From that day forward you have been considered to be the leader of this class, not only by me, but by all the senior officers and trainers. That night I telephoned your mother and told her of your heroics."

"You called Mother?"

"Yes, I did. I told her not to worry about you and that I expected you to pass this program with utmost distinction. I'm not sure those were the words she wanted to hear. I sensed she would have been happier if I'd told her we were sending you home. But I told her the truth."

Darwin struggled for words. "Sir, I am humbled by your encouragement. And I apologize for what I am about to say, but with the captain's permission, I should like to make one small request of you."

"By all means. What is it?"

"Captain, I know that our mission is highly dangerous. And as you said in your speech today, I sense that we shall be called into action sooner rather than later. I know there's at least a good chance I will never see my father again. And sir, if I don't see him again and you do, would you tell him about my time here, so that his last memories of me will be proud memories?"

Rudy hesitated. "Of course I will tell your father. But I'm betting you will be able to tell him yourself. Now if you'll come with me, there's a special guest in the administrative offices waiting to see you."

Rudy turned and led Darwin into the crowd. This was a scene Darwin had witnessed many times—a Royal Navy captain parting a military crowd down the middle quicker than Moses had parted the Red Sea.

Darwin looked down as his shipmates and other dignitaries stepped aside and made way for Captain Rudy with Darwin in tow. First it was the members of Parliament, and now the commanding officer was paying him an inordinate amount of attention. Darwin dreaded the ribbing he would get tonight from his shipmates. But he was even more curious as to the identity of the special guest in the admin offices.

Stopping outside the door of the offices on the other side of the old hangar, Rudy spoke to Darwin.

"Darwin, there's not a lot of time." Rudy looked at his watch. "We've got about thirty minutes before the briefing. Please stop by and see me later today."

"Aye aye, sir."

Darwin opened the door and stepped into the small and Spartan office. Inside was a battered desk, a well-worn chair, a clock, and a few gray cabinets. As he closed the door behind him, he felt the familiar arms wrapping around him from behind.

"Sally! You're here!"

"Of course I'm here. I was just in the water closet trying to fix my hair. You didn't think I would blow my chance to say good-bye, did you?"

The moisture in her eyes revealed she had been crying. Her hair was still a mess from the wind. He took her and gave her a long embrace.

"I looked for you in the grandstands, but all the faces blurred together."

"I was right in the middle of the crowd. Unfortunately, the crowd couldn't block all that wind. I know I look like a wreck."

Darwin smiled and playfully ran his hands through her hair. "You look fabulous, Sally Cameron. Redheads are supposed to have a little bit of a wind-blown look, you know. I'm so happy to see you. I didn't know if you were coming."

"You look so handsome in your dress uniform. And I love that green beret." She smiled, flirtatiously caressing the beret.

"Here, try it on." He put the symbol of the commandos on her head. "Actually, it looks pretty good on you. Red on green. Or should I say green on red? You remind me of Christmas in August."

"You always know the right thing to say. Christmas is such a happy time of year. I pray we can spend Christmas together some day."

He hugged her again as the tears streamed down her face.

"Someday, some way, we will be together again. I promise you that."

"How long do we have right now?"

"Not long. They're calling a military briefing in about twenty minutes. And I'm under orders to stop by the C.O.'s office."

"Does that mean you're leaving me now?"

He looked deep into her eyes. If God allowed him to survive this war, he would propose. Scotland would be their home. "Just for now. But we will be together again." He paused. It was time to go.

"I love you, Sally Cameron."

"I love you, Darwin."

32
FORT BRAGG, NORTH CAROLINA
AUGUST 8, 1942

Walter could not have lived with himself had he taken the medical deferment. Dr. Pap meant well, but in the end, he was accountable to God. Over Jessie's protests and tears, he ripped up his deferment letter and reported for active duty.

The nine months that had passed since Billy was killed seemed like a decade. After finishing boot camp and basic training at Fort Jackson, South Carolina, Walter was stationed at Fort Bragg, the huge military reservation near Fayetteville, North Carolina, just 162 miles from Jamesville.

Cumberland County, North Carolina wasn't what Walter had in mind in his pre-draft visions of the Army. He had envisioned going to France or Germany, winning the war, and then coming back to Jamesville to his job at the post office. But Uncle Sam had other ideas, at least for the time being.

While the Navy and Marines were fighting the Japs in the Pacific, Walter was plopped into a no-combat zone on a base in his own state as a corporal in the infantry. His routine was filled with daily target practice, marching, close-order drills, and spit shining his boots.

There were some advantages, however, to Fort Bragg. For

one, he enjoyed a decided advantage over many of the other recruits in dealing with heat and humidity. The Army's largest base, Fort Bragg was full of sand hills and pine trees and reminded him of his grandfather's farm, of the scorching humid days working in tobacco with Baldy, Billy, and Woodrow. In the late afternoons in Fayetteville, just like Jamesville, the temperature climbed to nearly a hundred degrees. Then the mosquitoes started swarming just before a cool late-afternoon thunderstorm washed them out of the air. When the heavy rain and thunder broke, a chorus of crickets would play background music for a symphony of lightning bugs during a cool respite. Then, in an hour or so, the heat and humidity climbed back to ninety degrees and ninety percent.

These "dog days," as the native Tar Heels called them, caused problems for many recruits, particularly those from California and other western states. All over the parade grounds, the western boys dropped like flies, suffering from heat stroke, exhaustion, or dehydration.

Medics rushed over the parade grounds during simulated combat exercises, loading the dehydrated Californians on stretchers and hauling them to sick bay, where they stuck smelling salts under their noses and poured water down their throats.

Though the westerners wilted like frail petunias in the hot sunshine, Walter remained tough during combat drills always among the first to finish the forced twenty-mile marches in full combat gear. He was also one of the most accurate marksmen among the new recruits—again, his experience on Baldy's farm paying off. His stamina caught the eye of leadership and had earned him a quick field promotion from private first class to corporal.

Walter also liked Fort Bragg because it was close enough for him to drive home on furlough. He had driven the four-hour trek at least every third weekend since basic training at Fort Jackson. He would have gone home this weekend but was scheduled for the evening watch and was stuck hanging around the barracks alone.

On this Saturday afternoon, Walter was lying on his rack in front of a large floor fan, trying to cool off and catch a nap before the evening watch, when Sergeant Todd Lewis stuck his head through the front door of the barracks.

"Corporal Brewer! Captain Patterson wants to see you. In his office! On the double!"

"Yes, Sergeant!"

In a brown tee shirt, green Army pants, and combat boots, Walter pulled out his pocket watch. It was three o'clock, or fifteen hundred hours, as he had learned to say in the Army.

Why would Captain Patterson want me at fifteen hundred on a Saturday afternoon?

"Better get a move on, Corporal. The captain sounded impatient."

"Yes, Sergeant. I'm on my way."

Breaking into double time, sweat beads rolled down his face and back as he jogged the quarter mile toward Company F's headquarters.

As he approached the front door of the tin can barracks housing Company F headquarters, a cool breeze chilled his face as thunder rumbled in the distance. Walter rapped on the front door.

"Corporal Brewer, reporting as ordered, sir."

"Enter, Corporal," Patterson snapped.

Walter stepped in and stood at attention as Captain Johnny Patterson, company commander, scribbled on some paperwork.

Patterson, a well-chiseled, blue-eyed, handsome officer in his early thirties, had been a star outfielder at LSU before entering the officer corps via the Army R.O.T.C. program in Baton Rouge.

Even after ten years, his forearms and biceps still retained the rippling muscles that had led to his .401 batting average his senior year and a tryout with the Yankees. They said Patterson was good enough to play for almost any team in the majors. But Patterson possessed a tough stubborn streak, and for him it was either start for the Yankees as a rookie or the heck with it.

As Patterson scribbled at his desk, Walter stared at the black-and-white glossy photo of *the Babe*, the legendary number three, with his big arms wrapped around the company commander's shoulder.

Patterson looked up and caught Walter engrossed in the photo.

"You like my picture, do you Corporal?"

"I'm speechless, Captain. I'd heard that you know Babe. I mean Babe is better known around the world than FDR himself."

"Babe's a nice guy. He's a great drinking buddy. But it's all political."

"Political? I don't understand, Captain."

"I mean baseball is political. I should have beaten Babe out. I mean, they invited me to spring training. I flat out told the manager I wanted to hit cleanup, that I was the man for the job."

"You went after Ruth's position, Captain?"

"Hey, to *be* the best, you've gotta *beat* the best."

"That's pretty ambitious, sir," Walter said.

"Hey Brewer, do you know what the state motto of Louisiana is?"

"No, sir."

"Union, Justice, and *Confidence.*"

"I like that, sir."

"Yeah, me too. Except it's too wordy."

"Too wordy?"

"Too wordy." Patterson took a swig of scotch. "Must've been written by a lawyer. You know, lawyers use three words when one will suffice. That's so they can charge more. He must've used three words so he could bill the state treasury triple rate."

Walter snickered. "So if I may ask, sir, which of the three words would the captain have kept in your state motto?"

"That's obvious—*Confidence.* Confidence should be the motto of every state, of this country, and of every member of this Army. That's what made Robert E. Lee the greatest general in history. They called him audacious. That means confidence.

"The captain makes a good point about General Lee, sir."

"Thank you, Corporal."

"So how did it go?"

"How did *what* go?"

"Spring training—with the Yankees, sir."

"Oh yeah; that's just it. I hit circles around Babe."

"You out hit Babe?"

"Sure. Confidence, Corporal, confidence. I was the *best* collegiate hitter in the nation. That's why they called me 'Madman Patterson.' I swung the bat with a reckless fury. And unlike Babe, who was a strike-out king, when I swung the bat, *I* made contact."

"That's impressive, Captain."

"Not really. Just business. Say, Corporal, would you like a scotch?"

"No thanks, Captain. I've got watch tonight."

"Suit yourself." Patterson poured himself another drink. "Anyway, in spring training of 1932—ten years ago—I clocked fourteen homers—count 'em, fourteen, out of the park. Babe hit nine."

"Sounds like you were on a tear, Captain."

"I was, Corporal. But that's my point. It wouldn't have mattered if I'd clocked a hundred homers. Babe had too much political clout. Don't get me wrong; he was still a great player. In '31 he led the majors in homers. But if the system was based on productivity, *I'd* be batting cleanup for the Yankees today."

"Captain, you should have made the team."

"I *did* make the team. See the picture? I've got on a Yankees uniform. But that's not the issue. I wasn't going to play second string to anybody, and that includes Babe Ruth. Not when I legitimately beat him out. And I told the organization that. As it turned out, Ruth was two years away from the end of his career with the Yankees at that point. They'd have been better off putting him on the bench and starting me." Patterson swigged more scotch. "See, that's what I like about the Army. You're promoted on merit. Not on politics."

Another swig. "Enough of that. Say, Brewer, there's a reason I called you in here."

"What's that, sir?"

"It's your transcripts."

"My transcripts?"

"Yes, your military service record. You left your college transcripts off your MSR."

"That's because I've never been to college, sir."

"Don't hand me that, Brewer. You're hiding something from us. Heck, you scored higher on your Officer Candidate School Test than I did, and *I* have a degree from LSU!"

"LSU is a good school," Walter said.

"A good school?" Patterson polished off his drink. "Heck, LSU's the Harvard of the Deep South."

"Yes, sir."

"Anyway, have you ever heard of a place called Crete, Brewer?"

"Yes sir, I believe it's an island in the Mediterranean."

"Very good. Do you know what's significant about this particular island?"

"It's off the coast of Greece. The apostle Paul made several missionary journeys there in the New Testament day."

"Again, very good. But can you tell me how it's been significant in more recent times?"

"I'm not sure what you're driving at, Captain."

"I'm driving at this—the Germans have taken an interest in Crete. Last July, they assaulted the island. They wanted it because of the British airfields there. They hit the island with paratroopers, and they captured it."

"Are we being ordered to Crete, Captain?"

"No. Not that I'm aware of anyway. See, Brewer, the Germans captured Crete, but they took heavy losses. Especially the guys dropping out of airplanes."

"I suppose the moral of the story, sir, is that man wasn't made to jump out of airplanes."

Patterson stared at him. "Soldier, that's not the way the Army reads it. See, even though the German's airborne invasion was costly, the Army thinks that with a few minor modifications, the assault could have been successful."

"What kind of modifications, sir?"

"Well, two things. The Germans dropped their men out of planes without weapons, at least with nothing more than pistols. The rifles and artillery were dropped separately. When the men hit the ground, assuming they weren't chopped up by British machine guns in the descent, they had to go running around looking for their rifles and ammo. In many cases, they were sitting ducks."

"What was their other problem, sir?"

"Their parachutes would not let them steer where they would land. Therefore, they might get lucky and land near their rifles and ammo, or they might drop a quarter mile away. If they dropped more than one hundred yards away, they were sitting ducks. Too much was left to chance."

"So what does our Army plan to do about all this?"

"Brewer, we believe we have the technology available to launch airborne assaults with much more accuracy and effectiveness than the Germans. I've been down to Fort Benning and tried out some of these parachutes. Our chutes will allow a man to steer and put him wherever he aims. Plus, our chutes are strong enough to let a soldier jump with full combat gear. It could be deadly for the enemy."

"You've actually jumped out of an airplane?"

"Sure I have, and in full combat gear. I've been getting some training on the weekends. It's a rush. You jump out, and you're free. The ground starts rushing up, closer and closer to your face, and you know you're going to die. Then at the last second, the parachute deploys and saves your butt, and you're floating like a feather. Like a cloud on the wind. You hit the ground, cut the line, and start killing Germans."

"I didn't know the Army had anything like that." Walter grew queasy.

"You're right, Brewer. The Army has never put much emphasis on airborne. But that changed after Crete. Now the Army is forming five brand new airborne divisions. Training will be at a new jump school in Fort Benning. We need officers to lead these troops. And that's why I called you here."

"But sir, I'm not an officer."

"Are you listening to me, Brewer?" Patterson snapped.

"Sorry, sir."

"Let me repeat myself. No, you're not an officer, but your

scores on the OCS tests and your performance here at Ft. Bragg tell the Army that you should be. The Army wants to send you to officer candidate school and then to jump school. We need you to be a leader in one of our new airborne divisions. Of course, nobody's going to point a gun to your head and force you to accept an appointment to OCS. You could stay here at Bragg. You probably wouldn't go airborne. Brewer, you're going to see combat either way. This is what it boils down to. You can hit them from the air as an officer, or you can hit them from the ground as an enlisted grunt. Trust me; you have better perks as an officer. I need your decision now, Brewer.

"Sir, I have just one question."

"What's that, Brewer?"

"These parachutes—they aren't suited for cold weather, are they?"

"They're perfect for cold weather. White parachutes. We could wear white uniforms. We could even paint our guns white. Heck, we could jump into downtown Berlin in a snowstorm and the Nazis would never see us. In fact, I would expect us to be deployed at all times of the year, including winter. What's your answer, soldier?"

Walter took a deep breath. He hated heights and he hated cold weather. What to do? This was happening so fast.

"I'll do whatever the Army needs me to do to best serve my country, sir."

"Good," Patterson replied, shoving papers at Walter. "Sign here."

Trying to keep his hands from shaking and trying not to think about jumping out of some airplane from who-knew-how-many thousand feet, Walter scribbled his name on the dotted line.

"Congratulations, Brewer." Patterson said. "You're now an officer candidate in the United States Army. Soon you'll be wearing railroad tracks on your collar. And trust me, the dames love that."

"Thank you, sir."

"Confidence, Brewer. It's all about confidence."

33
ARDENTINNY, SCOTLAND
AUGUST 15, 1942

Darwin and Sally had exchanged letters at least twice a week. But they had not seen each other since graduation. He missed her more than he thought he would.

Rumors were flying around Units C and D that combat was imminent, but he never shared this with Sally in his letters. Best to keep the letters upbeat and keep her from worrying.

Meanwhile, Darwin and his new buddy Richardson were assigned to Commando Unit D, where Darwin was named assistant beachmaster. The rumor was that combat would be in Africa, where the Eighth Army was having a rough go of it, having been forced back into Egypt from Libya by Rommel's powerful Afrika Korps.

The commandos were about to get their answer. A top-secret military briefing was scheduled in the hangar at HMS *Armadillo* at ten in the morning on Saturday, August 15.

When Darwin reported to the entrance of the hangar about quarter to ten, he was surprised to see such a high level of security around the building. Royal Marines, armed with live Enfield rifles, manned every entrance and patrolled the perimeter of the building. About seventy-five commandos were backed up on the parade grounds awaiting entrance to the hangar, a bottleneck having been created from the laborious process of checking everyone's identification. Darwin made his way to the back of the queue, waiting as his fellow commandos filed into the building.

When he passed through security and into the hangar just before ten o'clock, about eight hundred Royal Naval and Marine commandos were already seated and chatting. Their collective rumbling sounded like a light roar.

Darwin took one of the few vacant seats on the back row and listened for a moment. He could hear the word *Africa* mentioned in one sentence. In another, someone was speculating about Libya. Still another conversation speculated on the latest rumor which had started spreading this morning—that the commandos would be dispatched to the Pacific to assist U.S. Marines fighting in the Solomon Islands as a gesture of goodwill to the United States for FDR's "lend-lease" program.

Darwin did not participate in the pointless speculation. They would know soon enough, when the Royal Navy felt they needed to know.

"Attention on deck!"

Rumbling gave way to immediate silence, as Captain Rudy made his way across the stage. The captain's leather soles clicked across the hardwood floor and echoed throughout the hall, almost like a ticking clock counting down to the moment of truth. Two weeks ago today, the ceremonious graduation had spawned a spirit of celebration. Today's mood was somber, with grave tension filling the air.

"At ease, gentlemen. Please be seated."

Rudy grasped the podium as the commandos took their seats. With all eyes glued to him, Rudy began at a slow, measured pace.

"Two weeks ago today, during graduation ceremonies for RNC class number three, I said Britain will depend upon you. And I said that in some cases we will depend on you sooner rather than later."

Rudy stopped, allowing his words to echo throughout the auditorium. "Gentlemen, that hour is at hand."

Again pausing to let the moment soak in, he gestured to his left. "At this time, I present to you Commander Tom Miller, Chief Intelligence Officer for the Royal Naval Commandos."

Silence reigned as Tom Miller, a tall, wiry officer with a mustache, made his way to the podium.

"Good morning, gentlemen. As we are all aware, in the last couple of weeks we have experienced a frenetic pace in our amphibious landing exercises. All this round-the-clock practice, assaulting beaches, simulating attacks against rock walls, has fueled rampant speculation that one or more Royal Naval Commando units is about to be deployed into combat. Let me take this moment to address that now. Those rumors are true. Within the next ninety-six hours, RNC Units C and D will be deployed to a highly dangerous mission against German forces."

Darwin felt his heart rate double as Miller continued. "But before I give an overview of the battle plan, let me emphasize the reason for all the armed security surrounding the building today. It goes without saying that the details of this operation are top secret. Nothing may be leaked outside the halls of this auditorium. Your lives and the lives of your shipmates will depend upon maintaining secrecy. Any breach of security will be considered treasonous to the Crown and shall be dealt with accordingly."

Miller motioned as two petty officers entered the stage with a huge rolling map of the European and African theatres. The map was mounted on plywood and looked to be about ten-by-twenty feet. One of the petty officers handed Miller a long pointer and stepped out of the way, disappearing behind stage.

"Now then." Miller stepped from behind the podium beside the huge map.

"This, gentlemen, is a map of the Republic of France." With the pointer, Miller tapped the map twice directly at the Normandy coast.

"As you know, Jerry now occupies all of Western Europe. But France, mind you, is the crown jewel of Hitler's stolen possessions. The Nazis took France like a grown man would steal candy from a baby. There was virtually no resistance. Now I know that we British have had our differences with the French. Nevertheless, recapturing France will be a key element in driving Hitler back to Berlin. Eventually, it will be left up to us and to the Americans and Canadians to get the job done."

Darwin glanced around at his shipmates. Every eye was on Miller.

"Now on the subject of France. There has been a great debate among Allied war leaders. Stalin has pressured our government to attack the Germans in France so as to divert German forces from their war with Russia. The Canadian government has complained that their forces have not yet seen any action."

Miller continued. "Mr. Churchill and Mr. Roosevelt will not commit to a full-scale invasion until the time is right, and with the Americans only having recently gotten into the fray, the time is not yet right. Nevertheless, all this political rhetoric from the Russians and the Canadians has presented the opportunity for a smaller-scale operation which will have value to the war effort."

Miller again directed his pointer to the map.

"This, gentlemen, is the town of Dieppe."

Miller tapped at a little French town on the Normandy coast just across the Channel from Southern England.

"As you can see, Dieppe is on the English Channel, almost due south of Dover. For more than three months, the Second Canadian Infantry Division with more than five thousand men has been on the Isle of Wight, planning an attack against the Germans in Dieppe. That invasion was planned for last month but was scrapped for bad weather."

Miller again motioned for his enlisted assistants, who unrolled another huge map.

"The invasion will be rescheduled for Wednesday, August nineteenth, under the code name *Operation Jubilee*. There have been some changes from the original battle plan. Supreme Allied Command believes the operation has a better chance with more British support. Therefore, we have been ordered to supply Royal Naval Commandos and Royal Marines to reinforce the Canadians. A small group of U.S. Rangers will also join the battle."

Miller stepped to his right, pointer in hand, to the new map his assistants just rolled out. "This, gentlemen, is an enlarged map of Dieppe and the surrounding coastal areas. Just before dawn on the nineteenth, four days from now, we will begin our attack. Royal Commando Units C and D will attack the beaches to the east and west of town. You will destroy shore batteries flanking the town. You will be transported to within three miles of the coast by destroyers, where you will board landing craft and commence your assault. We will hold the town for twelve hours, take prisoners, and then retreat with prisoners in hand. You will receive more detailed information in your company briefings later this afternoon, but I will be happy to answer any questions at this time.

"You should know that we may be outnumbered. Our attack force will number just over six thousand men, and there are many more than six thousand German soldiers in France. But given the relatively short duration of the attack, twelve hours, we feel we can get in and get out before the Germans can bring overwhelming reinforcements. We want to show the Germans that we can attack on short notice and punish them.

"Second, the operation will be a dress rehearsal for any large-scale invasion that may follow. Finally, we solve some political issues with the Russians and the Canadians. Stalin gets his Allied offensive, and the Canadians no longer feel like the redheaded stepchild of the British Commonwealth, as their boys get to spearhead the battle force. You will be flown to Portsmouth the morning of the eighteenth. At eighteen hundred hours on Tuesday, you will each board destroyers and prepare to get underway. Commando Unit C will be assigned to the destroyer HMS *Invincible*. Commando Unit D, you will board HMS *Defender*."

Did he say HMS *Defender?*

Darwin felt his heart pound. He tapped the commando sitting next to him. "Excuse me. What ship did he say Unit D is on?"

"HMS *Defender*."

"That's my father's ship," he whispered with excitement.
"I thought it was *His Majesty's* ship," came the reply.
"Never mind."

Darwin was going to battle. But first, he would see his father again. His prayers had been answered.

34

WALTER BREWER HOME
JAMESVILLE, NORTH CAROLINA
SUNDAY AFTERNOON, AUGUST 16, 1942

For an afternoon, at least, the world seemed right again to Walter. God had granted a temporary reprieve from the oppressive Carolina heat and humidity and replaced it with gorgeous, fall-like weather for his three-day weekend at home. The Almighty's timing was perfect for what might become his last weekend in Jamesville for a long time.

Enticed by a cool breeze under a deep Carolina blue sky, Walter, Jessie, and Ellie, who had brought the kids up from Plymouth to play with their cousins, sat in the lawn chairs under the pecan tree in the backyard behind the big, white frame house.

Their conversation was not as pleasant as the weather.

"You're going to be doing *what?*" Jessie demanded.

Walter needled his fork into the rich slice of pecan pie Jessie had prepared for his homecoming weekend.

"It's called being a paratrooper," he said before sipping his iced tea. "It's an excellent opportunity to become an officer."

"Let me get this straight." A worried look crossed her face. "You're going to be *jumping* out of airplanes?"

He savored a bite of the ultra-rich dessert for a few seconds. Nobody could make pecan pie like Jessie. With a concoction of rich syrup, vanilla, sugar, pecans, and butter, Jessie's pecan pie recipe was a state secret in Jamesville that all the ladies in the church had tried cracking.

"Did I tell you how much I miss your pecan pie?"

"Did I tell you how much I do *not* miss you changing the subject when I ask you a question you don't want to answer?"

"Got me again, Jessie," Walter replied. "Okay, what would you like to know?"

She met his eyes then glanced at Ellie. Looking back to Walter again, she said in an even sharper tone, "I'd like to know if you're more likely to get killed getting shot at or jumping out of airplanes."

Walter pulled out his pocket watch, checking the time.

It's a long drive back to Fort Bragg. I need to get on the road.

He looked at Jessie. "Right about now, in Louisiana, the Army is inaugurating a brand new airborne division. They're gong to call it the 101st Airborne Division, and they want me to serve as an officer in it. The pay will be more than twice as much as I'm getting now. That's more money to send home to you and the children. It's a great opportunity."

She glowered at him. "You didn't answer my question."

"I give up, Madame Prosecutor. Your question, as I understand it, is this—Am I more likely to die jumping out of an airplane or getting shot at? And here's my answer—I am more likely to die getting shot at than jumping out of an airplane."

"Walter, you're afraid to use a stepladder to change a light bulb. You've got the worst fear of heights of anybody I know. And you expect me to believe you're going to jump out of an airplane?"

Thanks for reminding me about my acrophobia.

"The Army has this down to a science. We carry a parachute that is strapped to us. It's like a huge sheet that opens up when we jump out of the airplane. We are in a harness that's tied to the parachute by ropes. Then we float slowly down to the earth. It's sort of like a bubble or a snowflake floating through the air. It's very safe."

If that's true, why am I about to wet my pants just thinking about it?

"And just how many times have you actually tried this *safe* procedure, Walter?"

Why is this conversation making my hands shake?

"I pack my bags tomorrow morning and take a bus down to Fort Benning in Georgia. There, I'll go through both officer candidate school and then jump school. I'll leave there, Lord willing, commissioned as a second lieutenant in the United States Army. From there, I'll go to Louisiana to join up with the hundred and first, where I will take command of a company of other paratroopers."

"Louisiana?"

"That's where the airborne division is being formed, Jessie." He looked into her eyes again and saw them watering.

There were a few seconds of awkward silence.

"I guess that means no more coming home every other weekend." Jessie's voice started to crack. Walter reached over and took her hand.

"Maybe I should give you two a few minutes," Ellie said.

"No, stay Ellie," Jessie said. "The children are having a good time." She took her hand from Walter and wiped her eyes. "It's just that this change . . ." She swiped her hand across her cheek. "I'm not used to it. With the article in the *News and Observer* this morning and now hearing this, it's just a bit much."

"What article?" Ellie asked.

"About the war," Jessie said. "We're attacking some islands in the Pacific."

"Oh, I hadn't seen that," Ellie said.

"I'll go get you the paper." Jessie stepped into the house and brought back the Sunday edition of the *Raleigh News and Observer*, dated August 16, 1942. She handed it to Ellie. "If you two will excuse me for a minute, I'm going in the kitchen to make Walter a care package before he has to leave."

Walter sipped his sweetened iced tea and watched Jessie walk back into the house again. He knew what her care package would include—two slices of pecan pie, a batch of freshly-baked chocolate chip cookies, several fresh biscuits, lemon bars, and a couple of pieces of fried chicken for the road.

Walter looked at Ellie, who was dressed in a modest white spring dress and white shoes. She was sporting a healthy tan against her blonde hair. She was even more beautiful in her early thirties than when they were engaged. She did not look back at him. Her attention was on the lead article in the *News and Observer.*

U.S. Naval and Marine Forces Attack Solomons
From AP and Wire Reports

The Navy Department has announced that U.S. Naval and Marine forces have attacked the Solomon Islands chain, a strategically important island chain located in the South Pacific five hundred miles northeast of Australia.

Since the fall of the Philippines, the tropical chain is considered important in blocking the Japanese southerly drive through the South Pacific where an invasion of Australia is considered to be the ultimate Japanese objective in the region. General Douglas MacArthur, Supreme Commander, Southwest Pacific Ocean Area, has relocated U.S. Army headquarters to Australia after the fall of the Philippines earlier this year. MacArthur left his headquarters on Corregidor, an island at the entrance of Manilla Bay in the Philippines, on March 10.

According to a Navy Department spokesman, most of the fighting in the Solomons has centered around the island of Guadalcanal, where elements of the First Marine Division, supported by U.S. Naval gunfire and air power, launched an invasion August 7. As of this date, the Marines have established a beachhead on Guadalcanal and have captured a Japanese airfield. The source reported that the Marines had renamed the airfield "Henderson Field," in honor of a Marine aviator who lost his life at Wake Island. The airfield is now being used by United States forces in support of the war effort.

No information on U.S. casualties was available as of this writing.

Ellie finished the article and looked into his eyes. "Is this where they are going to send you Walter, to the Pacific like they did Billy?"

He looked at her and smiled. "I don't know, Ellie. There has been some speculation that this new airborne division may go to the Pacific. But then again, that may also depend on how things go in Europe."

She leaned over and put her hand on his. "I've already lost one Brewer brother to this war. I want you to *promise* I won't lose another one."

She yanked her hand away when the back porch screen door slammed.

"Here's you're goodie bag, Walter." Jessie was walking from the back porch to the chairs under the pecan tree where Walter and Ellie were sitting.

"Thank you, honey," Walter said. "Now I've got everything I need to hit the road."

"Are you packed?" Jessie asked.

"Everything's in the car." He pulled out the pocket watch Ellie had given him twelve years ago. "I hate to break this up, but this soldier must return to his duties, ladies."

"I'm going inside to give you two some privacy," Ellie said. This time Jessie did not argue with her.

Alone in the living room, Ellie looked out the window and saw Walter and Jessie standing by his Model A in the driveway. He was holding her in his arms, their eyes locked in an unbreakable gaze. She took her hand from his arm to wipe her eyes a few times. Then he reached into his pocket, pulled out a white handkerchief, and gently dabbed the tears dripping down her face.

The long, tender kiss reminded Ellie of years gone by, of her first kiss with Walter standing in front of Grace Episcopal in Plymouth at midnight after the country club Christmas dance. It also reminded her of the kiss Billy had given her the last time she saw him alive, before he enlisted in the Navy, before he shipped off to Pearl Harbor, and before he died a hero's death.

Jessie turned and ran toward the house. Ellie stepped back from the window.

I hope she didn't see me.

The back door flung open and Jessie, ignoring Ellie, called upstairs, "Children, your daddy's leaving. Come down and say good-bye!"

The rumble of excited feet bounding down the wooden staircase sounded like a small stampede. They flew through the living room right past Ellie, not noticing her at all. Out the squeaking screen door they rushed and into the backyard, toward the Model A.

There were six of them altogether. Four belonged to Walter and Jessie. Two—the cousins—belonged to her and the late Billy Brewer. Ellie looked out the window again. Walter was down on his knees accepting a rush of hugs and kisses from his four children and his nephew and niece.

I'm not going outside. I'm not going to spoil this moment.

Walter got into the car and threw it into reverse. Backing out of the driveway, the children followed the car to the street. Some were waving. The small ones were crying.

As the car backed out of view, Ellie ran to the front of the house to catch another glimpse, this time out of the dining room window. She got to the window just in time to see Walter turn right on St. Andrews Street. He drove slowly, waving out the window with his hand, and disappeared at the other side of Jamesville Christian Church.

Then he was gone.

Ellie stared out the window for a moment, her eyes focused on the brick facade of Jamesville Christian Church, just across the grass parking lot from Walter's house. She thought of her memories of that church and of its symbolism. The church had hosted her husband's funeral. Now Walter had disappeared behind it.

She felt the water running down her cheeks.

An ominous cloud floated in front of the sun, blocking the bright sunlight from the yard.

Lord, let him live.

35

The ninth chime from the grandfather clock downstairs reminded her that it was time. Ellie kissed her three-year-old daughter Margaret, who was already asleep, and then looked in on seven-year-old Little Billy.

The light streaming in from the hallway chandelier illuminated the eight-by-ten-inch black-and-white photograph of Billy in his navy blue sailor's uniform. The picture was sitting in a modest black frame on the nightstand beside the boy's bed. The hunk of a man he was, the photo made him look boyish. Maybe it was the white pixie sailor's cap or the sheepish grin. Whatever, Billy had been happy in the Navy. He died doing what he wanted to do. It was the last picture of him alive, and you could see the joy on his face.

"Billy?" Ellie whispered as she tiptoed into the bedroom. She gazed for a moment at the shape of her son under the white sheet. When her eyes adjusted to the dark, she saw the sheet rising and falling ever so slightly in perfect rhythm. Her eyes followed the contour of her son's body and rested on his face, where she judged his eyes to be closed and his mouth to be half open. She rolled her eyes over to the picture of Billy, then back to Little Billy. When the boy held his mouth half open like that, Ellie thought the resemblance to his father was striking.

Little Billy was a light sleeper. So she tip-toed toward his bed, kissed him on his forehead, left the room, and descended the grand staircase to the foyer.

She glanced at the grandfather clock before heading to the living room. It showed 9:05.

Five minutes behind schedule. But who cares? Peace at last.

The electric Victor Victrola sat on a mahogany table in the corner of the ornate living room. Ellie pulled two records from a cabinet beside the table. One was a recording of the London Symphony Orchestra from happier times, playing Beethoven's Fifth Symphony. The other was a recording by the Berlin Philharmonic of Beethoven's Ninth.

Hmm. What will it be, victory or joy? That is the question, Ellie Williams. Hold that thought.

She laid both records in the wingback chair beside the Victrola then walked into the kitchen and looked at the wine rack.

Decisions. Decisions. Pinôt noir or cabernet?

Ellie pulled a crystal wine glass out of the cabinet and reached for the 1931 Argentinean vintage Pinôt noir. She removed the cork and filled her glass half full. She closed her eyes and took a sip, savoring the warm path it made down her throat.

Billy's dead. Walter's gone. I need joy. The Ninth it is.

She walked back into the living room having made her selection and placed the big black record on the whirling Victrola. The needle made contact with the outer circumference of the spinning record, and through the sound of a few electronic scratches the soft violins of the enemy filled every corner of the living room.

The violins built to a rapid crescendo, and within thirty seconds woodwinds and brass instruments made their entrance with tympani exploding. Ellie took another sip of the expensive wine.

Did I hear something? Must've been my imagination.

Ellie sat in her velvet wingback and closed her eyes. She sipped the Pinôt and listened some more. She loved this musical masterpiece, the way it fluctuated in the beginning from soft to powerfully majestic within seconds, then soft again and then back to yet another full orchestral explosion. Alternating strong then subtle, all throughout the first movement. The music reminded her of herself. Hot and cold, all at once. Vulnerable and powerful, all at once.

The five raps on the front door were unmistakable.

Company? This late?

With wine glass still in hand and with the Berlin Philharmonic still filling the living room, she got up and walked to the front door.

"Jessie?" Walter's wife wore a long blue dress, and her normally-pretty face bore a twisted, contorted look of worry.

"I hope I'm not interrupting anything," Jessie's eyes darted toward the living room.

"No, I'm alone. I'm just listening to some music. Please come in."

"Thank you," Jessie said.

"I'd offer you some wine, but I take it your stance on alcohol is the same?"

"That's kind. No, I still don't drink. Although sometimes it's tempting."

"Maybe I could tempt you?" Ellie said.

"No thanks, Ellie. I'm not here to drink," she said. "I'm here to talk."

She looks serious. I wonder what this is about.

"Okay." Ellie spoke slowly. "Just have a seat." She pointed Jessie to the davenport in the living room.

Ellie sat across from her in the velvet wingback. There was a moment of awkward silence.

"Is everything all right, Jessie?"

Jessie sat for a moment, and then her eyes met Ellie's.

"No, to be honest, Ellie, everything is *not* all right."

Ellie sipped her wine. "Is there anything I can help you with?"

"I'll get to the point, Ellie. It's about Walter."

"What about Walter?"

God please let him be okay.

"Actually, it's about *you* and Walter."

Where's this coming from?

"Me and Walter? I'm afraid I don't understand."

"You were engaged to Walter."

"Yes, that was years ago."

"We've never talked about it," Jessie said.

"You've never broached the subject. I certainly wasn't going to. I thought it would make you feel awkward."

"Now that Billy's gone, to be honest, you being around Walter makes me feel awkward," Jessie said.

The comment struck her like a cold slap across the face. "I'm sorry you feel that way."

"Ellie, I want to know what your intentions are."

"My intentions? What do you mean by that?"

"Yesterday when the three of us were talking in the back yard, I left to go to the kitchen to make Walter's care package."

"I remember," Ellie said.

"When I was in the house, I was determined not to stare, but I looked out the back window. I saw what was going on."

"What are you talking about, Jessie?"

"What I'm talking about is what I saw out the back window."

Is she trying to trick me into admitting something here?

"Jessie, unless you tell me what you're talking about, I can't respond to it."

"The way you were looking at him. I could see it in your eyes."

"See what in my eyes?"

"Don't play games, Ellie."

"I'm not playing games."

"Maybe this is more than a game to you," Jessie snapped.

"You're here, upset because you think you saw something in my eyes?"

"Oh, it's not just your eyes, Ellie. I saw your hands too."

"My hands?"

"Yes, your hands. The way you put your hands on his

when I was inside. The way you snatched them away when I walked back outside."

"Jessie, I . . ." Ellie's eyes looked away.

"I'm sorry, Ellie. I don't mean to sound like a jealous fool. But this whole thing has been bothering me for a long time, this thing with you and Walter. And then yesterday. I had to get it off my chest."

"Jessie." Ellie lost her train of thought. The Berlin Philharmonic was about to commence the glorious finale of Beethoven's Ninth. "Let me turn that off." She stood up and stopped the record player. When she sat down, she took another sip of wine and focused her eyes on the Persian rug draped over the shiny hardwood floor. She felt her eyes well with tears.

Silence.

"Maybe I've said enough. I should go," Jessie said.

"No." Ellie hesitated. "Don't go." Ellie looked at her and touched her lightly on the shoulder. "Jessie, I'll talk about anything you'd like, including my feelings for Walter and our engagement if you wish. But first, there's something I'd like you to see."

"Okay," Jessie said.

"Wait here a second." Ellie left the room. About a minute later, she returned with a large, eight-by-ten-inch envelope. It was addressed to "Mrs. Ellie Williams Brewer." The return address was "The White House, 1600 Pennsylvania Avenue, Washington, D.C."

Ellie handed the envelope to Jessie. "Open it. I want you to read what's inside."

Jessie removed the heavily-bonded sheet of paper from the large envelope.

Navy Department
Washington, D.C.
December 19, 1941.

Award of the Navy Cross.

By direction of the President of the United States, the Navy

Cross is awarded posthumously to Seaman William L. Brewer, USN.

Citation: On December 7, 1941, while serving as a gunner's mate on board the USS *Arizona*, BB-39, during the surprise Japanese attack on the naval base at Pearl Harbor, Territory of Hawaii, Seaman Brewer, faced an enemy air force whose firepower outnumbered his and his shipmates by a factor of at least a hundred to one.

With complete disregard of his personal safety during a battle which would result in the sinking of his ship with a loss of 2,390 souls, he downed two Japanese Zeros and one Japanese Kate aircraft.

In the face of the unexpected and overwhelming enemy fire, Seaman Brewer manned his 50-caliber antiaircraft machine gun, and despite having been physically wounded from Japanese 20 mm canon fire, sprayed bullets into the teeth of the enemy aircraft screaming directly at him, demonstrated great personal valor by manning his duty station, and continued to fire at oncoming enemy aircraft despite explosions, smoke, fire, and enemy bullets all around him.

Displaying uncharacteristic bravery and valor as many of his shipmates slept, Seaman Brewer remained at his duty station until an enemy bomb exploded the ammunition magazine of his ship, instantly killing him and hundreds of his shipmates.

Seaman Brewer's superior professional skills and bravery reflect great credit upon himself, the United States Navy, and the Naval Service. Entered the Naval Service from North Carolina.

By direction of the President,

Frank Knox
Secretary of the Navy

Jessie looked up at Ellie.

"There's something else in the envelope," Ellie said.

Jessie looked into the bottom of the envelope again and found a small handwritten note.

Department of the Navy
Office of the Secretary
Washington

December 19, 1941

Dear Mrs. Brewer,

It is with both joy and sadness that I have, by direction
of President Roosevelt, signed the citation awarding your
late husband the Navy Cross. This is the highest award given
by the Navy for bravery. The President and I have personally
discussed your husband's actions. He has asked that I convey
to you his deep appreciation for the sacrifice your family has
made and to reassure you that your husband will never be
forgotten.

With warmest personal regards,
Frank Knox

"I've never shown that citation or the letter to anyone
before, Jessie. I had planned on showing it first to Little Billy
when he was old enough to read it and understand it."

Jessie looked up at her. "I don't understand."

"Come with me upstairs for a moment." Ellie motioned
for Jessie to stand. She gently laid her hand on Jessie's back and
walked with her, side-by-side up the stairs to Little Billy's bedroom.

With the soft light streaming in, Ellie glanced over at the
nightstand beside the boy's bed. As she suspected, the photograph of Billy in his sailor's uniform had been moved. She
whispered to Jessie, "Step into the bedroom with me. I want
you to see something."

The two women stood next to the boy's bed. He was
laying on his back, his face up, mouth still half open. On his
chest was what looked like the cardboard back of an eight-by-
ten-inch picture frame, which was being guarded by his little
hand.

Ellie gently pried the boy's hand from the photo and set
the official U.S. Navy portrait of Seaman Billy Brewer back on

the nightstand between the picture of the USS *Arizona* and the picture of Little Billy and Billy, Sr. together at the beach.

"He does this about every night," Ellie whispered. "When I checked on him thirty minutes ago, the picture was on the nightstand. But he usually wakes up wanting his daddy then reaches for the picture. He's been doing this since the funeral."

Jessie wiped her eyes.

"Come on, let's go back downstairs," Ellie said.

They descended the staircase back down into the living room. Ellie motioned for Jessie to sit down. Then Ellie did the same, took a sip of her almost-empty wine glass, and looked Jessie in the eyes.

"Jessie, I've never told you this. In fact, I've never mentioned it to anybody. But it's true. I married Billy for the wrong reasons. I married him to get back at Walter for dumping me for you.

"Not only did I marry him for the wrong reason, but I didn't love him. I was still in love with Walter at the time.

"But then something began to change. You and Walter started having kids, and well, I got pregnant. At first I was reluctant, since I wasn't in love with the baby's father. But when Little Billy arrived, something happened to my perspective.

"Billy was so very good with our son. And Little Billy worshipped the ground his father walked on.

"You know I grew up wealthy. I won't lie. I still am very wealthy. I was an only child. Somehow, the relationship Billy had with our son was something I never imagined having with my mother or my father.

"My mother and father are good people. My father is in many ways like Walter. He was sort of a country boy with a down-to-earth set of values. In fact, when Walter and I met, the gossip circles in Plymouth said we were an odd couple, and we were. Sort of like the aristocrat's daughter and a poor tobacco farmer's grandson. That's not the way I felt, but that's what my mother's blue-haired social friends were gossiping about.

"Anyway, I was in love with Walter. I'd never been in love

with anyone. Never been dumped by anyone. But I don't think he trusted me." Ellie looked down.

"The thing with Billy?" Jessie asked.

"You know?" Ellie looked surprised.

"Ellie, Walter hasn't said a whole lot about his background with you, but he did mention the incident at the barn."

"It was as if I had a self-destructive personality back in those days. I was dating a guy with real substance. It was a strange feeling. I'd always had luck in the men department, but most guys in the social scene were so superficial. Then Walter came along, but it was like I couldn't be satisfied. Like I couldn't settle for just one man.

"Billy and I had nothing in common. He was a good-looking, strapping athlete. In a perverse way, I thought it would be exciting to have a secret, physical thing going on with my boyfriend's athletic-but-dumber brother. So I'd meet Billy during the day then date Walter at night. Turns out, I was the dumb one. I got caught. Then I got dumped. That was a first, too. Are you sure you want to hear this?"

"Yes, I need to hear it," Jessie said.

"When Walter caught us stuck in the mud that day by the barn, he was furious. He dropped me like a hot potato and turned cold as ice. It was pretty soon after that his grandfather died. I think he and Billy started getting along after that, but he was still cold toward me. It drove me crazy. Made me feel ashamed. Then around Thanksgiving of that year, I did something I'd never done. I wrote him an apology letter. You wouldn't believe the pride I swallowed to do that. In the letter, I asked him if he would escort me to the Christmas Dance at the country club. He accepted. So I swallowed my pride on two fronts. First an apology—which I *never* did back then—and then asking a man for a date."

"Now you're getting into territory I'm not familiar with," Jessie said.

"Jessie, would you mind if I got another glass of wine? I think I'll need it."

Jessie smiled. "Only if you bring me some sweet iced tea."

"Done." Ellie walked into the kitchen, poured the respective beverages of choice, and returned with her wine and Jessie's tea.

"So, where was I?"

"The club dance," Jessie said.

"Ah, yes," Ellie said. "Walter took me to the dance, and that's when the romance sort of rekindled. By Christmas Eve, just three weeks later, we were engaged."

Jessie sipped her tea. "Then what happened?"

What happened is he met you.

"Our engagement started out with a fight between me and my mother. I wanted to get married on August 19, 1930, which was my birthday. My mother thought that was a bad idea because that day was a weekday. Anyway, we were two spoiled, strong-willed women locking horns in a debate over a wedding date, and I think that made Walter uncomfortable."

Ellie sipped her wine. "By April, he postponed the engagement. I'll never forget that moment. He had asked me to go for a walk down along the Roanoke River, behind the stores on Water Street. He suggested that we should 'postpone' the engagement until my mother and I came to an agreement on the wedding date. I got mad and threw his ring back at him."

Her eyes glanced down at the diamond on Jessie's finger.

I threw that ring on your finger back at him.

"I accused him of seeing someone else, which he denied. The next time I saw him was June at his house in Jamesville."

"I remember that day." Jessie said. "The day that father and I came to the back door asking Walter for help after our house was ransacked. And you were there," Jessie said.

"Right." Ellie met Jessie's eyes. "That was the first time I ever saw you. Or even knew about you."

"I remember that like yesterday." Jessie wiped her eyes. "I was shocked to see you at his house." Jessie's eyes were watering again. "I was already an emotional wreck from them tearing up our house and killing our dogs, but I kind of wondered about you too," Jessie said.

"I've often wondered what Walter must have been thinking at the moment," Ellie said.

"Now that I think back on it, it was rather amusing," Jessie said. "Walter was trying to hide one woman from the other, and we both showed up at the same time, uninvited, at his house on a Sunday afternoon."

Both women smiled. Then Ellie continued. "Anyway, I left his house that Sunday, June sixth, and I didn't see him again until that day in the train station in Rocky Mount when you returned from your honeymoon. I didn't even know he'd gotten engaged until I bumped into Billy, who informed me that he'd gotten married and was off on his honeymoon."

"You know, that wasn't right of Walter," Jessie said. "I mean the two of you had been engaged only nine months earlier."

"No, it wasn't. And I let him know. Anyway, I was hurt and mad. So I sort of coaxed Billy into proposing to get even. It was immature, I know."

"You two did appear to be a mismatch."

"We were. And I didn't love him, at least not at first. But over the years, though there was never much of a romantic spark between us, I grew to love Billy for who he was. He was very loyal to me as a husband. Yes, he lived in Walter's shadow, but he would have done anything for me. In his own way, he tried hard to please me. Like when he would pick flowers and give them to me. Or plan special trips, day trips, to Nags Head or to Greenville for a movie. Nothing made him happier than when he did something to bring a smile to my face. But I didn't smile at him enough. I was so darned hard to please. How I regret that now."

Ellie felt her eyes beginning to water. "But the thing I grew to love most about Billy was how he loved those children. He was so affectionate, always holding hands with Little Billy, always holding Margaret in his arms. He showered them both with kisses—thousands of kisses and hugs—all the time. Little Billy refused to go to bed until his daddy cuddled with him and helped him say his prayers."

Ellie dabbed her eye with a handkerchief. "What I'm trying to say to you, Jessie, is that Billy was a good man. I grew to love him for who he was and what he taught me about family. He taught me that there is nothing eternal on this earth except our relationships. He invested time in his family. Family, he taught me, is an institution far more important than any romantic spark we might be looking for. Billy created lasting memories with his children—with his family—that will never be forgotten. With Little Billy, he hunted, fished, and played baseball. With Margaret, he made cookies and took her on picnics down at Albemarle Sound. And he will never, ever be forgotten."

She glanced over at a picture of Billy in his Navy uniform, then looked at Jessie. "I say all that to assure you that I would never do anything to disrupt your family. I'm sorry I made you feel uncomfortable. And if you want me to stay away, I will."

Jessie stood, walked over to her, and embraced her. "I don't think that will be necessary."

36

ABOARD HMS *DEFENDER*
PORTSMOUTH, ENGLAND
AUGUST 18, 1942

This was the first day in five months that the *Defender* had seen port in England. Even still, the ship's visit to Portsmouth would last only a few hours, just long enough to refuel, take on members of Commando Unit D, and head to sea for *Operation Jubilee.*

With the ship's engines running and with members of the commando unit making their way on board, Captain Edward McCloud tried relaxing for a moment alone in his stateroom. On a destroyer, the captain's stateroom was by no means elaborate, but it was the only place where the skipper could find a few minutes of solitude away from the pressures of command.

On this mission, Edward would assume command not only of the *Defender,* but he had also been named Destroyer Squadron Commander, meaning that the skippers of the seven other destroyers participating in the mission would report to him.

He had just finished a phone conversation with his good friend and boss, Captain J. Hughes-Hallett, the commander of the naval task force for the impending attack. Hughes-Hallett had called to discuss the latest intelligence reports showing expected danger to the fleet. As usual, the major threats to the eight destroyers participating in the mission would come from the German Air Force and the ever-lurking presence of U-boats.

Edward sat on the small sofa and lit his pipe. One of the Royal Navy's most experienced and battle-tested commanders, he always tried to find time alone before combat.

Danger was nothing new to Edward McCloud. He had stared it in the face many times and defied it brilliantly. His personal key to success in battle was preparation. There could never be enough of it before combat. He would use every second to study and restudy the rules of engagement before the ship got underway.

He puffed on his pipe and again reviewed the battle plans spread out on the small table before him. To his surprise, the naval armada did not include any heavy cruisers or battleships, leaving most of the firepower to the destroyers and the RAF. Other than that, on paper, the plan looked sufficient, at least from the Navy's perspective.

Yet something was not quite right in the bottom of his stomach. Maybe it was the prospect of supporting an amphibious invasion without the heavy firepower provided by battleships and cruisers.

Edward couldn't quite figure out what was wrong about this mission. He just knew that his stomach was in a knot, something he had never experienced before in his career as a naval officer.

The knock on his stateroom door interrupted his thoughts. It was the Master at Arms, Chief Petty Officer David Arnold.

"Enter."

Arnold opened the door and was brief. "Pardon me, Captain. You have a flash message from Admiral Mountbatten via Captain Hughes-Hallett."

"Thank you, Chief. Wait there for a moment please."

McCloud opened the message, as Arnold stood at attention awaiting further instructions.

FLASH
TOP SECRET

From: Royal Naval High Command
To: Commander Naval Task Force Jubilee

Commander DESRON 6

Commanding Officer, HMS *Defender (H07)*
Commanding Officer, HMS *Impulsive(D11)*
Commanding Officer, HMS *Ardent* (H41)
Commanding Officer, HMS *Antelope (H36)*
Commanding Officer, HMS *Cavalier (R73)*
Commanding Officer, HMS *Highlander (H44)*
Commanding Officer, HMS *Fearless (H67)*
Commanding Officer, HMS *Intrepid (D10)*

Subj: Ground Force Casualty Estimates Operation Jubilee

Latest military intelligence shows expect heavy casualties to ground forces.
Stand by for additional medical supplies and body bags to be delivered to task force ships NLT 18:30 hours GMT 18 AUG 1942.
Task force ships are ordered under way at 19:00 hours GMT 18 AUG 1942.
All previously issued operational orders stand in effect.
Prepare accordingly.

Edward took a long draw from his pipe as he absorbed the message.
"Hmm." Edward said. "Chief, it seems that High Command expects our ships to become floating morgues. Maybe the admiralty should rethink its position and assign us battleships and cruisers to improve our ability to reinforce these boys hitting the beach. I'll bet Mountbatten would bring heavier firepower to bear if this were a British force instead of a Canadian force spearheading the invasion. Oh, well. He's the admiral, and I'm just a captain. I suppose he and Winnie know what they are doing."

"Let's hope so, Captain," the Chief said.

Edward looked up. "Chief, I want you to inform the XO, the CDO, the Medical Officer and the OOD that we are expecting a cargo delivery from Fleet Medical by eighteen thirty hours."

"Eighteen thirty hours. Aye, sir."

"Then inform the XO and the CDO that the captain will be on the bridge at eighteen forty-five hours, and we are to be underway at nineteen hundred hours."

"Skipper on the bridge at eighteen forty-five. Underway at nineteen hundred. Aye, sir."

"And Chief, there's one other thing. Please ensure that I'm not to be disturbed prior to eighteen forty-five unless the matter is urgent."

"Aye-aye, sir."

"That will be all."

The sweet-smelling smoke from the burning Prince Albert tobacco lurked through the air like a ghost, saturating the far corners of the captain's stateroom. With the commando unit already boarding the ship and with the ship's engines running idle, Edward took another puff. He watched the cloud of white smoke dissipate.

Two lone photos, framed in simple, black five-by-seven frames and sitting in the corner of his small desk, came into view. One was a photo of his ex-wife, Baroness Juliana McCloud.

The other was his only son, Darwin, the aspiring actor and weekend warrior with the Royal Naval Reserves. The sight of his only two family members momentarily distracted him from thoughts of his battle preparations. It had been nearly a year since he had heard from either of them. Edward missed them. He wondered where he had gone wrong.

Another knock on the captain's stateroom door interrupted his daydreaming. This time it was the command master chief with the latest status report on underway preparations.

"Sir, cargo from Fleet Medical has been loaded and stored in sick bay. Commando Unit D is fully boarded. Radar and fire control report ready. All hands on the bridge making underway preparations, awaiting the captain's arrival in fifteen minutes, sir."

"Very well, Master Chief. Is there anything else?"

"Yes, sir, there is one other thing."

"Speak."

"There's a young man on board. Looks to be about twenty years old. He has requested a moment with the captain, sir."

"A moment with me? Now? When we are preparing to steam into combat? Master Chief, the last I heard, the King and Queen only have daughters. And unless I've been so busy that I somehow missed out on the Royal birth of the Crown Prince of Wales, I'm afraid a visit at this time will be impossible."

"Sir. The young man claims to be *your* son."

"My son? That's impossible. My son's an actor. The last I heard he was doing weekend duty in the reserves. We're not taking any reservists on board for this mission, are we?"

"No sir, Captain, just commandos. The sailor claiming to be your son is a Royal Naval Commando."

"Darwin? A Royal Naval Commando? That's about as likely as me sailing across the Channel and joining the German Navy. This is no time for practical jokes, sailor. Especially not when we're about to sail on a combat mission."

"With all due respect, Captain, the commando in question identified himself as *Darwin*. He said his name is Darwin McCloud from Kensington. And the lad *does* bear a striking resemblance to the photograph in the corner of the captain's stateroom."

"Impossible." Edward was dumbfounded. "Send him in."

"Petty Officer McCloud, the Captain will see you now."

The knots in the captain's stomach intensified as the good-looking young man in battle gear stepped into the stateroom and stood at attention, determined to show utmost respect for his father's position as a Royal Navy captain and as command-ing officer of the *Defender*.

"Sir, Petty Officer Darwin McCloud, Royal Naval Com-mando Unit D is at your service, sir."

In the last two years, Edward McCloud had helped save the British Expeditionary Force from Dunkirk, had helped sink the French Fleet in Oran by order of the Prime Minister, and had helped sink the most hated submarine in the German Navy, U-47. He had fended off dozens of torpedoes, withstood aerial attacks from the Luftwaffe, and received numerous decorations for heroism. But none of his training, none of his experiences could prepare him for the shocking sight now before him.

"Darwin, what are you doing on my ship? This is a very dangerous mission, son."

"Sir, this petty officer is doing nothing more than his duty and is very pleased to follow his father in a glorious tradition of naval service to the Crown."

Edward stood speechless, gazing at the improbable sight of his son, the aspiring actor with no real ambition, standing before him in the uniform of one of the most elite forces in the British military. Edward McCloud, the great commander with the stomach of steel, suddenly felt his insides ripped by diametrically-opposed emotional forces. As a father and as a navy man, he felt a great surge of pride that his son whom he had long ago given up on had somehow become a member of such as highly-prestigious military unit. Yet as that same father and navy man, he felt unbearable apprehension as he thought about the extra shipment of body bags that had just arrived, knowing that he may be transporting his only child into mortal combat.

The captain had to somehow get hold of this—and fast. He was due on the bridge in ten minutes.

"Son. It's just me and you in the room. You can cut the military talk. I'm your father. And please, stand at ease."

Darwin seemed to welcome the opportunity to speak candidly. "I just wanted to show you the respect you deserve as commander of this ship. Over the past few months, I've grown to respect you and appreciate you more than you know for the great responsibility you have."

The son's words were melting the father's heart. All those years he had felt a lack of respect, a total disinterest in anything related to the Navy or anything else he had done. Darwin had always been his mother's boy. Now suddenly, out of nowhere, he had become his father's man.

"But son, a *Royal Naval Commando?* I . . ." Edward lost his words.

"I know, Father. You can't believe your eyes. It's okay. No one else thought it would happen either. Not Mother, not even Captain Rudy. But I've learned over the past few months that strength of mind and strength of the heart are far more important than strength of body."

"From the looks of things, it appears you've added a little body strength to boot."

"With the physical training they put us through, I suppose that was inevitable."

"But why the commandos, son? Why not surface warfare or intelligence?"

"I did it for you, Father. I wanted you to have a son in the most elite corps of the Royal Navy. I want your colleagues in the senior officer corps and at the admiralty to see how much your son respects you."

Edward could feel his eyes misting. This was no state for a destroyer commander to be in minutes before sailing into combat. He choked back his emotions. "I don't know what to say. I am honored."

"Father, you don't need to say anything. I know how you feel. You must go to the bridge now, and I must rejoin my unit. But before I go, I have two requests."

"Anything you ask, son."

"I won't skirt the issue. We both know this mission is dangerous and that I may not come back. You know how I feel about you and Mother. I know that asking you to reconcile may be too much to ask. But Father, will you promise me that if I am unable to, you will take care of her and support her if and when she is in need?"

"I will always love your mother, son. No matter what, I'll make sure she is taken care of."

"Thank you, Father. I have one other request." Darwin pulled a small envelope out of his pocket. "This is the address of a very special young lady I met in Scotland. Her name is Sally. If I am killed or wounded, would you contact her for me?"

"Of course."

Darwin looked at his watch. It was eighteen forty. The captain was due on the bridge in five minutes. "I suppose I must get back to my unit and you must get to the bridge now. So with the captain's permission, I should be going."

"Wait, son." Edward held out his arms and gave Darwin a long embrace. It was the first time Darwin could remember being hugged by his father.

37
THE RAID ON DIEPPE
AUGUST 19, 1942

Ellie sat up in bed and turned on the lamp at 10 p.m. The stroke of midnight would bring August nineteenth, her twenty-ninth birthday. Her mother was planning an elaborate birthday party at their Woodlawn Road estate the next day, hoping that an ol' fashioned bash might lead Ellie to a prominent bachelor. Invitations had been sent, and many single, wealthy men eagerly had accepted, at least the ones who had not been drafted or volunteered for the military. Billy died almost nine months ago, and her mother saw the bash as a way of easing Ellie's transition from being a young widow in mourning to a young woman who could hopefully feel the excitement of life once more.

Ellie went along with the party idea to appease her mother. If throwing a party made her feel better, so be it. Tonight, however, she wrestled with insomnia, and it wasn't the upcoming party that was keeping her awake. It was the card.

Never mind that it arrived a day early. And so what if the language wasn't suggestive of anything. He remembered her birthday. The card proved it. With so much on his mind, *he* had been thinking of *her*.

By the time she flipped on the lamp, she had read the card ten times already. Maybe one more reading would help her sleep.

Dear Ellie,

Happy birthday!

      I'm writing from the Army's Officer Candidate School at Fort Benning, Georgia. I miss Fort Bragg because it was easy to get home on the weekends. I knew that couldn't last forever.
      Oh well. Enough about me. How have you been? I know things are tough without Billy. I miss him too. But I'm grateful Becky is staying on with you a while longer.
      How are the kids? Be sure to tell them Uncle Walter loves them. Tell Little Billy I have some exciting things to tell him about next time I am home.
      Take care, and have a good twenty-ninth! Look forward to seeing you and the family soon.

Walter

Ellie folded the card and put it back in the envelope. It was late. She had to get some sleep. She turned off the lamp—again.

⁂

Over the dark, choppy waters of the English Channel, an impressive armada of British warships carrying more than six thousand Canadian and British soldiers steamed into the night, bearing down on the northern coast of France.

On the bridge of HMS *Defender*, Captain Edward McCloud scanned the horizon through his binoculars. All was still black except the stars and the running lights from other ships in the flotilla scattered out in a string over fifteen miles from east to west. *Defender* and her support vessels anchored the western flank of the armada, taking aim at German shore batteries on the beaches to the west of Dieppe.

Edward glanced at the clock on the bridge's bulkhead. Tee

minus fifteen seconds until 0400. With sunrise due at four fifty-seven, the armada was now battling against the clock.

Within the next half hour, the starry eastern horizon would fade under a pale grayish hue, a sign to experienced mariners that the sun would crest the water within the hour. To maximize surprise and effectiveness, the battle plans called for the surprise attack by the commandos to begin at sunrise.

On the fantail of the ship, several hundred British commandos stood, packed shoulder-to-shoulder in full battle gear. The cool wind whipped their faces as they waited to board the landing craft about to carry them into battle against the hated Nazis. The scene was the same all along the string of ships and landing craft which were now positioned along a wide front just ten miles off the French coast.

The hour was at hand. Captain McCloud turned to his helmsman.

"All engines half speed."

"Engines half speed, aye sir."

As *Defender* cut her speed to ten knots, Edward focused his binoculars on the back of the ship where the commandos were assembled on the fantail. He hoped to catch one more glimpse of Darwin. No such luck. With black grease smeared on their faces under the dark sky, all the commandos looked the same. The best thing he could do for his son right now was to make sure the commandos would be in position to attack by daybreak. Time was of the essence, but Edward was calm on the brink of the storm. His voice steady and sure, he issued the next order to the helmsman.

"All engines idle," Edward said.

"Engines idle, aye sir," replied the ship's helmsman.

"All engines reverse full, then maintain idle."

"Aye, sir."

With her propellers shifting into reverse to brake her forward movement, *Defender* halted her southern trek as the wake of trailing water lifted her stern a few feet.

Edward turned to his officer of the deck.

"Mr. Jones, status report on landing craft, please."

Edward again checked the clock. It was five after four and

still dark. To attack by sunrise, the commando unit needed to board the landing craft and be underway by four twenty.

"Sir, CDO reports all four landing craft now docking on our starboard and ready to receive commando unit."

"Outstanding," Edward said.

"Mr. Jones, convey message to commando team leader—landing craft ready for commandos. Please advise of your status."

"Aye, sir."

The bridge of a warship was the most comfortable place on Earth for Edward McCloud. In his long career, he had seen storms, war, and smooth seas. He had commanded hundreds of men, including the loyal crew he now carried into battle. He commanded their respect in part because nothing rattled him. His adrenaline flowed in the face of danger, sending him on an emotional high.

Yet the price was high for his loyalty to the Navy. His love for the rush of command in combat had cost him his marriage. Now, the command he was about to give might cost him his son. For the first time in his career, he did not relish the moment. The adrenaline was absent. The rush was gone.

He thought about the flash message from Captain Hughes-Hallett—*Latest military intelligence shows expect heavy casualties to ground forces. Stand by for additional medical supplies and body bags to be delivered to task force ships.*

He tried but couldn't shake the image of the body bags. He would rather face a dozen U-boats with a hundred deadly torpedoes than give the next order.

Why couldn't Darwin have remained an actor and just stayed in the reserves? If only I had been more supportive of his love for the theatre. If I had accepted and approved of his decision to join the reserves, if I had found more time for him, maybe he would not have been so driven to prove something to me.

The knots in his stomach intensified, but duty called. As commander of *Defender*, he would keep a cool appearance and maintain his composure. The lives of his crew depended on it.

"Sir, commando team leader reports Unit D ready for departure on captain's orders."

Edward took a deep breath. It was ten minutes after four. Launch now, and the unit would attack by sunrise. Surprise would be achieved.

"Very well, Mr. Jones. Send the order. Launch commando units."

"Aye, sir. Launch commando units."

Within seconds, dozens of Royal Naval commandos were crawling over the starboard side of *Defender* descending down large netted ropes and into four troop landing craft for the final push into Dieppe. Edward swung his binoculars down toward the commandos, looking for Darwin. He remembered that he was a ship's commander and had more to think about than just his son.

Edward again glanced at the clock as the last of the four landing craft pulled away from *Defender*. The commandos were now headed due south, right on time for their rendezvous with the Germans. It was twenty after four. With sunrise in thirty-seven minutes, the Eastern sky was beginning to lighten. Through his binoculars, Captain McCloud saw dozens of other landing craft preparing to launch.

He stepped onto the catwalk outside the bridge for a better look. The distant sound of approaching aircraft from the North riveted his attention toward the ship's aft. He searched the pre-dawn sky with his binoculars. Spitfires! Never had the Royal Air Force looked so good so early in the morning.

"XO, you've got the con," Edward said to his executive officer. "I'm going to look for our aviator friends."

"Aye, Captain."

Edward descended the ladder to the main deck and toward the ship's aft. The eight airplanes in the lead squadron came roaring straight toward *Defender,* about two hundred feet above the water. The warbirds passed low and turned east, flying over the line of ships that comprised the invasion force. This was a message of reassurance that air cover would be available on this hard day of battle.

Edward looked to the northern sky. Darkness faded into dawn. He spotted a second squadron of Spitfires on the way.

This was a good sign. Winston Churchill would give his

beloved navy plenty of air cover when the Luftwaffe pounced. Soon the roar of several hundred warplanes would stir enough commotion to wake the drunkest German.

The ship's loudspeaker broke the distant roar of more approaching aircraft.

"Captain, you're needed on the bridge."

Edward jogged up the main deck and back onto the bridge.

"What's our status, XO?"

"Not good, sir. We've spotted a squadron of three German torpedo boats—look to be T1 class."

"Location?"

"Two-four-zero degrees, range four thousand yards. Bearing a course of ninety degrees."

Edward scanned the southwestern horizon. The German torpedo boats were crashing through the waves at full speed from right to left. Through the binoculars, the swastika-laden Nazi banner flew off their sterns.

"They're headed straight for our landing craft," Edward said. "Our boys are sitting ducks."

"Yes, Captain. I'm afraid we've lost the element of surprise," the XO responded.

Edward had to act. He could not stand by and watch his son and hundreds of other British commandos sunk before his eyes. "Sound general quarters! All hands to battle stations!"

"Aye-aye, Captain."

The XO flipped a switch on the panel of the bridge and grabbed the microphone to the ship's intercom system. "General quarters! General quarters! General quarters! Battle stations! Battle stations!"

With alarm bells sounding all over the ship and with the XO's voice echoing in every passageway, crew members donned helmets and life vests and scrambled to machine guns, five-inch cannons, and depth charges.

"Sir, the torpedo boats are opening fire on our landing craft!"

Edward could see puffs of smoke coming from the German cannons, with splashes all around the landing craft to the far right. The XO was right. His son's landing craft was under fire.

"All engines full forward. Head course one-eight-zero degrees. Commence fire at will."

The helmsman pushed the throttle as *Defender* lunged forward toward the French Coast.

"Sir, five-inch guns are still out of range," the XO said.

"Time until we are in range, mister?"

"Estimate two minutes, sir."

Edward felt sweat beading on his forehead. His son was under attack, and his hands were tied.

"Sir, one of the landing craft has been hit!"

Through his binoculars, Edward saw smoke billowing from the landing craft on the far right.

"Estimate time until guns are in range!" he demanded.

"Approximately one minute, sir."

He again peered through the binoculars. The landing craft was listing on its end, with smoke still billowing like a steel mill.

This sight was familiar to Edward—the sight of a dying vessel breathing its last gasp before becoming engulfed by the waters of the ocean. Edward felt helpless. Unlike his son, he wasn't much on prayer. But watching the craft slide under the surface produced a quick silent bequest to the Almighty that Darwin wasn't on board.

"Sir, three remaining landing craft turning ninety degrees," the conning officer reported.

"Jolly good! They're taking evasive action," Edward said. "Get out of there, boys. Get the heck out of there!"

"Captain," the XO interjected. "May I remind you that if we proceed too far south toward France, we may sail out from under our air cover? We'd be naked targets for the Luftwaffe."

"You may remind me XO, but if we don't attack that convoy, our entire commando unit goes down. I can't let that happen."

"Sir, now closing to within range of five-inch guns."

"Very well," Edward felt a sense of relief. At least he could take action. "Open fire!"

"Batteries, release!"

Boom!

The shock from the simultaneous firing of *Defender's* five-inch guns rocked the ship. Edward, his XO, and the command duty officer all aimed their binoculars toward the three Nazi vessels chasing the British landing craft. Within seconds, they saw water splashing all around the torpedo boats as rounds from the first salvo dropped around their targets. The boat in the middle seemed to rock. Then smoke started pouring from her midsection.

"Tally ho!" cried the XO.

"One down, two to go," said the CDO.

"Reload batteries and prepare to fire again on my order!" Edward instructed.

"Batteries reloaded and awaiting the captain's orders, sir."

"We've got to close the gap more. We've got to sink those other boats with our next salvo. We need more power, Petty Officer Newell," Edward said to his helmsman.

"We're giving her all the steam we've got, Captain."

"That's not good enough, mister. Get engineering on the horn! Tell them I need more steam. Now!"

"Aye, Captain!"

"Sir! Forward spotter reports hostile aircraft approaching nine-zero degrees. Look to be two Messerschmitts."

"Warn antiaircraft gunners. Let's greet them with a wall of fifty-calibre fire," Edward said.

Edward looked out to the East as two German fighters came barreling in just above the water, headed for the ship's stern. *Defender's* fifty-calibre machine guns opened fire first, producing an ear-splitting staccato of bullets flying toward the Messerschmitts. The Germans retaliated, spraying machine-gun fire all over the back deck of the ship as they passed over.

Edward watched as the planes shot past and into the western sky, where they would regroup and come back for another attack on his ship.

"Damage assessment," Edward said.

"Two gunner's mates dead, sir. Antiaircraft guns manned and awaiting next round. Damage minimal."

"They'll be back," Edward said. "XO, call in air cover immediately."

"Aye, sir." the executive officer adjusted the ship's radio to the RAF's frequency and spoke into the microphone.

"HMS *Defender* to Spitfire Leader. We are under aerial attack. I repeat. We are under aerial attack. Receiving machine-gun fire from Messerschmitts. Request immediate assistance."

"Spitfire Leader to *Defender*. Stand fast. Help is on the way."

"Roger that, Spitfire Leader."

"At least the flyboys heard us, Captain," the XO said.

"Good, XO. But right now I'm more concerned about those torpedo boats than the Nazi fighter planes. We need to get off another salvo before the fighters make their next pass."

"Five-inch batteries are reloaded and awaiting your command, sir."

"Very well," Edward said. "Open fire!"

Defender again rocked back from the concussion of her own guns.

"Messerschmitts approaching! Two-seven-zero degrees!"

Edward looked due west. This time, the German fighters were aiming straight for the bridge of the ship.

"Hit the deck!"

A barrage of machine-gun fire raked through the bridge, shattering glass everywhere. Edward stood up. Two petty officers lay bleeding on the deck.

"Call medical," Edward instructed.

"Medics to the bridge! Medics to the bridge. We have casualties."

"Spitfire Leader to *Defender*. We've got your Nazi vultures in sight. Have a look off your starboard for the greatest show on earth."

Edward and his XO looked off to the right as five Spitfires dove out of the clouds and pounced onto the Messerschmitts' tails. Within seconds, the Messerschmitts were ablaze, like flaming comets spiraling to the ocean. Several other German planes exploded, igniting multiple fireballs that were brighter than the rising sun, then smashed into the sea.

Edward grabbed the radio mike. "*Defender* to Spitfire Leader. Good shooting, ol' boy!"

"Spitfire Leader to *Defender*. All in a day's work. And while we're at it, why don't you let us help with that last torpedo boat?"

In the chaos, Edward had not checked the results of the second round of five-inch fire. He glanced out at the torpedo boats.

A second boat was billowing smoke. The batteries had released seconds before the Messerschmitts attacked and struck one of the two remaining torpedo boats. Two down, one to go.

"*Defender* to Spitfire Leader. The third torpedo boat is all yours. We're enjoying the show so much, we're thinking of selling tickets."

"Spitfire Leader to *Defender*. Tickets are on the house today. Compliments of the Royal Air Force. Tally Ho!"

The five British planes swarmed around the torpedo boat like bees attacking a honeycomb. One by one, they took turns swooping down and spraying machine-gun fire into the bridge of the boat.

"Spitfire Leader to *Defender*. Your Royal Air Force is pleased to report that third torpedo boat is now dead in the water. But if you want her sunk, you must render the honors."

"*Defender* to Spitfire Leader. With pleasure. Thank you for your assistance."

"Call us anytime."

As medics loaded the two dead petty officers onto stretchers and carried them off the bridge, Edward turned to his XO. "Let's send her to the bottom."

"Aye, Captain. Five-inch batteries again reloaded and awaiting your command."

"Commence fire!"

"Batteries release!"

Boom!

The torpedo boat went up in flames. The immediate danger was gone, but the Germans had sunk one landing craft and delayed the commandos attack. Edward looked at the bridge clock. It was ten minutes after five, and the morning sun was blazing over the water. The element of surprise was gone.

With the torpedo boats out of the way, the three landing craft reversed their direction and headed back toward the rocky beach to commence their assault into the teeth of submachine-gun fire.

"Spitfire Leader to *Defender*. We've spotted survivors in the water near the sight of sunken commando landing craft!"

Edward felt his heart leap.

Earlier he prayed Darwin was not on the sinking landing craft. Now he prayed again that his son was alive and floating on the surface in a life preserver. Darwin's chances of survival were better in the ocean than facing the Nazi hornet's nest awaiting him on the beach.

"*Defender* to Spitfire Leader. *Defender* is commencing search and rescue operations."

"Roger that, *Defender*. Be advised that Spitfires will provide air cover for search and rescue."

"Helmsman, steer course one-eight-five degrees. Advise crew—prepare to pick up survivors."

"Aye, Captain."

By the time *Defender* had scooped up the last survivors from Landing Craft One, Darwin and the handful of commandos who had survived from Landing Craft Two were holed up behind a rock seawall on the beach outside Dieppe. The landing craft had been flooded with machine-gun fire as soon as it opened its doors on the beach. Blood, guts, and bullets were flying everywhere.

Darwin, Richardson, and several others scrambled over the side and into the surf, making their way underwater up to the beach. They came out of the water and sprinted across the beach to a rock seawall, dodging a rainstorm of bullets zipping by their heads as they ran.

The beachmaster, Ensign Winstead, had his brains blown out the back of his head as he sprinted with the commandos from the landing craft to the rock wall. His assistant, Darwin

McCloud, in his first combat exercise, was now acting beach-master and in charge of the squadron.

Most of the fire was coming from two rock pillboxes with machine guns about one hundred yards from the seawall. Darwin crouched down low with twelve other commandos around him and gave instructions.

"We must first take out those pillboxes. To do that, we've got to drop a grenade inside. I'll run for the pillbox and you all cover me. If I don't make it, Richardson, you take command."

"Unacceptable, McCloud," Richardson barked. "You're in charge of the operation. We need you. You stay here, and I'll go first. Besides, I'm the fastest runner here, and I've got the best chance of survival."

Richardson had a point. He *was* the fastest and had the best chance of making it through. Richardson could make the sprint in about fifteen seconds in full battle gear. Anyone else would take about twenty seconds. Five seconds could make the difference between life and death. Darwin had to make a snap decision. What would Edward do? Edward would command with his head rather than his heart. Richardson was right.

"Very well, Richardson. Stay low. We'll all cover you. On the count of three, I want all rifles pouring lead at that pillbox. Richardson, you sprint low down the middle. Ready. One. Two. Three!"

The commandos aimed their rifles over the top of the seawall and poured wave after wave of lead at the two pill-boxes. Shots ricocheted off the rock, but the audacious wave seemed to shock the Germans, as machine-gun fire from the pillboxes slowed momentarily.

"Now, Richardson! Go! Go! Go!" Darwin shouted. "Keep firing!"

Richardson scaled the wall and sprinted toward the pill-box. The machine-gun fire chopped him down at the knees less than twenty feet from the seawall.

"I'm hit! I'm hit!" Richardson cried. The big commando's legs had been shot off at the kneecaps. The next round of fire would take his head. Darwin had to do something.

"I'm coming, Richardson!" Darwin leaped over the seawall

and ran to his wounded friend. He jumped on Richardson to shield him from any more German gunfire.

The machine-gun bullets raking into Darwin's back stung and burned. For a moment, he could feel blood drenching the back of his shirt. The thought of Sally Cameron's face brought comfort like a guardian angel bringing peace. Then he saw a white light as the gunfire faded and the pain subsided.

Far off in sunlit places,
Sad are the Scottish faces,
Yearning to feel the kiss
Of sweet Scottish rain.
Where tropic skies are beaming,
Love sets the heart a-dreaming,
Longing and dreaming
For the homeland again.

38
DIEPPE, FRANCE
AUGUST 20, 1942

Heinrick gazed out the left rear window as the bomber taxied down the grass airfield. The lush, green fields of Northern France were a welcome change of scenery from the scorching sandstorms of North Africa. He had been in Libya so long it seemed he had forgotten what vegetation looked like.

But he wasn't complaining. The advantages of serving with one of the world's greatest military commanders had outweighed the inconvenience of living with camels and nomads. Just last week, General Rommel had promoted him from captain to major, meaning more pay, more prestige, and more power.

He had been so preoccupied with his military duties that he had not written Ingrid with news of the promotion. She would get the news when the increased paycheck arrived. All summer long, Afrika Korps was in a bloody tug-of-war in the desert against the larger British Eighth Army under the leadership of General Auchinleck. Yet despite their numerical disadvantage, Rommel's panzers had punished the British again and again in 1942. Heinrick was pleased with the German war effort in North Africa and was even more pleased with himself.

Today marked his much-awaited first mission on behalf of General Rommel as a major.

The propellers stopped as a ground crew moved a stepladder to the aircraft door. Heinrick would be met by Captain Rudolf Kleinstübber, the local intelligence officer for the Dieppe region.

Heinrick knew Kleinstübber and speculated that the captain would feel uneasy that one of Rommel's chief intelligence officers had been sent to probe the circumstances surrounding yesterday's attack by the Canadians and British.

Heinrick stepped out the door onto the top of the ladder.

"Heil Hitler, Major Schultz!" Kleinstübber was already in position at the base of the ladder, flipping the familiar Nazi salute to Heinrick.

"Heil Hitler, Captain Kleinstübber," Heinrick returned the salute as he walked down the ladder to the airfield.

"*Willkommen* to France, Major."

"The pleasure is mine, Captain."

"So what brings one of General Rommel's finest staff officers to France?" Kleinstübber asked.

"The general has a keen interest in what happened here yesterday," Heinrick said.

"What happened is quite simple. The Canadian Army attempted an invasion, and we crushed them. Our intelligence capabilities were sufficient, as proven by the magnitude of our victory. Surely General Rommel isn't concerned about our ability to predict British military operations, is he?"

"You know I can't read the general's mind, Captain," Heinrick said as Kleinstübber led him to a Jeep at the edge of the airfield.

"Major Schultz, perhaps you should remind the general that the losses to the Canadian Army were devastating."

"You are taking credit for whipping a paper tiger, Captain. It's not the Canadians the general is worried about. It's the British. You see in Africa, we know the British well. We know they can fight."

"Again, Major Schultz, perhaps you should remind the general that British forces also participated in this attack. They, too, were beaten back into the sea. We've even taken a number of British prisoners."

"Interesting you should say that, Captain. My report shows that some newly-formed British commando unit attacked our shore batteries to the east and west of town and that one shore battery was destroyed and the other heavily damaged."

"Does your report also show that our naval convoy intercepted one of the commando units offshore before the attack?"

"Do you mean the same convoy that was sunk by a British destroyer and a squadron of Spitfires?"

"Casualties happen in battle, Major. You know that. My point is that the naval convoy delayed the attack on the shore battery and kept it from being completely destroyed."

"I take it, then, that I should inform the general that the naval intercept to the west of town was a result of superior German intelligence gathering, rather than blind luck? So, if you want to take credit for that, Captain Kleinstübber, I know what the general will ask. He will ask if your intelligence was good enough to intercept the commando unit west of town, then why didn't you intercept the one east of town? And then he will want to know why you didn't inform the Luftwaffe and the Kriegsmarine of your intelligence so they could intercept the main invasion force and attack them in the sea."

"Major, please." Kleinstübber paused as Heinrick watched blood rush to his face.

Kleinstübber was probably thinking Heinrick had come to gather evidence for a court-martial against German intelligence officers in Dieppe. Surely, he knew well the penalty for dereliction of duty—the firing squad. "Please. I do not wish to take credit that is not due, but I implore you to assess our situation this morning. We still control the town. The enemy took heavy casualties and retreated into the sea. We have taken many prisoners, and hundreds of dead Canadians and British soldiers are still lying on the beaches even as we speak. The intelligence could have been better, as it always can be better in any military situation. But based on the results, I hope the major will agree that our intelligence operations here in Dieppe are hardly a failure."

What a pleasure to watch Kleinstübber squirm.

"Relax, Captain," Heinrick said. "I don't think you're going to lose your head or even your job for that matter. I'm not here to investigate the breakdown of German intelligence. General Rommel is interested in gathering intelligence on this new British Naval Commando unit that attacked our shore batteries. He's convinced we'll see them again. I'm here to oversee a battlefield assessment of the shore battery sites where the commando units were in action. I'll need the help of you and your men. If things go well, I'll be sure to mention your name in my report to the general."

Kleinstübber looked like a man who had just gotten a reprieve from the guillotine operator. "Why yes, Major. My staff and I will provide you with the fullest cooperation. If you wish, I will have our driver take us to the battle site west of town. It's only a couple of miles from here, sir."

"Yes, I'd like to see the battle site now, Captain."

"As you wish, sir."

The Jeep pulled up on the edge of the beach beside the bombed-out concrete shore batteries. Heinrick stepped out and stood for a moment, gazing at the sight before him, watching the gentle waves lap against the rocky beach. Except for the sound of the waves and an occasional chirping seagull, there was silence.

He looked north across the English Channel. He knew the French called this body of water La Manche or "the sleeve," since on a map it looked like a narrow sleeve separating continental Europe from the arrogant English. Were it not for "La Manche," the flags of the Third Reich would be flying over the houses in Westminster right now.

Somewhere over the horizon was the giant island-nation that had been Germany's principle nemesis for the last thirty years. Heinrick imagined what the scene would have been like twenty-four hours ago.

The enemy fleet was stretched out offshore, unloading poor Canadians whose bodies got chewed up by the German shore batteries.

Gone were the ships and landing craft which yesterday had wrought so much hell and destruction on their own troops. Gone was the Royal Air Force which had collaborated in the failed invasion. They had returned to their ports and airfields across the Channel to lick their collective wounds. They would be back.

Gone from this picture was everything British except for the massive heaps of human carnage left behind on the beaches. Heinrick looked east at the long stretch of rocky shoreline. Like the battle scenes in Africa, the dead British were joined by an equally-impressive number of dead Germans. In this war, death did not discriminate.

He had seen many battle scenes before, mostly in Africa, once in Crete. But the panorama before him was an unexplainable paradox of bellicosity against a backdrop of beauty. Were it not for the stench of rotting flesh and the sight of decapitated corpses with arms and legs strewn in every direction, this tranquil place by the sea would be serene enough for a picnic with Ingrid or even a family vacation with the girls.

"How long did the naval exchange take?"

"About twenty minutes, Major. We lost the aircraft and our patrol boats, but the skirmish gave us enough time to prepare our shore batteries for the invasion forces. With our patrol boats sunk, the remaining landing craft reversed course and hit the beaches right here in front of us at about 0500." Kleinstübber pointed to a spot on the shoreline about 100 yards from where he and Heinrick were standing.

"You mean, right in front of those pillboxes?" Heinrick asked.

"Precisely, Major. Our machine-gun operators were loaded and waiting for them. We mowed down a lot of them, as you can see, but there were too many to get them all."

"What happened next?" Heinrick asked.

"They started firing over the top of the seawall and began making charges at our machine gun operators in our pillboxes."

"You mean, they were running into the face of machine-gun fire?"

"Yes they were, Major—into the teeth of two submachine-guns."

"They were a brave unit," Heinrick remarked.

"Yes they were, Major, and effective in the face of such great odds. I understand why General Rommel is interested in them."

"Go on, Captain."

"As I said, they kept charging over the seawall. We chopped many of them down, but finally they made it to the pillboxes and dropped grenades inside, killing our machine-gun operators. They took control of the pillboxes and started firing at the shore batteries.

"Once they controlled the pillboxes, they brought reinforcements from behind the seawall. They launched mortar rounds and portable rockets at our shore batteries.

"Their mortars hit our batteries and knocked them out. So their attack was effective. We exchanged fire till about four in the afternoon. Then they retreated back to their landing craft and out to sea. I'd say we killed about half the force as they retreated."

"That's a remarkable story, Captain. We have to give the enemy credit for bravery, at least."

"Yes, sir. I agree with you."

"Captain, I want you to summon your squadron. I'd like a few words with them before we proceed."

"Right away, sir."

Kleinstübber whistled and motioned for the dozen sentinels who had been guarding the perimeter of the battle site to line up in front of the Jeep.

With the squadron lined up in two rows of six, Kleinstübber introduced Heinrick.

"*Guten morgen*, gentlemen. I am Major Heinrick Schultz from General Rommel's staff in Libya. I have just been briefed by Captain Kleinstübber on what happened yesterday. Let me say that the German High Command and General Rommel have an interest in this battle site because it contains the bodies of a new British special forces unit.

"From all accounts, this unit was a devastatingly-effective

fighting force. We expect to see this unit and others like it in the future. Therefore, we want to know everything we can about the unit. I want you to divide up into six teams of two. Then I want you to first check all the bodies and clothing for any written materials. Collect those materials in a box and notify me of anything suspicious. Then collect all weapons left behind by this unit. Once that is done, we will collect dog tags and have these bodies disposed of. Any questions? Very well. Go to it."

Heinrick leaned back against the Jeep and drew a cigar from his coat. "Care for a smoke, Captain Kleinstübber? I've found that the smell of good tobacco burning helps neutralize the stench of rotting flesh."

"Thank you, Major."

Heinrick passed Kleinstübber a large French cigar. The two officers turned their backs against the cool sea breeze to light up as the squadron scavenged through dead and rotting bodies.

"These men any good, Captain?" Heinrick asked, drawing a first puff from his cigar.

"Anything you're meant to find, I can guarantee that you'll find it, Major."

"Good." Heinrick drew another long puff. "That's what I like to hear. Confidence in the troops under your command."

"So what's it like, Major?"

"What?"

"Working for such a famous general. What is that like?"

Heinrick relaxed with a third long puff before answering. "Rommel is a great man. Maybe the greatest commander in the world. We are outnumbered in Africa, yet his panzers respond to him with swiftness and brilliance. I'm sure you are a student of military history, Captain?"

"Of course. Military history is the bedrock of good military intelligence."

"*Ja*. Well, Rommel is destined as a man of historic greatness. Whether Germany wins or loses, his tactics will be studied alongside the likes of Caesar, Napoleon, and Alexander the Great. He is the most brilliant military genius to come along in generations. The most exciting thing in my life is to serve General Rommel. You can feel the electricity around him. I am very lucky."

"I'm envious."

"Yes, envy." Heinrick took another long puff from the cigar. "Envy—the predominant driving force behind war—and greed, adultery, and territorial expansion. I suppose we'd both be out of a job without it, eh, Captain?"

"Sir?" Kleinstübber looked puzzled.

"Never mind."

"Major! Captain!" One of the soldiers on the beach motioned for the officers.

"What is it?" Kleinstübber yelled.

"This British commando has some sort of manual written in German!"

Heinrick stamped his cigar out and walked out to the beach. Kleinstübber was close behind.

"Don't open that till I get there," Heinrick ordered. "Where is it?" Heinrick approached the solider.

"Here, Major. As you can see, it is a little damp, but I haven't opened it."

"Give it here!" Heinrick took the book from the soldier. "Which body did you take this from?"

"That one," the soldier replied as he nudged the dead body with his boot.

"Turn him over," Heinrick ordered.

With the front of his boot, the Nazi sergeant kicked the dead commando over on his back. The uniform's name tag bore the inscription *McCloud*.

Heinrick looked a moment at the lifeless corpse. The dead man's eyes were frozen open—peering at Heinrick. He felt a chill shiver down his spine. He had seen thousands of dead men, but this man's eyes seemed alive and seemed to be peering into his soul.

Heinrick looked away.

Then he opened the book that had been taken from the commando's body. The words were in German. The text was strange yet had a compelling force to it.

[1] Im Anfang war das Wort, und das Wort war bei Gott, und das Wort war Gott.

[2] Dieses war im Anfang bei Gott.

[3] Alles wurde durch dasselbe, und ohne dasselbe wurde auch nicht eines, das geworden ist.

[4] In ihm war Leben, und das Leben war das Licht der Menschen.

"I want that man's dog tag."

"Yes sir, Major."

39

His chin and neck stubbly from a five-o'clock-shadow now five hours old, Heinrick sat on the side of his canvas cot dressed in his uniform trousers, black boots, and a white tee shirt. He rubbed his eyes then reached for a glass of clear liquid when he heard three sharp raps at his door.

"Enter."

Lieutenant Hans Kohlman, Heinrick's administrative assistant, stepped into the room dressed in full uniform and clicked his heels. "Heil Hitler."

"Lieutenant Kohlman. I should have guessed." Heinrick took a sip from the glass and responded with a less enthusiastic "Heil Hitler."

"Would my trusting assistant care to join his commanding officer in imbibing of some of the finest spoils of war?"

"Is that Libyan, sir?"

"My dear Lieutenant Kohlman. You know as well as I that the Libyans drink nothing fermented but camel's milk," Heinrick said. Kohlman forced an obligatory chuckle.

"This, Lieutenant, is some of the finest vodka in the world, captured by the German Army driving east toward Stalingrad.

Field Marshal Paulus had four cases flown here to Afrika Korps Headquarters—no doubt to stay in the good graces of Field Marshal Rommel. One of the bottles has mysteriously found its way into my sleeping quarters, resting only a few centimeters from the side of my bed. Imagine that."

"The spoils of victory," Kohlman said.

"To victory." Heinrick raised his glass, taking a sip. He poured a glass and handed it to Kohlman. "Now then, what was it that you said I could do for my trusted assistant at one hour before midnight?"

"The matter is delicate, *Herr* Major."

"And the hour is late, Lieutenant. Spit it out."

Kohlman took a sip of the Russian vodka. "There had been some concern about Afrika Korps withdrawing back to Europe."

"Concern, you say?" Heinrick raised his eyebrow.

"Yes, Major. By that I mean concern that Field Marshal Rommel may be disregarding the orders of the Fürher."

"Just what orders of the Fürher do you think General Rommel 'may be,' as you say, disregarding?"

"Word has it that the Fürher has ordered Afrika Korps to stay and fight the British to the death but that Rommel has decided to override the order."

Heinrick felt his blood boiling in anger all over his body. He polished off the vodka and poured another glass. "First, the Fürher has not been here. He has not seen the pummeling our forces have taken because we have been overmatched numerically. Rommel is a genius. But the British under Montgomery have 230,000 men. We have 80,000. They have 1,400 tanks. We are left with 500.

"So whose fault is it that we haven't the supplies to deal with the British Eighth Army? It wasn't Rommel's decision to send the rest of our panzers to the Russian Front. Now the Americans are landing, and in addition to Montgomery, Rommel must also deal with General Patton."

Heinrick took his first swig of the new glass of vodka. "Besides, if the Fürher had in fact given such an order, such an order would remain a highly classified matter—certainly not within the purview of a German lieutenant whose job responsibilities are the collection and analysis of battlefield debris."

"*Herr* Major, if Rommel in fact disregards the Fürher's order, such a decision could not only have an impact on the general's personal health, but also on the personal health of those allied with the general."

"That sounds like a threat," Heinrick said.

"Only an observation, sir."

"You act as if you *know* there is a disagreement between Rommel and the Fürher over the disposition of Afrika Korps."

"I have my sources," Kohlman said.

"So you're SS," Heinrick snorted.

"I can neither confirm nor deny the identity of my sources, *Herr* Major."

"And you've been sent to find out if there are sufficient rumblings within Rommel's staff to organize a mutiny."

"Let's just say that perhaps there are those in Berlin who are interested in knowing whether certain officers' loyalties lie with Rommel or with the Fürher."

"And just where do your loyalties lie, Lieutenant?"

Kohlman smiled sarcastically then raised his glass toward Heinrick and took another sip. "I am a German officer. I support the German objective of breaking through at El Alamein, marching east on Cairo, and then capturing the Suez Canal. With control of the Suez, we choke the Allies at one of their most vital supply lines while at the same time giving Germany quick access to Middle Eastern oil. If this is the Fürher's objective, then it is mine also."

"So we lead a revolt against Rommel, stay here and get slaughtered by the British and Americans, or we follow Rommel and risk a firing squad on charges."

"Perhaps the other alternative would be to stay here, await reinforcements, and slaughter the British. Retreat back to the continent would be fatal," Kohlman said.

"Lieutenant, there has been no officer ever in the German Army with a greater tactical genius than Erwin Rommel. I am on his staff and I take my orders from him. If he feels it would be in the best interest of Afrika Korps to withdraw, to regroup, and to then later attack again, I trust him totally. The Fürher is a politician. General Rommel is a professional soldier."

"Your loyalty is admirable, *Herr* Major. I detect a soft spot in your heart for General Rommel. Of course, that is not surprising."

Heinrick eyed his subordinate for a moment. "And what do you mean by that?"

"Perhaps I have said more than I should. After all, you are my superior officer. My apologies, sir. "

Should I throw this insubordinate, disloyal ingrate out of my quarters or pump him for information?

"Speak, Lieutenant," Heinrick snapped.

Kohlman hesitated for a moment. "I was thinking of the nomadic girl, sir."

"What about her?"

"Word seems to have gotten back to Berlin that one of Field Marshal Rommel's senior intelligence officers took time out of his duties to bury a dead nomadic girl during the course of an important intelligence gathering operation."

"No doubt an important piece of information the SS will use in justifying who goes before the firing squad when Afrika Korps is lost to the Allies."

"I make no judgment on your actions, Major Schultz."

"You certainly made a judgment on the day it happened. You said something about a nomadic girl standing in the path of destiny, as I recall."

"That was then. This is now. And then as now, my only purpose in coming here is to provide my commanding officer with information which may be helpful to him personally, sir."

Your purpose, you SS swine, is to ensure the execution of your commanding officer so that you can have his job under the direction of a new, sycophant field marshall who will jump at the Fürher's maniacal antics, which will result in the slaughter of the finest fighting unit in the German Army.

The job may be yours sooner than you think.

"The information you have provided is appreciated. That will be all, Lieutenant."

Kohlman clicked his heels, extended his arm, and snapped,

"Heil Hitler." When Heinrick said, "Heil Hitler," Kohlman left the room and closed the door.

Heinrick sat on the side of the bed, finished his vodka, and thought.

So here I am, in a losing army and falling out of graces with Berlin. I suppose I deserve this. After all, I am the murderer of an innocent little girl. I can no longer bear the pain.

He clasped his hands together and held his head down. Outside, the distant sound of mortar fire broke the peace of the nippy, evening air. *So this is the sound of a great army in retreat.*

He pushed himself to his feet and staggered to the sink. The cold water splashing against his face rushed some blood back into his cheeks and lips. He turned off the cold faucet and turned on the hot, holding his razor under the steaming stream.

It was a quick shave. He raked the top side of his index and middle fingers from his Adam's apple to his chin. Smooth enough.

His military dress uniform hung in the closet next to his bed, freshly pressed. It had been hanging there since his journey to Crete last summer. No need for a dress uniform in battle. The sharp, gray wool jacket and trousers were ceremonial—perfect for the occasion.

He looked in the mirror, straightened his medals, and firmly pulled the bill of his cap down even with his eyebrows. Unsnapping the holster draped at his waistline, he inhaled deeply. He felt his hands start to shake when he gripped the pistol.

He let go of the weapon and poured a final shot of vodka. The warm flow of alcohol draining down his esophagus and into his stomach had an instant, soothing effect. The shaking was gone.

Slamming the glass back down on the wooden table, he reached for the pistol with a renewed fearlessness. This time, he jerked it out of the holster and held it out in front of him. He snapped the bolt action, popping a bullet into the firing chamber.

Then he brought the barrel against his temple. It was a

cold feeling of steel against his flesh. He wrapped his finger around the trigger and pushed the barrel of the gun harder against his head.

"Die, you Nazi child killer!" He stared at his reflection in the mirror. His piercing eyes floating on a residue of tears, he jammed the barrel even harder against his right temple. Not even two shots of vodka could shield the physical pain of the barrel jamming against his brain. Good. This would be the death he deserved.

He closed his eyes and started a countdown.

"Five."

"Four."

"Three."

"Two."

"One."

"Read the book, before it is too late," came the voice from four years ago.

He opened his eyes and looked in the mirror, pulling the pistol away from his temple. No one was there.

"I've read the book. It causes me nothing but misery. It reminds me of what I did to you and your father."

There was no response. It must have been the vodka talking. He put the revolver to his temple and started counting again.

"Five."

"Four."

"Three."

"Do not stop reading. Your sins are forgiven," came the little girl's voice.

"I must be going mad," Heinrick said. "Who are you?"

He waited for a response. None.

"I know who you are. You are a hallucination prompted by the vodka, come to haunt me before I end this misery."

Still nothing.

"I am the daughter of Judah."

"Judah you say? I do not know him."

"You will know him."

"Impossible. I killed you and your father."

"I was only sleeping. Now I am here. And you did not kill my Father."

"Then where is your father?"

"He lives."

"What is your name?"

Nothing.

"Who are you?"

No response.

Heinrick laid down the pistol and sat on the cot.

40
LONDON, ENGLAND
JUNE 1943

As much as he hated every minute of it, Walter braved his way through jump school at Fort Benning and became a bona fide Army parachutist. Still, after hundreds of jumps out of an airplane, he never got over his extreme fear of heights. It was a fear he kept secret because his country needed him as an officer in the newly-formed 101st Airborne Division. By May of 1943, he was a captain in the U.S. Army and was assigned as a company commander within the division.

Walter expected to lead his company into combat. The question was when and where. Speculation was rampant. Some thought the division would join its big brother, the 82nd Airborne Division in Europe, for the European liberation against the Nazis.

Still others reasoned that the 101st was formed as a Pacific alter ego of the 82nd and would go to the Western Pacific to fight the Japs.

Walter did not waste his time speculating about the specifics of combat. Rather than guessing about where he would fight, he spent his spare time writing home. Almost daily he wrote to Jessie and the kids. He rarely wrote to Ellie, but he wrote to Little Billy and Margaret almost as much as he wrote to his own children.

In May of 1943, he got a surprise notice from the Army. He was being sent to England on special assignment—*without* the other members of his company and *without* his division. The Army had become infatuated with his high scores on the battery of tests administered to him during officer candidate school. He had aced the foreign language battery, and that had earned him orders to language school for three months at Supreme Allied Headquarters in London.

The Army never explained why he was being sent to England ahead of the rest of his division. Walter speculated that Uncle Sam would soon invade France, and the Army wanted a few of its officers able to communicate with the local population.

He reported to London on the fourth day of June. A week later, he wrote home with a report on his adventures.

June 13, 1942

Dear Jessie,

I arrived in London on Friday the fourth and reported to Supreme Allied Headquarters for my assignment to language school. Unlike my experiences at Fort Jackson, Fort Bragg, and Fort Benning, the line at the induction desk wasn't very long at all. Nor was the atmosphere so antiseptic and military-like.

The induction clerk, a young female British Army corporal, surprised me with a smile and an offer of either coffee or tea as I waited in the lobby for my papers to be processed. Unaccustomed to the concept of 'a spot of tea' in the afternoons, I opted for good, ol' fashioned American black coffee. It made me think of the early mornings in Jamesville around our kitchen table, the way you always got up and had a delicious hot breakfast ready before I would leave to go on my mail route.

I took my coffee and sat while the corporal processed my papers. As I sat and read one of the British newspapers, someone shouted "Attention." I dropped the paper and jumped to my feet along with all the other military personnel in the ornate lobby. The front doors flung open and a small cadre of British and American officers came walking through. General Dwight Eisenhower, the Supreme Allied Commander, was in the middle of the group! I'd never seen a five-star general before, and I suddenly felt like I was in the presence of a movie star.

Ike and his entourage walked through the lobby in a quick, businesslike stride. As they passed by, the general looked at me, smiled, and waved. His eyes locked with mine for a couple of seconds, and without saying a word, I sensed how much he cares for his men.

At that point, I lost my military bearing, right there in front of the most powerful military officer in the free world. How, you ask? Well, an Army man at attention should remain unflinching and display a stolid, poker face. But when I saw him smile at me, I couldn't contain myself. I tried to suppress it, but I smiled right back at him. He snickered and then he was gone. Poof! Like he vanished out of thin air. It reminded me of the line in the poem "The Night Before Christmas." You know, the last line that goes "I heard him exclaim as he drove out of sight, "Merry Christmas to all and to all a good night."

Anyway, the room returned to normal and the induction clerk called me back over. In her sweet little British accent she gave me some news that made me feel like it was Christmas in June. She informed me that the U.S. Army was sending me for a ninety-day assignment to take courses at the London School of Economics!

She announced that I would be taking courses with a handful of British and American officers. The Army had registered me for courses in French, military history, and French geography. It was like Ike had disappeared into the back of the building and waved a magic wand. Like good ol' Saint Nick, he was giving me what I always wanted—a chance to go to college—even if only for one quarter. I have never been so excited. So tell your daddy that I've been studying at his alma mater for the last week with some of the best professors in the world!

Today I attended church at St. Paul's. It was magnificent. I wish you could be here with me. I miss you and the kids and love you all.

I will write again soon.

Love,
Walter

On September first, four years to the day after Germany invaded Poland, Walter was transferred to Newbury, England, where he took command of E company of the 506th Parachute Infantry Regiment, part of the 101st Airborne Division. In the middle of the month, he penned another letter home.

September 4, 1943

Dear Jessie and children,

It's Saturday afternoon, and I'm writing you from my new quarters in Newbury, England.

I finished my schooling at LSE this past Tuesday (August 31, '43) and the next day was sent back to the 'real' Army.

I've been assigned as a company commander of a parachute infantry regiment. That's a fancy way of saying I'm the first one out of the airplane, and I get to give the guys orders when we hit the ground. I can promise you one thing—we will all hit the ground one way or another. You know what's funny about my assignment? You're the only one in the world who knows my dirty little secret—that to this day I'm still petrified of heights.

These guys think I'm their brave and fearless skydiving leader. I look the part, sound the part, and even fake the part. I wear a "Screaming Eagles" patch on my uniform sleeve, since "Screaming Eagles" is the nickname of the 101st Airborne Division. I make sure all my men have their patch sewn on too. As we are flying a thousand feet off the ground preparing to jump, I give them a little pep talk and remind them who they are—"Screaming Eagles." I remind them of the words of our commanding general, who says that the 101st has "no history, but we have a rendezvous with destiny."

Then I tell them that they should be "Screaming Eagles" and that they should scream as they dive out of the plane as a means of intimidating the Germans. Then I turn around, close my eyes, and leap out the aircraft with the loudest scream you ever heard. My men have no idea I'm screaming because I hate jumping out of the airplane. By the time my parachute deploys, I'm thanking God in heaven and hearing my men scream one by one as they leap out of the plane above me. It's sort of like tricking Billy all over again—God bless his soul. Like my dear brother did, I think most of my men have bought into my egocentric propaganda. But if it helps me get over being a secret chicken and at the same time helps them be better soldiers, so be it.

I've only had two jumps here in England so far. That's because my unit hasn't fully arrived yet. The division continues to arrive by ship every day. When everyone is here, the practicing will intensify, as will my prayer life.

Meantime, I'm enjoying the pastoral life here in this small village in the country south of London. I feel almost guilty in a sense because the officers' quarters are so much nicer than the enlisted. A lot of the enlisted guys are crammed into horse stables, tents, and metal Quonset huts. Plus, there was initially a shortage of food, leading some of the enlisted guys to shoot deer on some of these estates.

The officers, on the other hand, aren't having it so tough. We have plenty of food and great living conditions. I'm living in a manor house in the country with another captain, a major, and a lieutenant colonel. The home is owned by Mr. and Mrs. Robert Morgan and is known as Corbin Hall. The couple is in their sixties and treats us like their sons. From that standpoint, I'm glad I listened to Captain Patterson and went to O.C.S.

For the time being, we sit and we wait. Please pray for us all.

I miss you all and love you all.

Love,
Walter

By the weekend of September 25, 1943, Walter had been joined by most of Company E. His respite from jumping out of an airplane was over, as the company resumed their practice of what Walter thought of as suicidal leaping on Tuesdays and Thursdays. Walter and his men had completed eight parachute jumps over the bucolic, rolling fields of Southern England. All that practicing had done nothing to assuage Walter's fears of heights. But at least the guys followed his lead and screamed on cue as they leapt. The scream was sort of a blood-curdling battle cry, the modern day, airborne equivalent of the old rebel yell employed by Confederate troops at Pickett's charge. Stonewall Jackson would have been proud.

In fact, members of E Company became so enthusiastic about their signature war cry that they deemed themselves the "Screaming Es", the self-anointed, fiercest parachute company of the Screaming Eagles. The primordial scream became a focal point for company camaraderie and helped mold Company E into a confident fighting unit. Meanwhile, their fearless leader screamed because he was still scared out of his wits each time he jumped out of a plane.

On Friday afternoon on the 25th, Walter finished target practice with his company and headed to Corbin Hall for two days of well-deserved furlough. Many of his men were headed into London to revel in a weekend of British nightlife. London was still a novelty to most of them, as many had just arrived in England and had never seen the British capital city. Walter, however, had lived in the city for ninety days and wasn't in the mood to do Piccadilly Circle with a bunch of drunken American GIs. The country setting of Corbin Hall, with its rolling pastures and grazing livestock would be the perfect setting for a much-needed evening of relaxation.

He caught a ride in an Army Jeep with several other officers, including Major Richard Winters, the 2nd battalion XO, his good friend Lieutenant Frederick "Moose" Heyliger, and PFC David Webster, who served as the Company diarist and had tagged along with the officers. They headed to their respective manor houses. As he rode through the English countryside on this sunny autumn afternoon, Walter felt a serious twinge of homesickness. In two days it would be the fourth Sunday in September, homecoming Sunday at Jamesville Christian Church. He thought about all that he would miss out on the day after tomorrow—the fellowship, the fried chicken, and the dinner on the grounds after church. He longed for the laughing, the backslapping, and a good ol' glass of syrupy, sweetened iced tea instead of a "spot of tea." England was beautiful and the people were hospitable, but it wasn't home.

"Good afternoon, Captain Brewer." Margaret Morgan met Walter as usual with a tray of tea and a large assortment of cheeses, fruits, jellies, and toast. The attractive sixty-year-old always sported a sunny disposition, but this afternoon she seemed especially cheery to Walter.

"Good afternoon, Margaret." Walter hung his jacket on a coat rack just inside the door.

"I made you some tea and a little snack."

"You are too kind to me, Margaret. And that looks so delicious. But you know I can't eat all that good food. I love the large front doors here at Corbin Hall, but pretty soon I won't be able to fit through them."

"Oh this isn't all for you, Captain Brewer. You'll want to share some of this with your friend."

"My friend?"

"Yes, Captain." Margaret tried suppressing her grin. "She's in the parlor. Come right this way, please."

Walter had never been so curious as Margaret led him across the deep mahogany hardwood floors of the stately manor. Surely, this wasn't who he thought it might be.

Margaret pushed open the double doors to the parlor as the slim and beautiful visitor in the pink dress stood up with a wide smile on her face. Walter felt like he was going to have a heart attack.

41
ARDENTINNY, SCOTLAND
SEPTEMBER 25, 1943

Every crack, every blemish in the brick-and-mortar pathway caused the chair to bounce and squeak. Perhaps it was a design defect, Richardson thought as Captain Edward McCloud pushed him up the walkway. Whatever, the wheelchair did not function well rolling down the long, broken brick leading to the front door of the modest home. He felt every bounce and bump digging at him in all the places that still hurt.

The chilly Scottish breeze was making him cold. As Captain McCloud knocked on the front door, Richardson pulled the blanket up around the stubs which were formerly his knees, trying to get more comfortable. This was a visit he dreaded making, but it was a visit that *had* to be made. At least he didn't have to make the visit alone. And at least he was finally out of that dreaded hospital.

Richardson felt his heart racing as the door knob turned and the front door cracked open. The auburn-haired young woman was prettier than he remembered.

"Miss Cameron?"

"Yes. I'm Sally Cameron."

"I'm Captain Edward McCloud. This is Petty Officer Richardson. We're with the Royal Navy."

Sally looked at Edward with a hopeful twinkle in her eye. "You're Darwin's father?"

"Yes, ma'am," Edward replied.

Then she looked down at Richardson sitting in the wheelchair, and he knew it was a pitiful sight. His left hand had been amputated too.

She probably didn't recognize him from when she'd seen him with Darwin a year and half earlier.

"And you're . . ." Sally tried to hide the look of horror on her face. "You're Richardson?"

"I apologize if my appearance startles you, Miss Cameron," Richardson said. "I know I don't look the way I did before."

"I'm sorry for staring," she said.

"Apologies unnecessary, ma'am. I'm just grateful to be alive."

Sally looked back up at Edward. "Captain, where's Darwin? Can I see him?"

"May we come in please, Miss Cameron?"

"Of course, Captain."

Sally led the men to the small parlor as Edward rolled Richardson behind her.

"Please be seated," she said.

"Miss Cameron," Edward began.

"Please call me Sally."

"Very well. Sally, it's been more than a year since our attack against Dieppe, France. I'm sorry. We should have come to see you earlier. Unfortunately, the war doesn't stop. My ship has been deployed almost constantly and Petty Officer Richardson has been hospitalized until last week."

Blood seemed to rush from Sally's face. She had probably been hoping against hope. Darwin would not have contacted her since the last letter he sent just before the attack against Dieppe last August.

"I've prayed that perhaps he was in a hospital somewhere recovering or assigned on some long-term, top-secret mission in the Pacific," she said. "I hoped that some day he would come knocking on my door again."

"I'm sorry, Sally," Captain McCloud said. "My son was killed at Dieppe. He was by chance stationed on my ship just before the raid. I'm grateful to have spent some time with him just before he died. Our time on the ship that day was short, but it was one of the most meaningful moments I ever had with Darwin. He had two requests of me, Sally. One was that I take care of his mother. The second was that I deliver this letter to you."

Sally bowed her head and whispered, her words barely audible. "At home in the body, absent with the Lord. Absent from the body, present with the Lord."

"I'm sorry. I didn't hear you," Edward said.

"Just a Scripture verse from Second Corinthians."

"Whatever the verse was, I'm sure Darwin would have recognized it."

"Recognized it?" she said with tears rolling down her face. "He not only would recognize it, Captain, he's living it. Of that I am supremely confident. Your son is in a better place than all of us."

Edward hesitated. "If anyone made it to heaven, surely it was Darwin. He was a good person."

"Yes, he was good," Sally said. "But he's not there because he was good. He's there because of his relationship with our Lord and Savior—because there was a captain of his soul, so to speak."

"Yes, well. He was very religious. In fact, religion was one of the most important aspects of his life. And so are you, Sally. He left you this in his will." He handed her a black-and-gold King James Bible. "This book was the one he coveted most. He prepared a will just a week before he died and specifically instructed that this go to you. This shows how he felt about you."

Sally took the Bible and rested it in her lap. Tears were still rolling down her face. "I don't know what to say, Captain. I hate to take from your family such a personal heirloom."

"Don't be silly," Edward said. "We have plenty of

possessions to remind us of Darwin. There's one other thing I have for you, Sally. But before I give it to you, Petty Officer Richardson has something to say."

Sally looked at Richardson, and he choked back his emotions. She walked over to him and put her hands on his shoulders. "It's all right, Richardson. I understand how you feel."

"I feel so guilty."

"Guilty? Why, Richardson?"

"I feel like I took Darwin away from you."

"Took him away from me?"

"We were on the beach in Dieppe. We were attacking a German shore battery. A number of our shipmates had already been killed. We were huddled at the base of a seawall, ducked down. The machine-gun fire at our position was heavy. We had to get a hand grenade to a pillbox to take out the machine guns. Darwin volunteered to lead the charge into the teeth of their fire. But I said no. I told him we needed him too much. You see, our beachmaster had been killed and Darwin was the acting beachmaster at that point. I jumped over the wall and charged the pillbox. There was too much fire. The machine gun cut me off. Darwin should have left me there. But he charged over the wall. I was laying there helplessly on the ground, bleeding to death. The machine gunner took aim at me and started to fire, but Darwin jumped on me and covered my body with his. He took the bullets that should have been mine. I'd give anything if I could trade places with him and if he could be here with you."

Sally thought for a moment, seeming to absorb the impact of Darwin's heroics. Then she walked over to him, the big crippled man in the wheelchair, and kneeled down. "I'm not surprised, Richardson. It sounds just like something he would do," she said. "But don't feel guilty. We are all appointed to go at a certain time." Sally rubbed Richardson's shoulders as tears streamed down his face too. "Don't feel too badly for him, Richardson." She stood up. "Promise me you won't. He's in a better place."

"I know he is, Sally. I found Christ because of him. I am a changed man. He witnessed to me with his words. It was on the fantail of his father's ship, in the darkness of the morning before we boarded the landing craft for Dieppe. He told me that one or both of us would probably be killed. If he died, he said, he wanted me to remember his last words to me before battle, that Christ would offer me eternal life. He urged me to accept Christ, right there on the fantail of that ship, even as we crawled over the side of the ship and down into the landing craft. He kept saying 'Look to Jesus while you still can.'

"Even as we motored through those choppy waters toward the German pillboxes, he said, 'Turn to Jesus, Ian, before it's too late.' I let him down then. When I was brought back to the naval hospital, I had nowhere to go. So I began thinking about what he had said to me and what he did for me. I read through the Scriptures and came across the verse that says 'Greater love hath no man than he who would lay down his life for a friend.' It struck me there in the bed that day that Darwin gave his life for mine so I would have an opportunity to meet the Savior before I died. If I had to lose my legs to gain my salvation, so be it. God used Darwin to bring me home."

"I can tell you are changed," Sally said. "You know, Darwin and I used to pray for you when you were both in training. Darwin would come home with me after church on Sundays. We sat alone, just the two of us, right here in this room and prayed for your salvation. Darwin was so passionate in pleading with God to move on your heart. He loved you, Ian. Now I praise God that our prayers were answered."

Edward cleared his throat. "Sally, as I said, there is one other thing we have for you. Darwin's mother and I want you to have this." He handed the gift to her in a small, black box.

"It's beautiful," she said.

"Do you know what that is, Sally?" Edward asked.

"It looks like some sort of medal. The words *For Valour* are written on the cross. The cross has a crown and a lion engraved on it," she said.

"That, Sally, is the Victoria Cross," Edward pronounced the medal's name with reverence. "It's the highest medal awarded to a member of the Armed Forces of the British Commonwealth. It is awarded for heroism in battle. This was posthumously awarded to my son for his heroism at Dieppe, for his actions as described to you by Petty Officer Richardson. Juliana and I want you to keep it. It's yours."

Sally was speechless. The tears, which had dried up for a moment, were now flowing again.

"Captain, I'm honored that you and Mrs. McCloud would make such an offer to me. But Darwin was *your* son. This medal should be in your home. It is the highest honor which can be bestowed on a British military man. I know how much Darwin wanted to please you by his service in the military. I wouldn't feel right accepting such a priceless object."

"Sally, Juliana and I have talked about all that. You were the only woman my son ever loved. We believe you would have been our daughter-in-law had Darwin lived. Even though I'd never met you until today, and although Juliana has never met you, we feel like you are family. We have no other children. You will always be our last link to our son. Besides, we are keeping the citation signed by the King commemorating Darwin's actions in winning the Victoria Cross. It's already framed and hanging in Juliana's living room. That's enough of an heirloom."

"Captain, your gesture of kindness moves me," she said. "Perhaps I should consider keeping it but only with stipulations."

"Stipulations?"

"Yes," Sally said. "First, if at any time you or Mrs. McCloud change your mind and want the medal back for any reason at all, it's yours. I would give it back to you."

"I suppose that's reasonable," Edward said.

"There's one other thing," she said.

"What's that?" Edward asked.

"When he wrote his will, I'm sure Darwin would have never dreamed that he would be awarded Britain's highest medal. He would have wanted such a precious possession to go to his parents. I don't feel right about keeping the two most precious possessions that represented his life. So here's what I propose, Captain. I'll keep the cross if you and Mrs. McCloud will keep his Bible. It has so many markings and notes that he scribbled in the margins. It will be a treasure to remind you of your son."

"But Darwin willed that to you," Edward said.

"I know. And I also know how much he loved you." She hesitated and thought for a minute. "Tell you what, Captain. Why don't we handle the Bible the same way as we handle the cross? You take it, but if for any reason I'd like to come have a look at it to remind me of Darwin, you would let me do that, just like I'd give the cross to you if you ever wanted it for any reason. Deal?"

Edward smiled. "You drive a hard bargain, Sally. I suppose that would be fine. Perhaps if we each keep a treasured possession of his, it will give us incentive to keep in touch."

"A splendid idea," she said. "Every time I look at this Victoria Cross, which will be often, I will be reminded not only of Darwin, but also of you and Mrs. McCloud. I want you to remember that."

"Thank you, Sally." Edward's eyes started to mist. He appeared moved by her kindness. But he was the captain and could not afford to show emotions like Richardson could. They had done his duty. It was time to leave. "Now, then. Richardson and I have a long drive to make. We must be going now."

Sally hugged them both as they left. When their black car sped around the curve and out of sight, she looked down at the coveted cross in the palm of her hand. She stood there with her eyes closed and thought of Darwin.

42

Walter could not believe his eyes. "What are you doing here?"

"Is that all you're going to say?" She asked with a big smile.

"Come here," he said. They rushed into one another's arms as Margaret Morgan watched with joy.

"I'm so happy to see you," she said.

"I can't believe this," he said.

"England is *so* beautiful."

"It's a lot more beautiful with you here. But how did you get here? There are restrictions on civilian travel."

"Well, I knew you'd be all melancholy about missing homecoming weekend in Jamesville. So since you couldn't come home, I decided to bring home to you! We still have ships crisscrossing the Atlantic, you know."

"Crisscrossing the Atlantic filled with German submarines."

"Now Walter, have faith in our Navy. You're here, and now I'm here."

"But how did you do it? I don't understand. How did you cut through the red tape?"

Margaret Morgan cleared her throat.

"My apologies, Margaret. I'm so shocked that I seemed to have lost my good manners. Margaret Morgan, I'd like you to meet my wife, Jessie Brewer."

"We met earlier," Margaret said. "I don't know how you did it, Mrs. Brewer, but you have one happy Army officer here."

"Amen to that," Walter said.

"I'll leave you two alone. I'm sure you have some catching up to do."

Walter again took Jessie in his arms and peppered her with questions. "How did you afford this? And what about the kids?"

"The kids are with Ellie. And don't worry about all that, Walter. I'll explain at dinner tonight. I've only got two days here before I have to sail back. You're taking me to London tonight. We've got reservations at The Prince Albert Hotel in Kensington. Get packed and let's go."

Suddenly Walter's perspective about a weekend in London changed. "I think a weekend in London with the prettiest American in Britain is just what the doctor ordered."

Walter decided to spare no expense for the weekend. He still wasn't sure how Jessie had done it, but for her effort in getting to England, she deserved every penny—or in this case every pence—he would spend on her. He would take this weekend and give her memories she would never forget.

After a whirlwind tour of Westminster Abbey, St. Paul's, and Buckingham Palace, he took her to dinner at his favorite restaurant in London, the posh, French restaurant, *Palais du Jardin* in South Kensington. The food there was fabulous and expensive, and the atmosphere was romantic. Plus, he could show off his newly-polished French for Jessie.

The cab dropped them off in front of *Palais du Jardin* at eight o'clock. Walter took Jessie by the hand and led her into the posh lobby, where they were greeted by the French-speaking maître d'.

"*Bonsoir, monsieur et madam. Comment allez vous?*"

"*Nous allons tres bien, monsieur. Nous avons reservations pour deux personnes, s'il vous plait,*" Walter said.

"*Votre nom, monsieur?*" The waiter asked.

"Brewer," Walter said.

"*Ah, oui. Un moment, s'il vous plait.*" The waiter stepped away as Jessie put her arm around Walter's waist.

"I'm impressed," Jessie said. "But what did you just say to him?"

"I told him that you were my mistress."

"You did not."

"Oh yes, I did. Then I asked him what he thought of your legs."

"Oh, really? And just what did this little Frenchman have to say about that?"

"He said your legs and your smile are both ravishing." Walter snickered.

"It's good to see the Army hasn't ruined your sense of humor, Captain Brewer."

The waiter returned with two menus. "*Monsieur, nous avon un bon table près de la fenêtre pour vous. C'est d'accord?*"

"*Bien entendu, monsieur,*" Walter said.

"*Volià. Bon appétite,*" the host said as he walked away.

Happy to be alone with her finally, he reached across the table and took her hand. "So, I've got just one question."

"And what would that be, Captain Brewer?" She smiled at him again.

"Are you an angel, or are you real?"

"Your question presupposes that angels aren't real, Captain. Why couldn't I be a real angel?"

"You got me on that one, madam. Let me rephrase. Are you an angel, or are you human?"

"Do you want to take my pulse?"

"Now you're talking," he said.

Jessie laughed. "Frisky, are we?"

"Guilty as charged. But also curious. How? How did you do it? I mean you shouldn't be here. England is a war zone. Don't get me wrong. I'm glad to see you, but . . ."

"Okay. Let me get my purse." She reached down and

handed him a letter. "Three weeks ago, this came in the mail. This is how I did it."

Walter opened the envelope and unfolded the one-page letter.

Allison & Cranford, Attorneys
300 Neptune Road
Norfolk, Virginia 23502

Mrs. Jessie Brewer
St. Andrews Street
Jamesville, North Carolina 27846

August 31, 1943

Dear Mrs. Brewer,

Our firm serves as general counsel to the Reunification Foundation.

Founded by the generosity of an anonymous donor at the beginning of the war, the Reunification Foundation seeks to ease the pain of separation caused by war by providing spouses an opportunity to visit their loved ones on foreign soil during long periods of separation.

Because of the restrictions on civilian travel during wartime, the foundation must be very selective in the candidates it chooses for travel and works with the appropriate Federal agencies to ensure the maximum opportunity for safety.

We are pleased to announce that you have been chosen as a grant recipient for travel to England. Should you choose to accept, be advised that all expenses for your travel will be paid by the foundation.

In addition, the foundation will provide for two days and two nights at a London hotel of your choice and will afford you five hundred dollars cash to spend on the trip or in any manner that you so choose.

Please notify our offices immediately if you choose to accept. We will need two to three weeks to coordinate with the appropriate congressional and military authorities to gain a diplomatic exemption for you, which will allow you to travel on a United States ship back and forth to England. The trip will take ten days each way, so you should arrange your affairs accordingly.

Please accept our congratulations, Mrs. Brewer. We look forward to hearing from you.

Very truly yours,
F. Eugene Allison, Esq.

"This is amazing," Walter said. "I've never heard of this organization."

"I hadn't either," she said. "But Mr. Allison said the organization was very small and had to be very discreet in their operations. Otherwise, he said they would get a flood of requests they couldn't handle."

"But if they're in Norfolk and you're in Jamesville, how did they find out about you?"

"I don't know. I asked Mr. Allison about that, but he was very secretive. He said the organization would fail if it lost its anonymity. Plus, he said that the foundation's ability to work through Congress, the War Department, and the State Department might be compromised if too much information is revealed."

"I've never seen anything like this," Walter said. "But you're here, and that's all that matters."

"It's a miracle from heaven," she said.

"It has to be—that you, out of so many thousands, were chosen."

It had been a fairy-tale weekend for Walter and Jessie. Not even their honeymoon trip to Washington, D.C. all those years ago could compare to this. Unfortunately, Sunday morning came too quickly.

Walter grabbed Jessie's bags and took them down the elevator to the lobby of The Prince Albert Hotel. She had a ship to catch, and he had to get to his men for a parachuting exercise at noon.

He kissed her one last time. Then the black cab disappeared into the streets of London.

On Christmas Eve, 1943, Walter received a package from the United States. It was a fruitcake from Jessie.

December 10, 1943

Merry Christmas Sweetheart,

Thought I'd forgotten our Christmas morning tradition, did you? Not a chance. Think of us when you have a slice of this for breakfast with your coffee Christmas morning. We'll be thinking of you.

By the way, when you get back I have another present for you which has been specially ordered but isn't quite ready for transatlantic shipment.

In fact, this present was specially ordered from England. I'm sure this token of the U.K. will serve as a glorious reminder of your tour of duty in Europe.

This surprise present will be delivered, not by Santa Claus, but by the stork! The stork, by the way, prefers warm weather. He should be stopping by Jamesville sometime in June.

Congratulations and Merry Christmas. Number five is on the way!

Love,
Jessie

It had been years since Walter had a swig of Jimmy William's eggnog. Suddenly he was feeling the urge again.

43

Two years ago, Heinrick could not forsee Rommel's defeat in Africa. But the Allies poured in more men, more tanks, and dispatched two brilliant warriors—the American George S. Patton and the Briton Bernard Montgomery—to double-team the Desert Fox.

Heinrick thought Rommel was brilliant enough to single-handedly defeat either man in a one-on-one matchup. The chess match became unfair, however, with the entrance of George S. Patton, the American general from California whose aggressive battlefield tactics had earned him the nickname "Old Blood and Guts."

With Monty and Patton pounding his flanks, Erwin Rommel and his staff retreated from Africa and relocated in Normandy. There, Rommel took charge of building German defenses for the great invasion of Allied troops which was soon to come.

Rommel believed—and stated many times in staff meetings—that an invading force must be pinned down and beaten on the beaches, much in the way that the Canadians and British had been turned back at Dieppe. "Pin them down on the beaches," Rommel had said, "and the invasion will fail. Let them break through the lines, and the Reich's hold over Continental Europe is in jeopardy."

To pin them on the beaches, Rommel's engineers would build the great Atlantic Wall, an impregnable defensive system along the French coast that would thwart the great invasion of Western powers the whole world was awaiting. Rommel himself began designing the defenses.

Fields were flooded to drown paratroopers. Barbed wire, mines, steel spikes, and booby traps were laid all along the Normandy coast. Demolition charges were placed under bridges.

It was Christmas Eve in France. The war had been raging for four years. From his intelligence post in the town of Carentan, on the Cotentin Peninsula in Normandy, Heinrick thought about Ingrid and the girls. Then he poured over the huge map of the Cotentin Peninsula. The land mines and the booby traps were marked by red x's all along the coastline. Barbed wire was shown in green. Shore batteries and airfields were in black.

The fields that had been flooded were marked by vertical blue lines. This is where the Nazi's last stand would repel the Allies back into the sea and end the war.

Heinrick would use the map for a scheduled briefing with Rommel in one hour. Rommel would want all the details, down to the depth of water in the flood zones and the number of explosives on each bridge. Although he was satisfied with his preparations and was ready for any question Rommel might have, he felt a nagging depression in the bottom of his stomach.

He wasn't sure if his despondency was from losing to the Allies in Libya or from the fact that he had been away from Ingrid and the girls for a second consecutive Christmas. He reminded himself that he was at least on the same continent with his family this year. That didn't seem to help.

The only thing that lifted his spirits was the little black book he had taken off the dead British commando at Dieppe. He sat on his cot and opened it.

DAS EVANGELIUM NACH LUKAS

8. Und es waren Hirten in derselben Gegend auf dem Felde bei den Hürden, die hüteten des Nachts ihre Herde.

9. Und der Engel des Herrn trat zu ihnen, und die Klarheit des Herrn leuchtete um sie; und sie fürchteten sich sehr.

10. Und der Engel sprach zu ihnen: Fürchtet euch nicht! Siehe, ich verkündige euch große Freude, die allem Volk widerfahren wird;

11. denn euch ist heute der Heiland geboren, welcher ist Christus, der Herr, in der Stadt Davids.

12. Und das habt zum Zeichen: ihr werdet finden das Kind in Windeln gewickelt und in einer Krippe liegen.

Heinrick closed the book.
His soul was at peace.
He would sleep well tonight.

44

Dressed in full battle gear, Walter sat in the rear of the C-47 transport. Other members of E Company piled onto the plane, their faces smeared in black, guns strapped over their shoulders.

The whining of propellers was the only sound heard. This mission had been scrubbed several times over the last few days because of bad weather. All the practicing, waiting, and delays had grated on their collective nerve. The men of E Company were ready for their first taste of combat. If the weather cooperated, tonight all the training, firing, and practice jumps were about to be put to the test.

In the pit of his stomach, Walter knew this mission would go. The dark skies were clear of cloud cover. No reason for another delay. He glanced at the wallet-sized picture of Jessie and the kids then stashed it back in his shirt pocket when the plane started rolling across the grass airfield. Live or die, that's where the picture would remain. Just over his heart.

Within minutes, the C-47 was airborne, joining hundreds of other planes hauling thousands of paratroopers through the dark skies of Southern England. The planes assembled in geese-like V formation as they prepared to cross the English Channel. In a big steep loop, the plane banked out of its circular pattern. Walter's pocket watch showed five past midnight. It was time.

"Gentlemen, I've been ordered to read a top secret message from General Eisenhower."

Walter looked down the aisle of the aircraft, studying the blackened faces of his men. The whites of their eyes glowing against the black grease on their faces bored a hundred holes through his heart. Realizing that many of these men would be killed before sunrise, he choked back his emotions as he read.

> Soldiers, sailors and airmen of the Allied Expeditionary Forces: You are about to embark upon the Great Crusade, toward which we have striven these many months. The eyes of the world are upon you. The hopes and prayers of liberty-loving people everywhere march with you. In company with our brave Allies and brothers in arms on other fronts, you will bring about the destruction of the German war machine, the elimination of Nazi tyranny over oppressed peoples of Europe, and security for ourselves in a free world. We will accept nothing less than full victory! Good Luck! And let us all beseech the blessing of Almighty God upon this great and noble undertaking.

He sat down and peered out the tiny window in the rear door of the aircraft. Hundreds of green lights on the wingtips of the C-47s blinked in the night. Down below, the black, choppy waters of the channel glistened in the moonlight.

The plane descended dramatically as it approached the French coastline—easily within range of German antiaircraft batteries. Walter looked out again. The water below disappeared under a thick cloud cover. Turbulence rocked and jolted the aircraft.

From the cockpit, the plane's first officer signaled Walter.

"Ten minutes to drop zone, gentlemen!" Walter said. "Stamp out those cigarettes and be ready."

What felt like an instant later, the first officer flashed another hand signal.

"Five minutes to drop zone gentlemen," Walter shouted over the hum of the plane's engines.

The mid-air explosion under the wing knocked Walter to the floor. The plane yawed then rocked as the pilot struggled to regain control.

Walter pulled himself up and looked out the rear window. Tracer bullets from the ground lit the sky like fireworks on the Fourth of July. Two other transports in flames were nosediving toward the ground.

With the C-47 back under control, the first officer held up two fingers. "Two minutes to drop zone," Walter said. "Line up. Watch for the green light."

Another explosion rocked the right side of the plane.

"Mayday! Mayday! Mayday! We're hit!" The pilot's words reverberated throughout the fuselage. Through the tiny window, Walter saw the left engine in flames. He *had* to make a decision. They were not yet over the drop zone, but delaying the jump could cost them their lives.

"Jumpmaster! Open the door! Men, follow me!"

The rear door flung open as Walter leaped into the blackness, falling to an invisible earth. Tracers whizzed all around him. As his chute deployed, he looked up for his plane. Both engines were ablaze. A blinding explosion ripped the plane's underbelly. Walter grimaced as the fireball plummeted to the ground.

There's no way the whole company made it out.

Floating to the darkened French countryside below, he prayed for his men, dead and alive. Then he looked down. The vague images of some buildings slowly rose out of the black.

Looks like a farm building. Maybe a barn and a silo.

He heard machine-gun fire. He started falling faster. The bullets were shredding his parachute. Suddenly, his descent became a roller coaster ride. His stomach leapt through his throat. He was in a blind free fall. He couldn't tell if he was falling head first or feet first. He started praying again. A blow to his head ignited stars brighter than all the tracer bullets he had dodged. Then there was only darkness.

45

He awoke with great pain in his right ankle. He opened his eyes to find himself lying on his back on a cot in a dim room.

Squinting, he tried to make out the blurred images around him. He started to sit up. A hand came out of the shadows and grabbed him by the throat, shoving him back onto the cot. Someone held a pistol to his face.

"*Vous êtes américain ou vous êtes allemange?*" Are you American or are you German? The hushed demand sounded urgent and furious, and Walter couldn't tell if the angry whisper was the voice of a man or a woman.

He strained his eyes at the vague silhouette of a human figure.

The attacker pressed the pistol into Walter's skull and repeated the whispered demand, squeezing Walter's neck harder. "*Repondez maintenant! Vous êtes américain ou vous êtes alle-mange?*" Answer now! Are you American or are you German?

If the gunman were a Nazi or a German collaborator, a truthful answer could cost him his life. If he were French Resistance, no answer could mean the same fate.

As Walter hesitated, the attacker tightened his grip into a choking vice. Walter winced as the man's fingernails dug under the flesh below his throat.

"*Vous êtes américain ou vous êtes allemange? Repondez maintenant ou mourez maintenant!*" Are you American or are you German? Answer now or die now!

Walter *had* to answer. If he was going to die, at least he would die proclaiming his country. A verse of Scripture came rushing to his mind—*The truth shall set you free.*

Gasping for the breath necessary to muster a reply, he prepared to die. "*Je suis américain.*" I am American.

The attacker loosened his tight hold around Walter's neck, but the gun barrel remained jammed in his head.

Lord, if Your will is to take me tonight, please protect my family until we meet again.

He felt long hair brush across his face and heard a strange sniffling in the dark.

Either pull the trigger or remove the gun. Lord, give me wisdom.

Walter whispered, "*Vive La France!*" Long Live France!

Silence.

"*Repetez,*" the voice demanded.

"*Vive La France.*"

The sniffling turned to sobbing. The gunman removed his weapon as Walter took a deep breath

"*Vive l'États-Unis. Maintenant et pour toujours,*" the aggressor said. Long live the United States. Now and forever.

With the muffled sounds of mortar fire and rifle shots echoing in the distance, the gunman rested his head on Walter's chest.

Then the person whispered again. "*Je suis désolé. Je ne comprends pas la langue anglais trés bien.*" I am sorry. I do not understand English very well. The voice had softened, and the tone was feminine.

"*Ce n'est pas un problème. Je ne comprends pas trés bien le francais.*" That's not a problem. I don't understand French very well either.

Silence again. The sounds of war grew closer. Perhaps the Frenchman was distracted by the approaching sounds of war.

"Est-ce que je peux avoir de la petit lumière, s'il vous plait?"
Walter asked. Can I have a little light please?

"Oui. Un moment," came the whispered response. The
shadowy figure struck a match to a small candle beside the bed.
In the flickering candlelight, Walter saw that the long hair he
felt was not the ponytail of an eccentric Parisian artist but of
an attractive young woman.

He strained for a better look. The girl had disheveled
blonde hair and looked to be in her twenties. She was beautiful
in the candlelight. At first glance, she reminded him of Ellie.

She wiped her eyes and smiled at her first sight of Walter.
"Je m'appelles Marie Claire." My name is Mary Claire.

*"Moi je m'appelles Capitaine Walter Brewer, de l'armée de l'États-
Unis, à votre service, madame."* My name is Captain Walter Brewer
of the United States Army, at your service, madam.

"Enchantez, Capitaine." Pleased to meet you, Captain.

"Avec plasir." With pleasure. *"Quelle heur est-il* Marie Claire?"
What time is it, Marie Claire?

"Il est deux heures moin le quart." 1:45 a.m.

"Où sont les nazis?" Where are the Nazis?

*"Tout les nazi shiens sont pres ici. Je deteste les Nazis. Restez ici
s'il vous plait."* All the Nazi dogs are near here. I despise the
Nazis. Wait here please.

Marie Claire left the room, leaving Walter alone with the
flickering candle. He pulled himself up to look around. The
sharp throbbing in the back of his head intensified as he sat
upright. He could feel a very sore lump on the back of his head.

With the small flame burning, he saw the shadowy image
of his gun, the M1A1 retractable stock carbine issued to paratroopers. He pivoted around on the bed with his feet hanging
to the floor.

The pressure on his right foot felt like a knife jabbing his
ankle. It was stiff and swollen but not enough to keep him out
of action.

"Welcome to France, Captain." The sweet sound of the
English language, albeit with a thick French accent, came
rushing out of the dark. Marie Claire had returned with a short
balding man who looked fiftyish.

"My name is Jacques. I am with the French Resistance. I understand you have met my niece already."

"I didn't know Marie Claire was your niece, but it was a meeting I will never forget."

"I hope you weren't too startled, Captain. Since the air-drops started a couple hours ago, word has spread that Germans have stolen uniforms off dead American paratroopers and are masquerading as U.S. soldiers. There have also been rumors that the Germans are bringing in paratroopers from Berlin to reinforce the coast. So with all the chaos going on out there, we are trying our best to identify who's who."

"Marie Claire was able to do that," Walter said. "It's a good thing I could speak some French."

Jacques smiled. "My apologies if her tactics were too aggressive. She is paranoid because the Nazis executed her husband. She puts nothing past them and is slow to trust anyone."

"I'm very sorry. But right now I need to regroup with my unit to carry out our mission. Can you help me?"

"I will try, but there are no members of your company in the immediate vicinity. Our network indicates that the parachute drops have been sporadic—most landings have been between two and five miles from the coast. You are eight miles inland of Utah Beach. That's one of the reasons we thought you might be German. Your plane must have overshot your drop zone. This area is still crawling with Krauts, and other than you, no Americans have yet been spotted this far from the beach."

"My plane blew up and crashed. But I'm sure others jumped. They had enough time."

"They're dead, Captain. Other than you, we've found a dozen dead bodies of paratroopers in the fields. It looks like they were shot before they hit the ground. All dead. You were the only one we found alive. I am sorry."

Walter felt like he'd been punched in the gut. "I thought we had undershot the drop zone." Stunned by the cold, harsh reality of the death of his men, he wanted to cry but had to focus for the sake of his mission. "But this could play to our advantage, Jacques."

"How so?"

"As news of the paratrooper landings reaches the Krauts, they will re-deploy closer to the beaches, thus thinning out their position here and leaving us with more operating room. Our mission is simple. Before sunrise, we must destroy their communication lines. We must block their ability to communicate with Berlin or other outposts north and east of here. We need to strike the local communications hubs. Do you know where they are located?"

"Captain, both the local telegraph and telephone hubs are located at the train station. They are not heavily guarded. There is one German guard outside the station and two German officers operating the hubs in the same office. We need to take out three Krauts to get to the control boxes."

"How far away is the station?"

"About one mile, Captain."

"Any other men available?"

"My brother Pierre is next door. He can help. There are others, but it may take a while to round them up."

"We don't have time for that. Can Pierre handle a gun?"

"He's Marie Claire's father. He taught her everything she knows about marksmanship."

"I'm a believer, then." Walter smiled. "That would make it three on three."

"Three on three, assuming we can take out the Krauts, blow the facility, and then ward off the other three hundred within the six block vicinity," Jacques said.

"Jacques, we've got to disrupt those communications even if we die in the process."

"I'm willing," Jacques said.

Walter felt a surge of adrenaline. "Let's go."

46

GERMAN MILITARY COMMUNICATIONS HUB
COTENTIN PENINSULA
CARENTAN, FRANCE
0200 HOURS
JUNE 6, 1944

Inside the hub, Heinrick and his assistant Captain Adolf Rödl listened for telegraph and voice communications from the coast.

For the last two hours, there had been strange reports of parachute droppings around the coast at Normandy. Some of the drops, it turned out, were rubber dummies the Allies had used. These rubber dolls somehow, by the use of Allied electronic trickery, fired blanks and sparkled upon impact with the ground. Still, there were other reports of live paratroopers dropping at various points, and German antiaircraft fire had been active.

The situation was confusing, to say the least. It bothered Heinrick that General Rommel was not in Normandy. The field marshal had gone home for Frau Rommel's birthday, not expecting the invasion anytime soon because of inclement weather.

On paper, Heinrick agreed with his boss. A strike against Normandy on the heels of the stormy weather over the channel defied military logic. The German high brass expected the attack near Pas-de-Calais, one hundred fifty miles to the northeast, at the shortest point across the channel from Dover. Between Dover and Calais, the channel was about twenty-six miles across, close enough to swim.

Perhaps the Allied fireworks during the last couple of hours was a diversionary tactic designed to make the Germans think Normandy was a viable military option. Heinrick wasn't sure what it all meant. Still, he felt nervous about the whole ordeal as he and Captain Rödl monitored communications traffic from their command post.

"Any updates?" Heinrick demanded.

"*Nein, Herr* Major. Just sporadic parachute drops closer to the coast."

"Numbers, Captain. We need the numbers. Is this an exercise or a prelude to the real invasion? We must accurately assess the situation. I must inform General Rommel," Heinrick said.

"The field marshal is at his wife's birthday party, remember? I'm trying to raise Rommel now for you, sir," Rödl said.

"Keep trying. If we can't get Rommel, we must notify Berlin."

"*Jawohl, Herr* Major."

The gunshot from outside startled them.

The Nazi officers looked at each other in shock. They reached for their sidearms. The carbine pumped several rounds of 30-caliber lead into both their stomachs. As they slumped to the floor in a pool of blood, the intruder yanked the metal pin with his teeth and tossed the grenade at the communications control center. He stepped outside the door and held his ears. As the deafening explosion rocked the building, a woman rushed back into the room.

Heinrick's ears were ringing in a loud whine, almost like a muted siren. On his back on the floor, he managed to raise his right hand to his lower abdomen. He could feel the warm blood gushing onto his hand. He could feel the pain subsiding. His senses were becoming numb.

His vision blurred, but he could make out the silhouette of the woman bending over him. He could feel her hand reaching into his jacket, taking papers from his inside pockets.

He closed his eyes.

"Marie Claire, get out of there!" Walter shouted. "We've got to go! Krauts will be all over this place."

Dressed in black to camouflage her appearance against the darkness of the night, she rushed back out with some papers in hand. "Come with me, Captain!"

With sirens blaring and searchlights crisscrossing the front of the disabled communications hub, Walter hobbled into the streets behind Marie Claire as bullets ricocheted and riddled the rock and pavement around their feet. He had never seen a woman move so fast. Like an Olympic sprinter, Marie Claire darted to the left into a dark alley adjacent to the building. His eyes glued to her blonde hair bouncing against her black pullover, Walter followed in step.

The black gulf of the alleyway seemed to swallow her. From his position, he turned around and looked back into the streets. The place was crawling with German soldiers. He was a hunted man, suddenly lost and alone with no Allies in a foreign country. Returning to the street would mean suicide. He would take his chances in the alley. Pulling the carbine from his shoulder, he crouched down and jogged into the pitch blackness of the alley.

"Captain, here!"

Walter was never so relieved to hear a woman's voice. "*Où as tu, Marie Claire?*" Where are you, Marie Claire? "*Je ne peux pas vous vois,*" he whispered. I can't see you.

"*Ici. Ici!*" Here, here.

Marie Clarie's hand felt soft, like a guardian angel in the midst of hell. She led him like a blind man deep into the alley. After a few seconds, she placed his hands on something leather. It was the seat of a motorcycle.

"Get on," she said.

"What?"

"I said get on."

Walter got on the bike and wrapped his arms around Marie Claire's waist as she kickstarted the bike.

The rumbling of the engine echoed off the walls. Marie

Claire revved the engine, and she and Walter sped deep into the alley.

"Hang on, Captain," Marie Claire said. "This alley empties into a back street. If we make it there before the Germans, we'll turn right and head out into the countryside."

"You *do* speak English?"

The bike broke out of the alley onto the back street. Not a German in sight. Marie Claire banked to the right and sped out of town.

"What was that?" she asked, as her blonde hair blew all in his face.

"You speak English, don't you?"

"So what's the big deal, Captain? Obviously, you speak French."

"But you made me think you only spoke French."

"A girl must have some secrets. Besides, this is France. Why should I speak English in my own country?"

"But you were going to shoot me if I'd not responded in French."

"I'm not saying what I would have done to you, Captain. We'll have to leave that up to the imagination."

"But you made me think you were a man."

"I never said that. Are you disappointed I'm not a man?"

Walter ignored the question. "So what *would* you have done if I'd not spoken in French?"

"I would have lit a match to see what you looked like. If you were ugly, I would have shot your head off. If you were cute, I would have made you a slave to the French Republic."

"I'm not touching that one," he said. "So where are you taking me?"

"To a barn," Marie Claire said.

"A barn? I need to rejoin my men."

"That will have to wait till tomorrow, Captain. Right now, there are too many Germans between here and the coast. Besides, you've already accomplished your main mission. You've taken out the most important communications depot in this region. We will get some sleep tonight, and I will help you find the other Americans at sunlight."

"Who else is at this barn?"

"If you're worried about the Germans, trust me. They will never find us. Neither will anyone else. For tonight, it's just you, me, and the cows."

47
NEAR CARENTAN, FRANCE
JUNE 6, 1944

Marie Claire rubbed her eyes and lifted her head from the bed of hay. "What time is it?"

"Five a.m." Walter pulled out a cigar, then stepped away from the hay and lit it. He'd never smoked growing up but started lighting up an occasional stogie while stationed in England because the burning leaves reminded him of his grandfather's tobacco barn back home. "By now, it's started." He took a first puff.

"Started? I thought it started last night. At least it seemed that way to me."

"I'm glad one of us was able to sleep," he said.

"Last night was so exciting you couldn't even catch a little nap, *mon capitan*?"

"Right. We blow up a communications station, shoot three Nazis, the place is crawling with Germans, and I'm supposed to sleep."

"It wasn't like *this* place was crawling with Germans. I mean, I don't remember seeing anyone here except you and me."

"You wouldn't have noticed the Nazis if they'd walked in the front door," he said.

"I would hope not. Would you?" she asked.

"I'd hope *so*. I'm a soldier."

"I'm disappointed," she said.

"Why?"

"I thought *I* was the reason you couldn't sleep," she said.

Walter took another puff from his cigar. "You know what?"

"What?"

"You remind me of someone."

"Your wife?"

"Not hardly."

"Your lover?" The playful look on her face disappeared. "What's that booming sound?"

"I don't hear anything," he said.

"Listen." She opened the door of the barn. "In the distance. Do you hear it?"

"How far are we from the beach?" he asked.

"About eight miles."

Walter cupped his right ear and listened. "That is the sound of American battleships firing on the Germans. What you're hearing is the sound of freedom."

BOOM!

The sudden explosion rocked the side of the barn.

"The sound of freedom is getting too close for comfort," Marie Claire said.

The screeching of inbound rockets whistled through the air.

BOOM! BOOM! BOOM!

The barn rocked again.

"Hit the deck," he yelled.

"What's going on?"

"Sounds like mortar fire," he said.

"That's impossible. I'm sure the Germans don't know about this place."

"Somebody knows about it," he said.

"Who would shoot at a brick barn?"

"I don't think it's the barn they're shooting at. Are there any windows?"

"Up in the ceiling. There are openings in every direction. You can see all around."

"Can I get off a shot from there?"

"Yes."

"How high up is it?"

"About twenty feet," she said.

"How do I get up there?"

"You have to climb up the side of the wall. There." She pointed to the wall just beside where they were lying. "Put your feet in the holes between the bricks and hang on tight. But you can do it. I used to do it when I was a child many times."

"Great." He took a big gulp. "Stay here and stay low. Don't move."

"Kissing the dirt floor of a barn wasn't what I had in mind," she said.

"There you go again, Ellie Williams."

"What did you call me?" she asked.

"Nothing."

Walter held his breath and started climbing. Outside the barn, the sound of gunshots cracked the morning air. He reached the wooden loft just below the ceiling and peered through a ventilation hole.

"Looks like we've got company," he said.

"What?"

"German scout party. Seven or eight of 'em. Huddled in a trench about a hundred yards from us. That's the source of our mortar fire."

"Do they know we're here?"

"Don't know. They seem focused on something across the field," he said.

"What?"

"Hang on." Walter crawled on his belly across the wooden planks to the opposite side of the barn. "Good news. We've got a dozen U.S. paratroopers in a trench on the other side of the field. Looks like we're in the middle of a crossfire. I don't think either side can see the other too well because of the hill in the field. Problem is the Germans have the mortar launcher."

"What do you want me to do?"

"Keep kissing the dirt. I'm gonna get a shot off."

"Won't that reveal our position?"

"It might," he said.

"Be careful."

He crawled back to the other side of the barn and looked out again. Ten German soldiers were lined up in a ditch side-by-side. Their rifles were aimed at the Americans. To their right, two more enemy soldiers manned a portable rocket launcher.

Captain Walter Brewer had a perfect vantage point from which to fire on the Germans and enough ammunition. The problem was numbers. He could not afford to miss or be seen.

He cocked the carbine. Marie Claire flinched as the bolt action echoed through the barn.

His hand steady, he drew a bead on the German soldier's head to the far right of the trench. This poor soul was about to have his brains splattered by a 30-caliber round. Whatever happened after that would depend on Walter's marksmanship and how fast the Germans reacted to the sniper in the barn.

Ready.

Aim.

Walter felt his finger shaking against the steel trigger. He ripped off six shots in rapid succession, sweeping from left to right.

Six German soldiers lay slumped in the ditch, bleeding. He ducked behind the brick wall, expecting a mortar round from the Germans. When the mortar fire did not come, he looked out and saw American paratroopers charging across the field toward the barn, shooting at the retreating Germans.

Walter ducked back inside and cringed at the sound of two whistling mortars fired at the barn. The mortars exploded in the field just in front of the building, shaking the ground, followed by the sound of repeated rifle shots from outside.

"Stay down," he said, then crept over to the ventilation hole for another look. The Americans had overrun the barn and were shooting at the Germans' backs. The outnumbered enemy dropped under the barrage of American gunfire. Within seconds, it was over. An eerie silence blanketed the scene, as the American platoon stared at the bodies of the dead soldiers strewn across the field.

"American Paratrooper! In the barn!" Walter yelled.

The American guns turned toward the brick barn.

"Identify yourself, soldier," cried the company commander.

"Captain Walter Brewer, 506th Parachute Infantry Regiment, 101st Airborne, Company Z."

"You okay, Captain?"

"Yes, sir. The first six Nazis are compliments of my carbine, sir."

"Good turkey shootin', Captain. I'm coming in to get you. My men will cover."

Walter scampered back down to the ground as the officer opened the door of the barn.

"Captain Brewer. Is that you?"

Walter smiled at the familiar face of his old buddy from Fort Bragg.

"Lieutenant Colonel Patterson. It's great to see you, sir." The last time Walter had seen Johnny Patterson, he had gotten an earful about Babe Ruth, the Yankees, and how Patterson had embarrassed the Babe in spring training. Walter was a corporal then and Patterson a captain. As cocky as Patterson had come across, he looked like the face of a guardian angel now.

"I was wondering where our help was coming from. My men are good, but they aren't that good."

"In defense of your men, I was about a hundred yards closer to the Germans. If they'd seen me, this barn would be rubble."

"I remember your marksmanship scores at Bragg. That's one of the reasons we picked you up for OCS. But that carbine of yours isn't exactly a sniper rifle. I'll make sure you get a medal for this, Brewer. In fact, maybe I should put myself in for a medal for good judgment. Looks like my decision to recommend you for Airborne was a good one. Come to think of it, *all* my decisions are pretty good." Patterson laughed and slapped Walter on the back.

Standing unnoticed in the corner of the barn, Marie Claire cleared her throat loud enough to grab Walter's attention.

"Colonel, I want you to meet Marie Claire."

Patterson grinned even wider and slapped Walter on the back again. "See, I was right, wasn't I, Captain?"

"Sir?"

"When you were in my office at Bragg, I told you that being a paratrooper would make you popular with the dames."

"Sir, it's not what it seems. My plane overshot its target and we—"

"Save it, Brewer. I don't blame you. I'd do the same thing. I mean war's a stressful time. You were out here behind enemy lines at night without your unit. A gorgeous French dame comes along and offers you some 'refuge' until you can rejoin your army. Hey, maybe I should put you in for a medal for good taste and for diplomacy with our French allies." Patterson laughed and slapped Walter on the back yet again.

"But sir, I was on a military mission last night. And besides that, I'm married."

Patterson bent over laughing. "Brewer, we were *all* on a military mission last night. And we're *all* married. Don't worry about it. Besides, you just picked off seven or eight Krauts and probably saved the lives of everyone left in this company. You know what they say about all work and no play. So what if the play comes before the work? You sure earned your paycheck this morning. Yes, indeedy."

Walter gave up. Patterson was going to believe whatever his imagination dictated, and if that made him happy, fine. "Yes, sir, understood. Sir, request permission to join your company."

"Granted with pleasure, Captain. I could use a good XO. Grab your things. We're making our way toward the beaches."

Walter looked at Marie Claire. "Thank you for all your help. We couldn't have destroyed the communications depot without you."

"I want to go with you. I know the area, and I can help your company."

"Too dangerous. You stay here and take care of your uncle

and your father. Maybe we'll meet again. Our troops are coming back to rescue your town."

With tears in her eyes, she pulled an envelope from under her shirt and handed it to him. "Here are some things for you. A souvenir of France to remember our night together. Don't open it until you get back to America. Plus, my address is inside."

He hugged her and she kissed him on the cheek.

"Good bye, Marie Claire."

She stood by the barn, watching Walter and the Americans disappear over the hill, marching north to the coast.

"*Au revoir mon, beau ami. J'espere que vous retournez tot.*" Good-bye, my handsome friend. I hope you come back soon.

48
CARENTAN, FRANCE
JUNE 26, 1944

Walter sat on the stone bench in front of an old church. In the twenty days since he'd parachuted into this country, he had not stopped to think. There had been no time for thinking. Only time for fighting.

By the twenty-sixth of June, the Allies had seized control of the Normandy coastline and were pushing the German Army into a stubborn but steady retreat. Reinforcements from England had provided Walter's battalion with a day of much-needed furlough. It couldn't have come at a better time. They were all dog-tired and needed the rest.

While Johnny "Madman" Patterson and other members of the battalion staff spent their day off imbibing the twin delicacies of French living—wine and women—Walter puffed on a cigar and penned a letter home. It was his first letter since arriving in France.

Dear Jessie,

How war numbs the conscience of a man. As I write to you this afternoon, I find myself sitting in front of a small stone church in Carentan, France. It's a Catholic church, as most are here, and it's hundreds of years old.

You would think I would be here with some reverence. But here I am in the church courtyard smoking a cigar. Something I vowed never to do.

In my first two days here, I killed eight Germans. I shot two in the stomach and six in the head. I've shot dozens since then. These were men just like me. Some with families, I suppose. I know I had to do it, but why don't I feel guilty?

He reached into his shirt pocket for the picture of Jessie and the kids. The wrinkled snapshot had been his lifeline for the last month.

"Captain Brewer?"

The young communications clerk in the crisp, freshly-starched uniform with corporal's stripes was standing by the bench.

"That's me."

"Captain Walter Brewer, 506th PIR, Company Z?"

Walter peered for a moment at the young soldier with the enthusiastic look on his face. "You haven't seen any action yet, have you, Corporal?"

"No, sir. I just arrived from the U.K. But I'm looking forward to combat, sir."

"Welcome to France, Corporal."

"Thank you, sir."

"Anyway, you've got the right Walter Brewer. What can I do for you?"

"Sir, I have new orders for you."

"I've been expecting a reassignment. I'm a company commander without a company. They're all dead. That's what you are looking forward to if you're looking forward to combat."

"I'm sorry, sir," the corporal said after a moment of awkward silence. His enthusiasm for a war he had not yet seen firsthand had now been dampened.

"Let's see what you've got." Walter motioned as the corporal handed him an envelope. He unfolded the papers and studied them.

"England?" Walter was stunned.

"I've been ordered to accompany you there," the corporal said.

"I just came from England," Walter protested. "The war's in the opposite direction, Corporal. What's this all about?"

"All I know is that we have a Jeep waiting for you, sir, and a C-47 on the airfield with its engines already running."

"Is Lieutenant Colonel Strayer aware of this?" He was referring to Lieutenant Colonel Robert L. Strayer, Second Battalion Commanding Officer.

"Colonel Strayer is being informed of your situation right now."

"Very well, Corporal. Lead the way."

The C-47 lifted off the French airfield carrying only Walter, his escort, and the two pilots. As the plane banked over the green French countryside before heading back across the Channel, Walter wondered why he was being plucked out of France and why he rated a personal escort.

Whatever the reason, it must be significant. General Patton was still in England. Maybe he was being assigned to the staff of Ol' Blood and Guts.

Better yet, perhaps he was being called back to London for an assignment to Ike's staff. After all, he was briefly at Supreme Allied Headquarters last year while he attended the London School of Economics. That scenario made more sense.

As the C-47 touched down at Greenham Common airfield in Southern England, Walter mentally prepared himself to meet with the top brass in the Supreme Allied Command.

"Welcome back, Captain." The Army lieutenant standing at the base of the aircraft snapped Walter a salute.

"I wish I knew why I was back," Walter replied.

"We have a Jeep waiting for you, sir. If you'll come with me."

Walter and the corporal climbed in the Jeep with the officer and sped across the runway to a hangar. The lieutenant led Walter to a hallway inside one of the hangars.

"I'll take it from here, Corporal," the lieutenant said.

"You're dismissed. Report to headquarters and get washed up. Your next orders will be waiting for you there."

"Thank you, sir." The corporal shot salutes at Walter and the lieutenant. "Good luck, Captain."

"You too, Corporal," Walter returned the salute. "Godspeed to you."

"You too, sir." The corporal turned and walked away.

The lieutenant looked at Walter. "There's someone waiting for you inside this office, sir."

Walter checked his uniform and then opened the door. Were his eyes playing tricks on him?

"Ellie?"

She rushed to him and wrapped her arms around him.

He had not been so shocked since the day in Rocky Mount when he returned from his honeymoon and found Ellie with Billy at the train station.

"I don't understand. What are you doing here?"

She looked at him with those big blue eyes that had ensnared him in her web all those years ago.

"I'm sorry, Walter. I couldn't let you hear it from the Red Cross."

"The Red Cross? What do you mean? Spit it out, Ellie."

"It's about Jessie. She went into labor prematurely."

"What do you mean? Is she okay? Ellie, she *is* okay, isn't she?"

"She went into labor on June sixth. Dr. Papineau rushed to Jamesville and tried everything he could. They took her to the hospital in Plymouth. The nurses and doctors worked so hard, Walter. All throughout the night on the seventh they were with her. In her last breath, she called your name. I'm so sorry."

Walter stood speechless. With Ellie's arms still around him, he stared upward, watching a ceiling fan go round and round. There were no words. There were no feelings. Only numbness.

"We tried to notify you, but the invasion had started, and there was no way we could get through. Daddy tried with Congressman Bonner and Senator Smith. There was so much confusion surrounding the invasion that nobody knew where you were for a while. We had to bury her, Walter. She's resting just a few feet away from Billy."

Walter could hear Ellie's words, but he wasn't going to let them sink in. This was only a dream. He had seen enough death the last few weeks. His mind was playing tricks on him. The only thing that mattered for the moment was the ceiling fan. If he moved his eyes fast enough in a circle, he could see the blades. No way the Brits could manufacture a fan that could spin faster than his eyeballs.

"Congressman Bonner's office has been in contact with the War Department. The Army is sending you home on indefinite emergency leave to be with the children. The lieutenant outside has your orders. I'll help you get your things. I'm taking you home."

49

HOMECOMING SUNDAY
JAMESVILLE CHRISTIAN CHURCH
JAMESVILLE, NORTH CAROLINA
SEPTEMBER 23, 1945

"Cousin Walter, would you like another helpin' of barbeque?" Walter's first cousin, Eva Gray Askew, was already spooning a mound of the greasy pork concoction on his plate before he could answer.

"I believe I will, Eva Gray. Thank you."

"And here's some black pepper and hot sauce," she said.

"Thanks."

"Beautiful day for dinner on the grounds, ain't it?" she said.

"The sun's shining. The war's over. The children are well," he said.

"And I hope you're doing well today, cousin. I'm sure Jessie would be glad you came to homecoming."

"Last year was too hard, Eva Gray. It was just too soon after. You know." He held back his emotions. "A fellow's got to get out in public at some point though. And I don't know how I'd have made it this last year without you and Ellie helping me with the children like you have."

"Me and Ellie love them younguns' like they were our own."

"Speaking of Ellie, have you seen her?" he said.

"Not yet. But there are so many people out here, she's probably politicking. You know how she is. I'm sure she'll be here."

Walter forked his barbeque and surveyed the crowd. No sign of Ellie. The gathering of two hundred or so neighbors, farmers, and townspeople seemed vibrant as they crammed down hundreds of fried drumsticks and swigged gallons of sweetened iced tea. They had reason to be happy. Japan had surrendered less than two month ago. Germany had fallen only a few months before. The war was finally over. Everyone seemed to have a bounce in their step. The backslapping seemed more frequent than in recent years. Amidst all the euphoria, Walter thought of Jessie. She was never far from his thoughts.

"Brother Walter!"

Walter looked up at his old pal, J.W. Barber, who was balancing a plate of baked beans and barbeque mounded as high as Mount Everest.

"How you doin', ol' boy?" Walter asked.

"Good to see ya today, Walter. That was some sermon, wasn't it?"

"That's the first time I can remember that we've had a Baptist come speak. Where'd they say he was from?" Walter asked.

"From Richmond, I believe. From the Southern Baptist Foreign Mission Board. Said he speaks German and has been over there evangalizin' them Nazis." Barber, a middle-aged, pot-bellied sort, shoved half a plateful of barbeque in his mouth in one swoop and launched into his next question with most of the stuff still lumped on the back of his tongue. "What would your granddaddy think about havin' a Baptist speak at Jamesville Christian Church?"

Walter ignored the question. "Did you say he speaks German, J.W.?"

Barber chewed a mouthful of barbeque and washed it down with sweetened iced tea. "That's what they say."

"Hmm."

"So what would your granddaddy think?"

"Say it again, J.W.?"

Barber gulped down the rest of his iced tea. "What I said was what'd your granddaddy think about havin' a Baptist speak at Jamesville Christian Church?"

"Granddaddy Baldy'd be happy to have 'em as long as they preach the gospel. I guarantee it."

"You reckon he'd-uh been happy with that sermon today?"

"I'm not sure, J.W.," Walter said. "But that sermon struck close to home for me."

"I thought about that, Walter. I mean, there you were just a year ago in the war uh-shootin' Germans, and then this fellah comes in here and preaches a sermon 'bout how we need to forgive 'em and evangelize to 'em. I was wonderin' what you thought about that."

"I think he's right, J.W. That's what the Bible says, best I can tell."

"Yeah, I know. But it's just hard, you know, with all our boahs that was killed and then us uh-findin' them concentration camps."

"We killed a lot of their boahs too. I know that firsthand."

"I'll bet you do, Walter, with all them medals you won in the Army."

"I was just doin' my job," Walter said. "Besides, it's time to move on."

"Excuse me, gentlemen, I'm Wayne Poplin."

Walter turned around as the guest preacher from Richmond, in a spiffy pinstripe suit, extended his hand.

"Nice to meet you, Dr. Poplin. I'm Walter Brewer. This is my friend J.W. Barber."

Poplin smiled and shook both of their hands, then focused his attention on Walter. "Your pastor tells me your grandfather gave the land for this church."

"That's true. He was converted during the War Between the States. When he came home, he felt led by the Spirit to build a church, so he donated all this land."

"Speaking of war, I understand you fought with distinction

for our country in France. I wanted to let you know how much I appreciate your sacrifice."

"Thank you," Walter said.

Poplin put his hand on Walter's back and moved in closer, speaking softly. "There's something else I wanted to say to you."

"What's that?"

"Your pastor also shared with me about your wife. I wanted you to know how sorry I am and that we're going to put you on our prayer list when I get back to Richmond."

Walter felt his eyes welling up. "Thank you, Dr. Poplin."

"Please, call me Wayne."

"When do you have to be back in Richmond?"

"Not until Wednesday. I was planning on driving back this afternoon. Why?"

"Could I ask you a favor?"

"Anything," Poplin said.

"I heard you're fluent in German."

Poplin smiled. "Enough to get by, I suppose. I've been over there trying to establish a Southern Baptist presence in Bonn. Why do you ask?"

"The first night I was in France, on D-Day, there was a young French woman who was working with the Resistance. She and her family helped me in an attack on a German communications station in Normandy. Since I had been separated from my unit and was deep behind enemy lines, she took me to a barn for safety that night. Just after sunrise, there was a firefight outside the barn between some American paratroopers and a German patrol. Our side won, and I joined up with the American unit. But before I left, she handed me an envelope, but I didn't open it until recently. In fact, I hadn't thought much about it with my wife dying. I discovered that there's a letter of some sort written in German. I was wondering if you could come over later today and translate the letter for me."

"I'd be glad to. Where do you live?"

"In that big white house over there."

"Right next door to the church?"

"That's the one," Walter said.

"Is four o'clock good?"

"That would be fine."

Walter, Ellie, and Eva Gray were sitting in a semi-circle under the big pecan tree in the backyard when Wayne Poplin walked over from the church at four o'clock.

"This looks like a home where children are happy," Poplin said with a smile as he extended his hand to Walter.

"Jamesville is a place for cousins," Walter said. "At homecoming, at Thanksgiving, and at Christmas, you see cousins and all their friends running around picking grapes or playing Cowboys and Indians."

"Children are the most precious commodity God gives us. How many of these are yours, Walter?"

"Four are mine; the other two are just like mine. Wayne, this is my sister-in-law, Ellie. She lives in Plymouth, and the other two belong to her."

"Nice to meet you, Ellie."

"And this is my grown-up cousin, Eva Gray Askew. We used to run around the farm and throw pecans at one another when we were little. Now she lives across the street with her husband. She and Ellie have helped me this year more than they know."

"Sometimes God puts people into our lives in seasons of sorrow to give us comfort. It sounds like these ladies have done that for your family, Walter," Poplin said.

"I agree. I've been lucky from that standpoint."

"It's not a matter of luck, my brother. Nothing ever is."

"I believe that," Walter said. "Lucky was a poor word choice."

"So, I understand you have a letter you want me to translate?"

"I've got it right here."

Poplin sat down and began studying the letter. After a couple of minutes, he looked at Walter.

"Walter, can you tell me again how you came into possession of this?"

Walter recounted the story.

Poplin unfolded the letter and began.

June 3, 1944

Dear Ingrid,

By the time you get this letter, if you ever get it, the war will probably be over. All signs are pointing to the end, and the signs point to a defeat for Germany. I sense that I may never live to see you again.

It is hard to believe that three years have passed since I last saw you and my precious two daughters. It is my deepest prayer that somehow, someday, this letter will find its way to you, for there are some very deep and important truths I wish to impart to you.

Nearly two years ago, in August of 1942, I was stationed in North Africa with General Rommel. Word came that the British and the Canadians launched an attack on the little town of Dieppe in northern France. Our forces beat them back that day, but Rommel wanted a battlefield assessment from his personal staff, so he sent me to investigate.

I flew from Africa to France as the general ordered. I had seen dozens of battle scenes before, but this one was different somehow. There were hundreds of bodies lying by the sea and on the beaches. Both German and British bodies. Only the seagulls mourned for the dead.

We were most interested in the British dead. They were part of a new special forces unit that concerned Rommel. I ordered my men to comb their bodies thoroughly for weapons, papers, or anything else that would give us a clue about this new unit.

Soon after the search began, one of my men shouted that a dead Brit had some sort of manual written in German. I rushed over to see what the excitement was about. He handed me the manual. It was small, about the size of the palm of my hand.

At first, I thought it was part of a psychological ploy to distract our troops with religious propaganda. I wanted to know where the sergeant found the manual. He pointed to a body sprawled face-down in a pile of other bodies. I ordered him to turn the dead man over so I could see a name tag.

What I saw instead was his eyes. They were staring

directly at me. This dead corpse was peering into me. It was like he was alive. His eyes were locked with mine, challenging my soul. The name on his name tag was *McCloud*. I have seen thousands of dead men, but none had ever made me shiver like this one.

I looked away. I opened the manual, and my eyes fell upon these words:

'In the beginning was the Word, and the Word was with God, and the Word was God. In Him was Life, and the Life was the Light of Men.'

I closed the manual and told my men to look for others. There were none.

Procedure called for me to place the manual into our evidence bag and discuss it in my report to Rommel. Instead, I stuffed it, along with the man's dog tag, into my uniform and took them back to Africa with me that night. This was the first time in my career I blatantly defied military procedure. I could have been shot for this.

That night, alone in my quarters, I opened the book again. On the inside cover, there was a note. It was from the dead man. It was written in German. Here is what he wrote:

'To the one who finds this book. Today our governments are enemies. As a result of this, we find ourselves as soldiers fulfilling our duties on the opposite sides of a war. But right now, there is another war going on. It is a war of far greater significance than the war between Britain and Germany. This war of which I speak is a war for your soul. I don't know your name, but I have prayed that you and I will be on the same side in that war, that we will be soldiers for the living Christ. I prayed this in life, and I pray this for you even in death. Read this book. It is your battle plan for victory. May God have mercy on you – Darwin McCloud.'

This message tormented me somehow. As an intelligence officer, I was proud of my ability to sort through data, to figure things out and make reports. But in this case, I was perplexed. I could not understand the message from the dead man or the book we found on him.

What was the purpose behind this ploy?, I wondered. An insatiable curiosity grasped me. All through the night, I read it, wondering about this dead British commando and why I, of all the soldiers in the German Army, had found this book.

As the hours passed and dawn approached, I read something in his manual which brought chills to my body and sweat to my forehead. I was reminded of something horrible I had done. Something I must now tell you about.

Do you remember Fall of 1938? I was attending all those Party meetings in the evenings. Do you remember the night of November ninth? You had planned a special meal for me and had apple strudel for dessert and the girls were all excited to have a meal with their papa.

But instead, I came down the stairs dressed in black and rushed off to a Party meeting. That night, I was given a difficult assignment. It was an assignment which would prove or disprove my loyalty to the Party. Some Jewish boy had shot a German ambassador in Paris, and the Party was determined to retaliate. All over Germany, attacks were planned against Jewish homes and businesses.

My mission was to help burn a synagogue and terrorize the home of the Jewish rabbi. I did not feel good about this. I would have preferred to attack a military target, but I wanted to show my loyalty.

That night, as my comrades gassed the synagogue, I rushed across the street to the rabbi's home and hurled a brick through the front window. I was only trying to scare and intimidate the Jews. But the loud screams I heard from inside paralyzed me. I could not move. I froze and stood just outside the front window. Inside, I saw a mother and father crouched on the floor over their little girl. The child was unconscious with blood gushing from her temple. As the mother sobbed and wailed, the father looked up. His eyes locked with mine.

With the synagogue burning at my back, my comrades called me back to the truck. But I could not move. The father rushed out into the front yard where I was standing. He had a large knife in his hand. I watched him charge me in slow motion.

I could feel nothing but the hot flames of the burning synagogue behind me. To me, these were the flames at the gates of hell, for that was what I deserved for what I had done to this little girl.

As the rabbi raised the knife over his head preparing to plunge it into my heart, I heard a burst of rifle fire. The rabbi slumped over, bleeding from his stomach. My comrades screamed that they would shoot me also unless I came. Like a coward, I sprinted back to the truck and we escaped into the night.

My comrades wanted to celebrate for what we had done. We popped open beers in the back of the truck. But I did not feel like drinking. The men sensed I was feeling guilty. They admonished me not to show any remorse because they said the Jews had started this fight by assassinating our ambassador. They said that remorse might be construed as a sign of weakness and disloyalty to the Party. So I drank several beers and tried to forget about it.

But I could not forget the little girl with the red curly locks. I began to have nightmares. As I lay in our bed, I saw the little girl's face in my dreams. She did not have blood gushing from her brain. Instead, she had a sweet and innocent countenance. In my dreams, she would smile at me, but she never said anything. I would wake up in cold sweats. But at least when I woke up, she was gone.

Then one night, not long before I entered the Army, I was dreaming about her again. I rose up in bed in a cold sweat as usual. But this time, she was not gone. She was standing there at the foot of our bed. As I shook and trembled, she smiled and spoke for the first time. It was a short and strange message. She said, 'Read the book, before it's too late.'

I demanded, 'What book do you want me to read?'

When you woke up and asked me who I was talking to, she was gone. I never had nightmares about her again. But I have carried the guilt of my actions and the mystery of her message in my heart all these years.

The night when I got back from Dieppe, reading this manual of McCloud's, I saw a message which unveiled the mystery. The passage stated, "For I am not ashamed of the gospel of Christ: for it is the power of God unto salvation to every one that believeth; to the Jew first, and also to the Greek."

It was at that moment I understood the message from this little Jewish girl.

She was telling me to read McCloud's book before it was too late. It was as if she foresaw the future and knew the book would fall into my hands at Dieppe.

I could hardly sleep for several weeks. Each night, I

stayed awake until nearly dawn, reading and searching. The book had a magnetic hold over me I cannot explain in words.

One night in late September, as I was reading a chapter in the book called "Romans," I discovered a verse I did not understand. It said 'the wages of sin is death.' I started to think about what this meant. As I was thinking, I remembered what I had done to this little girl and that her father had been shot because of me. Even worse, I remembered neglecting you and our daughters, all for the sake of my career. As I thought about these things, a deep feeling of guilt descended on me.

With a burden so heavy I could not bear, I stopped reading. I wished that the rabbi had plunged the knife into my heart that night.

My soul felt twisted like wrecked metal, smoking and burning on a battlefield in the wake of a military slaughter. I wondered, with all the death I had seen, why my life had been spared. I could not bear the guilt. I wanted to be a corpse in a heap of dead bodies with buzzards picking at my flesh. That is what I deserved.

I was ready to stop—to end it all right there. The book had been sent to torment me for my past, to remind me that eternal death was my destiny. I looked at the table beside my bed. There was an unopened bottle of vodka that had been brought back from the Russian Front. I looked at my pistol.

The vodka would make this easier. On the other hand, I deserved to feel the bullet rip through my skull as my brains splattered all over the wall. After all, I had caused so much pain. Why should I not feel the pain of this girl and her father as I died?

For what seemed like an hour, my eyes shifted between the vodka and the pistol. Finally, I got up and put on my dress uniform. I adjusted all the medals I had received as Rommel's aide. I downed a swig of vodka. A little bit seemed the gentlemanly thing to do. As it burned my throat, I cocked my pistol. I put its cold, steel barrel up to my head. With my fingers on the trigger, I closed my eyes and began a countdown.

Five, four, three, two.

As I reached one, she spoke to me again. Her voice

startled me so much that I nearly pulled the trigger. Six years had passed since I had seen her at the foot of our bed. Her message was the same one that haunted me all these years.

"Read the book, before it is too late."

I looked and saw no one. For a moment, I thought it was the vodka talking. With the gun still at my head, I spoke to an empty room.

"The book has caused me nothing but torment," I said. "It reminds me of what I did to you and your father."

The voice came back. "Don't stop reading. Your sins are forgiven."

"Who are you?" I demanded.

She did not respond.

"What is your name? What do you mean, my sins are forgiven?"

There was only silence.

I laid the pistol on the table beside my bed. If this little girl told me to keep reading, I supposed I owed her at least that much before I shot myself.

I sat on the bed and picked up the book. I returned to the place on the page where I had left off. I again read that "the wages of sin is death." Then I saw the next part of the sentence. It said "but the gift of God is eternal life through Jesus Christ our Lord."

I closed my eyes and thought about this. As I wondered what this meant, I saw in my mind an image of Jesus hanging on the cross. His body was writhing in agony. His face winced in excruciating pain.

With my eyes still closed, I heard her voice for the last time. She said, "Do you see Him? He is taking the punishment for what you did to me and for what you did to my father and mother. All your guilt is heaped on Him. He wants to bear all your burdens. Let Him. He loves you."

I never believed in miracles before, but one happened at that moment. It was like an invisible hand came down from Heaven and lifted a ton of weight from my heart. The oppressive conviction that had driven me to the brink of suicide was gone.

I fell on my knees in the presence of a Holy God. The living author of McCloud's book had made His presence known to me. This book was not merely a historical account, nor was it a psychological ploy by British Special

Forces. It was living, like a two-edged sword, and its author is alive.

That night in Africa, Christ called me, a worthless murderer, unto himself. He used an enemy soldier and a little girl I probably murdered to draw me to Him. I am so unworthy of His Grace.

I tell you this for selfish reasons. I believe in my heart that I shall never see you and our daughters alive on this earth again. I want so much to be with the three of you again.

Therefore, I now implore you, my dearest Ingrid, to heed the message that was brought to me by the little Jewish girl. Read the book before it's too late. Get to know its living author. Ask Him to reveal these truths to you, and teach them to our daughters.

It is my prayer that somehow, someway, this letter will make its way to you, and that the four of us will be reunited in Heaven.

Good-bye my love.

I will love you always,
Heinrick

Poplin folded the letter as Ellie and Eva Gray dabbed their eyes. For a few moments, no one said a word. The foursome sat speechless, listening to the sparrows chirping in the tops of the pecan trees.

"I have never encountered anything like this before," Poplin said.

"And this is the man I shot," Walter said.

"Walter, I don't know how you're going to do this, but somehow this letter needs to find its way to that widow," Poplin said.

"But I'm the one who shot her husband," Walter said. "And besides, how would I find her? Is there an address anywhere on the letter?"

"There's no address."

"Then what can I do?"

"When I get back to Richmond, I'll ask some folks at the Foreign Mission Board if they have any ideas. But Germany is in shambles right now. Barring a miracle, I'm afraid that finding this lady will be like looking for a needle in a haystack. We will pray God opens the door."

50

ARMISTICE DAY
JAMESVILLE, NORTH CAROLINA
NOVEMBER 11, 1945

Before Wayne Poplin left Jamesville on Homecoming Sunday, he penned a copy of Heinrick's letter in English. For days, Walter found himself obsessed with it, reading and rereading the translation day and night. At night he lay in bed alone, wrestling with questions that could not be answered.

Poplin became a faithful friend to Walter. Each Wednesday since September, he called to say hello and to report that the Foreign Mission Board still had no leads on Ingrid Schultz.

After two months of no luck, Poplin encouraged Walter to try and put Ingrid out of his mind for the time being and get on with life. Wayne said that the children needed his undivided attention. He was right.

Walter did a good job of refocusing until Sunday, November eleventh, when Armistice Day brought an American flag to every house in Jamesville. From the pulpit of Jamesville Christian Church, Preacher Holliday delivered a rousing sermon of thanks for the veterans of both World War I and II. The Armistice Day parade that afternoon right in front of Walter's house evoked a flood of memories about the war. The ghost of Ingrid Schultz had returned.

To Walter, it seemed that Armistice Day, 1945 would never end. Because the Armistice had fallen on Sunday that year, Monday the twelfth was a Federal holiday. No mail would be delivered, which meant Walter was home from work. Idle time was not what he needed. What he needed was a distraction.

WILLIAMS RESIDENCE
WINDLEY-AUSBON HOUSE
302 WASHINGTON STREET
PLYMOUTH, NORTH CAROLINA

An hour later, Walter parked his car right in front of the Baptist church, looked both ways, and crossed Washington Street, stepping under the oaks blanketing the sidewalk on the other side. He walked up onto the porch of the historic old white house that had survived the Civil War in the 1864 Battle of Plymouth.

His heart was beating hard, but he didn't know why. Perhaps it no longer mattered why.

Taking a deep breath, he knocked three times on the door.

"Good morning!" Ellie greeted Walter and his four children at the front door of her house with a smile.

"Thanks for having us on short notice, Ellie. The kids were in a mood to come play with their cousins."

"I'm glad the kids were thinking of their cousins this morning," Ellie gave Hardison and Virginia big bear hugs. "Where's your car, Walter?"

"Daddy parked it down by the river, Aunt Ellie," Zack said.

"Yeah, he made us walk all the way down the street," Caroline protested.

"Now, Walter Brewer, there's plenty of parking spaces right out in front of the house," Ellie said. "There's not a car anywhere on Washington Street."

"I know, but these kids needed the exercise, so I figured we'd take a little stroll through downtown Plymouth," he said.

"Oh, I'm sure that's what you had on your mind, Walter—exercise for your kids! You're such a thoughtful father."

He looked down and blushed. "I try Ellie. Exercise is important to their health."

"Right." She winked at him. "I'll let you get your exercise on the grill in the back yard. I've got the charcoals going already."

"We're cooking out?" Walter asked.

"Hot dogs and burgers for the kids. Steaks for the adults."

"Are you sure?"

"Don't worry. The neighbors on both sides are gone for the holiday weekend. And Miss Inez Ange might be nosy, but she's too short to see over the back fence. Your anonymity will be protected, my dear."

"Daddy, what's an, uh, nu . . ." Virginia asked.

"Anonymity? That's just a big word Aunt Ellie knows. She probably learned it at that fancy college she went to up in Raleigh."

"Your daddy's talking about St. Mary's, sweetie. And it's not that fancy." Ellie grinned, as she leaned over to whisper in Walter's ear. "Do you think she'd understand the phrase *rumor mill*?"

"Go play, children! In the back yard now," Walter ordered.

"But Daddy, I wanted to know what that word meant," Virginia protested.

"We'll talk about that later. Now, go. Daddy and Aunt Ellie will be there in a few minutes."

The day with Ellie was the perfect tonic for Walter. By nine o'clock that night, Ingrid Schultz was a thousand miles from his mind. They exchanged hugs and Walter left with the kids under the cover of darkness. Exhausted from a full day's play at Aunt Ellie's, the kids slept on the short ride back to Jamesville.

By five o'clock the next morning, Walter was alone in the Jamesville post office getting ready for his mail run. As usual, he checked his personal post office box to see if anything had arrived overnight. There was a package postmarked from Norfolk wrapped in brown paper about the size of the Sears Roebuck Catalogue. Walter pulled out his pocket knife and ripped it open.

Allison & Cranford, Attorneys
300 Neptune Road
Norfolk, Virginia 23502

Mr. Walter Brewer
St. Andrews Street
Jamesville, N.C. 27846

November 7, 1945

Dear Mr. Brewer,

Our firm serves as general counsel to the Reunification Foundation.

Founded by the generosity of anonymous donors at the beginning of World War II, the Reunification Foundation was formed to ease the pain of separation caused by war by providing spouses an opportunity to visit their loved ones on foreign soil during long periods of separation.

While the original purpose of the foundation was solely dedicated to serving only the needs of United States servicemen and their families, our charitable scope was expanded at the end of the War to consider the needs of families from all nations affected by the war on a case-by-case basis.

Word has come to us through confidential sources that you have discovered a letter which you may wish to deliver to families who lost loved ones in Germany and Britain.

Our Foundation has considered this predicament and has for several weeks been working behind the scenes through our various contacts to seek a solution to best serve the needs of all the families involved.

I am pleased to report that we have located the addresses for both the German and British families involved. The German family is in the city of Nuremberg. The British family is in London. The Foundation has approved a five-thousand-dollar grant for you, solely for the purpose of traveling to Europe to deliver the letter.

We are also including three Bibles, translated into German, which you may wish to present to the Schultz family as a token of friendship and as a reminder of your trip.

Should you choose to accept our offer, you will need to travel within the next sixty days, as there is a possibility that the German family will be relocating after Christmas. We cannot be certain of their location beyond sixty days. Please contact our offices within one week and advise us of your intentions. We will provide you with a travel itinerary and specifics with regard to addresses.

Please accept our congratulations, Mr. Brewer. We look forward to hearing from you.

Very truly yours,
F. Eugene Allison, Esq.

Walter felt his chest pounding as he thumbed through the three German Bibles that had been included in his package. That night, as soon as he finished his mail run, he asked Eva Gray to come watch the kids for a couple hours after dinner. By 9 p.m., he was knocking on Ellie's front door.

"Walter! What a surprise!" Ellie beamed.

"I know it's late. I hope you don't mind."

"Where are the kids?"

"They're with Eva Gray," he said.

"You know if you keep parking your car in front of my house like this and if you keep showing up without the kids, people are going to start talking," she said with a teasing wink.

"I'm sorry. I'm just in a real rush."

"Don't apologize to me. I don't care if they talk," she said.

"I know you don't."

"Don't just stand there; come on in," she said.

"I won't stay long."

"It's not polite just to drop in and drop out." She took his coat.

"Ellie, I need to talk to somebody. There's something I need to show you."

He pulled out the letter from Mr. Allison and handed it to her.

She took a moment and studied it.

"Walter, I don't mean to sound negative, but this seems too good to be true. I hope this isn't a hoax."

"Ellie, it's not a hoax."

"I don't know, Walter. It sounds fishy. I mean . . . Wait a minute."

"What is it?" he said.

"Maybe Wayne Poplin's behind this. Didn't he say he was going to work some of his contacts for you?"

"I haven't spoken with Poplin, but I'm sure he's got nothing to do with it," he said.

"How can you be so sure?"

"I just am," he said.

"I'm sorry, but I'm skeptical, Walter. You've been through so much. I don't want to see you get your hopes up only to be let down. I mean, just because this is on an attorney's letterhead doesn't mean it's real."

"Ellie, there's something I need to tell you."

"What?"

"Remember when Jessie visited me in England during the war?"

"How could I forget? I had six kids running around my house for three weeks."

"And I never thanked you for that. I'm sorry."

"Don't be sorry. Your wife died. You've had more important matters on your mind," she said.

"Anyway, this same foundation provided the funding and cut through the red tape to get her there," he said.

Ellie paused and seemed to think for a moment.

"That's interesting. She never mentioned anything about a foundation when she asked me to watch the kids. She just said she'd run across some money and had found a way to take a ship over there."

"She didn't mention the foundation because of this attorney, Mr. Allison."

"What about Mr. Allison? I don't understand."

"He asked her not to say anything about it. He said that the foundation had to remain anonymous in order to function."

"If this is real, they've done a good job of operating behind the scenes."

"It *is* real, Ellie," he said with a slight irritation in his voice.

"Okay. Okay. I believe it if you say so. What are you going to do?"

"You and I both know the answer to that," he said.

"Yes we do. You're going back to Europe. And you're going soon . . . before you lose track of Ingrid Schultz," she said.

"You still know me better than anyone, don't you?"

"I'd like to take credit for that. And you don't even need to ask me to keep your kids, because you know I will."

"You've done so much for me already. I hate to impose."

"*Impose?* Are you crazy?"

"But I—"

"Shut up and come here." She opened her arms and gave him a long, sympathetic embrace. "You know I'd do anything for my favorite brother-in-law."

"I know."

51

LAW OFFICES OF ALLISON & CRANFORD
NORFOLK, VIRGINIA
NOVEMBER 25, 1945

On the Monday after Thanksgiving, Walter stopped by the law offices of Allison and Cranford. He needed to pick up some materials before setting sail for Europe that afternoon. He also hoped to meet Eugene Allison and at least try to find out who was behind all this.

Like the mysterious foundation it represented, Allison and Cranford seemed a bit mysterious also. Despite having an address on Norfolk's prominent Neptune Road, the small law offices were not visible from the street, but instead faced an alley in the back of a three-story office building.

The receptionist area was small but elegant, with mahogany furniture, a leather sofa, and brass lamps. An attractive and well-dressed young receptionist who looked to be in her early twenties was seated behind a desk in the waiting room. Behind her in the next room, Walter saw several law clerks milling about with papers in their hands.

"I'm Walter Brewer. I'm here to pick up some paperwork for a trip to Europe."

"Yes, you're the grant recipient," she said with a pleasant look on her face. "We've been expecting you. Mr. Allison asked me to give this to you." She handed him a large, leather satchel. "Inside you'll find a travel itinerary, tickets for the voyage across the Atlantic, tickets for the trains once you get there, a memorandum from the War Department on procedures for travel in Germany and a basic German phrase book. You may want to double check to make sure everything's there."

Walter thumbed through the package as the receptionist looked on attentively.

"Looks like this Reunification Foundation is an organized outfit," he said.

"There's one other package you'll need, Mr. Brewer." She handed him another envelope. "Please count this right now."

Walter had never seen so many greenbacks all at once. Fifty crisp, one-hundred-dollar bills had been clipped together inside. Just like the letter said.

"I count five thousand dollars," he said.

"Very well," she said. "Sign here acknowledging receipt."

"I sure would like to know who to thank for all this." He scrawled his name on the transaction log.

"No thanks are necessary, Mr. Brewer. The donor wants it that way. Secrecy is necessary to the success of this charitable organization."

"Donor? I thought the letter said this foundation was founded at the beginning of the war by *donors*."

The woman's face turned ashen. "To tell you the truth, this office handles so many charitable trusts that we can't keep all our donors straight. Don't read anything into what I just said. I can't say anything else."

"But you seem to know something about this organization," he said.

"Please, Mr. Brewer, I could lose my job if I say anything to undermine the privacy of our clients. Please just forget that silly comment. There was no significance to it."

"I'm sorry, Miss, I didn't catch your name."

She hesitated and looked down.

"I won't bite. I promise. I would just like to know who I'm talking to," he said.

"I'm Jane Swain."

"Miss Swain, I was wondering if I could have a moment with Mr. Allison."

"Uh, Mr. Allison is very busy today."

He leaned over the desk and whispered, "Miss Swain, I don't know what the big deal is, but I promise I won't breathe a word to him about anything you just said."

She looked into his eyes for a moment.

"I promise. I want you to keep your job. Your secret is safe with me." He flashed a disarming smile at her.

She hesitated. "Your face looks honest. All right, follow me."

They walked down the hallway to a large office where he was greeted by a trim, middle-aged man with wire-rimmed glasses.

"Welcome to Norfolk, Mr. Brewer. I'm Gene Allison."

"I know you're busy, Mr. Allison, but I wanted to thank you before I leave the country this afternoon."

"I wish I could accept your thanks. But our firm is just a conduit carrying out the wishes of our donors. Anyway, we wish you well."

"Mr. Allison, I know you can't tell me who's behind this, but there's something I want to say anyway."

"Go right ahead."

Walter noticed Jane Swain looking down at the floor. Her hands were trembling.

"It's about your receptionist."

"What about her?"

"I just met her, and—"

"Um, maybe I should excuse myself," Jane said.

"No, please stay, I want you to hear this," Walter said.

"What about her?" Eugene asked again.

"I find her to be extremely professional and courteous. She's a credit to your firm."

"Thank you, Mr. Brewer. We feel like we've got a good one," Allison said.

Walter noticed the look of relief and the smile on Jane Swain's face. "There's something else I need to say before I go," he said.

"Say anything you'd like."

"Two years ago, I was in England in the Army. We were training for the invasion of Europe. One Friday afternoon, I got off duty and came back to the manor house where I was quartered with three other officers. When I walked in the front door, I had a surprise visitor. It was my wife, Jessie. I couldn't believe it." He stopped as his eyes started filling with tears. "I took furlough and we spent that weekend together in London. It was the most wonderful weekend of my life. Jessie felt the same way. It was also the last time I saw her alive. She died during premature labor in June. I was in France. My last memory of her alive was this most wonderful visit. Your foundation provided the money and laid the groundwork to make it possible. Thank you."

"I'm glad the Foundation was able to help," Allison said.

"I realize that the donors wish to keep their identities a secret, but I wanted to thank them in a way that doesn't compromise their identity. So I've written a letter. Could you make sure they get it?"

"I'll be happy to forward it to the appropriate parties."

"And if there is *any* way I could personally thank them for the last memories they gave me with Jessie, I'd give anything. You'd have my word I would never reveal their identities."

"Mr. Brewer, I appreciate your persistency and I know you're sincere, but I'm afraid that would never be possible. The attorney-client privilege requires that I maintain my clients' confidentiality."

"Would you at least pass on my request anyway?" Walter persisted.

Allison put his hand on Walter's shoulder and smiled. "Mr. Brewer, as a husband myself, I understand your need to know. If I were in your shoes, I'd ask the same questions. Tell you what I'll do. I'll ask the client if they would like to meet you. But don't get your hopes up. My best advice is to go to Europe, deliver this letter to Mrs. Schultz, and then let it drop. Don't worry about things you can't control."

52

When Walter had come to Europe a year and a half ago, he had been on a mission of war. Now he was returning on a mission of peace to a ravaged land. Though he would not confront physical danger this time, he dreaded this mission more than his first. He would rather be shot at by German machine-guns than look into the eyes of the young widow.

On the week-long voyage across the Atlantic, he rolled and tumbled in his berth at nights. Little was on his mind other than Ingrid Schultz. What would she look like? What would he say? How would they communicate? He studied the German phrase book Eugene Allison had given him but was having problems concentrating. Ingrid Schultz's face—at least his imaginary version of her face—was always on his mind.

Maybe he would just knock on the door, leave the letter, and come home. That would fulfill his mission, wouldn't it? No point in establishing a relationship with the widow or the family. How would it help matters if she knew who shot her husband? She didn't need to know. Besides, they were thousands of miles from Jamesville. She would have the letter, and he would have fulfilled his duty.

Coward!

As he traveled by train from Luxembourg through West Germany and on to Nuremberg, he was struck by the devastation on both sides of the track. The destructive firepower of the American Army had left the landscape resembling the path of a killer hurricane, a raging forest fire, and a thousand tornadoes all converging on the same spot at once. Char, smut, bombed-out bridges, and dilapidated buildings were everywhere.

Lines for food stretched into the cold streets. Germany was literally an armed camp, with victorious British and American soldiers at almost every checkpoint and at every railroad depot.

As the train neared Nuremberg, a tranquil snowfall covered the ground like a white blanket hiding the body of a corpse. Maybe the fresh snow was a sign that God would be with him when he faced Ingrid. Otherwise, Germany was the closest thing to hell on Earth he had ever seen.

The snowfall became heavy as the train pulled into Central Station in downtown Nuremberg in the early afternoon. Walter noted the calendar. It was December 7, 1945. He thought of Billy then stepped off the train.

The sizable presence of British and American troops in the station reminded him of England before the invasion of France. The soldiers were in Nuremberg to maintain order and security in the midst of the International War Crimes Tribunal, which had begun just last week on November twenty-fifth.

Walter grabbed his bags and reported to the American military checkpoint in the station to ask for directions, where a young military policeman was manning the desk.

"Excuse me, Sergeant. I'm Captain Walter Brewer, 101st Airborne. I'm here on a non-military matter. Could you help me with some directions?"

"Could I see your papers and military ID?"

The MP studied Walter's papers. "Looks like you're on indefinite emergency leave from active duty, Captain."

"That's right, soldier. I was pulled out of Normandy when my wife died. That's why I'm traveling in civilian clothes. I expect to be transferred to the reserves at Bragg sometime next year."

"Papers look in order. What can I do for you, sir?"

"I'm looking for this address."

"Hmm. I think that's in the British-controlled sector. Let me check our map." The MP stepped away from the counter then returned. "I was right, Captain. It's about eight miles from here in the British sector of the city. There's a nice little hotel about three blocks from this address which probably has some vacancies."

"Thanks, Sergeant. What's the best way to get over there?"

"There's not a good way with all this snow we're getting right now. But the major says we can have someone run you over there in a Jeep if you'd like."

"Send the major my regards and my thanks."

"Glad to do it, sir. Normandy vets get the royal treatment around here."

The American Jeep dropped Walter off at the Hotel Turmberg, a three-story, older facility off the beaten path from the hustle and bustle of downtown Nuremberg. This residential section of town seemed far removed from all the talk about the war crimes trials.

There was little traffic and little sign of occupying Allied forces. Walter saw no sign of the military at all save a bored-looking British Army corporal sitting behind the check-in desk with a young female German clerk.

Walter approached the front desk and decided to try out some of the German he had been studying on his transatlantic voyage.

"*Haben sie ein zimmer?*" Do you have a room?

"*Für eine person?*" the clerk asked. For one person?

"You must be American," the British corporal interrupted.

"It's that obvious?" Walter said.

The sergeant chuckled. "I'm Corporal Montgomery, British Army Intelligence."

"Captain Walter Brewer, U.S. Army. One hundred and first Airborne."

"The pleasure is mine, Captain. You're welcome to try out your German on Gretel here. But if you'd like to expedite matters, I'd be happy to translate. That's why the Army has me here, to translate for the BBC correspondents covering the war crimes trials. It's been a slow afternoon. I may as well earn my paycheck."

"No argument here," Walter said. "Tell Gretel I need one room for two to three nights."

The corporal spoke to the clerk and handed Walter a key. "Room 201 just upstairs, sir. Is there anything else I can help you with?"

"Yes. I'm looking for this address." He handed the corporal a piece of paper with the address written on it.

"Ten minutes by foot. Go out the front door of the hotel. Turn left and go three blocks. Turn right on Bayernstraße. That address should be on the left."

Walter checked into the room and fell on his knees. *Lord, You say that You will liberally give wisdom to anyone who asks. Well, right now I'm asking. I don't have a clue about what to say to this Ingrid Schultz. But I believe You've brought me all this way for a reason. Give me the strength and wisdom to do and say the right thing, that Your will may be done. In Jesus's name. Amen.*

Wrapped in a heavy black trenchcoat, boots, and wool gloves, he headed outside onto the frozen sidewalks. In the fifteen minutes since he had checked into the hotel, the weather had turned to near-blizzard conditions.

Trudging through the mounting snow drifts, he squinted to see ahead and thought briefly about the date—December 7, 1945. Four years ago on this day in a sunny, tropical place thousands of miles away, his family had been thrust into this war when brother Billy was killed on a battleship in Hawaii. Now in a winter storm halfway around the world in an Axis nation conquered by the Allies, he would deliver a letter which he hoped would bring this war to an end—at least for him.

Walter cupped his hands over his eyes and strained to see the street sign at the far corner.

Bayernstraße. This is it.

He crossed the desolate main boulevard and turned onto the small cobblestoned street where Ingrid Schultz was last reported to live. The two-story houses were narrow and homogeneous, cottages built elbow-to-elbow with only a narrow alley separating them by no more than six feet. The house numbers were painted on posts outside the front stoops above the snow line and were still visible in the darkening afternoon.

200, 202, 204, 206. He double-checked the address on the card provided by Allison's office.

Ingrid Schultz, 206 Bayernstraße, Nuremberg, Germany.

With his heart pounding against his overcoat and his lungs sucking up blasts of freezing air, Walter thought he was hyperventilating. He walked past the house a few yards, trying to regain his composure, then turned around and walked straight to Ingrid's front doorstep. Inside, a soft light beamed through the downstairs windows. His hands shaking from both the cold and his nerves, he balled his fingers into a fist and rapped three times on the door.

He waited.

His only answer was the wind, howling and whipping ice into his nostrils and against his frozen ears. Otherwise, nothing.

As he raised his numbing knuckles to bang out another three knocks, the doorknob started jiggling. Inside, someone fidgeted with the deadbolt lock. He took a deep breath—and prayed.

53

SCHULTZ HOME
BAYERNSTRASSE
NUREMBERG, GERMANY
DECEMBER 7, 1945

The melodic strain of a single violin from inside the house froze the image in time. He stepped up out of the snow and onto the front stoop and wondered for a second if he were really here. He stood there for a moment, taking in the snowscape that had blanketed the small German house on the narrow, cobblestone street.

A surrealistic aura overwhelmed him.

He knew, in that instant, that he would never forget this moment for the rest of his life.

The violin stopped, and the door swung open.

But for her icy blue eyes cutting into his conscience, her face was expressionless. Like a golden frame adorning a masterpiece, her curly, blonde locks caressed her cheeks and shoulders.

"Guten tag, Fräulein," he said. Good day, miss.

"Guten tag," she replied. Good day.

"Ich heiße Walter Brewer." My name is Walter Brewer.

"Ja?" Yes?

"Ja," he said. Yes. *"Wo ist Frau Schultz?"* Where is Mrs. Schultz?

"*Kommen innen*," she said. Come inside.

"*Danke*," he said. Thank you.

"*Entschuldigung, ein moment*," she said. Wait here a moment.

Walter stepped inside and closed the door as his teenaged welcoming committee of one scampered up the stairs with her violin, leaving him alone in the foyer.

His eyes darted around the living room as he waited for Ingrid. In some ways, the room could pass for an American living room in Martin County. A music stand stood in the middle and a lighted Christmas tree in the corner.

Smoldering embers in the fireplace generated just enough heat to break the chill in the air. He gazed at the red-hot coals and smoldering ashes in the hearth. More firewood was needed. The logs were probably buried under three feet of snow outside.

His eyes roamed to the mantle just above the fireplace. The glossy black-and-white photo of the German military officer above the fireplace riveted his focus away from all else.

Walter's eyes locked on the photograph. Maybe the blinding snow had strained his eyes. No, it was real! The eyes of the man in the photograph were following him around the room.

Walter shut his eyes. Surely, he wasn't going mad. *This is just my imagination.*

His eyes still closed, he visualized the events of the dark morning hours of June 6, 1944. It had happened so fast. He had stormed the communications station, shot the stunned German officers, threw his grenade at the electronics console, and ran.

The explosion and subsequent escape had dominated his memory all these months. All else was blurred—until now.

Now the photograph was triggering images buried deep in the crevices of his memory. The stunned gaze. The surprised look on the soldier's face. He could see clearly now— in living color.

It was this man's eyes that Walter had forgotten—or suppressed.

Their gaze was one of helplessness, a sudden foreknowledge of imminent death. Maybe Heinrick had seen him. Maybe not. Perhaps his life had been flashing before him in his mind. Possibly his thoughts had gone to his wife and children.

No matter. The eyes in the photograph and the eyes of the dead German officer were one and the same.

"You were admiring my husband's picture?"

Walter looked up, wiping the tears from his eyes, to the sight of a pretty, well-figured, redheaded woman who looked to be in her mid-thirties.

"Is everything okay?" the woman said.

"You speak English?"

"I am an English teacher here in Nuremberg. My name is Ingrid Schultz."

"I'm Walter Brewer. I'm an American."

"Yes, I know," she said.

"You know my name?"

"I knew you were American."

"You did?"

"I overheard your conversation with my daughter, Leisel. Your accent gave you away. Most Americans try and speak German with a cowboy accent."

Walter smiled. "I'm not a cowboy. I know only a few phrases. I studied German on the ship coming over here."

"So if you're not a cowboy, then you must be a correspondent covering the war crimes trials. The only Americans we see here are from the press or the Army. I hear the war crimes trials are done for the week. So, what brings you to this part of town on such a freezing afternoon?"

"I have no interest in the war crimes trials. I *am* here because of the war, however."

"What do you mean?"

"Frau Schultz, was your husband Heinrick Schultz?"

"*Ja*. What about Heinrick?"

"Was Heinrick by any chance assigned to General Rommel's staff?"

"*Ja*, what about him? Have they found the body? Did the Americans find his body?"

"I'm afraid not, but we did find a letter. We think it was written by your husband to you. I've come to deliver it."

"No body? Just a letter? Then maybe he is still alive, no?" Her green eyes twinkled and lit up with optimism. "They never confirmed him dead. He is still listed as missing in action."

She probably thinks Heinrick wrote this from an Allied military hospital.

He could not look her in the face and glanced instead at the pictures on the mantle above the fireplace. In one, Heinrick and his two smiling daughters were in a swing, his arms wrapped around each of them. Another was a family portrait when the girls were toddlers. Then there was a picture of Heinrick and Ingrid at their wedding. They looked so happy together, he in his tux and she in a long flowing gown.

Maybe I should tell her about the attack.

He looked into her eyes again and melted.

I can't do it. Not now. I'll just give her the letter. Surely, she'll read between the lines and figure out what happened.

"Would you like to see it now?" he asked.

"The letter?"

"Yes, ma'am."

"I'm so—how do you say in English?—nervous. I want to read it, but I'm afraid of what I may find. When was it written?"

"I don't read German well, Frau Schultz. But we've had a translator look at the letter, and we think it was written in June of last year."

"Where was it written from?" She looked nervous, like she wanted him to tell her that its contents offered hope of his survival.

"France."

"France?"

"Yes, ma'am."

"That wasn't so long ago, June of last year. If the Americans didn't find a body, maybe he was captured by the British. Maybe *they* have him, no?"

"Frau Schultz, I think it would be best if you just read it. Maybe the letter will give you some clues."

She hesitated, seeming to think about what he just said.

"You're right, Mr. Brewer. I must face this now, whatever

the outcome. I should have face it long ago. Thank you. Please have a seat," she said.

He handed her the envelope. "Frau Schultz, I think you need some privacy. I notice your fireplace is about to go out. Maybe I could get some more wood for you while you're reading it."

"Thank you. The wood is out back."

As Walter stepped out into the snowstorm, he looked over his shoulder at Ingrid sitting alone on the sofa, unfolding the letter from her dead husband. The blizzard had gotten worse. He pulled out his pocket watch.

Three thirty. I'm gonna give this lady plenty of time alone with that letter before I go back inside. Even if I get frostbite. She deserves that much.

At this latitude at this time of the year, the days were short. Darkness was already descending on Germany. He turned left out the front door, then turned left again into the narrow alley, making his way into the small back yard. With a back porch light casting a dim glow over the snowscape, he spotted a mound of snow and ice protruding from the back of the house.

With his hands, he knocked at least a bucketful of snow and ice from the mound. He pushed more of the ice out of the way. His gloves might have been adequate for carrying the mail in the mild winters of North Carolina, but not here. The gloves grew soggy with cold slush. His fingers ached and felt numb.

With his arms, he pushed yet another wave of snow off the mound. Then he felt what he was searching for. Firewood.

He dropped to his knees. The snow by now was so deep that it covered him up to his waist. Tears streaming down his face and dripping off his nose felt like they were burning, then freezing.

The burden of death heaped on his shoulders by this war was now a heavy weight, crushing him deep down into the snow. First Billy. Then his baby daughter, Mona. His true love, Jessie— he had not even attended her funeral. And now the pictures on the mantle of a father with his daughters. The frantic face of an enemy soldier's widow, desperately wanting her husband back. A family shattered by the bullets of his own rifle.

He buried his face in the snow and wailed—for Billy, for Mona, for Jessie, for Heinrick, and for both of their families. Then he thought of Darwin McCloud, a man from England he'd never met, and cried for his family too.

Fifteen, maybe twenty minutes passed.

You've got to be strong, Walter. Right now, you're her only link to her husband and to her future.

He looked at his watch again.

Four o'clock. I've been out here a half an hour. Time to go in.

He got up and cradled a load of firewood in his arms. Mercifully, the snow had stopped falling. He walked back around to the front of the house and tiptoed in the front door without knocking. Ingrid was sitting on the sofa, her hands buried in her face. The letter was lying beside her on the cushion.

"Frau Schultz, may I come in?" he whispered. She sat without moving or answering.

"I brought you some more firewood," he said.

"*Danke*—I mean, thank you," she whispered back.

She would not—or maybe could not—look up. No matter. He walked softly across the living room floor to the fireplace and laid the wood in a basket on the hearth. Then he laid a couple of the drier logs onto the hot coals. With an iron poker, he jostled the red, smoldering embers under the grate. The oxygen reignited a small flame which, like a burning tongue lapping from the ashes, slowly wrapped around the fresh firewood.

With orange flames dancing around the two new logs, Walter placed a third one on. Within a minute, there was a loud pop followed by cracking and the roar of a resurrected fire.

He imagined the heat on the back of her hands and the top of her head felt good to Ingrid. Good enough to thaw her out of her shock. Slowly, she moved her hands to her lap and looked up at Walter. He saw the glistening residue of tears, but there was also a very slight smile.

"Thank you, Mr. Brewer," she said. "Thank you for helping me with the fire, and thank you so much for bringing me this letter. I know it is a long shot. But the recency of the letter gives me hope that maybe he is alive."

She's missing the point. Heinrick told her in the letter he thought he would die. She's embracing a hopeless hope. Tell her, Walter. Tell her what you know about Heinrick. She needs to get the substance of his message. It's not fair to give her false hope, to leave her wondering.

Ingrid dabbed her eyes with a handkerchief and revealed a more definite smile. *She looks like Jessie when she smiles like that.*

"Tell me, Mr. Brewer. How long will you be in Germany?"

"All weekend," he said. "I catch a plane from France to England Tuesday night. I spend a few days there and then back to the States."

"I look like such a wreck." She wiped her eyes again.

"You look great, especially considering the news you've just received."

"You've been so kind," she said hesitantly, "to come so far. The girls and I would like you to have dinner with us. But tonight is not good. You understand."

"I do. And please don't go to any trouble for me, Frau Schultz."

"You can call me Ingrid if you'd like. And if you could come back tomorrow night, the girls would love to serve you their father's favorite dessert, *Apfelstrudel.*"

"That isn't necessary, Ingrid. You've just gotten some disturbing news. I should be cooking for you."

Please, Ingrid, take a hint so I don't have to tell you. I said disturbing news.

"Nonsense. The news is good. A letter from my husband. He may be alive. At least it wasn't from the Army announcing his death. Now, we insist on showing you some hospitality if you are free. Please, can you come back at seven? We want to thank you for bringing this letter all so far."

Walter thought for a moment.

This is against my better instincts. I've done my duty. I've given her the letter. Sooner or later, she'll realize he's dead. He'll never come home, and she'll figure it out. Maybe it's better to leave now, go to England, and find Darwin McCloud's family. No real point in prolonging this.

He looked into her eyes again.

"Yes, ma'am. I'll come back tomorrow night."

"Good," she said with a smile that once again resembled Jessie's.

"But before I leave tonight, I have some gifts for you and your daughters." He reached into the package Eugene Allison had given him. "Your husband's letter referred to reading the 'book.' Some friends in America wanted you to have these copies of the book your husband was referring to. They are written in German." He handed her the three Bibles. "Inside the cover of your copy, there's an envelope with the address of the family of Darwin McCloud in England, just in case you may ever want it for any reason."

"This is so kind of you, Mr. Brewer," she said.

"If I get to call you Ingrid, you have to call me Walter," he said.

"With pleasure, Walter." She gave him a hug, and he walked out the door into the moonlit snowscape.

54

Walter rolled over and looked at the ticking alarm clock. It was 8:30 a.m. Between the lumpy mattress and his dilemma over what to tell Ingrid about Heinrick, he was operating on three sporadic catnaps of maybe fifteen minutes apiece. The lousy bed aside, his insomnia was mainly over Ingrid.

By 9 a.m., he was staring in the bathroom mirror at a face half covered with shaving cream. His hope for a relaxing, hot shave was chilled when the hotel's "hot water" felt more like a splash of iced tea from back home. At least the hotel's steam heat was working; so well, in fact, that the room was getting downright hot.

As he scraped the razor across his face, the same questions that had tormented him all night pounded the inside of his skull so hard that he experienced something rare for him, a headache.

Should I tell her or not? If so, should I admit that I killed Heinrick? I know I shot him. I don't really know that he died. I mean, I ran out of there. No one took his pulse. For all I know, the German medics could have pulled him out after we ran and resuscitated him. I don't know what happened to him.

He dragged the razor across the pronounced dimple on his chin, drawing blood—again.

Come on, Walter. You fired half a dozen rounds into the stomachs of each one of those officers. Then you tossed a live grenade at them. The grenade blast alone would have taken them out even if the bullets did not rip their internal organs to shreds. It's a miracle the letter didn't get shredded or charred. Don't fool yourself, Walter. Of course he died. Both of 'em did.

He redirected the razor in a path from the midpoint of his throat just above his Adam's apple to just under his chin.

Ouch! Blasted freezing German water!

Tapping the razor three times against the white tile basin, he flushed a heap of stubble down the drain.

Besides, I've already accomplished my mission by delivering the letter, haven't I? It's not my fault Ingrid read it wrong and won't see the obvious. I mean, a reasonable person would've concluded that Heinrick died. She doesn't need me to tell her that, if he had survived, he would be home by now. Why not meet the children, have a nice dinner, and get the heck out of here? I came here to make sure that a dead soldier's last message got to his wife and kids—not to masquerade as a messenger of death and certainly not to confess to being the killer!

Dragging the blade across his face for one last swipe, he nicked his chin once again.

He wiped the blood with a cold washcloth, stuck some toilet paper on the nicks to clot the bleeding, then walked to his window and looked out at the street below. The sound of mechanized armor turned out to be a British Army bulldozer plowing ice and snow off the streets. Yesterday's storm was gone, yielding to clear skies and an eastern sunrise.

He decided to take a walk to try and clear his mind. He threw on a pair of long johns, a thermal undershirt, a flannel shirt, jeans, boots, and an overcoat. His gloves were mostly dried out from the night before though still a bit moist in the fingertips. At least it was warm moisture. The hot steam radiator in his room ensured that everything he was wearing felt warm.

He went downstairs to the front desk where a slim but otherwise very plain British female corporal had taken over the morning shift at the front desk.

"I'm Walter Brewer. I'm staying upstairs in room 201."

"Ah yes, the American. I believe it's *Captain* Brewer, isn't it?"

"Word travels fast," he said.

"Corporal Montgomery mentioned you were here. We don't get too many Americans in this hotel. Mostly just BBC. Could I offer you a cup of hot coffee, Captain?"

"Thank you, Corporal . . ."

"Stephenson." She handed him a cup. "Is there anything I can do for you, Captain?"

"Corporal, I'm going to take a walk, I think. Anything worth seeing around here?"

"We aren't very far from the old city centre. About ninety percent of it was leveled to rubbish by our respective air forces back in early January. You might enjoy some of the sights down on the river. A few medieval castles are left standing."

"Ironic, isn't it? A city that's the cradle of Protestant Christianity becomes a cesspool for the Jew-hating, bellicose rhetoric of Adolph Hitler and winds up getting bombed to smithereens," he said.

"So true. From Martin Luther to Adolph Hitler. One must wonder how what was once such a beautiful city could have, in just a period of four centuries, hosted such diametrically-opposed philosophies. They once called Nuremberg *das Deutschen Reiches Schatzkästlein*, which means the Treasure Chest of the German Empire. Anyway, I'm afraid you won't find much sympathy from me, Captain. My uncle and two cousins died in the Nazi blitz against London."

"My condolences for your loss. And my compliments on your knowledge of the area."

"Thank you, sir," she said.

"Those big Nazi rallies—Where were they held?"

"To the southwest of the city. Not within walking distance of here, I'm afraid. We're told that nearly half a million people came out to support that Austrian corporal." She spoke with a tinge of sarcasm in describing Hitler."

"That Austrian corporal. What an appropriate description of the little bloodthirsty megalomaniac," Walter said.

"Actually, British intelligence has learned that some of the more moderate elements in the German High Command, such as the late Field Marshal Erwin Rommel, disdainfully referred to Hitler behind his back using that very phrase."

"I take it you're with British Army Intelligence?" Walter asked.

"Yes, sir. The Army has a number of us stationed here because of our fluency in German."

"My compliments to the British Army. And it's been a pleasure chatting with you, Corporal Stephenson."

"Captain, before you go out into the cold on your walk, why don't you let me sketch you a map? You may find it useful. It'll just take a second."

"You're right. I'd gotten so carried away by our conversation that I forgot to ask for directions," he said.

"The pleasure is mine, sir." She sketched out a simple map and handed it to him with a smile that transformed her looks from plain to pretty. When he smiled back, she blushed. "Cheers, Captain."

"Cheers to you, Corporal," he responded then took the map and headed out the front door of the hotel, walking north in the general direction of the Pegnitz River.

The cold air felt invigorating to his face, but the sun reflecting off the snow was blinding. He donned a pair of shades, then headed north on Färberstraße, past Breite Gasse, Ludwig, and turned right on Käiserstraße.

Let's see, the river should be near here.

As he glanced at the primitive map for the first time, his eyes barely noticed the lines that had been drawn representing the streets around the hotel and leading to the river. It was the handwritten note scribbled on the bottom of the page that grabbed his attention.

I enjoyed meeting you, Capt. Brewer. Hope you enjoy your stay. My number is 08-97651. Feel free to call if you need anything or if you would just like to talk. Cheers!

Alice Stephenson

He read the note again. Then he reread it once more. "Alice," he mumbled to himself.

Not Corporal Stephenson, but Alice. A signal that she would like to remove the formal barrier of military rank separating us? An officer isn't supposed to be fraternizing with an enlisted person, but then again, I'm not on active duty and she is British, not American. Plus, she is so knowledgeable—a fascinating conversationalist. And that accent and her smile. I'd forgotten how much I enjoy the company of intelligent women. It's amazing how much prettier she became within a period of about thirty minutes.

Mission accomplished. Walter was trying to get Ingrid off his mind for a while. Alice Stephenson had done just that.

I wonder if I should call her before I leave. Nah, she's got to be ten years younger than me. Of course, she's bound to have figured out there's a slight age difference here. Maybe I should suggest a lunch. Or maybe a dinner? Ellie would never know. Wait a minute. Why should I care if Ellie knows? I'll have to think about it.

He strolled along the banks of the Pegnitz most of the morning, thinking. It was a refreshing walk. His mind wondered and soared. He thought of Alice, of Ellie, his children, the war, and yes, Ingrid.

By early afternoon, after having walked seven or eight miles up and down the river, he headed back to the hotel.

"Captain Brewer?" the British corporal smiled as Walter walked to the front desk.

"Yes, I was looking for Alice." Walter had mustered enough confidence to suggest at least a lunch to the young-but-well-spoken and smiling Brit. If he could find her.

"Alice?" Corporal William Montgomery, British Army Intelligence, looked confused. Then the light bulb seemingly ignited. "Ah, yes. You mean Corporal Alice Stephenson. I'm sorry, Captain. She's off for the rest of the afternoon. Is there something I could help you with?"

Walter was disappointed. He could not, however, respond to Montgomery's question with a *no*. To do so would suggest that he wanted Alice for something other than official business.

"Ah, yes. Corporal, I didn't get much sleep last night. I'm

going to bunk down for a few hours. But I need to be up by eighteen hundred hours. Do you suppose you could ask the clerk to give me a wake up call then?"

Montgomery spoke to the clerk in German then looked at Walter. "You can expect a ring at eighteen hundred hours, sir. Anything else I can do for you?"

You can ask Alice to give me a call.

"No, Corporal. Thank you."

55

At six o'clock, or eighteen hundred hours in military jargon, the phone rang. Walter rolled over. The mere thought of Alice Stephenson had helped him relax enough to catch up on some of the sleep he'd missed. At least he felt a thousand percent better.

As much as he'd tried to avoid thinking of Ingrid today, the clock would no longer cooperate. He was due back in one hour. He got up and got fresh.

The fifteen-minute walk from the hotel to Ingrid's house was easier than the night before with no blizzard to contend with.

He was greeted at her front door by the appetizing smell of German cooking and the lovely sight of a smiling Ingrid Schultz in a knee-length, well-fitting, red dress, a shade darker than the color of her hair. Wearing short black pumps and a simple strand of white pearls matching the pearly-white smile that reminded him of Jessie's, it was obvious she had gone to some effort to make her appearance special for the evening. The result of her efforts was dynamic. Were it not for the circumstances and the two curly blonde-headed teenage girls standing in the background and prepared to chaperone, Walter might have thought she was ready for a date. The way Ingrid looked, he just might have gone along with the idea.

Maybe this will be easier than I thought.

"Welcome back, Walter," Ingrid said. "I'd like you to meet my daughters, Stephi and Leisel."

"A pleasure, ladies," Walter said. "I believe I've already met Stephi."

"Yes. Stephi was your welcoming committee yesterday. The girls speak some English. I'm afraid I may have to translate though."

"*Guten abend, fraulines.*" Good evening, ladies.

"*Willkommen.*" The girls giggled at Walter's southernized German accent.

"I understand that much." He smiled at them. "*Danke, fraülines.*"

"You . . . ahhr . . . velcumm." Stephi stepped forward, smiling and giggling some more.

"Could I take your coat?" Ingrid lifted the heavy bridge coat from his shoulders before he could answer.

"Thank you," he said.

At least the atmosphere is a little more lively tonight.

"Something smells spectacular," he said.

The fraulines Schultz giggled again, this time at his southernized English.

"We've made a special meal of bratwurst and schnitzel, which is Heinrick's favorite meal. And for dessert, apple strudel. I think the apple strudel is what you must be smelling."

Ingrid and the girls led Walter into the small dining room, where a feast of German delicacies had been set around the long table. Walter was seated at the head with Ingrid at his side. Stephi was at the far end with Leisel to Walter's right, sitting across from her mother.

Ingrid raised her glass as soon as they were all seated.

"Before we begin, I would like to do something reserved for the host. But since our host is not here tonight, on behalf of Major Heinrick Schultz of the German Army and also on behalf of my two sweet daughters, I would like to propose a toast to a man who brings us news and hope from our Hein-rick, wherever he his, who has come all this far at great time and expense because his heart is good. To Captain Walter Brewer of the United States Army."

Stephi and Leisel appeared tickled to be part of an official toast and clanged their apple cider against their mother's glass of red wine. Walter, embarrassed at the notion of being toasted by an enemy officer's wife—even a pretty redheaded one— looked into his plate and forced a smile of appreciation.

I'm afraid the only hope I bring for Heinrick is that he's in Heaven. A likely scenario, assuming that the contents of his letter are genuine. The sooner you accept that, the better.

"You are too kind, Frau Schultz." Walter pretended to sip the red wine she had poured for him.

"It is *you*, sir, who are kind. Because of the letter you brought us, we feel like Heinrick is here with us tonight. So in his honor and in yours, we have prepared the very same meal that was prepared for him seven years ago on the night in November 1938 that he spoke of in his letter. Let this be a night of hope and celebration."

She raised her glass again, in a follow-up toast to her orig-inal toast.

"Hear, hear!" Walter mimicked the phrase he heard members of the British armed forces mutter over drinks back in the English pubs when one member would make a comment that others agreed with.

We don't do a lot of toasting back in Martin County. Not much point in clanging Mason jars of sweetened iced tea.

But you're not in Martin County, Walter. You're in Europe. You know how the Europeans are. When in Rome, or in this case Germany. I suppose international custom would now require me to propose a toast. Oh well, what the heck?

Raising his glass, he grasped for words to return the honors. "And let me propose a toast." With the eyes of three German women expectantly on him, he hesitated for an instant then spoke slowly. "To peace and friendship forever—between our countries and between our families."

"To peace and friendship," Ingrid said as she touched her

glass to Walter's. The girls clanged their ciders together and giggled again.

"You choose your words with great tact and diplomacy, Captain." Ingrid looked sadly into his eyes.

"My words are from the heart," Walter smiled, again feigning a sip of wine. "And that's the first time I've heard you call me Captain."

"I sometimes called Heinrick that before he was promoted to major. I hope you don't mind."

"Not at all. I've been called that for nearly four years now. You get used to it when you're in the Army."

He broke eye contact and stared for a moment into his plate, where the cabbage, potatoes, and bratwurst had not been touched. "My wife, her name was Jessie. She died when I was fighting in Normandy. The Army sent me home on emergency leave before the war was over. By the time I got home, she had already been buried."

He took a deep breath. What had made him mention Jessie? Whatever the reason, his own words about her were like a knife to his soul.

"I'm very sorry about your wife." She gave him a smile that showed kindness and compassion. "Do you have children?"

"Four."

"Then you're alone as a parent," she said.

"It gets lonely."

"I know that to be true from personal experience," she said. "And I'm sorry."

"They look happy," he said.

Stephi and Leisel Schultz were whispering back and forth in German between chewing their bratwurst. In a world of their own, they were ignoring Walter and Ingrid.

"They have each other, but they miss their father."

They miss him because I shot him. Of course, if I hadn't shot him, I'm sure he would have shot me first. I wish it had been me. Then again, if that had happened, my four children would be with no parent at all. I'm sure Ellie would have raised them, but it's not the same.

They would be the real victims here, fatherless and motherless. Maybe it was a good thing I pulled the trigger first. I can't believe I'm thinking that. What a selfish attitude. But if I'm being selfish over my children, so what? This is too complicated. This is not happening. Maybe I should drink a little of that wine. No, don't do that. Alcohol isn't the answer here.

"Walter, are you all right?" Ingrid asked. "You look like you were a thousand miles away."

"Maybe not quite a thousand," he said.

I wonder how far it is from here to Normandy. Probably more like six or seven hundred.

"Since our time together is short, perhaps we should think of pleasant things. We should try to cheer each other up. After all, the beautiful snow is on the ground, the full moon is out, and Christmas is in the air."

He looked into her eyes. "I'm not a drinking man, Ingrid. But I'll drink to that." He lifted his glass and tapped it against hers.

"I hope you like my cooking," she said. "The girls are almost finished, and we haven't even started."

"Then I think we should make up for lost time," he said. She smiled again, took a sizable swallow of her red wine, and began nibbling her bratwurst between their delightful small talk.

By the time Walter and Ingrid had finished eating, Leisel and Stephi had excused themselves and had been upstairs in their bedrooms for nearly an hour.

"That was delicious, Ingrid. The best dinner I've had in years."

"You are most welcome, Captain. The meal was my pleasure. Your compliments are appreciated. It's been a long time since I have been complimented." She gazed into his eyes, again with a longing sadness. "Anyway, I hope you saved room for apple strudel."

"You won't have to twist my arm on that one," he said.

"Are you ready for it now, or would you like to wait a few minutes?"

"I'm sure it would be equally delicious now or later. I'll defer to your judgment on that one."

"Very well, I say lets go into the living room and talk for a while and save the dessert for later. And if you don't care for the strudel, we have some other desserts you might like better."

Ingrid led him into the living room on the same sofa where last night she had been sitting with her face buried in her hands. She directed him to sit first, and when he did, she sat down in the chair beside the sofa.

For some reason, the room seemed more vibrant than the night before, perhaps because the fire in the hearth was roaring with a fury. On the coffee table just in front of the sofa were the three German Bibles from Eugene Allison's Reunification Foundation.

Ingrid saw his eyes wandering toward the coffee table.

"Interesting, these books," she said. "Of course, we've heard of the Bible but never read it. We've been too wrapped up in our everyday lives. Tell me. Do you think the claims in it are true?"

Walter looked at her and smiled. "Yes, I do," he said.

"I don't know. The part about Christ rising from the dead. That seems a bit far fetched to me," she said.

"Sounds like Heinrick must have concluded it *is* true."

"Maybe so. Which would be unlike Heinrick to believe in something supernatural like rising from the dead. He was—" She caught herself. "He *is* an intelligence officer. He is a proud man. To harbor such a belief would contradict his nature. But this letter, which is clearly in his handwriting, suggests that he may have formed such a belief. Anyway, I shall read it. And my girls too. We will have discussions each night. Sort of in honor of Heinrick. Plus, we will read in honor of you too, Walter."

"Me?"

"*Ja*, you too." She smiled.

"I don't know why you would read in my honor."

She looked into his eyes and began to tear up as she spoke. "Walter, you are an honorable man. You fought for the enemy but have come all this way to bring this letter from my husband. Not many would do this for the wife of an enemy soldier. You have given us hope again that Heinrick may be alive. I sense that you have been truthful. I sense that you are a man of your word, that you would never lie to me."

I would never lie to you? I'd just let you go on thinking your husband is alive when I know better.

"Ingrid, I don't think you should read that book in honor of me. I'm nothing but a mailman delivering a letter from a long, long distance away. Read it for Heinrick. Read it for yourself and your girls. But not me. I'm but a fallible man. I would let you down if you knew the truth about me."

"You are too modest, my friend." Looking into his eyes, she leaned toward him a bit. "Your coming all this far—I sense there is more to it than just a mailman wanting to deliver a letter."

She paused and smiled again. "I sense there is something driving you from deep within. I don't know what. But whatever it is, maybe it is the same thing that drove my husband to write this letter, to share his experiences about the little Jewish girl who came to our room in the middle of the night. Somehow I sense that though you were enemies you have something forever in common, you and Heinrick. Perhaps it is because you were honorable officers. Or maybe because of some sort of common dedication to this book of which he speaks. Perhaps you both are convinced that this book you have given me is the one book of truth."

He looked back into her eyes and said nothing.

The one book of truth. You are beautiful, Frau Schultz. And perceptive. I have given you the one book of truth, but I haven't told you the truth.

His eyes broke contact with hers and wandered to the mantle, to the photograph of the officer in the German Army uniform whose eyes bore down on him.

Here I am, sitting in your house with your wife. I'm here for her. I'm here for your daughters. But I'm also here for you. What would you have me tell her? Should I tell her what I did to you?

Now gazing into the roaring fire, he remembered the stories of fire in the book he had just given her, of the burning bush seen by Moses, of the fire over the tabernacle in the desert at night, of the blaze on their heads on the Day of

Pentecost. Her gaze was still on him as a silent voice came to his ear.

You shall know the truth. And the truth shall set you free.

He looked back into her eyes and took her hand in his.

"Ingrid, there's something I need to tell you."

"What is it?"

He stopped, searching for the right words.

"I can't give you this book of truth and not tell you the truth."

"What do you mean?"

"There's something I have to tell you about Heinrick."

"What about him?"

"I'm sorry, Ingrid . . ." he felt himself choking up and looked down at the floor to avoid her eyes. "Like so many brave Germans and Americans and British men . . . Like my Brother Billy . . ." he wiped his eyes and stopped.

"What are you saying, Walter?" she demanded, looking nervous. "You are making me afraid. Just tell me."

"I'm sorry to say that Heinrick lost his life in the war."

"No. You are wrong," she protested. "You said the Americans haven't found his body. And if the Americans haven't found him and the Germans haven't found him, I'm not ready to give up. I cannot. His daughters need him."

"It's true, Ingrid."

"No. Are you saying a body was found?"

"No, I don't think a body was found."

"Then how can you be so sure?"

"Because," he said looking into her eyes, "I was there when he died."

"What do you mean, you were there when he died?"

He paused again, uttering a silent prayer for wisdom in his choice of words before proceeding. "I was a paratrooper, Ingrid. Do you know what a paratrooper is?"

"No, I don't know the word. What about it? What happened?"

The pretty face now twisted with consternation. The fear in her eyes grew with each word he spoke. "A paratrooper is someone who jumps out of airplanes."

"*Ja, ja.* With a parachute. I know what that is. Just tell me what happened. Please tell me now."

"In June of 1944, I was in England with thousands of American, British, and Canadian soldiers. We had been there for months. But on the night of the fifth, the weather cleared enough that General Eisenhower ordered the invasion to proceed. I was among the first to be dropped in."

"Wait a moment, please." She got up and walked into the kitchen. When she returned with her glass filled to the brim with red wine—this would make her second glass of the evening per Walter's count—she sat on the far end of the sofa. She took a big sip, put the glass on the table, and looked at him. "Okay, I'm ready. Please continue."

"Just seconds after midnight on June sixth, hundreds of airplanes filled with paratroopers started taking off from England headed to France. Everyone was quiet on the flight. We looked around the plane, at the faces of our friends. Many of us had wives and children. We knew that not all of us would make it, that some of us, maybe all of us, were going to die.

"Then, when we broke out of the clouds, the Germans started firing at us with everything they had. There were explosions all around our plane, bursts of fire in the air, under the aircraft, and around the wings.

"Our plane was headed for a drop zone several miles behind the beaches. Five minutes before we reached the drop zone, we were hit by antiaircraft fire from the ground. "We threw open the back doors and started bailing. No more than five seconds after I jumped, there was an explosion. I looked up. Our plane was engulfed in flames. My chute deployed, and I started floating toward the ground."

Walter relived each moment of the invasion as he told Ingrid, from the plane being hit to his split-second decision to jump—everything.

Ingrid said nothing the entire time, her face a mask of fear, horror, and sadness.

"I thought I was going to die. I dropped like a rock in the dark. I hit the ground hard and was knocked out. When I woke up between one-thirty and two in the morning, I had been rescued by several members of the French Resistance. They had taken me to a small house nearby."

"What do you mean by 'French Resistance?'" Ingrid gulped down the last drop of wine glass number two.

"French Resistance—native Frenchman, just ordinary citizens, who were giving active assistance to the British and the Americans," he said.

"You mean they were working against Germany," she said.

"That's right, Ingrid. They resented having the German Army on French soil. They were willing to die for France."

"I thought the French hated the British," she said.

"There's some truth to that. But these resistance fighters, they disliked the German Army even more," he said.

"They hated the Germans, no?"

"To be honest Ingrid, yes they did. One of the women who rescued me said that her husband had been executed by the Nazis. She wanted to kill Germans more than anything. Unfortunately, sometimes there is hatred in war."

"If you will excuse me, Walter. I have to go to the bathroom."

Ingrid rose and walked across the floor, past the fireplace and toward the kitchen. When she returned a few minutes later, she was holding in her hand a new bottle of red wine, freshly opened. She plopped the full bottle down on the coffee table and sat down beside him.

She poured her wine glass full for the third time. Taking a sip, she looked into his eyes.

"I hope you understand, Walter. If you are going to tell me that my husband was killed by these resistance peoples, I am going to need some more of this." She took yet another swig.

Now she thinks the Resistance killed Heinrick. She probably wants me to say I joined in and fought beside Heinrick against the evil Resistance. Anyway, she'll probably be too drunk to comprehend by the time I tell her what really happened.

"Are you going to be okay?" he asked.

"What do you mean? About the wine?"

"I just don't want you to feel bad in the morning," he said.

"Don't worry about that. We German women can hold our wine fine. I promise not to take advantage of you just because I am drunk and you are not."

She took another swallow. "Now if you want to take advantage . . ." She paused. "Perhaps you are right. Perhaps I *am* drinking too much. And you were trying to tell me about these resistance peoples and my husband. I should be embarrassed." She took yet another drink, reducing a glass that was only moments ago filled to the brim to a glass that was now about half full.

Looking into his eyes, she spoke again. "Now that I have been to the bathroom and gotten a fresh bottle of wine, maybe you can finish the story, no? Are you going to tell me what they did to him?"

"When I was rescued by the Resistance, I asked if there was a communications station nearby that could be attacked. They told me yes, there was a communications hub near the train depot in a nearby town."

"What was the name of the town?" she asked.

"Carentan, in Normandy."

"What happened next?" She started sipping her third glass of Pinôt noire again.

"They said that the communications hub was crucial to the German ability to communicate on the peninsula. Take it out, and we could disrupt telegraphs from the beaches to Berlin. They said it wasn't heavily guarded, so we planned an attack.

"Three of the Resistance fighters led me into an alley just beside the communications hub. Remarkably, it was unguarded. Still, we knew that at least two German officers were inside running the hub. Our first objective was not to harm the officers, but to destroy their equipment. But we knew that they would kill us to stop us. We knew we would have no choice.

"There was a woman with me, a French Resistance fighter. She was the woman I told you whose husband had been executed by the Nazis. The woman rescued me and helped me survive the night."

"The woman who hates the Germans?" Ingrid asked.

"She's the one. Anyway the two of us waited a few

minutes to see if anyone would show up, any guards or anything like that. We ran across the street and into the front door. Sure enough, two German officers were manning the control center, a major and a captain. Shots were fired and we tossed a grenade onto the control center, destroying it.

"I ran out the front door, but the woman, this Resistance fighter, stayed behind. I wasn't sure why. I yelled for her to come out. I needed her to guide me out of the area, which I wasn't familiar with. Finally, she came out and we ran for our lives. By now, other German units had descended on the area. Searchlights were everywhere. We could hear troops running to the communications depot.

"This woman led me deep into the dark alley I told you about. There, the Resistance had a motorcycle waiting for us. I hopped on behind her, and she sped out the back of the alley, into the country out of town. We escaped that night to a barn somewhere. We spent all night in the barn.

"Next morning, just after sunrise, some American paratroopers and some German soldiers converged on the field outside the barn where we were hiding. There was a firefight. The American unit wiped out the Germans, and I was rescued by the Americans. The colonel commanding the American unit invited me to join him as his executive officer, and as the second highest ranking officer there, I accepted.

"Before leaving the barn, the woman gave me an envelope. She said it contained some papers off the body of one of the dead German officers. Soon afterwards, my wife died and the Army shipped me out of France and back to America. I didn't pay any attention to the papers the woman gave me until over a year later. Just three months ago, in September, a guest minister came to our church. He was fluent in German, so I asked him to translate the papers. It turned out to be the letter from Heinrick to you, the letter I gave you last night."

Ingrid sat on the sofa, staring into space. Tears streamed silently down her face. "Then it's true. He must be dead."

Walter put his hand on her shoulder. "Yes, I believe it's true. And I'm sorry. Nobody could have survived the gunshots and the grenade blast. I'm sorry to give you this news."

She looked at him and wiped her tears with her hand.

He reached into his pocket and offered her a handkerchief.

"This woman who killed my husband, what was her name?"

"I'm not sure that it matters, but the woman's name was Marie Claire." He looked her in the eyes. "But Ingrid, it wasn't Marie Claire who shot Heinrick."

"What do you mean?"

"What I mean is, I'm the one who had the gun, and I'm the one who had the grenade."

"Do you mean . . ." She pulled her hand away from his and stood up.

"Yes. Ingrid. I am so sorry."

"You . . ." She covered her mouth with her hand.

"I couldn't come here and give you this book of truth and not tell you the truth."

A look of astonishment crossed her face. "I thought these resistance people hated Germans. I thought *they* killed him. I thought you were going to tell me what *they* did to him and that *you* were going to be my friend."

"I did. I do want to be your friend. I wanted you to have Heinrick's letter. I wanted to give you the books."

"You came into my home. You were friendly to my daughters! You were friendly to me. You ate at my table! Why would you do all this if you were the one who murdered my husband?"

"I didn't murder him, Ingrid. It was war. I didn't know who he was. The last thing I'd ever want to do is harm you. If my wife were alive, I'd gladly trade places with Heinrick right now if I could, but I can't."

He stood, putting his hand gently on her shoulder.

"*Fassen sie mich nicht an!*" she said and immediately pulled away.

"Ingrid, please."

"*Sie sind eklig!*" Tears dripped off her cheeks, splatting on the floor.

"I don't understand," he said.

"*Lassen sie mich in rue! Ich möchte alleine sein!*"

"I'm sorry, Ingrid. I don't understand anything you're saying."

She wiped her eyes and stared at him. "Out! Now do you understand? Get out! I want you out of my house now, or I'm calling the police!"

She walked to the mantle, took Heinrick's picture down, and hugged it against her chest, sobbing.

Walter turned, grabbed his bridge coat, and walked out the front door.

56

Ellie was rubbing her hand across the little boy's warm forehead when the doorbell rang.

"Daddy!"

"Daddy's home!"

"Aunt Ellie! It's Daddy!"

Ellie placed a cold compress on the boy's head then tiptoed out of the room and down the wooden plank stairs, where Walter was getting mugged with hugs from Zack, Caroline, and Virginia. When his eyes met hers, she thought she noticed an extra little sparkle.

"There's Aunt Ellie," he said.

"Welcome home, world traveler."

"It's good to be home." He accepted a barrage of kisses from Zack and the two girls. "Where's Hardison?" he asked.

"He's upstairs, asleep," Ellie said. "He's been under the weather. He still has a mild fever, but Dr. Pap says he'll be fine."

"What's the matter?" The smile on Walter's face evaporated into a look of concern.

"The flu," Ellie said. "It's been going around. Dr. Pap says it's got to run its course. But he thinks the worst is over. Doc says he should be good as new by Christmas Eve."

"Thank the Lord for that," he said.

"Daddy, guess what?" Virginia beamed at him.

"What, sweetie?"

"We bought Mommy a Christmas present!"

"You did what?"

"And guess what else, Daddy?" Caroline's smile was even wider than Virginia's.

"I'm almost afraid to guess." Walter's fake smile looked plastered across his face, as if trying to mirror the smiles from his grinning girls.

"I wrote Mommy a letter. We taped it on her present. Right now it's under Aunt Ellie's Christmas tree. But when we get back to Jamesville, we'll put the package and the letter under our tree. Aunt Ellie says Mommy will be able to read the letter from Heaven!"

He looked up at Ellie.

She knew exactly what the raised eyebrow meant. She had seen it a hundred times before.

"I think we need to talk," Ellie said.

"Why don't you kids look in the bag on the floor? Daddy has a little something for all six of you from England. Just don't open Hardison's yet. Right now, Daddy needs to talk to Aunt Ellie for a few minutes."

The kids scampered for the cloth bag containing souvenir tea sets for the girls and wooden, hand-carved Big Bens for the boys. Ellie put her hand on Walter's back and led him into the living room.

"Here, let me take your jacket."

"Thanks."

"Have a seat."

"Don't mind if I do." He sat in the pink wingback across from the sofa and looked at her.

"I bet you're probably wondering about the present for Jessie," she said.

"The thought crossed my mind," he said.

She looked at him for a moment, studying his face. "When

you left, they started missing you terribly. Little Caroline was worried about you not coming back. She didn't believe the war was over. When I finally convinced them you would be coming back soon, they started talking a lot about Jessie."

Ellie stopped for a moment, choking back tears. She continued, "Last Friday night, little Caroline was sitting alone by the Christmas tree. No one else was in the living room. I walked in and saw tears in her eyes. I asked her what was wrong, and she said it was about the presents. I asked her what she meant, and she said that everyone had a present under the tree except for her mommy.

"I didn't know how to handle it, so I let her sleep with me that night. She was very clingy to me. And she's a real cuddlebug.

"The next morning, just to give all the kids a change of environment, we decided to walk downtown to do some Christmas shopping. I wanted to make sure they had a little something to put under the tree for each other in Jamesville. I thought they could sort of tell Aunt Ellie what they wanted and then I could go back later and take care of things."

"That's kind of you, Ellie, but you didn't have to do that," he said.

"I know, but it's something I wanted to do. Besides, I knew you wouldn't have much time to play Santa Claus when you got back with such a short time before Christmas."

"You're right. Thank you," he said.

"Anyway, we first went to the dime store, and the girls saw all kinds of dolls they liked. Then we went over to the hardware store, because I heard that Mr. Gurkin had gotten in a shipment of toy airplanes and ships that the boys might like. We spent about an hour in each store. The boys were bored in the dime store, and the girls were bored in the hardware store. But we got through it, and I took a mental note of what all six said they wanted.

"When we finished at the hardware store, it was time for lunch. They all said they were hungry and wanted to walk down to the drug store for a big soda and some candy. Since I hadn't cooked anything at home, I agreed to the soda but told them they would have to settle for one of Mr. Arp's delicious chicken salad sandwiches instead of the candy. After some complaints from the peanut galley, they realized Aunt Ellie wasn't going to budge, so they agreed to eat the sandwich. Then we started down Water Street toward the drug store.

"As we passed Ligget's Jewelry Store, I felt a tug on the back of my jacket. I turned around, and it was Caroline. She asked if we could go inside. I asked her why, and she said she saw something in the window she wanted to look at. I knew the kids were hungry, but she was giving me that look with those big, brown puppy-dog eyes of hers."

"I know the look very well," Walter said.

"Anyway, you know the effect that look has on you."

"Yes, I do, very much so," he said with a big smile.

"So we all walked in the jewelry store, all seven of us. It's not a very big place, and I think Mr. Ligget felt a bit overwhelmed."

"Raymond Ligget overwhelmed? Best I remember, that guy was always Mister Cool and Calm," Walter snickered.

"I just think a lot of children around all that valuable jewelry made him nervous at first. But when he asked how he could help us, Caroline looked up at him with that irresistible face."

"Let me guess. He was putty in her hands, just like you were?"

"I've never seen such a transformation. She walked up to him and said, 'My name is Caroline Brewer. I'm ten years old, and I'm from Jamesville. I would like to see the gold necklace on the mannequin in the front window please.' Walter, he melted on the spot like candle wax. He looked at me and smiled and said, 'Yes ma'am, anything you'd like,' and then he handed her the necklace.

"She held it in her hands a few minutes then held it up to the light. It was adorable the way she was examining it, like she was a certified gemologist or something. Then she looked at me and said, 'Aunt Ellie, this is the present I want to give my mommy for Christmas. I know she can't wear it up in Heaven, but I know she'll know I gave it to her.'

"I looked down at her, and she looked up at me and said, 'It can be from all of us children. And I promise to pay you back. I can get the money from my daddy or get a job at the dime store. Please.'

"What could I say, Walter? That her mother wasn't coming back? I've never experienced anything like that before. She was just tugging on my heartstrings. I looked over at Mr. Ligget. His eyes were filled with tears. When I told her okay, she literally jumped for joy right there in the store. Then the other kids started getting excited too, even the boys.

"I just had to buy it for her. Mr. Ligget wrapped it, and we brought it home and put it under the tree. Later, she came up with the idea of writing the letter. The letter was just from her, not the other kids. I have no idea what she wrote. She just brought me an envelope with *Mommy* written on it and asked me to tape it to the package. I hope I haven't stepped out of line here."

Walter wiped his eyes with a handkerchief.

"She has a heart of gold," he said. "And no, you certainly weren't out of line. You've been wonderful to these children, Ellie."

"I'll be happy to keep them any time you want to go to Europe," she said. "And speaking of which, tell me how things turned out. I've been dying to know."

He hesitated, as if he were far away in thought.

"Walter?"

"Sorry," he said. "It's a long story, and I know you're ready for me to take these kids off your hands. Maybe I could give you the abbreviated version now with more details later."

"Wrong about the kids, Walter. In fact, I was hoping you could all stay for dinner."

Another faraway look. Was he having flashbacks from the battlefield?

"Are you all right, Walter?"

"Sure Ingri—Ellie. I'm sorry."

She shot him an inquisitive look. She'd never heard him botch her name with the name of another woman before.

"I'm going to go get you a glass of sweet tea and a slice of pecan pie," she said. "Maybe then you'll remember that you're back in Eastern North Carolina and remember *my* name. You know, your sister-in-law and former fiancée? And then maybe, just maybe, you can remember enough about what happened in Europe to, shall we say, share a bit of information?"

When she plopped the slice of pie and glass of tea on the coffee table in front of the sofa and then plopped herself down beside him, a change came over him. The faraway look disappeared. Life returned to his eyes. He seemed ready to talk.

"I'd evaluate the trip in two parts. Germany was disappointing. England was a delight."

"Why was Germany disappointing? Weren't you able to deliver the letter?"

"Yes, I found her at her home in Nuremberg on December seventh in the middle of a snow storm. When I got there, her daughter met me at the door. She has two adorable blonde daughters. They are twelve and fourteen years old."

"What about Ingrid? What was she like?"

"Early thirties maybe. Red hair, green eyes, average figure," he said.

"Is she pretty?"

"Not ugly. Not the prettiest I've ever seen," he said. "Actually, she was attractive. She also speaks pretty decent English. She's an English teacher in Germany."

"That must've helped," she said.

"It did. Anyway, I introduced myself and told her who I was. She invited me in and I gave her the letter. I also gave her the Bibles. It was hard telling her the truth about her husband."

"How did you handle that?"

"She'd been asking me some questions about the Bible—if I believed its claims are true. I said yes, of course. I felt awkward telling her the Bible is true and hiding the truth about what happened to her husband. I figured she deserved to know. So I came out with it. I told her I had fired the rifle at Heinrick and I had thrown the grenade."

Ellie felt her eyes widen. She thought for a second, stunned by what must have happened next. "I can't believe you did that, Walter."

"I didn't feel I had a choice. She deserved the truth, Ellie."

"How did she react?"

"By this time she'd consumed close to a bottle of red wine. She stood up, started yelling something in German and crying. I couldn't understand her. But I could tell she was upset. When I asked her to translate, she chastised me for coming into her home, having dinner with her, and then announcing that I killed Heinrick. She ordered me out of the house. I felt sick. I left and went back to the hotel. That was the last I saw of her."

Ellie sat for a few minutes, trying to absorb what she had just heard. "I'm sorry it turned out that way, Walter. But you did your duty. You delivered a priceless letter that a dead soldier wrote to his wife and children, and you gave them the Bibles. Maybe something good will come of it yet."

"Thanks for your encouragement, Ellie."

"Speaking of which, didn't you say your trip to England was a bit more encouraging?"

"Yes." He speared a wedge of pecan pie and washed it down with iced tea.

"Well?" She studied his face, trying to figure him out. "Walter, you look like you're in the Land of Oz. What's the matter? Are we off to see the wizard?"

"Sorry, Ellie. England. Yes. It was good. Maybe the best part about it is that I found the parents of the young British commando who had the German Bible Heinrick found. They're very nice people, but they're divorced. She is from royalty—sort of. She is a duchess. Her name is Duchess Juliana McCloud. She lives in a flat in one of the nicer parts of London, in Kensington. Her ex-husband is a Royal Naval captain. His name is Edward McCloud. He was a destroyer squadron commander in the war and now has taken command of a British battleship."

"They sound like fascinating people," she said.

"They are. I spent quite a bit of time with them both. Juliana had me over several afternoons for tea, and Edward took me to dinner one night. I gave them both copies of Heinrick's letter, translated into English. They were very appreciative and moved by the impact their son had on an enemy soldier. They told me that their son, Darwin, had been killed at the battle of Dieppe, on the coast of France in 1942 and that he was posthumously awarded the Victoria Cross."

"I should know what that means," Ellie said.

"That's the highest medal given to a member of the British military for heroism and valor. It's the equivalent to our Congressional Medal of Honor."

"They must be so proud of Darwin," she said.

"They are," he said.

"So your trip to England was a success."

"Yes. I struck up a friendship with the McClouds. We exchanged addresses and telephone numbers, and they said that if we . . . that if I ever want to come to England, that there will be a free place to stay."

To try and make Christmas seem more like Christmas, Walter and the kids spent a lot of time with Aunt Ellie and the cousins. The group of eight spent all day together on Christmas Eve at Ellie's in Plymouth and all day New Year's Eve at Walter's in Jamesville. The combined family get-togethers were good for all. The kids loved playing together, and Walter, as always, enjoyed Ellie's company.

Walter had a tough time New Year's Day. He and Jessie had a tradition of taking down the tree on New Year's Day. But on January 1, 1946, for the second straight year, he performed the honors alone. A single, unopened package was left resting on the floor, with a few pine needles having been shed on it. It was from Caroline.

Walter took the little package and the unopened note taped to it and locked them in a fireproof safe. He wondered how many gifts to Jessie the safe would hold in future years.

57

The first purple martin sighting of the year and the sweet fragrance of early-blooming azaleas meant that spring had arrived in Martin County. The warm weather had come not a day too soon as far as Walter was concerned. Maybe the change of seasons was just what he needed to get his mind off Ingrid Schultz.

With his car window down, enjoying the late afternoon sunshine, he pulled into Widow Edna Overholtz's driveway to drop off her mail. It was his last stop of the day.

He turned around on the rural road and headed back to Jamesville, where he would stop by the post office and check his own mail before picking up the children at Eva Gray's house.

Sorting through the usual assortment of bills, he noticed one of the envelopes had an unusual postmark.

The stamp bore a picture of His Royal Majesty, the King of England.

His curiosity piqued, he ripped it open first.

Captain Edward McCloud, Royal Navy
&
Baroness Juliana McCloud

Request the Honour of Your Presence
At Their Marriage

First Presbyterian Church
Ardentinny, Scotland
Saturday, April 13, 1946

Two o'clock In The Afternoon

Reception To Follow At Officer's Club
HMS *Armadillo*
R.S.V.P.

Folded inside the invitation was a handwritten note on Juliana McCloud's stationary.

March 6, 1946

Dear Capt. Brewer,

I know this would be a long and expensive trip for you to make, but I wanted to extend an invitation to you and a guest because it was your visit which is largely responsible for our reconciliation.

The letter you brought us written by the German officer made us both realize the eternal impact that our son, even in death, had on people. We were deeply moved. His prayers have been answered. Thank you.

Very truly yours,
Juliana McCloud.

Alone in the post office as the late-afternoon sun streamed through the front windows, Walter broke into a big smile.

The Lord does work in mysterious ways. I went to Europe for Ingrid Schultz, and it looks like the result is that the McClouds are getting remarried. Maybe it was all worth it after all!

He felt like doing a jig. First, he needed to pick up the kids. Then there was somewhere he needed to go.

Ellie looked out the door. She looked at her watch. It was 8 p.m.

Walter and all four kids were waiting on her steps. Seeing the whole crew show up on a weeknight was unusual. She opened the door.

"What a delightful surprise," she said.

"I know it's a school night, but I need to show you something," Walter said.

"Come on in," she said.

Ellie sent the kids upstairs and brought Walter into the kitchen, where she was in the middle of baking Jessie's German chocolate cake recipe. He handed her the invitation and letter from Juliana.

"This *is* good news," she said. "I don't know these people, but I'm happy for them. I'm also happy for you. See, your trip paid off in ways you didn't even expect!"

"You're right," he said. "And I didn't expect to get invited to a wedding in Scotland."

"Wait a minute." Her stunning face suddenly looked puzzled. "I thought you said they were from London. I wonder why they're getting married in Scotland."

"I bet it has to do with their son. Juliana told me when I visited with her that his commando training was in Ardentinny. She even showed me a few letters he wrote her from there. Apparently, he had attended a Presbyterian church there."

Satisfied with his explanation, she looked at him and smiled. "So . . . are you going to do it?" she asked.

"Do what?"

"Go to the wedding, of course. You've got an invitation. Why don't you go?" she asked.

"To Scotland?"

"Of course, to Scotland," she said.

He hesitated for a moment, his eyes on the floor. Then he looked at her. "Well, there *is* something I wanted to talk to you about."

She grinned at him. "Then you *are* thinking about going. That would mean a lot to the McClouds. And you don't have to say another word, because the answer is yes!" she said.

"Yes?" he asked.

"Yes! Of course, I'd love to keep the kids while you're gone. In fact, by that week it might be warm enough for a trip to the beach. I'll rent a cottage at Nags Head and take the six of them to the ocean. They'll love it. In fact, I've just gotten a letter from Becky that she'll be off for spring break. I think I'll see if she'd like to come too. That's a pretty good deal for a college girl, a free week at the beach in exchange for a little baby sitting assistance. She'll jump at the chance. And then—"

"Ellie!"

It wasn't like Walter to cut her off midsentence. He normally let her ramble until she ran out of gas. She looked surprised at the sudden interruption.

"I didn't bring the kids over here on a school night to ask you to babysit," he said.

"You didn't?"

"No." He paused for a moment. "I came to ask another favor."

"Really? What is it?"

"I don't want you to watch the kids, Ellie. I want you to come with me to the wedding."

Her mouth dropped.

"Well, well. I get to witness something about as rare as a solar eclipse—Ellie Williams Brewer speechless."

"Did I just hear you right?" she said, still half dazed and now half smiling. "Did you just compare me to a solar eclipse, or did you just ask me to go to Scotland with you?"

"Actually, I asked you to go to a wedding with me. The wedding, of course, just happens to be in Scotland. Now, if you go to the wedding with me, it would make sense to travel to Scotland with me. Unless, of course, you'd rather have the Williams Trust charter separate yachts. To me, that wouldn't seem to be an efficient use of resources. But then, what do I know? I'm just the mailman."

"And a very conservative mailman who is usually overly

concerned with what people think." She felt herself smiling. "Not that I particularly care, but if I go to Scotland with you, you know people will start talking. I thought that was a big concern of yours."

"We'd do some damage control before we left. We can reserve separate cabins on the ship and get separate rooms wherever we stay. Then we'd announce our intentions of having separate quarters to all the little old ladies in the bridge club to try and minimize the gossip."

"I don't know, Walter. This separate quarters business sounds like an inefficient use of Williams Trust Fund resources." She winked at him. "Anyway, if you think that story will stop the gossip, I've got some news for you."

"I know it's kind of lame, Ellie. But I'll bet people have probably been talking about us for a while anyway. I mean, I bring the kids over to play all the time. The little old ladies probably imagine something's going on over here anyway."

"No!" she said facetiously. "Say it isn't so!"

"Smart aleck!"

"I just think it's kind of funny," she said. "Watching you worry about gossip about you!" She chuckled.

"You know what? I'm not worried about it any more. We know our intentions are honorable. So, what we do in Scotland or over here, or anywhere else for that matter, is none of anybody's business," he said.

"I like the way you're talking, baby," she said.

"You haven't called me 'baby' in years," he said.

"About fifteen or sixteen by my count."

"So what's your answer, baby?" he said.

"Who would watch the kids?"

"Eva Gray's already agreed to take all six. She's sworn to secrecy," he said.

"In that case, I can't think of anything more fun than to stir up the gossip mill. Yes, I'd love to go with you to Scotland. And I promise to be good."

58
FIRST PRESBYTERIAN CHURCH
ARDENTINNY, SCOTLAND
APRIL 13, 1946

Based on the invitation announcing the marriage of *Captain* Edward McCloud to *Baroness* Juliana McCloud, Walter figured the ceremony, like so much of the pomp and pageantry that made Britain distinctly British, would be formal. He had purchased an expensive black tux with tails just for the occasion. On the morning of the wedding, he got up, shaved, and showered. He put the tux on and stood before the full-length mirror in the small room in the historic Ardentinny Hotel.

The tux fits fine. And I sure spent enough money on it. I'm sure the baroness and the captain would approve, and Ellie would like it. So why don't I feel right wearing it? I feel like a woman, unable to make a decision about what to wear. I think I'll try the other option.

He stripped out of the tux and slipped into the other option he had brought along, just in case he changed his mind. Adjusting the silver star he'd been awarded for attacking the communications depot on D-Day and the bronze star for combat in Normandy, he again stood before the mirror.

The British are our closest allies, and the war's barely over. We've all been through so much together. For those of us who were at Normandy, British and American, it felt like we were in hell together. I'll wear the dress uniform of the United States Army out of respect for Captain McCloud and his son and all the other British naval personnel who will be there today.

With a handkerchief, he polished a fingerprint smudge off his captain's bars and headed downstairs to meet Ellie for brunch on the veranda overlooking Loch Long.

At 1:15 p.m. under sunny skies, the black cab carrying Walter and Ellie stopped on the narrow, cobblestone street in Arden-tinny.

On one side of the street was the small, brown Presbyterian church where wedding preparations were underway. To accommodate the overflow crowd of military officers, members of Parliament, and other family members, about a dozen white canopies had been erected on the lush, green grass outside the front doors.

White folding chairs were lined up in rows on each side of a center aisle. The tents and chairs extended the sanctuary onto the lawn to accommodate the captain and baroness's long guest list.

On the other side of the street, just across from the church, two Royal Marines, armed with Enfield rifles, stood at attention flanking the guard station of the entrance to the Royal Naval Commando's Training Facility. Off in the distance behind the marines, perhaps three blocks down a hill, Walter could see the sparkling blue waters of Loch Long. Scotland was the most beautiful place he'd ever seen.

Handing the driver three pounds, he walked around the cab to open the door for Ellie.

Wearing a formal ivory dress with a strand of white pearls around her neck, Ellie took Walter's arm and let him escort her to the end of the line. It seemed that the entire Royal Navy Officer Corps, decked in dress choker whites, was waiting to get in.

If not for her diamond broach glistening brightly in the afternoon sunshine and her deep tan, Ellie fit right in with the sea of white uniforms, dresses, and shoes snaking around the green grass.

Walter noted that none of the British women with their pale complexions were any match for *his* escort, who at thirty-five, looked even better to him than the day he met her at the FCX in Plymouth sixteen years ago. In his fleeting moment of pride at escorting the prettiest woman in sight, he failed to notice the small military band assembling on the lawn on the other side of the white canopies.

"Your invitation, sir," the young ensign took Ellie's arm and led the couple to a seat along the grassy aisle under the canopy but just outside the door to the church.

"I was hoping we'd get inside the church. I can't see inside too well from here," Walter said.

"We're here. That's what counts," Ellie whispered. "I know Juliana will appreciate you coming. Besides, with these loudspeakers out here, I think we'll be able to hear just fine."

Sure enough, within a few minutes organ music was piping over the loudspeakers from the chancel area, and the amplified sound enabled the guests outside the sanctuary to hear better than the VIPs seated inside.

By one forty, the organ was getting some competition from several long, black automobiles which had just pulled up on the cobblestone street in front of the church. Their engines running in idle, Walter looked to his left across Ellie to see who was inside. The tinted glass made that impossible from his vantage point. He did notice, however, that a platoon of Royal Marines was sealing off all access to the cars.

I wonder what all the commotion's about.

At one forty-five, the organ stopped and the loudspeaker let out a momentary squeal. The squealing stopped, and a booming voice rang out over the loudspeakers.

"Ladies and gentlemen, would you please rise for the introduction and arrival of our distinguished guests."

As soon as everyone rose, the booming voice returned.

"Ladies and gentlemen, Commanding Officer of His Majesty's battleship, HMS *Victorious.*"

The military band now made its presence known, blaring a trumpet fanfare followed by a melodic march. A British Navy captain, escorted by an attractive woman who looked fortyish, strode down the aisle just past Walter and Ellie and into the church.

"Ladies and gentlemen, Commanding Officer of the Royal Naval Commando Training Facility, HMS *Armadillo*."

As the military band repeated the same ruffles and flourishes afforded the first officer, a shorter Navy captain, escorting his wife, walked down the grassy aisle. Walter noticed his breastplate bore the name *Rudy*.

"Ladies and gentlemen, the Second Lord of the Admiralty."

This time the trumpet fanfare sounded a bit longer, with more flourishes and higher notes.

"This guy is one of the highest officials in the British military," Walter whispered to Ellie. The official walked by to the tune of a stately military march, donning a sophisticated blue uniform with gold braiding draped over each of his shoulders. The hat was that of an eighteenth-century mariner, high like a camel hump in the middle with long and narrow flat bills extending in the front and back. The fancy garb, complete with a white ostrich feather stapled to the black felt hat, looked like something Napoleon or John Paul Jones would wear, reminiscent perhaps of the British Navy dress uniform from the American Revolutionary War era.

When the man with the fancy hat was inside the church, the military march stopped. In its place, a snare drummer commenced a long drum roll, as two young naval ensigns dressed in choker whites rolled a white carpet down the grassy aisle and up the front steps into the church.

"I'll bet this means the bride is here," Ellie whispered to Walter as the drum roll continued.

Walter looked at his pocket watch and whispered back. "It's five minutes to two. I bet you're right."

With the ensigns now out of sight and the drum roll continuing, the man with the distinctively British voice came back on the loudspeaker.

"Ladies and gentlemen."

The drum roll stopped.

"L-A-D-I-E-S AND G-E-N-T-L-E-M-E-N."

The announcer paused for a few seconds, as if he had forgotten what he was going to say.

"Her Royal Highness, the Princess of Wales, accompanied by Lieutenant Philip Mountbatten."

"Oh my goodness," Ellie whispered. "Did he say what I think he said?"

Even Walter's heart nearly jumped from his chest at what he just heard. He turned around and looked back down the aisle. Standing there, accompanied by a young naval officer, was the Crown Princess to the throne of Britain, Elizabeth II. Never in combat had his heart raced as fast as it was racing now.

The twenty-year-old princess, with a shy smile on her face, stepped forward as the herald trumpets blared a long and regal fanfare befitting only a monarch. She walked right past Walter, so close he could smell her royal perfume.

Ellie was so excited that she grabbed Walter's hand as the princess passed by. She let go only when Elizabeth disappeared inside the church.

"L-A-D-I-E-S AND G-E-N-T-L-E-M-E-N."

What now? Walter wondered. I wonder if this is the prime minister or the king himself!

"L-A-D-I-E-S AND G-E-N-T-L-E-M-E-N."

"Would you please remain standing for the entrance of the bride, Baroness Juliana McCloud, escorted by her uncle, the Earl of Dorchester."

To the stately march of "Pomp and Circumstance," Juliana McCloud strode slowly down the aisle in a modest wedding dress. Next to Ellie, the fair, blonde baroness was definitely the second prettiest woman there.

With a beaming smile, her blue eyes roamed the crowd of guests under the canopy. Her smile brightened when she made eye contact with Walter.

Juliana disappeared into the church, leaving Walter and Ellie still so dazed from having seen the princess that they hardly noticed anything until about twenty minutes later, when eight junior naval officers in white uniforms and white gloves lined up in two rows of four, facing each other on the church steps.

"Swords, arch!" The command came from the officer at the bottom right step.

"Ladies and gentlemen," the voice on the loudspeaker had returned.

"Captain and Mrs. Edward McCloud!"

Edward and Juliana appeared at the top of the church steps, kissed, then ducked under the glistening arch of stainless steel swords. They walked down the steps and onto the white carpet in the midst of the guests who were seated under the outside canopies. They broke their stride only when Juliana reached Walter's seat.

"Thank you so much for coming so far," she said in an elegant British accent, smiling at Walter. Then she grabbed Edward's arm and quickly left the canopy area, where a horse-drawn carriage was waiting to take them to the reception across the street at the base.

59

The Officer's Club banquet hall at HMS *Armadillo* was arranged so as to make the British social and military hierarchies visibly evident. On the far side from Walter and Ellie was the head table, surrounded by senior military officers and other VIPs of blue-blooded lineage. Members of Parliament and mid-level politicians were generally in the center. Junior officers and others lucky enough to be on the guest list, including Walter and Ellie, were on the side closest to the entrance.

During the succulent lunch of beef Wellington, a number of guests on her side of the room were straining their necks to try and get a glimpse of the Princess of Wales. Even Ellie appeared to be sucked into the unaccustomed habit of star gazing. After finishing lemon chiffon wedding cake, Walter noticed that the short Royal Navy captain who had marched down the aisle—the one with the name tag that read *Rudy*—was headed to the podium.

"Ladies and gentlemen. I am Captain Al Rudy, commanding officer of the Royal Naval Commando Training Facility here in Ardentinny. On behalf of the Royal Navy and on behalf of my good friend, Captain Edward McCloud and his better half who is also my good friend, Baroness Juliana McCloud, I welcome you all to HMS *Armadillo.*

"We are pleased that you have joined us on this momentous occasion, an occasion where my good friend, Captain McCloud, has proved he has gotten smarter over time by once again tying the knot with Baroness Juliana, who unlike Edward, gets prettier and prettier over time!"

"Hear!! Hear!" A hearty round of approval followed, then a host of champagne glasses were raised to the sky.

"As you know, Princess Elizabeth was here with us today, helping us celebrate this beautiful ceremony. The Princess has asked me to convey her regrets that she could not stay for the reception, as tomorrow being Palm Sunday, she has a number of duties back in London. However, before she left, she handed me a telegram from Buckingham Palace and asked me to read it to you this afternoon."

Rudy carefully unfolded the Royal telegram, holding it high above the audience for everyone to see, masterfully building a moment of theatrical tension.

"Hmm. A telegram from Buckingham palace. I've been trying to decide whether I should actually read this." The crowd laughed. "Oh, all right, if you insist.

"To Captain Edward McCloud and Baroness Juliana McCloud.

"Please accept my heartfelt congratulations on this your wedding day, as you renew your commitment and again dedicate your lives to one another. Your service to our nation has not gone unnoticed. As a couple, your devotion to our military and to charitable works has made Britain stronger, safer, and better. Through it all, you raised a son who laid down his all for the Crown and, in doing so, rightfully received the Victoria Cross, the highest award the Crown has to offer. Many thanks to you forever and may God bless you in all your endeavors. With Greatest Respect, His Majesty, King George."

Applause broke out, followed by a prolonged thunderous standing ovation. As the clapping subsided, Rudy again spoke.

"Now, then. We shall open the floor to toasts to the bride and groom. So, I pose this to you. Who would dare be the first to follow the King?"

More chuckling from the crowd.

Rudy spoke again. "Come now. If no one speaks up, I shall have to read the *real* telegram from Buckingham Palace, wherein His Majesty expresses his true thoughts about our friend Edward here."

As the crowd broke into nervous laughter again, a slim young lady, who looked to be in her twenties, walked down the center aisle toward the podium.

"I see we have a taker," Rudy said. "Young lady, the podium is yours, and my colleague Captain McCloud thanks you for preventing me from having to read the king's true thoughts about him."

The crowd laughed, as the young lady sporting a shy smile and carrying something in her right hand stepped to the microphone.

"It's hard for a girl to follow a king or even a telegram written by a king," she said. "I know you're all wondering why, with so many majestic cathedrals in our capital city, you would get hauled all the way to a little town in Scotland and sit crammed together like sardines in a tin can while the captain and the baroness tie the knot."

The crowd laughed, which seemed to embolden the young lady with confidence.

"I must confess I am partially to blame. My name is Sally Cameron, and I am a member of the First Presbyterian Church of Ardentinny. You see, the McClouds' son Darwin, whom the king spoke of in his letter, and I would have been married in the same church where the captain and the baroness were married today. But the war got in the way, and Darwin is now in a better place."

Sally stopped and dabbed her eye. "I am sorry. Even four years after his death, the mention or thought of his name quickly draws tears to my eyes."

She paused.

The crowd went silent. All eyes were now riveted on the podium.

"They awarded Darwin with the highest honor Britain bestows on her finest sons, the Victoria Cross. Captain

McCloud, you told me—a lowly Scottish girl from Ardentinny—to keep the cross, our nation's highest honor, if only for a while."

Sally stopped, choking her emotions back.

"And I have done as you asked. I have looked at it every day, and it served as a reminder to me to pray that this day would come. Captain, the cross has now served its purpose. Today is the day Darwin would have me give it back to you, where it rightfully belongs. What you've done today by marrying the baroness is not only an answer to his prayers and mine, but Darwin would tell you it is an act far more heroic than anything he ever did in battle."

She walked over to Captain McCloud, who sat speechless at the front table, and pinned the cross on his uniform. The thunderous and emotional standing ovation surpassed even the reaction that followed the king's telegram only moments ago.

Walter felt goosebumps crawl down his spine. Beside him, Ellie was patting her eye with a handkerchief.

As Sally left the podium, Captain Rudy returned.

"Thank you, Miss Cameron. Darwin McCloud, a Royal Naval commando, became a leader of men. A hero among heroes who gave his life for a friend and for the Crown. A young man lives today because Darwin sacrificed his own body by blocking machine-gun fire aimed at his friend. Darwin McCloud—I say this from personal experience—combined the very best of both his mother and his father."

More applause.

"Now then, are there other toasts and tributes?"

In the far left corner at the opposite side of the room from where Walter and Ellie were sitting, Rudy pointed to a redheaded woman raising her hand.

"Yes, ma'am, in the far corner. Please come down."

Rudy yielded as the attractive redhead took the microphone.

"My name is Ingrid Schultz. First, I would like to thank the baroness for having me here today."

An eerie silence cascaded through the building at the sound of the distinctive accent of the defeated enemy—a

German in the midst of her British conquerors. Walter looked at Ellie then in disbelief looked at the woman whose husband he had killed.

"Perhaps you wonder why a German woman would come to a British wedding so soon after the war. I come at the invitation of the baroness, a wonderful woman who has become my friend."

With every eye riveted on her, Ingrid's words reverberated across the large hall.

Walter leaned forward. How could this be happening? Why was she here? Did Ingrid even know that he was in the crowd? Would she go into an angry rage if she spotted him? Surely the baroness must have warned her.

He felt Ellie's hand touching him assuredly on his shoulder. Ellie whispered in his ear. "It's going to be okay."

"Like Baroness McCloud's son," Ingrid continued, "my husband was killed in the war. A letter came that my husband wrote to me before he died. He wrote that letter because of a gift Darwin McCloud gave him. That gift was a Bible, written in my native language of German. Darwin never met Heinrick, but he wrote a note inside the Bible, and he wrote it in German. Here is what Darwin McCloud wrote to my husband."

Ingrid read the words Walter knew by heart. "We may be enemies on the battlefield, but I pray that we may be brothers in Heaven one day. Give your life to the One who died for you and rose again. And please, read this book every day."

Ingrid laid down the bible and unfolded the letter from Heinrick. "My husband—his name was Heinrick Schultz, a major in the German Army—took the advice of Darwin McCloud and began to read this book. Then he wrote a letter to me saying that the book had changed his life. He urged me and my daughters to read it too.

"In December, just five months ago, a very nice American officer named Walter Brewer brought me this letter all the way from America. When I found out that this officer was involved in the operation that killed my husband, I am ashamed to say I did not treat him well. I threw him out of my house and treated him badly. For that, I am sorry."

She stopped and searched the crowd. And when her eyes found Walter, she smiled.

"But this American, Captain Brewer, he then came to England and told the baroness the story of how her son impacted my husband. Captain Brewer told the baroness where I lived.

"Baroness Juliana began writing me and calling me, and she showed an interest in me. She called me once a week to encourage me and my girls.

"In the meantime, I began to take the advice of Darwin and then my husband, to read the book. I discovered that the Word of God is a living and breathing thing and that the Son of God, He loves me and He loves you.

"Today, all of you have come to a great reunion, a reunion of friends and colleagues to see the captain and the baroness reunited in marriage.

"But someday, thanks to Darwin McCloud and Baroness Juliana and Walter Brewer, for me and my girls there will be an even greater reunion in Heaven. A reunion with Heinrick and an even sweeter reunion with our Lord. Thank you."

The crowd sat stunned as Ingrid stepped down. The clicking sound of her heels walking across the marble floor back toward her table in the far corner of the room was the only sound heard. At the head table, the baroness wiped her eyes with a napkin. Then, as everyone seemed uncertain what to do, Juliana stood up alone and began to applaud Ingrid. Others followed, one by one, and soon the entire room was affording Ingrid the same response that had been afforded Sally Cameron, a thunderous, sustained ovation.

"I need some air," Walter said to Ellie. "Come with me."

Walter put his hand on Ellie's back and he led her out of the banquet hall into the courtyard.

"Let's go for a walk," he said.

"But Walter, the reception's not over. Don't you want to see Ingrid or speak with Juliana?"

"Maybe later. Not right now." He put his hand on her back and led her down the central street of the base, down toward the sparkling blue waters of Loch Long.

They walked past the green parade grounds where Darwin graduated from commando school and past the Union Jack and the Royal Naval Ensign fluttering in the wind. When they got to the water's edge, they stopped.

"There's something I've been thinking about, Ellie." He looked straight out over the water.

"What's that?"

"I've been thinking that none of this would be happening if it weren't for you."

"I don't understand," she said.

"I mean Ingrid getting Heinrick's letter, Edward and Juliana getting married, Princess Elizabeth coming to the wedding, and Ingrid becoming a Christian."

"I'm sorry. I don't follow you."

Still staring at the water, Walter continued. "When I got back to Norfolk in December, I paid another visit to Mr. Allison. As hard as I tried, I got nothing out of him about this Reunification Foundation. I had a little cash left over, so I thought—what the heck—I'll go see a private detective. Five hundred dollars later, I found out that this mysterious foundation spent thousands of dollars lobbying congressmen and senators and working other foreign contacts to clear the way for Jessie to go to England, to track down Ingrid Schultz, and to track down Juliana McCloud."

"Wow," she said.

"I also found out a little bit about the contributors to the foundation."

"You did?"

"Seems as if our mysterious foundation has but a single anonymous source of sugar."

"Really?"

"As if you have to ask." He turned his gaze from the water and onto her face. "Why, Ellie? Why did you do it?"

She looked away from him and gazed out at the water. "You know," she said.

"Tell me," he insisted.

"I wanted the best for you, Walter. And my feelings haven't changed in sixteen years."

He stood there beside her for a while, watching several sailboats dart circles in the water just in front of them. From behind them and up the hill, they could hear the faint sound of applause and laughter from the reception.

"Ellie?"

"Yes, Walter?"

"You wonder what's been going on in the gossip mills back in Plymouth right now?"

"You mean about the two of us being here?" she asked.

"Yes," he said.

"I'd love to be a fly on the wall at Mary Lib Johnson's Thursday afternoon tea," she snickered.

"We should *really* give 'em something to gossip about," he said.

"What do you mean, Walter?"

"I mean I saw the Presbyterian pastor in the restroom at the reception. He was leaving the reception early to head back over to the church to get ready for tomorrow. He said we were welcome to stop by this afternoon if we needed him for anything."

"What are you saying, Walter?" she asked.

"I'm saying let's take a walk up the hill."

He took her hand and they headed back up the hill, past the wedding reception, out the front gate, across the cobblestone street, and into the doors of the little brown church.

ABOUT THE AUTHOR

A former U.S. Navy JAG officer, Don is the author of the Navy Justice series and the Pacific Rim series. Paying no homage to political correctness, Don's writing style is described as "gripping," casting an entertaining and educational spin on a wide range of current issues, from radical Islamic infiltration of the military, to the explosive issue of gays in the military, to the modern day issues of presidential politics in the early twenty first century.

Don graduated from the University of North Carolina in 1982, and after finishing law school, continued his post-graduate studies through the Naval War College, earning the Navy's nonresident certificate in International Law. During his five years on active duty in the Navy, Don served in the Pentagon, was published in the Naval Law Review, and was also a recipient of the Navy Achievement Medal, the Navy Commendation Medal, and the National Defense Service Medal.

Visit his website: www.donbrownbooks.com

DISCUSSION QUESTIONS

1. Who was your favorite character and why?

2. Can you see God working in Heinrick's life even as a devoted Nazi? Talk about the people and events God used to reach him.

3. Compare Billy to Walter. How are they different?

4. How does the war change Ellie Williams?

5. Do you agree with Darwin's decision about pacificism? Why or why not?

6. Which people are most affected by the role the Bible plays in the story?

7. How does Walter show himself to be an honorable man? In what ways?

8. What was your favorite scene in *Destiny*?

9. What surprised you the most as you read the story?

10. What did you discover about World War II that you didn't know before reading?

11. Of all the characters, who would you most like to sit down and have dinner with?

12. How does the title *Destiny* play out in the book?

Visit the Mountainview Books, LLC website for news on all our books:

www.mountainviewbooks.com

Printed in Great Britain
by Amazon